Take Money

BY

Tony Moda

This novel is a work of fiction. Names, characters, places, and incidents either are the product of the author's imagination or are used fictitiously, and any resemblance to actual persons, living or dead, businesses, companies, events, or locales is entirely coincidental.

Tony Moda/Take Money
Library of Congress Control Number: 2012935033
ISBN: 978-0-9851931-0-2

www.tonymoda.com
www.storylinebks.com

CHAPTER 1
NO WAY OUT

Outside a condo complex in Edgewater, New Jersey, two men sat behind the tinted windows of a dark blue, late model Lincoln Navigator. Both men in the SUV silently watched the door of reputed drug dealer Angel Gomez. It took nearly fifteen minutes for them to see what they'd been waiting for.

"There goes his man Ramos," the driver said as they watched the black Escalade pull into the parking space in front of Angel's condo. They continued to watch as the shadowy figure exited the SUV with two large duffel bags before shutting the door.

The two men stared into the dimly lit parking lot at Ramos struggling with the large bags. They could've easily snatched him on the spot but that wasn't the job. They wanted Angel. Even though they'd dealt with him numerous times over the last few months, this would be their last encounter with him.

The men inside the Navigator were brothers from Cleveland, Ohio. Their names were Asad and Ahmed Sparks. Asad, the older of the two, looked at his Breitling that read 9:52 p.m. He removed two pair of black batting gloves from the top of the pizza box located on the dashboard then handed a set to his brother before putting on the other pair himself.

"Grab the tools," he said in his low monotone voice.

Ahmed reached in the back seat, moving a large black towel revealing two identical Heckler & Koch MP5-K submachine guns, along with two 40-caliber Glock handguns. He gave his brother one of each, while keeping the remaining two for himself. Asad took a quick look around the parking lot. Seeing it was clear, he opened the black book bag on the passenger floorboard and took out a red pizza delivery jacket and hat. He put both items on before reaching back inside the bag, this time he pulled out four metal cylinders. After passing his brother two of them, the only sound that could be heard inside the SUV were the silencers being attached to the HK's and Glocks. When they finished putting the sound suppressors on their weapons, they folded the stocks on the HK's to make them even more concealable.

After chambering rounds into their guns, they turned toward one another. It must've seemed like glancing into a mirror because they looked so much alike. The only minor differences were Ahmed stood slightly over 6'2" and weighed 220 pounds while Asad was a little over 6 feet and weighed 190 pounds. Asad also had a faint inch and a half long scar on his cheek. Both men were caramel complected and, by anyone's standards, extremely handsome. But, the same faces that made women want them, made their men shiver in fear.

Ahmed broke the silence in the same monotone voice as his brother. "Let's go to work."

Asad grabbed the pizza box off of the dashboard and they both quickly exited the Navigator.

$$$

Inside the condo, Angel watched as his two lieutenants Ramos and Boogie separated the cocaine he had just returned with, from Angel's Dominican connect Manny Ortiz. Sitting on the black leather sofa, with the open duffel bags in front of them, the two took out brick after brick of cocaine stacking them neatly on the hardwood floor. It totaled fifty when they finished.

"Boogie." Angel called as he took a seat on the black leather recliner. "When will you be done wit' that work I gave you last week?" he asked.

"I'll have all the money to you by tomorrow night," Boogie answered.

Ramos stared at Boogie, waiting for him to initiate conversation about them getting more money. Realizing he wasn't going to, so he did.

"Angel," Ramos called.

Angel, who was reclined in his chair, looked over at him.

"Dig Angel, I'm tired of workin' for Manny! It's time we go fo' self, Papi" he vented while looking at Angel for a response. Not getting one he continued. "It's like we take all the risk and he gets most of the money. That shit ain't right." Ramos finished, staring Angel in the eyes.

"First of all, let's get somethin' straight. You don't work for

Manny. You work for me!" Angel said angrily. "And secondly, we're all makin' good money..."

"Some more than others," Boogie chimed in cutting his eyes at Angel.

"So, this, what's it about?" Angel asked somewhat upset. "I'm disappointed in y'all," he continued, pointing an accusing finger at his childhood friends. "Boogie, didn't you just buy two fuckin' BMW's, a 745i for yourself and a 330i for your girl, Angie?"

Boogie broke eye contact with Angel, turning his gaze toward the floor before speaking. "Angel, I move no less than twenty keys a month for you while you sit up here in Jersey, without a worry in the world. Me and Ramos stay on the grind runnin' around N.Y., dealin' wit' crooked cops, crazy Ricans and foul niggas. All you do is sit back servin' your outta town clientele. No disrespect Papi, but I think me and Ramos should get a bigger piece of the profits."

Angel took his gaze from Boogie turning it to Ramos who nodded his head in agreement. Angel sat there, quiet for a moment. He had to think fast because Boogie and Ramos were the crew's muscle. He knew without those two, it would be hard keeping people in line. Other crews would try to run his boys out of the Bronx along with the other spots he'd controlled for the past few years.

After listening to Boogie and Ramos, a thought he'd pondered for quite some time came to him again. Maybe it *was* time for him to turn everything over to them. *I've made enough money to live like a king in my home country the Dominican Republic. And, besides, I haven't had time to enjoy the ocean front villa I built there last year.* He also thought of the beautiful women the island had to offer. A smile came to his lips as he made his decision.

"What's so funny?" Ramos asked, seeing the silly smirk on his face.

"Eduardo, Javier," Angel said using their first names. Ramos and Boogie stared at him because he hadn't called them by their names since they were kids. "Listen up," he started. "I got some good and some bad news. The bad news first. As of this very moment, I'm out the game."

Ramos and Boogie stared at each other in disbelief, not

wanting to believe their ears.

Angel continued, "I'm finished! I've made enough money. I'm 32-years-old and never seen the inside of a prison. And, being the type not to tempt fate, I'm gettin' out while I'm ahead," he finished, looking from one man to the other.

They both stared back with the same thought on their minds. They believed, without Angel, Manny wouldn't work with them, especially knowing how picky he was about the people he dealt with. Boogie sat in silence. He regretted even bringing up the subject of more money. In hindsight, the money they got with Angel was good, but had come to an end because they wanted a bigger cut.

"Hey, don't y'all wanna hear the good news?" Angel asked, breaking their train of thought. With stressful faces, both men glared at him without answering. "C'mon, y'all breakin' my heart wit' those pitiful looks," he said.

"*Que pasa?*" Ramos asked, tired of seeing the grin on Angel's face.

"You two know I love y'all like *hermanos* and I would never leave y'all out in the cold without heat," he said, looking from one to the other. "So, once we're done wit' this package, I'm gonna take Manny his money and break the news to him and vouch for you two *cabrons.*"

"How do you know he'll go for it?" Boogie questioned as a feeling of joy swelled up in his chest.

"Look, I've made Manny and his people *mucho dinero.* They don't want all that money to stop comin' in so he'll go for it. Now, all of the problems that comes wit' this level of the game is yours," Angel said, wiping his hands of it.

The two men weren't concerned with the potential problems. Their only thoughts were on all of the money to be made once in charge. With smiles on their faces, they both got up from the sofa and rushed Angel. Boogie put him in a bear hug lifting him off the floor as he and Ramos shouted their thanks.

"You won't regret this," Boogie said happily as he put Angel down.

"Let's celebrate our new beginnings," Angel exclaimed,

joining in on the festive mood. "Boogie, go grab a bottle of Patron outta the kitchen."

"Don't worry 'bout nothin'. We won't fuck this up," Ramos promised from the sofa before getting lost in his thoughts of riches.

Angel stood in the middle of the room with his thoughts on the Dominican Republic and the things he would do upon his return. As he stood there, a knock at the door interrupted his thought process.

"Stay there, I'll get it," he said, stopping Ramos from getting up from the sofa. On his way to the door, he looked over his shoulder at Boogie, who came from the kitchen drinking liquor straight out of the bottle. "Don't get that shit on the floor you fuckin' *borracho*," he jokingly said as he reached the door. In his joyful mood, he made a fatal mistake that would cost him severely. Looking over his shoulder, playfully cursing Boogie, he started to open the door without seeing who stood on the other side.

As soon as it opened, he realized his blunder but it was too late. Asad rushed in, pushing Angel back into the house simultaneously throwing the pizza box down. He grabbed Angel by his shirt, jamming the Glock under his chin. Ahmed, who was right behind him, quickly closed the door before hurrying toward the living room.

The men moved so quietly and quickly, the others inside the condo were oblivious to their presence until Ramos spotted the gunman in the entryway of the living room. He was the first to go. Ahmed blasted him with a three round burst from the silenced HK. Two bullets hit him in the chest with the third tearing into his throat. Before his body hit the floor, Ahmed turned his attention to Boogie who stood frozen from seeing his childhood friend gunned down. Ahmed let loose another three round burst. Two hit their mark. One struck Boogie under his left eye exiting the back of his head as the second split through his forehead, causing him to drop the bottle of Patron. The third shot missed high, going harmlessly into the wall. It didn't matter. Boogie was dead before his body hit the floor.

Lowering his weapon, Ahmed looked over his shoulder at the stone face of his brother and the frightened face of Angel, who stared at the bodies of his deceased partners.

"Angel," Asad said into his ear, it's only one way out of this. Tell us where everything is and don't make me have to ask you twice."

Glancing from one brother to the other, Angel's mind raced. *Why did I open the door? How did they find my place?* He couldn't believe what was happening. Over the last couple of months, he'd dealt with them numerous times since Charm introduced them and their money was always good. He couldn't understand why they were doing this, then it hit him. They had been setting him up all along.

Realizing the obvious, his mindset changed from fear to survival. He figured if he told them about the money under the kitchen sink and his plan to retire to his home country, he might make it out of this alive.

"Sam," he said regaining his composure, calling Asad by the false name Charm introduced him by. "You and Chuck can have everything. There's 1.2 million under the kitchen sink. Inside the cabinet it's a false bottom, just pull it up. I don't want no beef wit' you guys."

Without word, the brothers communicated. Asad nodded at Ahmed who went to the kitchen. Once inside, he walked over to the sink and knelt down to open the cabinet. He looked around moving the cleaning supplies to the side. After displacing them, he pushed one end of the board, which made the other end pop up. He took the board out, placed it against the cabinet, reached into the hollowed bottom and pulled out a large black duffel bag, and then unzipped it.

"Jackpot," he said, looking inside at the bundles of rubber-banded money before closing it back up.

Reentering the room with the duffel bag slung over his shoulder, he nodded a confirmation to his brother. While Ahmed was in the kitchen, Asad had Angel put the kilos back into the duffel bags. When he finished, Asad ordered him to sit on the love seat. As he sat there looking at the bodies of Boogie and Ramos, his mind couldn't get over the quietness that death brings. He looked on nervously as the two killers stood next to one another staring at him.

Angel watched in horror as the man he knew as Sam

walked over to the bodies of his dead friends, firing two shots a piece into their heads. All hope of making it out of this alive quickly faded from Angel's mind. He knew there was no way out. He closed his eyes to say a quick prayer when he saw Sam coming toward him. But, before he could finish the prayer, two .40 caliber bullets ripped through his face.

After gathering the drugs and money, they gave the room a once over then picked up all of the spent shell casings and making sure nothing incriminating remained. Once everything appeared to their liking, they picked up the duffel bags and left the condo smelling of gunpowder and blood, before exiting it as fast as they had entered.

CHAPTER 2
DERBY WEEKEND

It was a Friday morning inside the Bank of Hamilton, located in downtown Cincinnati, Ohio. The four bank tellers quietly attended to the few customers who arrived early to expedite their transactions. Sitting on a stool by the entrance, an obese, overage white security guard looked through a brochure about a retirement community in central Florida. Inside the vault, bank manager Robert Pamplin took inventory of the transactions retrieved from the drop boxes from the previous night. Thursday night, for some reason was the night most of the businesses in the area dropped off their two-day earnings, this pattern didn't go unnoticed.

The so far normal day, instantly turned violent when two masked men in black overalls stormed into the bank.

"Lay it down muthafuckas!" The robber with the large black tennis bag over his shoulder yelled as he ran toward the tellers, leaping the counter with a Mac-10 in his right hand, herding them into the corner.

As soon as the first robber entered the bank, the security guard got up from the stool fumbling for his gun. Before he could pull it, another robber came up behind the guard and viciously pistol-whipped him to the floor. The second gunman held the bloody stainless steel Ruger on the now unconscious bleeding guard.

"Everybody on the floor," he ordered. Everyone complied.

The first robber quickly ordered the four bank employees down into a corner telling them not to move. He then rushed into the vault catching the bank manager off guard. "Respect this robbery," he demanded while grabbing the man by his suit jacket collar and throwing him to the floor.

"One minute," the second robber shouted in the direction of the vault.

The first robber was already in the process of dumping stacks of money into the oversized bag. He stuffed it with as much as he possibly could, barely able to zip it closed. Robert Pamplin sat on the floor staring at the Mac-10 that hung on the shoulder strap of the robber and prayed he wouldn't get shot. Just as the thought entered his mind, the robber rushed out of the vault and jumped over the counter.

"Don't anyone move for five minutes," the second robber barked as he and his partner backed their way out of the lobby. Once between the double glass doors, they took their ski masks off replacing them with oversize sunglasses and hats before casually exiting the bank. Outside, they made their way up the street to where the stolen car was parked, quickly getting in and taking off. Even at 9:17 a.m., in downtown Cincinnati, the men went unnoticed. It was a clean getaway.

Parked in a supermarket parking lot, the robbers removed their overalls as well as their ski masks then placed them into a black garbage bag. Young Curtis, the Mac-10 wielding bandit, grabbed the money as his partner Ducci picked up the garbage bag. The men got out of the stolen car and headed down the parking lot to where Ducci's black 1996 Chevy Impala SS was parked. After disarming the alarm on the car, both men got inside and proceeded to their next destination Louisville, Kentucky. But first, they needed to stop at a rest area to dump the garbage.

Abdullah "Ducci" Martin and Curtis "Young Curtis" Houston had known one another for most of their lives. They were more like brothers than friends. Life had basically dealt them the same hand. Both grew up in fatherless homes and were raised by strong, caring Black women. However, when the streets called, neither could resist its allure. They began by selling rocks, then went onto robbing dice games. But, nothing was more successful for them until Young Curtis came up with the bright idea to rob banks. That worked for the two. Aside from them being bank robbers, their personalities were the total opposite. Ducci, 6'3" yet slim built, with a brown complexion, was well liked by everyone he met. Other than robbing banks, he lived a structured life. With the money from the three heists him and Young Curtis pulled that year, he started a small realty company.

Young Curtis, on the other hand, was a ghetto celebrity. He stood 5'8" with a cocky build. He was light-skinned with boyishly good looks. He got his name from his youthful appearance because he was twenty-years-old with the face of a fifteen-year-old and had the temperament of a four year old. He was arrogant and obnoxious. Unlike Ducci, he was disliked by almost everyone except for his other best friend, Fly Ty and his younger homie CCW. Since they started seeing real cash from their robberies, Young Curtis spent his money on things Ducci considered stupid. He bought hundred-thousand-dollar cars as well as gaudy platinum and diamond jewelry. But despite all of Young Curtis' shortcomings that Ducci attributed to their three-year age difference, he was the most genuine friend he knew. Ducci always understood, no matter what, Young Curtis had his back. That's why he took him under his wing years ago. In Cleveland, Ohio, where they were born and raised, Young Curtis and Ducci's unity was rare.

As they neared the Louisville exit, driving on I75, they both began to get the feeling of excitement and anticipation that always came when they entered different cities. Young Curtis was on his cell phone when he saw that they were approaching downtown Louisville. He was ready to end his call.

"Hey, check this out Trina. I'll be back in the city in a couple of days, so keep that pussy tight and right for a gangsta. I'ma holla at you then."

"Aw Young Curtis, don't hang up. I'm not finished talkin,' and if you do, you won't be gettin' none of this when you get back," she said playfully.

Not in the mood for games or being blackmailed, Young Curtis shouted into the phone, "Holla back, bitch!" before he pressed the end button.

"Why do you talk to them broads like that?" Ducci asked, glancing over at him.

"Man, don't no hoe mash the gas on Young Curtis. I'm tellin' the bitch, 'I'll holla,' then she gon' say if I hang up she's not gonna fuck me when I get back home. That bitch must be crazy, I'm Young Curtis. She should be honored to suck this dick!"

The car filled with laughter from his statement because both men knew him to be serious. After it ended, Young Curtis looked out of the window realizing they were on Muhammad Ali Blvd. "Since we're already down here, we might as well hit the Galleria and buy some fits for the weekend," Young Curtis suggested.

"Let's drop this money off first," Ducci replied as he navigated the car through traffic.

"Man, that money is cool where it is. Plus, once I get to the telly, I'm goin' to sleep. So let's get this shit out the way."

Instead of arguing, Ducci headed to 4th Street Live, where the Galleria was located. Once in the parking lot, he cruised around looking for a space. As he drove, he spotted a silver Lexus GS 300 backing out close to the entrance. He pulled into the spot after it was vacated. After they parked, the two men got out of the car and headed toward the shopping center then slowed their pace when they noticed the Lexus coming back their way.

Young Curtis and Ducci looked inside the car seeing three men.

"I see y'all ain't from 'round here," the dark skinned driver stated. Ducci and Young Curtis just stared at the man. "It aint no beef, I just wanted to say I like yo lil ride. Is those twenties?"

"Naw playa. Twenty two's," Ducci answered, realizing he was no threat.

"Yeah, yo lil ride is cool but it's 2004 and bruthas need to step their game up," the driver of the Lexus replied with his hand out of the window, rubbing the car door as if it was a Bentley.

"Let's bounce," Young Curtis said tired of seeing the lame showboating. As he and Ducci turned to walk away, he stopped in his tracks and turned back around, then walked up to the Lexus before the driver could pull off.

"I forgot," he said, making his way to the car. The driver smiled at him, flashing his gold grill. Young Curtis returned the smile, flashing his four top front platinum and diamond teeth. "Hey playboy, tell yo' woman she's kill 'em," Young Curtis smiled.

"What cha say?" The driver asked, instantly getting angry, along with the other two men in the car, who glared angrily also.

"Nigga, I know this piece of shit gotta be yo' baby mama's cuz real niggas don't ride nothing with 3's on 'em." Before the men could respond, Ducci pulled Young Curtis away to avoid them getting caught in an out of town beef.

"Man, these corny ass niggas tryin' to stunt. Ridin' bullshit, thinkin' it's hot," Young Curtis spat angrily as they walked to the entrance. "Fuck that, I'm havin' my shit brought down here today to show these chumps how to do it."

"Nah, we're only here for a couple of days. Let these chumps shine," Ducci reasoned, shaking his head in disagreement.

"Fuck all that!" Young Curtis barked. "I want my shit down here today and that's that."

Ducci left it alone. After that outburst, he knew when his young homie got like this it was no sense in trying to talk him out of it.

$$$

After spending close to an hour inside the Galleria shopping, Ducci and Young Curtis walked toward the exit with their bags in hand. On the way out, Young Curtis spotted an attractive, nicely built brown complected female. She wore a light gray, form fitting, strapless dress that fell slightly above her knees. On her feet were a pair of gray "come hit it" pumps. She had long hair with auburn highlights that hung just below her shoulders. Seeing how she was up to his standard in the looks department, he went at her.

"Hey Ms. Lady. How you?" he asked, walking beside her.

"I'm fine," she replied while sizing him up.

"My name Young Curtis. What's yours?" he questioned, making eye contact instead of staring at her full breasts.

Seeing potential in him from the platinum and diamond teeth as well as all the bags he carried, she could smell the money on him. "My name is Ms. Karen," the woman replied with a sexy smile. "You're not from around here, are you?"

"Nah, I'm here for Derby weekend."

She thought to herself, *he's cute with money. This should be fun.* "Well, Young Curtis, if you want somebody to show you around, maybe we can exchange numbers."

"We can do that," he said, pulling out his cell phone. She did the same. After programming their numbers into one another's phones, they said their goodbyes.

"Who was that?" Ducci asked when Young Curtis rejoined

him.

"Some bitch by the name of Ms. Karen," he answered as they headed for the exit. "I just knocked her off, and, by tonight, she'll be suckin' me off." Young Curtis laughed and gave Ducci dap. "Aint nothin' hotta," he smiled referring to his game, as they made it to the car.

$$$

After dropping Young Curtis off at the Seelbach Hotel, Ducci drove to the east end of the city where his girlfriend lived. Pulling into the driveway, he noticed her car wasn't there. He got out of his and walked around to the back of it, then opened the trunk to retrieve the black tennis bag. After closing the trunk, he went to the back door of his car to get the shopping bags. On his way up the stairs to the porch, he enabled the car alarm before going inside the house.

Once inside, Ducci carried all the bags to the first floor bedroom then placed them in the corner. He took the tennis bag over to the bed with him and kicked off his shoes then sat down. He unzipped the bag, removed the Mac-10 and Ruger that sat on top of the money, and laid the guns on the bed next to him. He then turned the bag upside down, dumping all the stacks of money out onto the floor. "Damn," he exclaimed, looking at the cash on the floor. It was much more than he expected. "I betta get to work," he said to himself, picking up a stack of the money.

$$$

Sitting on the burgundy sofa in his hotel suite, wearing a white Terry cloth robe, Young Curtis' usually braided hair was in a wild afro. He sat there finishing off the last of the cheeseburger and French fries he'd ordered from room service. "That shit was hittin'!" he said, sucking his teeth. He leaned back into the sofa, putting his bare feet on the coffee table before closing his eyes to get some rest. As soon as he got comfortable, his cell phone rang.

"What's happenin'?" he answered.

"May I speak with Young Curtis?" a sexy, mildly accented, southern female voice asked.

"This him. Who this?"

"Hi baby, this Ms. Karen. I met you at the Galleria earlier

today."

"Yeah, yeah. I know who this is. What's up wit' chu?" he asked going into mack mode.

"Nothing much," she said. "I was calling to see if you wanted to have a good time tonight. I'll be at the Velvet Rose Club so, if you can, stop through?"

"My people should know where it's at. I'll come through just for you," he laughed.

"Well, I'll see you tonight," she said in a sultry voice.

"Ai'ight Ms. Lady. I'll be there," he smiled, ending the call. Once he hung up, he dialed another number. It took four rings before the phone was answered.

"Who this?"

"What's up Unc? This Young Curtis. Where you at?"

"I'm up here at Dough Boy's, droppin' Kenya's car off so he can fix it," June Martin answered. June, who was actually Ducci's uncle, was referred to as Unc by everyone in the hood.

"Unc, I need you to do me a solid. I need you to bring my automobile down here to Louisville."

"What! Are you crazy?" Unc asked, not wanting to drive all the way down to Kentucky.

"Unc, I need my shit down here today, so put it on the flat-bed and bring it to me." Young Curtis said flatly. "Dig, I'll make it worth the trip" he added, tempting Unc with the promise of money.

Unc knew he could easily walk away with a grand messing with Young Curtis. "Okay boy, where do you want me to drop it off?" Unc asked finally giving in.

"Listen Unc, I don't need my shit 'til 'bout three in the mornin.' I want you to ride down here with the tarp on it. I want you to drop it in the middle of the street in front of a club named the Velvet Rose."

"Boy, you one crazy muthafucka," Unc managed to say through his laughter. "I'll be there. Just remember, the meter will be runnin," Unc warned before hanging up.

Young Curtis pressed the end button on his phone then laid it back on the coffee table. He smiled to himself, thinking, "I'll teach these niggas how to stunt."

$$$

Pulling into her driveway, Missy Frost smiled when she saw Ducci's car. She got out of her silver "04" Chrysler Sebring and quickly walked around to the passenger side back door to get her four-year-old son out of his car seat. After removing him, she closed the door with him in her arms. "Look, Ducci's here, Poo-Poo," she said pointing at his car. The little boy looked, as his eyes got big with excitement. "Ducci, Ducci, Ducci," the child said, bouncing happily in his mother's arms.

As soon as the two entered the house, they saw Ducci coming out of the bedroom. She watched him move toward them in just his jeans and white socks, showing off his slim 6'3" frame.

"Hey baby," Missy said with a smile on her pretty light-skinned face. When he made it to her, they engaged in a passionate kiss. Ducci broke their embrace then took Poo-Poo out of her arms.

"Give me kiss." The boy smiled at Ducci, who gave him a peck on the lips.

Ducci wasn't the boy's father but he loved him like his own. He held Poo-Poo in his arms. As the boy told him about an episode of "Sponge Bob," Ducci listened intently. After listening, he put the boy down so he could go into the front room and watch TV.

Once Poo-Poo was out of sight, Ducci pulled Missy to him by her small waist and gave her another kiss. He whispered in her ear, telling her how bad he wanted her but he knew nothing could happen as long as Poo-Poo was in the house and wide awake.

"Poo-Poo is staying the night at my mother's tonight, so we'll have same quality time for ourselves," she said, staring up at him.

"Yeah, I'm gon' put it on you tonight," Ducci smiled.

"You put it on me every time," she shot back, giving him a quick kiss on the lips. "Let me go check my answering machine," she said walking toward the living room.

She sat down on the blue micro-fiber sofa; leaning over the arm, she checked the answering machine that sat on the end table. She played two messages. The first was from Poo-Poo's father,

Daren. The other was from her friend, Rosalyn.

"Where is Young Curtis?" she asked with a puzzled look on her face.

"He's at the Seelbach," Ducci answered, sitting on the sofa next to her.

"Did he drive his truck?" she asked, thinking she could probably talk him into taking Rosalyn out again.

"Nah, we rode down together,but that fool saw this chump in a baby Lexus tryin' to flex so he sent for his ride."

"Oh, he wants to outshine them in his Range Rover huh?"

Ducci shook his head. "Nah, he got a new car a few weeks ago. Our homie, Fly Ty, turned him onto this car dealership that will give a hustler the hook-up for a fee. Now Curt wants all these exotic ass cars."

As if on cue, Missy's phone rang. "Hello," she said into the phone.

"What's up, y'all muthafucka's gon' fuck all day and leave Young Curtis stuck in the hotel?"

"Boy, ain't nobody doing nothing," Missy laughed. "I just got in. But, since you're lonely, I'm going to send Rosalyn up there to keep you company."

"Fuck that! Her pussy stank! Y'all better come get me," he ordered.

"I might let Ducci come get you if you take Rosalyn out," Missy bargained.

Before he could respond, he heard Ducci in the background saying that he's on his way. "Dig Missy," Young Curtis started. "I'm not fuckin' wit' your girl. I just knocked this broad off named Ms. Karen. Do you know her?"

"Yeah, she's a gold digging boojie bitch so you better watch her nasty ass."

"Shiiid. If that's the case, I'ma fuck the shit outta her and make her boost me some fits," Young Curtis chuckled.

"Bye," Missy said, laughing herself off the phone.

"Hey baby," Ducci said as he entered the room with Poo-Poo in his arms. "I'm taking little man to the barber shop with me.

"Okay, when will y'all be back?"

"In about two hours," Ducci replied. She gave him and Poo-Poo a kiss before they left.

$$$

Standing in front of the full-length mirror in the bedroom of his hotel suite, Young Curtis checked his appearance. He wore a red and gray Roc-A-Wear jogging suit. Pleased with how it fit, he sat down on the bed putting on a crispy pair of Air Force One sneakers. He looked at his platinum and diamond Rolex, wondering what took Ducci so long. When his cell phone started to ring, he pulled it from his hip and answered it. "What's up?"

"I'm out front homie, come down," Ducci said.

"'Bout time," Young Curtis shot back hanging up.

$$$

Pulling into Creative Cuts Barber Shop, Ducci and Young Curtis noticed the stares of a few thugs checking out the SS as they parked. Getting out of the car, they ignored the looks and went into the shop. Inside, they were greeted with southern hospitality. After the three were seated, KeKe, who was Missy's cousin, walked over to Poo-Poo and gave him a kiss.

"So you're getting your hair cut like a big boy?" She smiled at him. He shook his head yes. She then gave Ducci a friendly hug while Young Curtis stared at her nicely shaped butt as she bent over in a pair of skintight jeans.

"That's my people over there," Ducci said, pointing at Young Curtis. "Hey Curt, this Missy's cousin KeKe." Young Curtis looked her up and down liking what he saw.

She walked over to him with her hand stuck out. "How you doing?" she asked as she shook his hand.

"I'm good baby," he answered, shaking her hand and staring at her thick thighs in the skintight jeans she wore.

She smiled but pulled her hand back from him when he started to softly caress it.

"Where you find him at?" she asked Ducci with a smile on her lips. Ducci returned the smile, shrugging his shoulders.

KeKe ran her hand through Young Curtis' big, soft, wild

afro. "I guess you want your hair braided?"

"Yeah," he answered flirting with his eyes.

KeKe smiled again, realizing that she liked the attention she received from the young, fly guy. "What style do you want it in?" she asked.

"Baby, it's only one way gangstas wear braids and that's straight to the back."

"Well okay, gangsta," she said in a low sexy voice before grabbing a chair cloth and putting it around him.

Ducci, who finished getting his hair cut along with Poo-Poo, stood at the counter looking in the mirror at his one in a half blade haircut and fresh line-up. While he stood there, making sure his line-up was even, he felt Poo-Poo pulling on his pant leg.

"You wanna check your cut to?" he asked while looking down at Poo-Poo, who shook his head yes. He picked the child up holding him in front of the mirror, watching as the boy turned his head from side to side, mimicking his action.

"It's cool?" he asked the child.

"Yeah. It's cool," he answered in his little voice as Ducci put him down.

"We'll be in the car watching Sponge Bob," Ducci told Young Curtis, who still had a few braids to go, as him and Poo-Poo walked out of the shop.

Young Curtis stared at KeKe's reflection in the mirror while she stood behind him putting the finishing touches on his braids. "What time you get off work?"

"Nine o'clock. Why?" she asked, looking at him through the mirror while twisting the last of his eight corn-rolls.

"Cuz, I wanna take you out to dinner."

"Oh. If you would've asked me this a year ago, I would've had to take you up on the offer. But, I'm in a really good relationship right now," she said sincerely.

Young Curtis couldn't do nothing but respect her because he knew a lot of women who would've rode with him regardless of having a man or not. "I feel you KeKe, but if dude ever fuck up, not realizing what he got in you, Missy knows how to get in touch wit' me," he said, getting out of the chair. He looked in the mirror, nodding his head in approval, and turned around to give her a hug. "Don't forget what I said," he continued while enjoying the feel of her soft body.

"I won't," she said, breaking their embrace watching the young gangster leave. Even though she was in a committed relationship, it felt good to know she still had what it took to pull a high caliber brother.

$$$

It was almost midnight when Ducci pulled into the crowded Velvet Rose parking lot.

"There's a spot up there, baby," Missy said, pointing up the aisle at a space where a black "72" Cutlass on 22" wheels pulled out. Ducci eased up the parking lot that had a club like atmosphere itself since people were dancing to the music that came out of the different car systems while others smoked, drank, and talked to the women who gathered around.

"Damn! I see these Louisville boyz doin' their thang," Young Curtis commented as they drove up the aisle with an assortment of candy painted cars, old and new school, that all set on twenties or better. After parking, they all got out of the car and made their way to the front of the club, then headed inside to enjoy themselves.

Entering the packed club, Missy spotted some of her girlfriends at a table. She waved happily, and they waved back. "I'm going to get us a seat baby," she said to Ducci before walking off toward her girls.

"Got damn! Look at them muthafuckin' boppas on the dance floor," Young Curtis said into Ducci's ear over the loud music. Ducci looked at the three sexy women, surrounded by an onlooking crowd, as they bumped and grinded on one another.

"I gotta be a part of that," Young Curtis said before going to the dance floor. Ducci watched as he made his way through the crowd toward the three females. No one seemed to object to him joining them. A blind man could see he wasn't much of a dancer. He just grabbed handfuls of butts and breasts as the women started bumping and grinding on him.

From across the club, Ms. Karen spotted Young Curtis getting sandwiched by three hoodrats. She tapped her girlfriend Ebony on the shoulder. "There go that young boy I was telling you about," she said then pointed at him.

"Who? The nigga wit' the three rats?" Ebony asked, staring at the scene.

"Yeah," Ms. Karen answered while smiling before walking across the club to pull Young Curtis away from the women and show him her own provocative moves.

Webbie's "Gimme Dat" started playing as Ms. Karen turned around and pressed her big, soft butt on his manhood then rolled it in a circular motion. When Young Curtis started getting hard, he asked, "you rollin' wit' me tonight?"

"How you get here," she shouted back over the music, turning back around to face him.

"I rolled wit' my people but..."

Before he could say another word, she looked at him with her face frowned up, then leaning forward, she shouted in his ear. "I thought you were the one but I see you're only a two. Baby, you gotta get some wheels before you can take me out. Ol' broke ass nigga," she laughed as she pulled back from him.

"What bitch!" he shouted, caught off guard by her statement. She smiled as she danced away from him, snapping her fingers.

Ducci, who saw the whole scene play out, approached Young Curtis laughing. Young Curtis stared at him then shouted. "That broke ass, fake Prada shoe wearing bitch, gon' tell Young Curtis I aint the one. That bitch got me fucked up," he said as he shook his head in disbelief.

Ducci smiled, looking over at the table Missy shared with her girlfriends. He watched as a man approached it. He stood over Missy, saying something, before sitting in the empty chair next to her. When Ducci noticed he made unwanted advances, he made his way to them.

"Here go my man right here," Missy said, looking up at

Ducci who stood over the table. The would-be player stared up at him as well. "Now, you better get up outta his seat before he kick yo ass," she threatened.

"No disrespect, bruh," the man said before getting up to leave.

Ducci just nodded, taking the seat after he left. "I see you had company," he said joking.

"Boy please," she shot back, smiling.

After drinking and dancing the night away, Missy wanted to call it a night. "Where is Young Curtis?" she asked Ducci, who pointed to the dance floor. They both looked on at Young Curtis in the middle of the dance floor, swaying from side to side with a bottle of Dom Perignon in his left hand. He routinely poured some in the glasses for the pretty women dancing around him. He stopped moving for a moment when he saw a thick, light brown-skinned woman coming toward him with a glass in her hand.

"Can I have some of your champagne?" The pretty dime piece asked sweetly.

"Damn baby, this one is almost empty," he said staring at her.

"Well, can I have the last dance with you?" she boldly asked.

"No doubt," he answered without thinking twice. He grabbed her by her small waist, going into his gangster sway.

"What's your name?"

"Shukela," she shouted over the music. "But everyone calls me Shu."

"My name Young Curtis and I'm the realest, flyest nigga you gon' meet," he hollered. "So, what's up? Are you out all night?"

"Should I be?" she asked while loving the young, good looking gangster's swagger.

"Have you ever sat on suede wit' yo' feet on mink?" he asked.

"No," she smiled not sure what he meant.

"Well, stay up all night wit' Young Curtis and you will. When the song ended, the deejay told everyone the club was closing. Young Curtis headed to the bar to buy a bottle. After talking the barmaid into selling him some Dom Perignon, he walked toward Shukela. Before he made it to her, his cell phone vibrated.

"Hello," he answered.

"Young Curtis, this Unc. I'm dropping her off the bed right now."

He smiled to himself. "I'm on my way out now," he said while taking Shukela's hand in his.

"Damn, what is everybody looking at?" Missy questioned as her and Ducci fought their way through the large crowd out front of the club. Ducci saw his uncle's tow truck pulling off and smiled to himself. Once they made their way to the front of the crowd, Missy saw what held the peoples' attention.

Parked in the middle of the street, blocking northbound traffic, sat a candy apple red Mercedes Benz 500 SL with a wide body kit. The convertible top was down on the luxury automobile, giving the spectators a look at the red and tan suede seats. Red mink mats lay across the floor. The 21" chrome Davin rims made the car look even more appealing. Throughout the crowd, you could hear the same question being asked. Everyone wanted to know who owned it. When Ms. Karen finally made her way to the front, she stood next to the Benz and looked around.

"Where is this nigga at?" she asked, thinking she could work him.

Ducci leaned over whispering into Missy's ear.
"That's Curtis."

"That boy is too hot," she smiled.

"Excuse me, pardon me," Young Curtis said as he came through the crowd with Shukela and the bottle of Dom Perignon. He got inside the car; lifting up the armrest and taking the keys from under it. He leaned over, opening the door for Shukela. "Take your sandals off baby so you can see how good that mink feels on your feet," he said before she got in.

Shukela sat in the passenger seat, taking her sandals off, as drivers in the cars behind them blew their horns and cursed angrily. Just when Young Curtis got ready to pull off, he noticed Ms. Karen on the curb staring at him.

"Bye bitch! What cha sleep to? I am the one," he said then drove off laughing. As he pulled off, his cell phone vibrated. "Yeah," he answered.

"It's me, homie. I'm cool on breakfast. Me and Missy is going home," Ducci informed.

"Cool, cuz I'm to the telly. I'll see you in the mornin'," Young Curtis said, ending the call.

$$$

Inside the suite at the Seelbach, Young Curtis and Shukela planned to order room service. Instead, she went to the refrigerator and found the fruit salad he'd ordered earlier.

"I'll just eat this," she said, walking over to the sofa and sitting down next to him.

"You smoke?" he asked, pulling out a blunt of Dro from his jacket pocket.

"Naw, I'm cool," she answered forking through the salad while he lit the blunt.

As Young Curtis puffed on his blunt, Shukela told him a little about herself. He found out that she attended the University of Louisville, where she studied Business Administration. It was easy to see that Shukela was a girl with her head on straight. But, like most good girls, she had an infatuation with bad boys.

"Dig Shu, I'm 'bout to go to bed," Young Curtis said, standing up from the sofa.

"Listen Curtis," she said softly then stood up. "I'm really feeling you, but I'm not ready to have sex with you."

Young Curtis looked at her with a smile. "I can respect that. How 'bout we get to know each other better first," he said, running game. "But, for now, we can at least sleep in the same bed," he said. He took her hand and led her into the bedroom.

$$$

It was 11:53 a.m. when Ducci woke to the smell of scrambled eggs, turkey sausages and toast. He got out of the bed then headed to bathroom to wash up and brush his teeth.

"It smells good in here," he said while walking into the kitchen where he saw Missy at the sink, wearing nothing but a T-shirt as she washed out a frying pan. He stepped up behind her and gave her a kiss on the neck.

She smiled, looking back at him. “Didn’t you get enough last night?”

“No,” he said, pulling his boxers down. At the same time, he lifted her T-shirt and Missy up, so that he could slide his manhood inside her from the back. She released a soft moan as he grabbed a hand full of her hair with his right hand and used his left to grip her waist.

“Yeah, take this work,” he whispered in her ear as their bodies clapped together.

$$$

Ten minutes after him and Missy finished their quickie in the kitchen, someone knocked at the front screen door. Ducci went to answer it. He smiled at Young Curtis before letting him in.

“What the fuck y’all in here doin’?” he asked, staring suspiciously at Ducci as he entered.

“Fall back with all the questions lil homie,” Ducci laughed.

“I know y’all ain’t been in here fuckin’ all over Young Curtis’ food?” he asked with a frown.

“You trippin’ Curt,” Ducci smiled going into the kitchen with Young Curtis following.

“Where Missy at?” Young Curtis asked, grabbing a clean plate off of the table. He went over to the stove and filled his plate with scrambled eggs with cheese, turkey sausages, and toast.

“Here she comes now,” Ducci replied, hearing her footsteps.

Missy entered the kitchen, wearing a pair of pink shorts with matching footies and a fresh T-shirt. “Who lookin’ fo’ me,” she said, mimicking one of Young Curtis’ favorite lines.

“I’m lookin’ fo’ you,” he shot back. “Get me some orange juice,” he stated, sitting down at the table with Ducci.

“‘ Scuse you?” Missy went into her ghetto girl pose with her hands on hips and shifted her weight to her back leg.

“Okay, please,” he playfully begged, getting a smile out of her.

"You want some baby?" she asked Ducci, who nodded his head as she went to the refrigerator.

"Oh yeah, Missy, I gave that broad I met last night your number. So when you come up to the city, bring her wit' cha," he said as he put strawberry jam on his toast.

"That girl has your nose wide open already?" she asked while pouring him and Ducci orange juice.

"Nah, it ain't like that. Shu just good peoples."

"All right. Whatever you say. I'm coming up there next week so give me her number so I can tell her to be ready.

Young Curtis nodded his head. He then turned his attention to Ducci. "Where's Unc?"

"He stayed the night at my Aunt Joanne's house. I told him we're pullin' out tonight so he's on standby."

"Oh yeah, I forgot to ask. What we do yesterday?"

"Two hundred and fifty three," Ducci answered, putting a fork full of eggs in his mouth.

Young Curtis looked over at Missy, who was busy at the stove with her back to them. "A quarter mill?" he whispered with a surprised look on his face.

"True story," Ducci smiled.

After eating, Ducci and Young Curtis played five games of Madden Football on Ducci's PS with Young Curtis winning three out of the five.

"Dig, I'm 'bout to go drop a few stacks on this horse at the Derby. After that, I'ma shoot up to Shaunee Park," Young Curtis said, standing up from the sofa.

"What horse you gon' bet on?"

"They got a horse named Smarty Jones. That shit sounds like an ol' school gangsta's name. Plus, the broad I met last night, her last name is Jones.

"Alright homie, I'll see you tonight," Ducci said, walking him to the door.

$$$

Shaunee Park was filled with families picnicking and other groups of people there to enjoy themselves. In the parking lot near the basketball court, another type of gathering took place. That side was unofficially designated for the city's hustlers, ballers and gangstas. The lot looked like a car show from all of the candy painted old schools, SUVs, and foreign luxury cars.

Young Curtis, sitting on the hood of his Benz and talking on his cell phone, received a lot of attention from the females. He was dressed in a white and red Eddie George, Ohio State football jersey, along with white Nike jogging pants. A pair of red suede Nike Cortez's, that Cleveland and Akron dudes called Dope Man's, donned his feet. As he sat there with the phone to his ear telling his young homie CCW about the previous night, he saw Ms. Karen along with another woman coming his way from across the picnic area. He continued talking as they walked up.

"Can we talk?" Ms. Karen asked as if pleading.

He held up one finger, talking a little longer on the phone before hitting end. "What's up?" he asked while putting the phone in his pocket and staring at her. *Damn, this bitch looks good,* he thought. She wore a pair of light blue booty shorts with a matching halter-top and a pair of matching platform sandals.

"You look like a rapper," her friend, Ebony said with a smile. At the same time, she stared at the diamond and platinum chain around his neck with the capital YC emblem embedded with diamonds, then looked at his platinum and diamond Presidential Rolex.

But, what was to be a compliment backfired. "Dig bitch, don't disrespect me like that. I ain't no punk ass rapper. I earn my paper by puttin' my life on the line out here in these streets. So, if anything, them niggas look like me."

Ebony stared at Young Curtis, thinking *I know this nigga just didn't call me a bitch.* She was about to say something else to him but changed her mind, instead, she whispered to Ms. Karen, "This nigga is crazy. You can fuck wit' him if you want but I'm gone."

With that said, she walked back across the picnic area.

"Now, what's up wit' you?" he asked, turning his attention to Ms. Karen.

"I just wanted to apologize for my behavior last night. I would like to make it up to you." With those words, she had his full attention. "It's getting dark. Let's get outta here," she said, seductively then went around to the passenger door.

This boppa must wanna fuck, he thought.

He walked around to the driver door and got inside. He started the car with Ms. Karen proposing that they get onto the freeway. Young Curtis drove while listening to her tell him about herself. He was surprised to find out she was thirty years old. He entered the freeway leading to 175, maintaining a speed of eighty miles per hour.

Ms. Karen realized she bored the young hustler with all of her talking. She knew she had to make a move because her plan was to make Young Curtis her little play thing slash ATM, so she threw caution into the wind and went for broke. She leaned over, pulled his penis out of his jogging pants, and stroked it until it was hard enough to stand on its own. Young Curtis kept his eyes on the road as a smile spread across his lips when he felt her wet, warm mouth engulf his manhood. She bobbed her head up and down, slobbing all over him, then stopped long enough to tongue the head of his penis. After a few minutes of the spectacular head job, he let off in her mouth with her swallowing every drop.

'Damn this ho' got a cold ass head game on her,' he thought while pulling his pants back up.

"Where you wanna get dropped off at?" he asked, looking over at her.

"I wanna stay with you baby," she said, rubbing his thigh.

"Dig, you got one choice and stayin' wit' me aint it. Now, where you want me to drop you off?"

She couldn't believe he played her, so she reluctantly gave him the directions to her apartment.

After dropping Ms. Karen off, Young Curtis pulled out his cell phone. On the third ring, Ducci answered the phone. "It's me homie," Young Curtis said. "I'll be there in twenty minutes. Let's blow this city," he said then smiled while zooming up the freeway.

CHAPTER 3
THE SPARKS FAMILY

Back at home in their Hunting Valley townhouse, Asad and Ahmed planned their day. It had been four days since the Jersey job while the money and the drugs safely made it to Cleveland. They put the cash in a secure location and now all they had to do was get rid of the drugs.

"Ahmed," Asad called as he came down the stairs going into the family room, where his brother sat on the gray suede sofa before a sixty-five inch television. He played Seal Com on his Xbox. He was so caught up in the game that he didn't hear Asad call his name.

"Ahmed," he said again, this time standing in the room.

"What's up bruh?" he asked, putting the game on pause before looking over at his brother.

"Did you talk with Charm?"

"Yeah, he's coming in tomorrow to pick us up."

Charm was a hustler from Detroit, who turned the brothers onto Angel. Over the last few years, he gave them information on quite a few hustlers across the country. Once he supplied them with the details, their job was to come up with the best plan to carry out the murders and robberies. They kept everything they found from all the jobs they pulled. It was a good arrangement for both sides. Charm got rid of his competition and people who crossed him as well as his Bolivian friends. In return, the brothers made a small fortune. The men had been introduced to one another by Charm's cousin, Rasheeda, an old girlfriend of Asad's.

Charm wanted something taken care of in Ohio. He needed two people eliminated. It wasn't as if he couldn't send his own people to take care of it. He just didn't want the embarrassment. The two people he wanted hit was a man named Billy who worked for him and Sherri, a woman he once loved.

Billy and Sherri met during a dangerous time in Charm's life. The man he trusted to protect her on a daily basis betrayed him. Charm never knew the two were having an affair right under his nose. If they would've just left it at that, he would've simply washed his hands of the matter by firing Billy and kicking Sherri out of his house. But, when they disappeared together, along with four hundred twenty-eight thousand dollars of his money from a stash in one of his houses, they had to go. It took close to six months before he found out that Billy snuck into Detroit to buy drugs to take back to Canton, Ohio and sell. That's when he called Rasheeda, asking if she knew anyone in Cleveland who wouldn't mind getting their hands dirty to make some money. Thinking over the question, she instantly thought of Asad. Rumors swirled around the streets that he and his brother were behind a string of murders and robberies of some well-known hustlers in the city. At first, she didn't believe any of the rumors because she dated Asad for a year and he didn't seem like a gangster to her. She knew he and his brother killed two men in front of their grandmother's house as youngsters but it was still hard for her to believe some of the things she heard. To her, Asad was an intelligent, respectful, soft-spoken brother. She never once heard him use foul language. To her, he appeared square but the streets held a different opinion. People from all over the city knew of Asad and Ahmed Sparks and they all said the same thing. "Those two brothers aren't to be messed with."

Once Charm met the two, he explained what needed to be done. After listening to him, the brothers agreed to do the hit for fifty thousand a piece. Charm agreed because Billy was a dangerous man who wasn't easy to take down. To his surprise, two days later, Asad called to tell him the job was done. He even told him that they found most of his money. Charm told them to keep it because it was never about the money as opposed to the disrespect.

"What time are we supposed to hook up with Ty?" Asad asked.

Ahmed looked at his stainless steel Submariner Rolex, "At five o'clock, over Aunt Joy's house."

Ty was Tyrone 'Fly Ty' Sparks, the brother's younger cousin and unarguably the richest twenty-year-old hustler in the city. They brought him in two years earlier to get rid of all the drugs they acquired from their robberies. He was perfect for the job. He had already made a name for himself as a hustler three years before they took him to a higher level in the game.

"I'm about to jump in the shower. When I'm done, we'll hit the city," Asad said.

Ahmed nodded his approval before turning his attention back to his game.

$$$

"Tyrone," a female voice sang from the master bedroom to the adjacent bathroom.

"What's up baby?" he asked, entering the room then plopping on the bed next to his beautiful woman Tamiko. He gave her a long, passionate kiss.

He still remembered the first time he'd met her. It was three years earlier, on the west side of Cleveland, at a get together for a guy he knew.

$$$

It was cool. Fly Ty stood in the living room of the gambling house. He stared at a large crowd of boys in front of an open bedroom door. They peered inside at a female as if she was Halle Berry. When he made his way over to the door, he saw what all the fuss was about. He glared in at the beautiful woman with an appearance of annoyance on her face as she tried to ignore all the boys at the door. *Forget about Halle Berry, this had to the most beautiful woman in the world,* he thought.

She had an exotic look to her, from her long straight jet-black hair to her slightly slanted eyes. Her natural copper toned skin was the color white women spent hours in the sun trying to get. As he stood there, caught up in the woman's beauty, they locked eyes for a split second. That second was long enough for him to feel something. He walked away, heading to the basement to shoot dice so he could get the attractive woman off of his mind.

After dropping two hundred dollars in the game, he went upstairs to get something to drink. He opened the refrigerator quickly, finding what he wanted. A nice cold beer. He closed the door and was surprised to see the pretty woman standing there. He flashed a perfect white smile at her but it wasn't returned. Now, standing face to face, the thing that stuck out the most besides her beauty was her height. He figured she had to be about 5'11" because he was 6' even and they almost stood eye to eye. He continued to stare, thinking she had a strong likeness to Ice-T's first wife Darlene, the one on a few of his album covers back in the day.

"Aren't you too young to consume alcohol?" she asked with her arms folded across her chest.

"*Damn, she proper*," he thought. "I aint too young fo' nothin," he replied.

She laughed at his terrible grammar.

"What's so funny?" he asked out of curiosity.

"You are," she said. "How old are you anyway?"

Fly TY thought about lying for a second because he could tell she was older than he was but he reasoned against it. He never had to lie to get a woman and didn't want to start, so he told her seventeen with pride.

"You're just a baby," she said in a condescending manner with a smile on her face.

Fly Ty felt himself getting angry, and, in his defense, he asked, "How old is you?"

"Twenty one."

"Shit, you're only a few years older than me," he shot back, taking a sip of his beer.

"We might be close in age, but, in maturity, I'm at least ten years older than you are," she replied.

From listening to her talk down on him, along with the beer starting to kick in, he snapped, "Well, why in the fuck you sittin' up here wastin' your time talkin to me? Cuz I aint sweatin' you and I ain't pressed to kick' it wit' yo' stuck up ass." With that, he went back to the basement, leaving her in the kitchen with a shocked expression on her face.

Fly Ty sat alone at the mini bar lost in his own thoughts. *Why did girlie try and dog me like that? Like she's better than me or something. I don't care how good she looks. She bet not pull up on me with that bullshit again.*

"Hey Fly Ty," a chubby, light-skinned boy named Will said,

breaking his train of thought.

"What's good fam?" he asked with a somber look on his face. "Dig, I enjoyed your get together but I'm 'bout to head back on my side of town." He stood up from the barstool.

"Al'ight homie. But, before you leave, my sister's friend wanna holla at 'cha," the boy said. He then gave Fly Ty some dap and left. *What does she want?* Fly Ty thought, heading toward the stairs.

Leaning against the wall, halfway up the stairs with her coat on, Tamiko became somewhat nervous when she saw him coming.

"What's up?" he asked smugly, leaning against the wall across from her.

"Do you have a car?" she asked, already knowing the answer. Lisa, Will's older sister, gave her the 411 on him. She found out he was a hustler from the east side who lived on Miles Avenue and everyone called him by his nickname. She also told her he was one of the top ranked amateur boxers in the country, who many believed would bring a world title to the city once he turned professional. Tamiko wasn't sure why she was interested in him. First of all, he was four years younger. Secondly, he was average looking but cute in his own kind of way. She also knew she could have any man she wanted but something in his eyes made her want to get to know him.

"Yeah, I got a car. Why?"

"Because, I wanted to know if you could take me home, Tyrone."

He stared at her for a moment, thinking it over. "I'll give you a ride, but you can cut that Tyrone shit short. You don't know me like that."

She couldn't do anything but smile as he walked past.

Outside, Fly Ty used his key chain remote to disarm his car alarm, making the lights on his candy painted purple two door "86" Cutlass Supreme, flash.

"You have a nice car," Tamiko said, walking toward it while looking at the twenty-inch chrome and gold Daytons.

"Thanks," he replied, opening the passenger door for her.

On their drive to Rocky River, a west side suburb of Cleveland, Fly Ty found out Tamiko stayed with her parents and fifteen-year-old brother when she wasn't in school in Columbus, Ohio. She also told him she was multi-racial. Her father was Black and Native American and her mother was a Japanese American. She was back in town for the Thanksgiving holiday, from Ohio State University, where she was in her second year of medical school, studying to become a pediatrician. The more she talked, he started to realize she wasn't just a pretty face but probably the most intelligent person he ever met. She was a worldly person who spent most of her teenage years traveling abroad as a foreign exchange student. She could even speak five different languages fluently. At the tender age of sixteen, she accepted an academic scholarship to OSU instead of Harvard because of its proximity to Rocky River and would be allowed to join the track team as a walk on. After earning her degree a year early in Biochemistry, she took the MCAT which was the medical school entry exam and scored in the 98th percentile. After listening to her open up to him, he did the same. He let her in on a secret. He was tired of boxing and wouldn't try out for the 2004 trials. When she asked him why, he told her it wasn't fun anymore and he chose not to tell her that he was making a name for himself in the streets as a bonafide hustler. They sat in her driveway, talking throughout the night and have been together ever since.

$$$

Tamiko broke their kiss, smiling at Fly TY. That brought him back into the present moment. "Are you going to kiss my other lips?" she asked seductively.

He answered her by kissing her on the mouth before helping her out of the over sized T-shirt, revealing a work of art. Her body was beautifully toned from years of running track. Her copper colored complexion appeared smooth and flawless. She had nice full breast with light brown areolas and nestled between her thick firm thighs was a perfect mound of jet black, silky smooth pubic hair. But Fly Ty's favorite part of his woman's body was her firm round butt.

He slowly and softly kissed her breasts, licking and sucking each one. He eased down further to her flat, slightly muscular stomach. She released a sexy moan when he reached his destination, sticking his tongue inside her. She arched her back and pushed forward as he used his tongue to spell out his name on her clitoris while loving the taste of her body. Before too long, she pulled him up and gave him a passionate kiss.

"It's your turn baby," she said switching positions with him.

Once she was on top, she grabbed his erect penis with her right hand and brushed her long hair over her shoulder with her left. She looked up at him, showing her beautiful smile before she inserted his manhood into her mouth.

Fly Ty closed his eyes as she did her thing, loving the feeling. She slowly sucked his penis from the base to the head, gently holding the head between her teeth ever so softly while lightly grinding them back and forth over it. This drove him crazy. She worked her way back up his body with kisses.

"Put it inside me," she whispered as she straddled him. Fly Ty grabbed his manhood and guided it into her warm, wet love canal. She eased herself down, taking him all the way inside. She started to roll her hips as he palmed her ass with both bands, guiding her up and down. She moved his hands, pinning them down by his wrists. "I'm running the show today." She stared down at him as she made her vaginal muscles contract.

He closed his eyes in ecstasy, enjoying the feeling of his woman. After close to an hour of lovemaking, Tamiko rested on top of Fly Ty, kissing him.

"You know we can do this all day but I gotta meet Asad and Ahmed over at my mama's house. I need you drop to me off over there."

She stared at him, thinking he must have some business to handle. She actually hated what she suspected him of doing to make money, but that was the only part of his life he refused to discuss with her.

During their three-year relationship, she never witnessed him doing anything illegal. She never saw drugs or large amounts of money but could tell by their lifestyle he had to be one of the biggest dealers in the city. During their time together, he went from living with his mother and driving an Oldsmobile to driving a Mercedes and owning a half a million-dollar condo on Lake Erie. He somewhat put her mind at ease when he received two large checks from an investment firm, one went into his account and the other into hers. That's how he tried to convince her he wasn't doing anything illegal, but she knew better.

She kissed him again on his full lips, rolled off of him, then got out of the bed and headed to the bathroom. Fly Ty laid there, watching the gentle sway in her hips and the slight bounce of her butt thinking he would never get used to seeing her nude. "Come on, we can share the shower to save time," she suggested.

$$$

Turning off of Miles Avenue, onto Lotus, Fly Ty's white AMG Mercedes Benz, CL 55 shined in the spring sun as the 21" Lowenhart wheels beamed. In the street, a group of little boys playing football scurried out of the way when Tamiko tapped the horn. She eased down the nicely maintained road and pulled into to Fly Ty's mother's driveway behind a black Hummer H2. Fly Ty ignored his cousin Ahmed's Hummer. He was more interested in the '03 champagne colored Ford Windstar packed with the drugs.

When they stepped out of the car, he was instantly surrounded by the neighborhood kids.

"Hey Fly Ty, give us some money?" Devon asked for the pack of nine and ten-year-old boys.

"I aint got no money," he shot back at the group. Dig, my mother told me y'all little busters been runnin' through her grass, so I aint givin' y'all nothin'."

"C'mon man," the group said in unison, knowing Fly Ty was a sweet lick. But this day, he stuck to his guns.

"No! And, if I hear y'all been in this grass again, I'm gonna bring my little cousin Boo-Man over here to take a look at y'all."

The crowd got quiet because they all knew Boo-Man from staying the night over Fly Ty's mother's house and he had already beaten up most of them.

Once they realized they had nothing coming, their attention went to the pretty lady who stood by the driver's door. She wore a lavender color Baby Phat jogging suit that hugged her body. Little Eric, who lived down the street, walked up to her. "You're pretty, is you Fly Ty's girlfriend?"

"Yes, I'm Tyrone's girlfriend," she answered smiling at the boy's boldness. "Why do you want to know?" she questioned.

"Because, if you wasn't, I was gon' make you mine," the boy blushed.

"I should kick yo..." Fly Ty said, in mock anger, going after the boy. He chased him around the car a few times and both of them laughed. Tamiko looked on smiling because she knew he was a big kid at heart.

"You better be lucky I ain't catch you," Fly Ty said as him and Tamiko headed inside the house.

As the two walked through the house, the smell of food filled the air. Tamiko followed him into the kitchen where Asad and Ahmed sat at a small oak table, eating Black Angus steaks, macaroni and cheese, Spanish rice and sweet rolls. They both wore tank tops, showing off their ripped, muscular bodies. Fly Ty noticed the light brown and gray short sleeve silk shirts hanging on the back of their chairs.

"Did y'all leave me anything to eat?" he asked.

His cousins both smiled at him. "You know your mother would kill us if we didn't," Ahmed answered.

"Where she at anyway?"

"She went around the corner to Ms. King's house," Asad answered. Tamiko waited for the men to stop talking before she walked passed Fly Ty, giving Asad a hug and a kiss on the cheek.

"Now I'm jealous," Ahmed said, standing up with open arms.

"Hi Ahmed," she said, going over to give him a hug and kiss on the cheek as well.

"Y'all two gon' quit gettin' hugs and kisses from my woman every time y'all see her." Fly Ty smiled.

"What, you want a hug and kiss?" Ahmed asked, before grabbing him. Fly Ty tried with all of his might to break out of the bear hug as Ahmed puckered up, acting as if he would really kiss him.

"Let... me... go..." Fly Ty said, barely able to breathe. Once Ahmed let him out of the vice like grip, Fly Ty stared at him.

"Damn Ahmed, you need some pussy or somthin'." Tamiko slapped him on the back for using the foul language. "He almost crushed me," Fly Ty said turning to face her.

"Come here baby," she cooed, rubbing his back once he made it to her. She gave him a goodbye kiss before leaving, telling Asad and Ahmed she would see them later.

"You're lucky, Ty. You don't only have a beautiful and intelligent woman, she's also a good one," Asad said gazing at him.

"Yeah, she's the last of a dying breed," Ahmed added. "You don't find too many classy women anymore."

Fly Ty already knew all of this so he changed the subject. "What do y'all got for me?"

"All together, it's going to be fifty," Asad informed him as he stood up from the table putting his shirt on. "We have twenty-five in the van. We'll give you the other twenty-five when you're ready."

"Check this out," Fly Ty said, staring at him. "I'm gon' give y'all all the ends up front. I know y'all don't like fuckin' wit' that shit anyway."

Asad and Ahmed looked at one another for a moment, but weren't totally surprised by their younger cousin.

"Do you have a half a million on hand?" Ahmed asked.

"Yeah I got it," Fly Ty smiled.

That made Asad think for a second. "How much are you worth?" he asked.

"The last time I checked, it was a little over three mill."

Ahmed walked over and gave him a pat on the back. "That's good. You're almost up there with us," he smiled.

"I wish," Fly Ty said. He didn't know he was just a few million off.

"You should seriously think about stepping away from the streets," Asad suggested. "After two more jobs, Ahmed and I are done.

Fly Ty looked from Asad to Ahmed, who nodded in agreement. "I've been thinkin' 'bout that a lot lately," Fly Ty said. "And, wit' Miko goin' back to Columbus for medical school soon, I was thinkin' 'bout spending a lot of time down there at her off-campus apartment. So, wit' y'all gettin' ready to step away from the game, it's not even a hard decision. I know the Sparks family name has protected me over the years and y'all two are the main reason niggas ain't tried me out here. I know these lames hate to see me gettin' all this money. I'm twenty-years-old and got mo' paper than niggas who been in the game ten years," he continued. "And the city has turned into the snitch capital. The only reason one of these lames haven't sent their people at me is cuz they know they would have to deal wit' y'all."

Asad nodded in approval, proud of how his younger cousin recognized everything for what it was.

"Yeah," Fly Ty said. "Since y'all have a couple more jobs, y'all gon' still need somebody to get rid of that work. So, y'all last job will be my last." The Sparks men all agreed to this plan. "Well I'ma get this shit outta my mama's driveway. Come let me out Ahmed."

"We're about to leave with you," Asad said, heading for the side door with Ahmed and Fly Ty in tow.

Outside, the cousins gave each other dap before going to their vehicles. "I'll see y'all tomorrow," Fly Ty said as he opened the door to the Windstar. "What time do y'all wanna hook-up?"

"Around five-thirty," Asad said, before getting into the Hummer. Ahmed slowly backed the big SUV out of the driveway. He waited in the street for Fly Ty, who backed out then pulled off with the Hummer following. At the corner of Lotus and Miles, Fly Ty blew his horn with Ahmed doing the same. The Windstar turned right while the Hummer turned left.

The further Ahmed drove down Miles Avenue, the more it looked like any other ghetto across the country. Old dilapidated buildings littered the entire neighborhood along with a bar or two here and there.

"What are you getting into tonight?" Ahmed asked,

breaking the silence.

Asad smiled, looking over to his brother from the passenger seat. "It sounds like you're trying to get rid of me."

"Never that, big bruh. I was planning on hooking up with this female I met a few weeks ago but, if you wanna hang out, we can."

"Nah, I'm not going to step on your action like that." He smiled. "Take me over grandma's so I can pick up my car. I need some down time myself."

"Who are you gonna call?" Ahmed asked, cruising down Miles.

"I might hit the XO. See what's happening there."

Turning off of Miles Avenue onto 114th Street, where the brothers were raised for most of their lives, Ahmed drove further before making a left onto Olney. The brothers couldn't help but notice the porch full of girls as he parked.

"We better go inside to see grandma," Asad said while getting out of the car.

Stepping up onto the semi-darkened porch, illuminated by the street light in front of the house, the conversation between the girls instantly stopped at the sight of Asad and Ahmed. All the girls on the porch ages ranged from seventeen to nineteen. One of the girls was their nineteen-year-old cousin Isis Nicole Sparks. When she saw them coming up the stairs, she stood up from the banister with a smile on her face and rushed over to give Asad a hug and a kiss on the cheek first then did the same to Ahmed. "About time you two made it over here," she said, giving Asad another kiss on the cheek.

"Is grandma up?" he asked, giving her a fatherly hug.

"Y'all know she goes to sleep early," she answered, standing between them and the door.

"Y'all can't speak?" Ahmed asked, looking around the porch at the young females whispering and giggling.

The girls broke out in to a chorus of *"Heeey* Ahmed, *Hiii* Asad."

They both spoke back before going inside the house.

As soon as they were out of hearing range, a brown-skinned girl named Tammy spoke. "Mmm, Isis, your two cousins are sexy as hell."

"I'll take either one of 'em," a light-skinned girl named Mimi said, with the other girls voicing their approvals. Suddenly the mood on the porch changed.

"They're fine and all but they're crazy as hell." Tonya, who grew up across the street, said. Isis cut her eyes at her but she continued, going into a whisper. "I remember it was like eight years ago..." She stopped to think for a second. "Yeah, it was about eight years ago because me and Isis were eleven-years-old when Asad and Ahmed killed two people in front of this house."

None of the girls were surprised by the news because they had all heard this but no one knew the details on what happened.

"How you know what happened, Tonya? Was you there?" Tammy questioned

"No, but my brother seen everything from his window..."

"Tonya, don't say anything else about my cousins because you don't know what you're talking about. So, shut your fake, two-faced ass up before I shut you up," Isis said, getting off of the banister. She stood over Tonya, who sat on the top stair of the porch. Everyone on the porch got quiet as Isis went back, and sat on the banister, thinking about that day eight years ago.

$$$

Isis' mother, Kimberly Sparks, was a beautiful woman with a voluptuous body that no man could resist. Seeing her, it would've been impossible for anyone to tell she was a crackhead. It was no secret in the neighborhood that she smoked but, thanks to her two older brothers, she couldn't pay a dope boy on the block to sell her anything. It was rumored that James and Raymel Sparks killed a neighborhood dope boy for tricking with her. When they put the word out that if anyone sold her drugs their mamas might as well buy some black dresses, Kimberly was blackballed by every dope boy in the hood. So, she took her show on the road, moving across town where no one knew her and putting plays down on unsuspecting hustlers.

Basically, she was the reason two men were murdered in front of the family's home. Kimberly showed up at the house one day, showering Isis with all types of gifts and hoping she could repair the damage her crack addiction did to their relationship. The then seventeen-year-old Asad stood in the living room, watching his aunt as she went through the clothes and gifts with her daughter. He could tell she was high and it hurt his heart to see his beautiful aunt destroy herself in that way. As he continued to watch, he wondered where she got the money to pay for all the gifts.

No more than an hour after Kimberly showed up, trouble followed. While Grandma Sparks and Isis sat on the couch looking over her gifts, the screen door flew open and in barged three men.

"Where is that bitch Kim?" Charlie, Kim's boyfriend, angrily asked while standing over Grandma Sparks and Isis.

"Get outta my house!" Grandma Sparks shouted at the three men as she held Isis close to her.

By this time, Asad came upstairs from the basement and entered the room with a look in his eyes that should have been a warning to the intruders.

"Who is this?" he questioned his grandmother.

"They looking for my mother," Isis cried. Seeing her cry only added to the fire inside of him.

"He's Kimberly's boyfriend," Grandma Sparks added.

"That bitch stole six thousand dollars and a quarter bird from me and I want my shit now!" Charlie roared. Asad heard enough. He looked at Isis' teary face, then turned his attention to Charlie. Without saying a word, he went at him. Asad quickly closed the distance between them, hitting Charlie with a thunderous right hand, left hook combination that sent him to the floor. Charlie's partners Man and Tim stood by the broken screen door surprised by the boys move. They backed out onto the porch to get more room to battle when he came after them.

He followed without saying a word, with a calm expression on his face. Kimberly heard the commotion downstairs and ran to Asad and Ahmed's room, where Ahmed listened to his stereo. She opened the door without knocking and blurted out, "Ahmed, Asad is outside getting jumped!" His eyes widened with shock as he stood up from the bed and rushed to the closet.

Outside, the two men back pedaled off the porch into the street in an attempt to get away from the fast, hard punches the young, slim boy threw. Once in the street, Man could see Asad knew something, and whoever taught him how to throw his hands, trained him well. Plus, he was as quick as lightning. *He must've knocked Charlie out with that wicked combination in the house*, Man thought as the two squared up in the street. As they circled one another, looking for an opening to attack, Man gave Tim a slight nod. He waited until Asad's back was to him then made his move. As soon as he neared, Asad pivoted on him and threw a blistering left up, right hand hook, left hook combination. The left up landed under Tim's right eye, instantly bursting it open with the right hand and left hook connecting with his head. The punishment he took gave Man enough time to rush Asad to the ground. The force of the two hundred and ten pound Man hitting the one hundred sixty-five pound Asad was enough to knock the wind out of him when they hit the ground but this didn't stop the fight. The two fighters started tussling on the ground. To Man's surprise, the young boy was almost as strong as him. While the two wrestled, Man could see that Tim was leaning against the railing, yet trying to get himself together, from the blows he took. Out of his peripheral vision, he saw Charlie stumbling down the stairs of the porch with gun in hand.

"We got 'cha now nigga,'" Man said, using all of his strength to hold down Asad, who was trying to wiggle free. As Charlie got closer, Asad stopped struggling when he saw his younger brother run up on Charlie.

Charlie saw movement to the left of him. When he turned his head, a young kid with a gun didn't hesitate. Ahmed pulled the trigger twice on the old snub nose .38 handgun, hitting Charlie two times in the face. He was dead before he hit the ground. Man, who had just witnessed his homie murdered, froze in shock. Asad took this as an opportunity to flip himself over on top of him. Man held on to Asad with a look of fear on his face as he tried to keep the young boy from getting his right hand loose. Asad put his left forearm into Man's throat after getting his right arm free. He stuck it out and, without a word, Ahmed handed him the gun. Man braced himself, locking his arms around Asad's upper body in hopes he could keep him from shooting. His plan didn't work. Asad placed the .38 to Man's temple and pulled the trigger. The ten to fifteen people, who gathered around to watch the fight, were shocked to see part of the man's head blown off. After it was over, Ahmed helped his brother out of the dead man's hold then the two walked back to the house to check on their grandmother and Isis as well as wait for the police to come.

During all of the drama, Tim ran off and Kim was nowhere to be found. Once the police showed up and started questioning people, they all claimed they didn't see a thing. The detectives found it hard to believe, that in the middle of a hot June day in broad daylight, no one witnessed the incident. What the police didn't know was James and Raymel Sparks made it to the scene shortly after the murders and warned everyone on the street to keep their mouths shut. Everyone did as they were told because no one wanted any trouble out of the two highly respected gangsters.

The only eyewitness accounts of the crime came from the brothers, their grandmother and their eleven-year-old cousin. The police couldn't dispute the fact that the two dead men forced their way into the Sparks' home. The grandmother claimed the intruders demanded money, which seemed strange because both of the deceased men had large amounts of money on them. As soon as the men entered the house, they were confronted by the seventeen- year-old. That caused a fight to occur, which spilled out into the street. During the fight, Asad along with one of the men ended up on the ground. The evidence supported the fact that one of the deceased, identified as Charles Jones, was in possession of a firearm at the time of the offense. Seeing this, the fourteen-year-old Ahmed Sparks shot the man twice to protect his brother but the recoil of the gun made him drop it. Once the gun hit the ground, Asad Sparks and the other perpetrator fought over it with the older Sparks boy winning.

Asad and Ahmed spent two weeks in the detention home before the city prosecutors ruled that both deaths were justifiable homicides and the boys wouldn't be tried. The detectives and everyone who worked the case believed they did the right thing. No one at that time could've known that those two murders would be the first of many for the brothers.

$$$

Asad and Ahmed came out of the house and noticed the look on Isis' face. "What's wrong with you?" Asad asked with concern.

She looked at him with a frown on her cute face. "Nothing," she answered, forcing a smile. "Oh yeah, I need some money," she said, getting off of the banister and walking over to her cousins. Both men dug in their pockets and pulled out a thin fold of bills. Each gave her two, one hundred dollars.

"Thanks," she said, flashing a genuine smile as Asad and Ahmed went down the stairs.

"Tell grandma we'll stop by tomorrow," Asad said to her over his shoulder.

"Okay." Isis waved.

$$$

"I wanna see how your car looks with the new rims on it," Ahmed said, following his brother inside the garage. He helped Asad remove the cover, revealing the triple black '04 Dodge Viper SRT-10. "Those rims set the whole car off," Ahmed continued, referring to the Maya rims.

"Junior put them on while we were in Jersey." Asad smiled, opening the driver's door to let the convertible top down.

"I'll see you in the morning," Ahmed said, giving him a manly hug before leaving.

"Alright little bruh, watch yourself out there," Asad warned then got inside the Viper and started it up. The powerful sports car came to life with a roar. He shifted it into reverse, releasing the clutch as he hit the gas. The new age muscle car bolted backwards almost hitting Isis' red VW Beetle in the driveway. Being only his second time driving it, he almost forgot its power. *This is going to be fun* he thought then threw the car in first gear and burned rubber up 114th Street.

$$$

Inside a small, well-maintained home in Bedford, Ohio, a suburb of Cleveland, Fly Ty was in the basement of a house only his mother knew about; he took stacks after stacks of money from the Heritage safe he embedded into the floor nine months earlier. He had just ended a call with Tamiko, telling her to meet him at his mother's house in an hour. After placing the money in a dark blue duffel bag, he walked over to the wall that had a large piece of plywood resting against it. He lifted the board and placed it over the Heritage safe. It fit perfectly. He then rolled the green rug over the plywood that blended flawlessly. Then he pushed the pool table over the rug before getting the hand crank off of the sofa. The last thing he did was to walk back over to the pool table and stick the crank under the front end of it then turned the crank until the front wheels on the table disappeared into the legs. He did the same to the back legs, thinking it would take five people to move the table if they knew where to look. He stood back, glancing over the room. Once pleased, he picked up the duffel bag on his way upstairs and headed out of the side door to the garage. Inside the garage, he opened the driver's door of the Windstar and got inside to start it up. As the van idled, he turned the defroster on then pressed a button on the radio and held it for seven seconds before hearing the decompression of air in the back. It was a little known fact that an airtight compartment could defeat a law enforcement narcotic's canine every time. All of Charm's transport vehicles were made to that standard. Fly Ty threw the money into the compartment before shutting it then climbed over the seats to get back to the driver's side. He hit the garage door opener before slowly backing out and pressed it again to close it. Fly Ty watched as the door closed before pulling off, guiding the Windstar up the street.

$$$

Asad sat in the back of the XO Prime Steakhouse at a table facing the door. He routinely checked out the beautiful black, working professional women who socialized throughout the lounge. He tried to ignore all of the subtle looks he received from women as well as men. It was rare for him or Ahmed to go out and even rarer to see one without the other.

He sat at his table having second thoughts about being at the lounge until he noticed a tall, cocoa brown-skinned sister stealing glances at him. He scanned the woman's body, loving the way her long, shapely legs gave way to a round butt. He continued his inspection of her, working his way up to the open back sundress. He liked how her skin color contrasted with the white fabric. When his eyes traveled further up, he noticed the woman watching him watch her. They both smiled. He looked on as the beautiful woman whispered something into another female's ear next to her, then picked up her purse and made her way toward him.

"Excuse me," the woman said in a sexy, husky voice. "Do you mind if I join you?"

"You can if you want but I'm not sure how much longer I'll be here," Asad answered, taking a good look at her.

The woman walked around the table and took the seat closest to him. That's when he got a better look at her. She had bright, clear hazel eyes like Isis' but there was something else vaguely familiar about her as if he'd seen her somewhere before.

"My name is Dayna," the woman said, extending her hand.

Asad took the woman's hand in his then leaned forward giving her a kiss on the cheek. "Mine is Asad and I hope I didn't offend you, but I don't shake hands with females."

Somewhat surprised by his action she smiled. "I'll have to remember that."

When she smiled, it dawned on him why she looked so familiar. She and the former beauty pageant winner, Kenya Moore, could easily pass for sisters.

"Asad, that's Arabic for lion isn't it?" she asked.

Asad smiled at her, surprised because he'd never met a woman who knew that fact. "You're correct."

"Well, Asad, are you some type of celebrity around here? For a second, I thought LeBron James came in." She smiled.

"I didn't notice," he said, deflecting the question.

"Okay, I see that you're going to be one of those mysterious brothers," she responded, raising her virgin strawberry daiquiri to her lips. She looked over the rim of her glass, checking out the man with male model good looks. *This man is so attractive that the scar on his cheek was even sexy*, she thought.

A couple of hours passed as the two socialized, with Dayna doing most of the talking. She told him that her work as a corporate accountant had sent her to Cleveland as a promotion, and that she had only been in town for a few weeks, with this being her first time out. He also found out she was in her twenties and had ambitions of working at the company's headquarters in New, York. Asad, on the other hand, was much more secretive about his past and future but this only made him more interesting to her.

Asad, who grew tired, looked at his watch and realized that it was almost two in the morning. "I enjoyed your company but it's late and I have to go. Do you need a ride home or anything?"

"No, but I would like to see you again," she said while going into her purse and pulling out a platinum colored card with gold lettering on it. "This is a rare card. I don't give them out to just anyone so don't lose it," she said as she handed it to him.

Asad looked at the card with her home phone, cell phone, email address and business phone number on it. He pulled out his wallet placing the card inside.

"I didn't know it was this late. Would you be so kind as to walk me to my car?" she asked with a smile.

"Of course," he said, standing up from his chair.

Once in the parking lot, Dayna led Asad to a steel gray BMW X5 SUV. "Well this is me," she said as she stood by the driver's door. Both of them remained there for a moment, having that awkward feeling of what to do next.

"Can I have a hug?" Asad asked, taking the lead.

Dayna smiled. Stepping into a gentle embrace, she felt herself getting excited from the strong, muscular feel of his body. She gave him a soft kiss on his cheek. "Call me whenever you get a chance," she said.

Asad broke their embrace. "I will," he replied as he opened her door. When she was in, he shut it before heading to his car.

Dayna sat in her BMW, watching Asad as he crossed the parking lot to a convertible sports car and wondered what the future had in store for her and the mysterious man.

CHAPTER 4
A CHARMED LIFE

The city of Cleveland felt like a sauna. It was another unusually hot day in May. It was a little after three in the afternoon and from the looks of it, the heat wasn't going anywhere anytime soon. Ahmed guided his pearl white Cadillac DTS through the after school traffic as Miles Elementary had just let out. He stopped at the light on 120th Street and smiled at the group of small kids passing in front of the car. Asad, who was in the passenger seat enjoying the air conditioning, turned the volume down on Jazzmaster's "See you in July."

"What happened with you last night?" Asad asked.

The traffic light turned green and Ahmed pulled off. "That sista I met a few weeks ago, lightweight tried to hold me hostage," he answered without taking his eyes off of the road. "Dig bruh, when I first met her downtown coming out of this fitness club, she played the soft spoken innocent role."

"How does she look?" Asad interrupted

"She's nice, on the brown sugar side, about 5'5" and hundred forty pounds. Thick like granny's cake mix. You know how we like 'em," Ahmed responded, glancing over to his brother with a smile.

Asad grinned, knowing the Sparks' men had a fetish for women with nice butts.

"So anyway," Ahmed said, bringing his brother's attention back to his tale. "I take the sista out to eat and she's still playing the game, acting kind of shy and nervous. I figured I'd give her until dinner to loosen up but that never happened. During dinner, I realized I wasn't vibing with her so, after leaving the restaurant, I took her home. When we got to her condo in Mayfield… I'm a gentleman like grandma taught us to be… I walked her to the door. Now this is where the story gets good. Once we got to the door, I told her that I enjoyed myself and I hope she did as well. That's how I was going to leave it. No hug, no kiss, nothing. So when I turned to leave, she grabbed my arm and asked if I could come in for a while because she wanted to show me something. I'm staring at her while she's shyly looking at the floor smiling. To make a long story short, I went inside," Ahmed explained while glancing from the road to his brother. "Now check this out, as soon as we get inside, she runs off to her bedroom. She took off so fast I didn't have a chance to ask her what's up. So while I'm standing in the living room, my mind started to race. I got paranoid and pulled out my gun, thinking this might be a setup."

Asad said nothing as he stared at his brother and listened to his story.

"So peep, I started looking around the condo. It was one of those single floor structures so the only place anyone could hide was the bathroom or her bedroom. I checked the bathroom. Nothing! I went back to the front door and put the safety chain on to make sure no one could creep in on me. When I turned around, I see girlie standing in the doorway of her bedroom wearing a short, red silk robe. It was open!" Ahmed said, looking over to him. "This sister's body was on point, she had it all. So, guess what I do."

"What?" Asad asked, turning in his seat to face him with a grin on his face.

"Man, I rushed into the room, knocking girlie to the floor. I had my gun out but I didn't point it at her. I told her not to move while I checked the closet. It was empty. Girlie is on the floor asking me, 'what the hell are you doing?' I ignored her as I checked under the bed. Once again, nothing."

Asad was in the passenger seat, dying laughing, but managed to say. "You scared that woman to death."

"Nope, check this. After I get up from checking under the bed, I looked over at her standing by the door breathing heavy like she was having an asthma attack or something. But when she took off her robe, I realized she was turned on by all of the action. She walked over to me, saying she wouldn't do anything to hurt me. Now I'm really tripping. I can't believe this is the same woman I was with earlier. She pulled up on me, reaching for my gun hand. I pulled it away from her. She apologized by going for my belt buckle. Needless to say, I didn't stop her," he smiled.

"Yeah, all the gangster stuff went out straight the window," Asad laughed.

"Right," Ahmed chuckled. "Man we went at it all night. Every time I tried to leave, she said, one more time. The only reason I'm here now is because I snuck out on her," Ahmed said, pulling into his Aunt Joy's driveway. He turned the car off then they got out and headed to the house.

"What's up cuz?" Asad asked Fly Ty who came out of the front door.

"Nothin' much," he answered, stepping down the stairs dressed in his hustling gear. He wore dark blue sweat pants, an oversized white T-shirt, and a pair of wheat colored Chukka Timberlands. "Where y'all goin?" he asked, noticing their attire. They both wore light linen outfits. Ahmed had on a cream colored, short sleeve shirt with matching pants and a pair of brown, closed toe gator sandals. Asad basically had the same thing on but his outfit was light gray and his gators were dark gray. He could tell they both had their brushed waved hair freshly cut and lined up.

"We're about to meet Charm at the airport and fly down to Miami to celebrate his birthday with him," Ahmed answered.

"Yeah?" Fly Ty said, not knowing it was his birthday. "Tell him I said happy b-day and I'll have something for him the next time I holla at Juan."

Charm was Fly Ty's connect outside of his cousins and Juan was one of Charm's people.

"The money in the car?" Asad asked, pulling out a set of keys along with an address and instructions on where to find the other twenty-five kilos in an apartment in Warrensville Hts.

"Yeah, it's in the compartment."

"Dig Ty, I need you to do me a favor," Asad said as they walked up the driveway to the Windstar. Fly Ty opened the driver's door and got inside while Asad opened the sliding door. Fly Ty went through the routine to open the secret compartment. Once it released, Asad picked up the duffel bag opening it.

"Are these in stacks of ten thousands?" he asked, knowing his cousin's money wrapping preference. Fly Ty nodded his head while watching as Asad took twenty stacks out of the bag. Ahmed stood behind the van, making sure no one walked up as Fly Ty and Asad handled their transaction.

"Could you go grab the duffel bag that's on the back seat of Ahmed's car," Asad said to Fly Ty, who got out and retrieved it. He made it back to the van with the bag then handed it to Asad.

"Take the rest of this money with you and put it in the same spot where you'll get the drugs from," Asad said, putting two hundred thousand dollars in the bag Fly Ty gave him. After shutting the compartment, he got out of the van.

"I got 'chu," Fly Ty said, following him to the car.

"Today is Friday," Ahmed said, looking at his watch. "I guess we'll see you Monday."

"Ai'ight, I'll hold the city down while y'all gon'," Fly Ty said before his cousins got into the Cadillac and drove off.

$$$

Ahmed parked in the long-term section of Burke Lakefront Airport. After getting their bags out of the trunk of the car, they went inside the small airport. As soon as they entered, they both spotted Charm sitting by himself in the practically empty lobby with a cell phone pressed against his ear. When he saw the two men walking his way, he stood up with a smile on his face and ended his call.

$$$

Ellery 'Charm' La'Vette was a small, handsome, light brown-skinned man who stood 5'6" and weighed one hundred and forty-six pounds. One look at him and it was easy to see he took pride in his appearance. He wore his hair in a short tapered afro and sported a full, neatly trimmed and lined up beard slightly thicker than a five o'clock shadow. To many, he was one of the most charming and charismatic men a person could know. He had a way with people. That was his strong point. He could put anyone at ease with his non-threatening appearance and manner, making everyone he met instantly like him. That was one of the reasons he achieved success for so long.

Back in his earlier days, folks considered him a hustler's hustler. During the early nineties, he shot to superstar status in the streets of Detroit as a true Kingpin. In the late eighties, Detroit's drug culture had been ravaged by State and Federal investigations that sent most of the city's drug crews to prison for long stretches while leaving others on the run. The streets were left wide open and in a relatively short time span, Charm went from a low level dealer who hustled out of a small apartment building, to becoming one of the country's biggest distributors of cocaine. Legend told it that in the spring of 1990, Charm started off with a quarter ounce of crack cocaine and worked his way up to two kilos within a month. People who knew him back then said he never thought of selling coke as a hustle but looked at it as a business. He ran his operation as if it was a Fortune 500 company. His main objective, ever since he began selling drugs, was to minimize risk and losses while maximizing product and profits. That motto made him super rich over the years.

His first big break came from, his then connect, Big Rick. Charm's drug empire expanded so quickly that Big Rick was having a hard time keeping him and his other customers supplied. That eventually led to him doing something he would later regret. In a rush to make it onto a scheduled flight to Jamaica, Big Rick's Mexican connect unexpectedly showed up in town and needed to dump thirty kilos before going back to Texas. However, he couldn't get to the drugs until later. Instead of cancelling his trip or simply telling his connect it was not a good time, he came up with a plan. Off of each kilo, he stood to make thirty-five hundred so he figured he could dump them all on Charm for five hundred less and have him go pick up the drugs that night. He thought this would be the easiest ninety thousand he ever made. Charm agreed to the deal and met the Mexican but, by the end of the night, he became his man in Detroit. No one could've known at the time that this would lead Charm to a direct connect with an up and coming drug cartel family in Bolivia. It was practically unheard of for them to deal directly with a Black man but that was before they met Charm and fell under his spell.

As his wealth and status grew in the streets so did the hatred of his enemies. And, with Detroit being a city of hustling gangsters, the streets were about to get hot. Charm, more of a money getter than a gunslinger, made his enemies think he would be easy to get rid of, but he had a few things working in his favor. He was smarter than all of his adversaries and far more dangerous than they gave him credit. He recognized all the signs in the streets and knew most of the other hustlers were aligning themselves to put an end to his reign. Before they could put their plans in action, Charm took a two week vacation to the Bahamas and left precise instructions for his lieutenants to be passed down to the hitters he brought in from Chicago. Charm's crew was relatively small compared to others in Detroit but, what they lacked in numbers, they made up for it with money and influence. He was about to pull off a stunning coup that no one saw coming. When the plan was executed, it became one of the bloodiest three days in Detroit's history.

Charm had planned everything perfectly. He got rid of the two men who hated him the most, Mercedes Moe and Big Rick. Mercedes Moe, along with his bodyguard Bink, was machine gunned to death inside his beloved S600 at a stoplight on the corner of John R and State Fair in broad daylight. Two days after, the police started finding arms and legs that turned out to be Big Rick's. He was murdered then dismembered with his body parts spread throughout the north end area of the Motor City. During the three days, Charm's men killed thirteen people without losing one of their own.

When he returned home from his vacation, he was met at the airport by a five-car motorcade. He was placed in the middle car with the other four cars positioned to shield him from any possible attacks. One car led the way, two followed behind him, and the fifth one stayed on the weak side of Charm's vehicle to keep anyone from pulling up on him. All of the cars in the motorcade contained two shooters in them each.

Charm was only back in town for a week before the calls started coming, asking for a truce. He agreed to a meeting with the other major hustlers in the city because the stunt he pulled brought so much heat and attention from the police and the media that everybody's pockets started to hurt.

The meeting took place at NorthLand Mall on a Saturday afternoon, at a time when it would be crowded. Charm knew that they chose the meeting place for that particular reason. That meant one thing. They feared him now. Charm and the other four men, who asked for the meeting, walked through the mall with numerous shooters in shouting range just in case things got out of hand. The scene in the mall was tense. As the five men walked and talked, each with a group of their own men following trying not to be noticed. The average shopper could tell something major was happening by looking at the scattered groups of rough looking men who kept their eyes glued on the five well-dressed men who talked in hushed tones. There was one person from Charm's entourage who went unnoticed, a young teenaged boy who stopped at every store ahead of Charm and the other men. No one seemed to notice that his girlfriend's shopping bag was heavier than normal. It carried a short Ak-47 that Juan had locked, loaded and readied to shoot, but that day it wasn't needed.

It didn't take long for all of the men to agree to a cease fire, vowing that they would all sit down to solve their problems if any further misunderstandings arose. They all shook on this agreement, ending the beef.

That occurred shortly before Charm met Asad and Ahmed. The contract he made with the men didn't sit well. He knew all four of them took a part in plotting his death. Not knowing if he could trust them, Charm figured, instead of waiting for them to get the courage to come after him again, he should get rid of them. Since he gave his word it was over, he had to do it in a way that wouldn't lead back to him. That was where Asad and Ahmed came into play. So impressed with how the youngsters handled Billy and Sherri, he decided to use them on the hits.

Before sending for the brothers, he spent big money compiling information on the targets that was usually paid to a scorned mistress or a disgruntled employee. By the time Asad and Ahmed made it to Detroit, Charm knew everything he needed to know. He knew where the stash houses were and the best places to catch the men. One by one, all four of the men were murdered over a six-month time period. Everyone in the city thought a crew of stick-up men, just released from Jackson State Prison, preyed on the city's biggest ballers. No one suspected anything else, the plan was classic Charm.

$$$

"How's my two favorite brothers?" Charm asked with a smile while clipping his cell phone to his hip just before giving each man a hug.

"We're good," Ahmed answered while handing him the duffel bag with the money in it.

"What's this?" he asked with his trademark smile then unzipped it.

"It's your birthday gift," Asad replied. "You don't know how hard it is to find a gift for a man who already has everything. We figured to just give you the money and you could decide on what you wanted to do with it."

"I knew y'all loved me," he joked zipping the bag closed. "Are y'all ready? The jet is on the tarmac waiting."

"Let's get outta here," Asad said, letting Charm lead the way.

$$$

On the Gulf Stream V, Asad and Ahmed took their seats in the comfortable light gray leather captain chairs. They both looked around the small cabin of the luxury private jet, wondering how much it cost.

"I spare no expense when comes to enjoying the good life," Charm said, reading the brothers' expressions. "Not to mention, this charter is a tax write off from It's A Charmed Life Promotions.

In Charm's earlier day, when he started becoming a bonafied money getter, he knew he needed a way to clean all of the illegal money he made. From that problem came the birth of his promotion company. He started promoting concerts and boxing matches in the U.S and South America, making himself well known throughout the boxing and entertainment world as an honest and fair promoter. The company, originally started to solely launder his dirty money, ending up becoming a profitable business itself.

On the boxing side, he promoted two world champions and also had a heavyweight who was going through his division like a hot knife through butter. It was no doubt in Charm's mind that his heavyweight would become a title holder within a year or two. Not to be outdone, '03 was a banner year for the concert promotion wing. A Charmed Life Promotions put together the hottest Hip Hop and R&B acts for a national tour, which became the highest grossing urban tour ever. In deed, he led a charmed life.

As the Gulf Stream taxied for takeoff, Charm told the brothers to get some rest because once they touch down in Miami, the party would start.

"Well, I'm about to go to sleep. I'll see y'all in a few hours," Ahmed said, leaning back in his seat to get comfortable. Asad closed his eyes but sleep was the last thing on his mind. His thoughts were on the beautiful woman he met the previous night.

$$$

Sitting with the car idling in the driveway of a house on Gardner, a street in Warrensville, Fly Ty looked at his watch that read a quarter to midnight. *Damn I didn't know it was this late,* he thought. His plan was to drop off the twenty-five kilos but he ended up staying longer than he expected. Just when he was about to put the car into reverse his cell phone vibrated.

He reached into his sweat pants pocket pulling it out. "Speak on it."

"Aww, what's good my fly fam?"

"Young muthafuckin' Curtis! What's poppin,' playboy?" Fly Ty said happily, instantly picking up on his voice.

"Aint shit homie. I'm just callin' to check on you."

"When did 'chu get back in town?" Fly Ty asked while backing out of the driveway.

"A few days ago but fuck all that. I'm tryin' to see if you wanna kick it tonight."

"Dig Curt, I've been out runnin 'round all day. I gotta get home to my woman. But we can do something tomorrow."

"Damn fam! You lettin' Tamiko put it down on you like that?

Fly Ty smiled. "Man, sometime you gotta let them think they're puttin' it down. So when you do it, they can't argue."

"Fam! Young Curtis aint wit' that soft shoe shit you on. I mash the gas on all my bitches. But I can feel you. You pussy whipped boy," Young Curtis said getting a laugh out of Fly Ty.

"Dig we'll hook-up tomorrow on everything, Curt," Fly Ty promised.

"Ai'ight fam. We gon' pull an all nighter so I don't wanna hear that I gotta get home to my girl shit."

"Stay down," Fly Ty laughed as he hit end on his cell.

$$$

It was 12:23 a.m. when Fly Ty arrived at the Bay Village condo he shared with Tamiko. Once inside, he made sure he took his boots off in the foyer. That was one of Tamiko's rules. She didn't allow shoes to be worn inside their home. She said it was unsanitary and didn't want anyone tracking up the white carpet. After taking off his boots, he placed them in line with a pair of her running shoes and a pair of size twelve, red and black Mike Vick's. He knew that meant her younger brother was visiting.

When he walked into the living room, he saw the eighteen-year-old Tanaka sitting on the floor in front of the big screen TV, playing NCAA Football on his PS2.

"What's up Tee?" Fly Ty asked approaching him.

"What's going on Ty?" He asked happily, quickly getting up from the floor rushing to him.

"Nothin' much Mr. Football," Fly Ty said, giving the tall boy a brotherly hug. Tanaka was the male version of his sister, from his slightly slanted eyes to his copper toned complexion. The only difference was his hair was curly instead of straight.

"It looks like you're gettin' bigger," Fly Ty said, looking at the 6'4" 218 pound man child.

Tanaka flexed his arm muscle. "I've been hitting the weight room hard," he smiled. I'm getting ready to go down to OSU for spring practice."

"I saw that on the news a few days ago," Fly Ty said.

Tanaka Youngblood was the top rated quarterback prospect in the country, who many of the experts considered a can't miss recruit. Every major college program in the nation sent recruiters to Ohio to try and land the phenom. He chose OSU over the other perennial powerhouses because his sister was finishing her medical studies there.

"What cha doin' over here?" Fly Ty asked curiously.

"I couldn't find the cleats I wanted in none of the stores in Sandusky, so I called Miko to come and get me. She's taking me to Beachwood Mall tomorrow. She did some checking around and the Footlocker there has them."

Fly Ty smiled because it seemed like every since his parents moved to Sandusky to be closer to the Ford plant where his father worked as a supervisor, he always found a reason to come to Cleveland. "Where's Miko?"

"She's upstairs studying."

Fly Ty walked over to the sliding glass door that led out to the balcony. He looked over the calm lake thinking about the conversation he'd had with his cousins. In his heart, he felt ready to step away from the streets and the people in them. As far as Hollywood and Bay Bruh, the two members of his hustle team, he knew they would always be tight no matter what. Then the thought of one other person he couldn't see himself walking away from came to mind.

"Hey you." The sound of Tamiko's voice broke his train of thought. He turned toward her as she approached. She wore a light yellow, long sleeved, button up sleeping shirt with matching footies. She gave him a quick kiss on the lips before turning to say something to Tanaka.

"What I tell you 'bout kissin' me like it's a routine?" Fly Ty asked, grabbing her by the waist when she tried to walk past him.

She turned around giving him more of a passionate kiss. "Are you happy now?" she asked with a smile.

"Nah, I ain't happy," he said, returning her smile. He pulled her closer, giving her a longer kiss.

"Getta room," Tanaka said, not taking his eyes off of the television as he played his game.

Fly Ty broke their kiss then picked her up in his arms. "You heavy," he said, looking down at her.

"I didn't tell your skinny butt to pick me up," she laughed.

"You ain't that heavy fo' real." He smiled before taking off running with her in his arms.

"You better not drop me Tyrone," she warned as he stood at the bottom of the stairs.

"Well you betta hold on," he shot back, before running up the stairs with Tamiko holding on tight. She laughed as he struggled to get to the top.

CHAPTER 5
JT AND MEL

Ducci lay asleep in his bed, getting the much needed rest he longed for until the ringing telephone disturbed the silence in his room. He tried to ignore it, but after the tenth ring, he rolled over and took a look at the caller I.D. He smiled as he picked up the phone. "What's up son?"

"Hi daddy," Ducci's eight-year-old said. "You know what today is don't you?" Abdullah 'AJ' Martin Jr. asked.

"Yeah, it's Saturday," Ducci answered, acting as if he didn't know what his son was alluding to.

"Daddy! We're supposed to go go-kart racing today."

"I know little man," Ducci laughed, looking at the clock on the nightstand. "It's only ten o'clock in the morning. I'll pick you up at one o'clock on the dot."

"Okay daddy. I'll see you at one o'clock on the dot."

"I love you AJ."

"I love you too," the boy replied.

I'll see you in a little bit," Ducci said before ending the call. He laid back down pulling the cover over his head to get a couple extra hours of sleep before his day began.

$$$

Young Curtis drove twenty miles over the speed limit on the freeway in his Range Rover while talking on his cell phone. He was headed to Cleveland from his Solon, Ohio condo.

"So all they got 'chu for is drivin' wit out a license?" he asked his sixteen-year-old homie, CCW, who grew up two doors down from him in the hood.

"Yeah, all you gotta do is get it outta the impound."

For CCW's sixteenth birthday, Young Curtis gave him his custom painted, black cherry '87 Buick Grand National as a gift. Since the car was still in Young Curtis' name, he would have to go get it.

"Dig C, I'll go get it but you need to get your license. I'll come and swoop you Monday. Stay up lil homie," Young Curtis said, ending the call. Just when he was about to set the phone down it started ringing.

"What's up?" he answered.

"Hi Curtis," said Shannon, the mother of his four-year-old daughter.

"Where's Amani?" he asked.

"She's in her room taking a nap," she answered. Instead of beating around the bush, Shannon got to the reason she was calling. "I need some money, Curtis," she said bluntly.

"Now bitch, you know I don't fuck wit' you like that. I told your scandalous ass years ago if it aint 'bout my daughter don't ask me for shit."

Outside of Shannon being the mother of his daughter, he couldn't stand her. To him, she was nothing but an unfaithful money hungry hoodrat who slept with a couple of dudes from his neighborhood while they were together. But the real reason he despised her so much was because he loved her and it hurt him to find out that she wasn't the woman he thought her to be.

"You're so typical, Curtis. You're so quick to talk crazy to me when the money is for me and Amani..."

"Hold on bitch! My baby don't want fo' nothin' so you can kill that shit."

"I wanted to take her to get some new pictures and I was going to buy me something to wear. And, I wanted to know if you could come with us so all three of us can get in a few together."

Young Curtis thought for a moment. "Yeah, we can do that," he said, taking some of the aggression out of his voice. "Whose idea was this?" he asked.

"Our daughter's," Shannon answered.

"I'll be over there in a couple of hours. Be ready to go when I get there," he said, hanging up.

$$$

After parking in the driveway of a house on Beachwood Avenue, Ducci went inside.

"Hey Abdullah," Monica warmly said as she walked up and gave him a kiss on the cheek. Monica was Ducci's high school sweetheart and the mother of his son.

"I'm in the kitchen," she said, walking past him.

He followed behind her smelling pizza in the air. He went to the refrigerator, taking out a bottled water while Monica took the left over pizza out of the microwave.

"Abdullah, you know your son wants a go-kart for the summer?" she asked as she sat down at the kitchen table.

Ducci stood by the refrigerator drinking his water.

"He hasn't told me, but as much as he likes going go-kart racing, it makes sense."

"I already know you're gonna buy it. Just make sure you get my baby a helmet and let him know you're keeping it at your house," she informed him.

"Where's he at anyway?" Ducci asked.

"Yolonda, next door, took him to the store. They should be back soon," she answered before taking a bite out of her pizza.

Ducci looked at her with a sly grin. "What's up with a quickie before he comes back?"

Monica almost choked on her food, laughing. "Boy, you done lost your mind," she finally managed to say.

"I had to shoot my shot," Ducci said with a silly grin.

"Yeah, and you missed," she shot back, smiling at him.

There was no doubt that the two still had feelings for one another but they decided years ago that the love they once had as teens wouldn't last through adulthood, mainly because of Ducci's infidelities.

"Oh yeah, before I forget." Ducci reached into his pocket and pulled out two thousand dollars in cash, handing it to her. This was something he did every month to help with the bills and their son.

"Daddy, where you at!" AJ yelled from the living room.

"Boy, quit all that hollering. He's in the kitchen with me," Monica said.

AJ came rushing into the kitchen. "Let's go daddy."

"Okay little man. Give your mother a kiss bye."

He ran over to her. "See you later mommy," he said, giving her a kiss before leaving with his father.

"We have a couple of stops to make first. Is that cool with you?" he asked his son as they came off of the porch.

"Where we going?" AJ asked, walking around to the passenger side.

"We have to stop by grandma's hair salon. I need to pick up the keys to our apartment building on Union. The contractors just finished the piping and wiring last week. Now, we can start making money off of it."

"Okay, daddy, as long as it don't take all day," AJ said as they backed out of the driveway.

$$$

"Tanaka, pick out what shoes you want so we can go eat!" Tamiko demanded.

"Hold on Miko," Tanaka pleaded as he tried to decide on the pair of Nike's he wanted.

"Tee, just get both of 'em," Fly Ty said , tired of the siblings going back and forth all day.

"I can get both pair?" Tanaka asked with a big smile.

"No, you cannot," Tamiko said, stepping in while looking from her brother to her man. Tanaka looked at Fly Ty with a 'help me out' look on his face.

"C'mon baby, let him get both," he said turning to her. "I'm gonna pay for them so it shouldn't bother you."

"Tyrone, Tanaka will never learn the value of a dollar as long as you're around. We came in here for a pair of cleats. He has them. Now, he's sitting over there with two pair of sneakers that cost over one hundred fifty dollars each."

"I feel what you're sayin' but he deserves to be rewarded for being a good kid," Fly Ty countered.

She looked at him unmoved by his words. "Nothing you just said had any effect on me whatsoever. I'm going to let you buy them because I don't feel like going through this anymore and plus I'm ready to go eat."

Just when Fly Ty was about to give Tanaka the good news, she stopped him. "Make this the last time you go against me in front of my little brother."

Fly Ty turned toward Tanaka. He smiled and gave him a wink.

"You can wipe that smile off of your face," Tamiko said from behind him.

He spun around straight faced, "What 'chu talkin' 'bout?" he asked, innocently.

Not in the mood for his antics, she walked over to the sitting area across from the shoe store.

"Hey my man," Fly Ty called to the sales clerk.

"How may I help you?" The young Black clerk asked as he approached.

"Give me those two pair of shoes over there," he answered, pointing at the boxes in front of Tanaka. "And I need these in a size ten," he said pulling a pair of orange suede Cortez Nike's from the display rack.

$$$

"Man this shit is crazy. The city aint been this dry in awhile," JT said to his partner Mel as they walked through the mall.

JT and Mel were a couple of known hustlers from 131st who made a reputation for themselves as being major money getters years earlier. JT was a short, slightly chubby brown-skinned man with braids. Mel was a tall, skinny man with a dark brown complexion and brush waves. They both were good looking and considered ladies men. However, few people knew of their shady business dealings or the rumors of snitching. Their once strong West Coast connect cut them off because of it. Now, the two were just living off of their old reputations. Nevertheless, they still had a lot of pull in their hood with countless young soldiers willing to do anything they were told.

"Yeah, I feel that shit JT. The only muthafucka's wit' work is that nigga Hollywood and Bay Bruh. I heard they been sellin' O's for twelve hundred a piece."

"You know where they're gettin' that shit from don't 'chu?" JT asked.

Mel stopped walking. He stood there with a puzzled look on his face, trying to rack his brain for an answer. "How the fuck should I know where those lames get their shit," he said angrily.

JT stared at his best friend, knowing that he wasn't that bright but he was loyal and that's what counted.

"Mel, those nigga's is gettin' that shit from that nigga Fly Ty," JT said, letting him in on the secret.

"There that nigga go right there," Mel said, pointing into the Footlocker.

JT watched as Fly Ty and the tall boy came out of the store. "Hey Fly Ty," JT said, getting his attention before he walked past.

"What's up?" Fly Ty asked while giving each man dap.

"Let me holla at you fo' a minute," JT said, with a smile on his face.

"Go over there with Miko. I'll be over there in a second," Fly Ty said as he handed Tanaka his bag.

As JT and Fly Ty walked out of hearing range from Mel, JT put his arm around his shoulder. Fly Ty wanted to shrug it off because they weren't that cool even though he used to buy dope from him and Mel back in the day. Since he's been the man for the last few years on their side of town, he'd sold them a few bricks on more than one occasion. But every time they copped from him he could detect the jealousy in their eyes and he'd heard of the moves they'd been putting down, so he really didn't trust them. *But, who can you trust in this game?* Ty thought to himself. With that, he heard him out.

"Dig Ty," JT said, "you know the streets been dry for the last few days. And from what I've been hearing from my people, it's gonna be that way for a minute. Ever since terrorism started, it's been harder and harder to move dope."

Ty looked at JT, knowing where his conversation was leading. *He wanna cop*, he thought. He didn't mind serving them, he knew he was in a power position. He wasn't the only hustler in the city with work but he was the only one with major weight. And since he was close to exiting the game, this was the best time to get it off.

"Dig, Mel and I wanna spend some paper with you."

"Tyrone, we're going to be late," he heard Tamiko yell. He turned to see her and her brother waiting.

He turned back to JT. "Dig, we can hook up later. I'm goin'

to The Fame tonight so come through and we can see what we can do." He slapped JT on the shoulder then walked over to Tamiko and her brother.

Mel pulled up on JT and asked, "What's up with Ty?"

"We're goin' to The Fame tonight to meet him. We gonna talk there." JT turned to Mel and asked, "Who's that bad bitch he wit?"

"That's his broad. I don't know her name but I seen them out a few times."

JT watched as Ty and the beautiful woman walked through the mall, then with malice his heart, said, "It seems like Young Ty done come all the way up."

CHAPTER 6
M&S YACHT SALES

Charm's Mediterranean Villa was located in Miami Beach, Florida in a private gated community on Star Island. The palatial estate was built for a king. The home featured twenty-foot floors, most featuring tan marble imported from Italy, and transparent glass ceilings. The expensive furnishings were accented in tan, white, and brown. Outside, the landscape looked like a lush tropical oasis with palm trees and there was a waterfall by the swimming pool created to look like a lagoon.

Charm was true to his word when he said they were going to party as soon as the plane touched down. He had a limousine pick them up at the airport whisking them off to the Forge restaurant for a late dinner. After eating, they immediately started club hopping. They hit three different spots on South Beach and didn't make it to Charm's estate until a little after five in the morning.

Charm woke up from his slumber feeling a little woozy from the night's activities. He sat on his huge king size bed trying to clear his head before standing up. As he sat there, a smile came across his lips when he thought about all of the beautiful women who kept approaching the table he shared with Asad and Ahmed but those two weren't any fun. Every club they went to the brothers just sat there, stoned faced, watching everything and everyone around them. *I'm gonna have to show them two boys how to loosen up*, he thought while getting out of the bed and walking across the plush cream colored carpet to the master bathroom to take a shower.

After taking a shower and having his Jamaican housekeeper fix him a sandwich, he headed outside to the pool area. For it to have been a little after one in the afternoon, it was already hot. The sun shined and the sky was clear, another typical Miami day.

Charm approached the canopy, constructed by the pool with lounge chairs under it, where Asad and Ahmed relaxed.

"Good morning," he smiled, taking the lounge chair closest to Ahmed.

"What's up," the brothers said in unison looking toward

him.

"How y'all like the spot?" Charm asked, smiling.

"This is nice. It seems like paradise out here," Ahmed answered. "Asad and I have been out here for the last hour watching all these rich people ride by in their boats," he continued, nodding toward the waterway behind Charm's estate.

Charm stared out at the waterway for a second before turning his attention back to the brothers. "So what do you two wanna do today?"

"You're supposed to be the host and you don't have anything planned?" Ahmed questioned.

"Oh I have something planned." He smiled. "Tonight we're going to Club Caliente."

"I heard that was one of the hottest clubs in Miami," Ahmed replied.

"Yeah, and tonight, Ocean Drive is gonna be packed with groupies, gold diggers and boppas. Tonight one of the top rap magazines is throwing a party at one of the clubs so a lot of recording artist will be there and you know how that goes. One rapper with an entourage of twenty-five. You do the math."

"I can tell you now, Asad and I are not trying to hang around no rapping cats, are we?" he asked looking over at his brother.

"He's right. I'm not trying to be around them people tonight," Asad said.

"Don't worry," Charm said. "Club Caliente caters to a different type of clientele. This spot is super exclusive. If it's not Diddy or Jigga, they're not getting in. Plus, I'm meeting some very important people there tonight," he said, looking from Asad to Ahmed.

"You know we're coming," Ahmed smiled. "Whatever you wanna do, birthday boy, we're gonna do it. But you know we don't feel comfortable without heat. Asad and I don't like to hang out in strange cities naked."

"I know and I already got that taken care of. I got two Sigma arms 40 cals with extra clips. How does that sound?"

"We can work with them," Ahmed answered. He looked

over to his brother who was lost in his own thoughts. "Asad," he called.

"What's up?" Asad asked with an annoyed look on his face.

"Charm has two Sig 40's for us."

Asad nodded his approval then looked over to Charm. "I need to use your phone," he said, getting up from the lounge chair and heading toward the house.

Charm and Ahmed watched as he entered the mansion. "What's up with your brother?" Charm asked turning to Ahmed.

"I don't know. He's been out here all morning daydreaming. I'll look over at him every now and then and he would just be staring into space, sometimes with a smile on his face."

"It's only one thing that would make a brother do that," Charm said.

"What?" Ahmed asked with concern.

"Some woman has your brother's attention," he smiled.

$$$

Inside the mansion, Asad walked into Charm's den and closed the door behind him. He looked around the den at the huge mahogany built-in bookcases filled with books. He wondered how many Charm had actually read. He walked around the desk and took a seat in the brown leather chair then looked at the card in his hand that read Dayna Hawkins.

$$$

Dayna walked inside her bedroom from the bathroom then took her damp towel off dropping it on the floor. She grabbed a bottle of baby oil off of the dresser and poured a generous amount into her hands before rubbing it all over her gorgeous nude body. Once she finished, she looked at her reflection in the full-length mirror and ran her hands through her long flowing hair. She turned to the side examining her figure, liking what she saw. Her stomach was still flat, her breasts were high and perky, and her butt was round and firm.

"Not bad," she said, smiling until the ringing telephone interrupted her. At first she thought about ignoring it because it was probably her new co-worker. Kelly was cool but all she wanted to do was go out man hunting every other night. She walked over to the phone to look at the caller ID. When she read private, it piqued her curiosity. She picked it up. "Hello," she said in her sexy husky voice.

"Hi, is this Dayna?"

Butterflies instantly swelled up in her stomach. She sat down on the side of her bed. "Yes, this is she."

"This is Asad, the brother you met at XO a couple of nights ago."

"I knew it was you," she smiled.

"How did you know?" Asad questioned.

"Well, first of all, you have a very distinctive voice. You talk in a low cadence. Secondly, you're the only man I've given my home number," she laughed.

"That's good to know," Asad smiled, liking the last remark. "Well let me say, it's an honor to be the only man in Cleveland with your home number."

They both laughed at his comment.

"So to what do I owe this call?" she asked.

"Nothing, I was just thinking about you and decided to call." He thought for a second, "You're not busy or anything because I can call you back later."

"No, no, no," she said a little too anxious for her own liking. "I mean no, I can talk. Just give me a second to put my robe on."

"You need a robe to talk?" Asad asked with a chuckle.

"No, but I don't like sitting around nude talking to a mysterious man."

For a moment, he tried to picture what she looked like naked.

"I'm so glad you called," she said coming back to phone. "I don't know what it is you did to me but I can't get you off of my mind," she said, finding herself being very candid.

"I was thinking the same thing about you," Asad replied, instantly feeling uncomfortable about the way he felt for the woman he didn't know. For him, this was out of character. He couldn't figure out what was going on but he wanted to see where it all would lead.

"Hey, I have an idea," Dayna said. "How about you let me

treat you to dinner. I know where this really good soul food restaurant is."

"I would really like that but, right now, I'm out of town."

"When will you be back?" she asked, a little disappointed.

"Monday," he answered before an idea came to mind. "What time do you get off from work?"

"Most of the time around five-thirty."

"Well how about I pick you up at six-thirty and we go out to dinner?"

"I'd like that. Take down my address."

"Hold on," he said. When he returned, they continued to talk for another five minutes before ending their call.

After hanging up the phone, Dayna rested on her bed and thought about Asad. She started to wonder if there was any truth to some of the things she'd heard about him. "Oh well," she said to herself as she got up and disrobed to get dressed.

$$$

By the pool, Asad could see Charm and his brother laughing hysterically. "What's so funny?" he asked while taking his seat.

Ahmed looked up at him and could see he was more relaxed and sociable than earlier. "Charm was telling me about how two call girls tried to rob him in Vegas."

Charm glanced at his black and gold Ulysses Nardin watch before looking over to the brothers. "Do you fellas feel like taking a ride with me?"

"How long will we be out?" Asad asked.

"About an hour or two."

"Yeah we'll roll. I'm tired of sitting out here anyway," Ahmed said, speaking for the both of them. The men all got up from their chairs and left the pool area then walked across the lawn to the four-car garage. "Where we going?" Ahmed asked.

"You'll see when we get there," Charm smiled as he lifted the third door on the garage. He went inside while the brothers waited. He backed out in an off-white Escalade EXT.

Ahmed looked inside the garage and saw a 2001 white

silver Seraph Rolls-Royce, a red 2003 Ferrari Spider, and a 1993 AMG enhanced E500 Mercedes Benz.

"What's up with the old Mercedes?" Ahmed asked as he got into the back passenger side seat.

"That Benz has a lot of sentimental value," Charm informed. "It was my first big purchase. I got it back in '92. It was the hottest Benz in the city. And don't get me started on how the women used to act when I pulled up in it," he said with a laugh then pulled out of the driveway.

It was almost closing time when Charm arrived to his destination, M&S Yacht Sales. Inside, walking around the showroom, Charm pointed out a speedboat he liked. "I think I'm going to eventually get one of these also," he said as he and the brothers looked at a yellow and white Cigarette speedboat.

"What, you're about to buy a boat?" Asad asked.

"No. I already have a yacht in the back getting customized. It's nothing too fancy. A 72 foot Conados. It's going to be my introduction into the world of yachting," Charm said in an uppity voice before laughing.

As the men stood around the speedboat talking, Charm saw Mike Guerrero, the owner of M&S. He walked their way with a big smile on his round face.

"How are you Mr. La'Vett?" he asked, shaking his hand.

"I'm fine," Charm said returning the smile. "These are two of my associates, Jack and Brian," he said, pointing at Asad and Ahmed.

"How are you two gentlemen," the short overweight man asked with a big fake smile plastered on his face. "Are you two twins," he questioned after looking at them for a second. Both of the men shook their heads no.

He continued to stare at them a little longer before turning to Charm. "You're early Mr. La'Vette. Your yacht will not be finished until Wednesday..."

"I know Mike," Charm said, cutting him off. "I have my friends in town for the weekend and I'd like to show it to them before they leave. If you don't mind, take us in the back so they can see it," he said, walking toward the double doors to the work area. To all of their surprise, the short, fat, balding man moved quickly in front of the door and stopped them.

"Wait a minute Mr. La'Vette. This is really not a good time. The workers are busy back there and it could be dangerous with all of the heavy materials they're using. Plus, it's closing time. How about you come back Monday and ask for Jim. He'll be sure to give you and your friends a tour."

Charm stared at Mike for a moment. "You're not going to be here?"

"No, I'll be on my long overdue vacation." He smiled. "I leave tomorrow and will not be back for two weeks."

"What, taking the wife and kids to see grandma?" Charm asked, turning on his charm.

"Oh no, nothing like that. I never married and I don't have children."

What Charm and the brothers didn't know was that Mike Guerrero was on his way to Costa Rica as a sex tourist. He had a thing for underage girls and Costa Rica was a place he visited twice a year because of its abundance of young prostitutes and lax laws.

"Well check this out, Mike," Charm said, putting his arm around the man's shoulder. "Look, you see those two over there," he said nodding to the brothers. Mike nodded as he looked at the two men. Charm went on. "Well, they are thinking about purchasing water vehicles but you see how you treat me? I was telling them all of these good things about you. Now you can't even give me the time of day and I've already spent three point five on aftermarket..."

Mike interrupted him. "Mr. La'Vette, don't think for one second that we here at M&S Yacht Sales don't appreciate your business. You are a valued customer that we look forward to doing more business with in the future."

Charm stared into the man's eyes, seeing the sincerity and playing on it. "Well you shouldn't mind us going back there," he said while walking off with the brothers right behind him. Mike didn't try to stop them.

Damn, I have to make this fast, Mike thought, as he

followed the men through the doors.

Once they were behind the double doors, the men stepped into the expansive service area and looked at all the different shapes and sizes of watercrafts. There were only four boats on the floor. The rest were on lifts or lined up at the docks in the back. One of the boats on the floor belonged to Charm. He was so caught up on talking about his yacht that he didn't seem to notice the reaction of the two men standing by an office door all the way at the other end of the huge facility. One of them hollered something to Mike in Spanish with him responding back in Spanish. Asad looked at Ahmed to see if he picked up on the scene. Ahmed acknowledged him with his eyes as they walked toward the yacht.

"We must hurry. We're not supposed to be back here," Mike said to the group of men.

"It won't take but a minute," Charm responded, climbing up the back of the large yacht with the brothers following. He gave them a quick tour, showing them the stateroom, the bedroom, and the galley.

After walking around for a few minutes, Ahmed told him it looked better than he and Asad's place.

Standing outside the yacht, Mike anxiously waited for the men to finish their tour. Just as he finished his thought, he saw Charm coming down the back ladder.

"Are you pleased, Mr. La'Vette?" he asked as Charm came off of the boat with his friends.

"Yeah, everything is coming along really well..." His sentence was broken by the sound of a car by the open garage door in the back.

A black, convertible Aston Martin came to such an abrupt stop that the white cargo van following almost ran into it.

Getting out of the Aston Martin was a tall, slim, suave looking Hispanic man dressed in a gold Versace shirt, cream-colored pants, and a pair of brown alligator cowboy boots. After shutting the door of the car, he lifted up his sunglasses and stared down the long garage at Mike as well as the three men with him. The man didn't say one word but Mike knew it was time for the men to go.

"We really must get going," Mike said, leading the men to the double doors.

Back on the showroom floor, Charm thanked Mike for the tour and told him to have a nice trip before he and the brothers headed out to the parking lot. Mike stood on the showroom floor, watching Charm and his buddies leave. Once they drove out of the parking lot, he turned to go upstairs to his office when Raul came through the double doors.

"Chico wants you in his office."

Mike's heart sank. "Okay," was all he could manage to say.

Inside the office, Chico De'Jesus stood behind the mini bar, preparing a Rum and Coke. Mike came into the room, looking around nervously.

"How you doing, Mike," Chico asked as he came from around the bar. He took a seat on the dark blue leather sofa.

"I'm fine, Chico," Mike answered from the door.

Chico patted the seat next to him before taking a sip of his drink.

"Raul, get the bags outta the van," Chico said, sending the man out of the room. As soon as he left, Chico turned to Mike who sat on the sofa next to him. He stared at him for a moment, taking another sip of his drink before he began talking.

"Chu know the rules, Mike, so tell me what were those *cabrons* doing back here?"

Mike cleared his throat. "Chico… the short, Black guy has a yacht here that we're customizing. He brought his friends here as potential customers."

With a wave of the hand, Chico dismissed his excuse. "You know that nobody is allowed back here during this time." As he spoke those words, Raul and Jose entered the room with two large, burlap sacks each. Chico told them to put the bags behind the mini bar.

"I know Chico," Mike said. "But this guy has spent three point five million dollars on aftermarket things alone..."

"Mike, you know I don't give a shit about that. My job is

to use this place for the next ten days without any problems while I'm collecting your cousin's money, who just happens to be my boss. So during this time, no one is allowed back here during closing hours. You understand me?" Chico roared.

Mike nodded his head passively, hoping Chico wouldn't tell his cousin.

"I hear you're going on a vacation." Chico smiled.

"Yeah, I need one," he responded as he got up to leave.

"Mike," Chico called, stopping at the door. "Bang one of those little girls in Costa Rica for me."

Mike stared at him in shock, wondering how he knew about his secret. It was a tense moment in the room before Chico and his goons had a good laugh at Mike's expense.

Mike dropped his head as he left the office. *Who does that punk Chico think he is? Sereno only gave him a job because he's sleeping with his slut sister,* Mike thought.

"I swear, one day, I'm gonna get that little punk," Mike uttered while walking back to his office.

CHAPTER 7
THE FAME

The brothers huddled in a guest room back at Charm's villa and discussed what they saw.

"It's something big in that yacht spot," Asad reasoned.

"Yeah, I knew something was going on when dude didn't want to let us go back there. Then, when we did, the two guys by the door body language screamed gangsters."

Asad nodded in agreement. "And the guy in the Aston Martin, followed by the van, didn't it make it any better," Asad said with his words trailing off as he thought.

"So what do you wanna do?" Ahmed questioned.

Asad thought for a second longer before answering. "I'm going to make a run to one of the public libraries and Google Michael Guerrero's name. If that don't work, I'll see about getting the two license plates numbers ran that were in the employee's parking spaces. Hopefully, one comes back with Mike's info."

"If we're going to move on him, it's gosta be tonight. Remember, he told Charm he was going on a vacation."

"Let me check some things out first and we'll see if it's a go or not."

"Alright, while you work on that. I'm going downstairs to spank Charm in a few games of pool," Ahmed said before leaving.

$$$

A group of young men stood in the parking lot of Hank's lounge surrounding a 2003 platinum colored Range Rover on twenty-four inch Asanti rims.

"Man, I swear to God I'ma get me one of these," said Demo, from 93rd and Anderson.

"Nigga, the only way yo' broke ass will get one of these is if you steal it," Young Curtis responded, getting a laugh out of the group.

"You know what? For you to be a nigga who don't live 'round here, you be doin' a lot of hollerin'," Demo said, getting mad.

"Nigga, my cousin used to run this block. And when he

come home in '06, he gon' run it again. So I don't have to be from over here nigga!"

Young Curtis' older cousin, Mark Hudson, had the whole hood on lock before he went to prison and his name still carried weight in that neighborhood.

"But on the fo' real nigga," Young Curtis said, getting angry from how Demo tried to play him. "I got a ghetto pass to go anywhere in the city," he said then pulled out a compacted stainless steel Smith & Wesson .45 semi automatic. "What nigga? You gon' run me outta yo' hood?" he asked, glaring at Demo.

"Damn, man, I was just fuckin' wit' you," Demo said, losing his heart.

"Yeah, I thought so," Young Curtis continued before getting inside his Range Rover.

As soon as Young Curtis put the car in gear to pull off, his cell phone vibrated. He took it off of his hip answering it.

"Yeah."

"What's up family?" Fly Ty asked.

"Shit, I was sittin' up here at Hank's lounge fuckin' wit' these suckas," Young Curtis replied. "Where you at?"

"I'm drivin' up Miles to my mama's house. Oh yeah, they shootin' dice at The Fame tonight. You wanna go up there a bust them lames?"

"Hell yeah," Young Curtis exclaimed. "You want me to meet you up there?"

"Nah, pick me up at my mama's. I'ma ride up there wit' chu. I wanna show you somethin.'"

"Bet, I'll be there in 'bout five minutes," Young Curtis said, ending the call.

$$$

Parked in front of Fly Ty's mother's house on Lotus, Young Curtis sat in his Range Rover, recounting the thirty-five hundred dollars he had with him for the dice game. As he started separating the hundreds and fifties, he heard a loud car system playing T.I.'s "Look What I Got." The car's booming sounds were so strong he could feel the bass as it got closer. *Who the fuck is that*, he thought, looking in the rearview mirror. In it, he saw an orange, candy painted Porsche 911 Turbo Cabriolet shot up in Fly Ty's mother's driveway with the top down.

"Hell nah!" Young Curtis shouted before getting out of his car to walk over to Fly Ty.

"Damn fam! You're hurtin' the game wit' this one," Young Curtis said while looking at the interior. The steering wheel, dashboard, and seats were done in a combination of orange and white suede.

Fly Ty turned his music down, looking up at Young Curtis with a smile on his face. "Look at the kit on this muthafucka Curt. That alone cost me, but it's worth it." He smiled, getting out of the car as Young Curtis admired the wide body style of the Porsche.

"How long you had it?" Young Curtis asked.

"Since February. This was my birthday gift to myself."

"You had this all that time?"

"Yeah. But, when all the paper work was done on it, I had the dealer send it to this spot in Detroit so they could hook it up. I was gon' wait 'til the summer to bring it out. But, since it's been so hot, I said fuck it."

"Your old girl ain't home. You ready to bounce?" Young Curtis asked.

"Yeah, let me pull this further up in the driveway then we can go," Fly Ty said, easing up the driveway.

$$$

In front of The Fame bar, Young Curtis waited as a blue Cadillac pulled out of its parking space in front of the bar before he pulled in. Before getting out, he and Fly Ty observed the scenery. Young Curtis took his Smith & Wesson .45 from under the armrest and jacked a round into chamber before tucking it in his pants waist line.

"Aw man, you don't need that strap in The Fame," Fly Ty protested.

"Shid fam. I keep my strap on me at all times. My last name ain't Sparks. These nigga's subject to try me out here," Young Curtis said, getting out of the car.

Tony Moda

The Fame was packed with people from every neighborhood in the city but this wasn't your average run of the mill hood hangout. One look at the cars in front and around the bar, anyone could see this was the place where "players" played and "ballers" balled.

"Look, there go Fly Ty," a brown-skinned girl named Fatima excitedly said to her girlfriend Shauntae.

"I told 'chu all the money gettin' niggas would be here for the dice game. I just saw Tuna and some of his "Down The Way" niggas go in the back" Shauntae replied while taking a sip of her drink.

"I ain't thinking 'bout nobody in here but Fly Ty and I'm going to do everything in my power to take him home," Fatima said, watching him make his way through the crowd.

"What 'chu drinkin' fam?" Fly Ty asked Young Curtis, as they stood at the bar.

"Get me a double of Cordon Bleu," Young Curtis answered as he checked out a female who walked passed him with a big butt.

After finishing their drinks, the two left the bar and walked to a door in the back of the club. Fly Ty knocked. It opened and an overweight, Black bouncer with braids looked at the two men. Fly Ty wore a burgundy Phat Farm jogging suit with a platinum chain that had a 3.0 piece covered in diamonds hanging from it around his neck. People always asked about the significance of the numbers but he never told them that he had it made when he hit his goal of three million dollars.

Young Curtis wore a white Cleveland Browns number "92" jersey, brown jogging pants and a pair of white suede Nike Cortez's. On his wrist sat a Rolex and a platinum chain hung around his neck. Pegging them as money getters, the bouncer stepped out of their way and allowed them to pass.

Stepping into the muggy room that seemed ever hotter from the twenty-five to thirty men who stood around drinking, smoking weed and placing side bets, Fly Ty and Young Curtis made their way to the front where all the real action took place.

"Hey, there go my nephews," old man Pete yelled at the

sight of them. Pete was the owner of The Fame and a highly respected old school hustler.

Fly Ty looked up and saw Tuna with a handful of money. Tuna was from Unwin and had the Carver Park Projects on lock.

"What's up Big Tuna," Fly Ty said to the 6'6" Ray Allen look-a-like.

"Oh, it's nothin'. I'm in here bustin' these niggas," he replied. "Hey Fly Ty, we need to hook up."

"Hit me up tomorrow," Fly Ty said, figuring he wanted to buy some work. "New money shoot?" he asked while walking deeper into the circle of men.

"You know it. This boy here is 'bout to fall off," Pete said, watching the shooter crap out on cue.

"Yo' ole ass did that Pete," the shooter said, making his way to the wall.

"Who got me faded?" Fly Ty asked then stepped in the center of the circle of betters picking up the dice.

A hustler name Jazz and his man Rio showed up. Jazz and Fly Ty had sort of a friendly rivalry going. If Fly Ty came down in a new car, Jazz had to get one. Whatever Fly Ty did, Jazz would try the same to prove his money was just as long.

"I'll fade him," Jazz said, coming through the crowd.

"I hope you holdin' heavy, cuz I'ma bust this muthafucka up," Fly Ty said, making his first bet five hundred dollars.

Jazz smiled and pulled out a stack of hundreds. "Shoot yo' shot," he said, peeling off five one hundred dollars bills then dropping them on the floor.

The whole room got quiet. Everyone knew, just from side betting, they could all come up off of Fly Ty and Jazz because both of them weren't that good.

But, that night was the wrong night to bet against Fly Ty. He stayed on the dice for twenty minutes, passing sixteen consecutive times before he crapped out. When he finally fell off, he had money all around him from the side bets he'd won.

"Y'all know I don't do this shit fo' real," a sweaty Fly Ty said as he got his money together. "But I can't stay here all night. So to keep it thorough, here you go Gee and Ant." He gave two broke players five hundred each to get back into the game. "Now my fam over there gon' bust this bitch up. This what he do."

"These niggers ain't sleep to me," Young Curtis replied. As he started shooting, the door to the crap game opened. Most of the men in the room looked up. Stepping into the room was Rose and Cha Cha, two of the most beautiful women in the entire city.

Rose was a short, thick light-skinned female with green eyes. Many of the men in the room would've paid big money to get between her thick thighs. Cha Cha, who drew more than a few stares herself, stood in the room trying to ignore all of them as they lusted over her but who could blame them. Her bronze complexion made her a Puerto Rican goddess with a body men longed to touch and other women dreamed they had. At 5'6" and 145 pounds, her shapely figured seemed out of this world. She had it all; breast, hips and an ass that could put Jennifer Lopez's to shame.

Fly Ty stared at the sexy Puerto Rican woman with the long, wavy, dark brown hair that hung to the center of her back. He tried his best not to but couldn't help it. Her clothes looked as if they were painted on. She wore a white midriff that read Baby Phat in pink strained letters across her big breasts. The pair of tight pink Capri pants hugged her body from the waist down, showing off every curve. On her feet was a pair of pink leather Jimmy Choo's open toe stilettos that wrapped around her shapely calves and accentuated the French pedicured toenails.

Fly Ty wasn't the only man staring. The beautiful exotic dancer mesmerized a lot of men, but unlike most, it took more than false promises and the lure of money to gain her companionship.

"Hey you! The girl in the pink pants," Fly Ty said, as he looked around the few people standing in front of her.

She stared at him, pointing to herself, knowing he couldn't have been talking to her.

"Yeah you."

She walked over to him with an annoyed look in her big, pretty brown eyes. "What?" she asked with an attitude.

"Will you do me a favor and go get me two bottled waters

and a few paper towels please?" he asked, holding out a five-dollar bill.

She stood there, staring at him for moment. *Why did he have to say something to me*, she thought before snatching the bill from his hand. "I'm gonna do this cuz you look busy," she said seeing all of the money around him. "But I'm called Cha Cha not 'Hey Girl in the pink pants,'" she informed him, then turned to leave the room with Rose right behind her.

As soon as the door shut, the room broke into laughter. Even the men who were losing got a kick out of it.

"That bitch lightweight checked you," Young Curtis said, looking up from the dice game with a chuckle.

"Dig Fly Ty," old man Pete started. "I know you're a fly money gettin' youngster, but that woman is outta your league. I know of many players she's gunned down. So, at least you got her to do what you asked," Pete said giving him dap.

$$$

At the bar, Cha Cha asked the barmaid for two bottled waters and a few paper towels then handed her a five dollar bill. When the barmaid went off to get her order, a man approached her.

"Hey Cha Cha." JT smiled.

"What's up JT," she shot back, putting on a friendly smile.

He looked her sexy body up and down before saying, "you." It was no secret between the two that he tried to get with her for the longest.

"When you gon' let me take you out and show you a good time?" he asked.

"I would love to go out with you, but I know you have a girl at home and I don't get down like that," she said as if she was serious. Over time, she got used to lying to men. The same ones she lied to came in the clubs she worked and spent big money in attempt to impress her. When the barmaid handed Cha Cha her order, she opened one of the bottles and took a sip.

"I'll leave my woman to be wit' you," JT said seriously.

He must be crazy, she thought as she stared at him. "Aw don't do that," she said as if she was concerned about his relationship.

"If the time ever comes, we'll see what's up then," she continued before grabbing the other bottle off of the bar. She told JT to take care, instead of leading him down a dead end road.

By the time she made it back to the dice game, Fly Ty was at the mini bar. He had gathered all of his money and put it into two big stacks. She walked over and handed him the bottled waters and paper towels then left before he could say 'thank you.' He glared at the two bottles and took the one that looked as if someone drank from it. He opened it, quickly drinking what was left. After wiping his face and neck with the paper towel, he put his jacket back on.

He walked over to Young Curtis, who was now a side better in the game, and handed him a bottle. "I'll be out front," he said.

"Ai'ight. I'll be out in a second," Young Curtis said, not taking his eyes off of the dice.

Fly Ty stepped out of the back room and made his way through the small crowded bar. While working his way through the people, he spotted Cha Cha at a table by herself. He attempted to make a beeline in her direction but a woman who hugged him stopped him.

"Hey Tyrone," a drunken Fatima said, looking up as she held on to him.

"What's up Fatima," he asked, smiling.

"I'm hoping that dick," she hollered in his ear while grabbing a handful of his manhood. "Ooh, is that all you?" she asked, squeezing him.

"C'mon, chill out Fatima," he said. He moved her hand when he felt himself starting to stiffen.

"I wanna go to the telly with you." She stuck her tongue in his ear.

He pulled back, trying to pry the woman off. At the same time, he noticed JT and Mel staring at him from a booth across the bar. *Damn, I forgot I was meeting them up here,* he thought. "Check this out, Fatima." He finally broke out of her hold. "I got some business I'm takin' care of tonight so I'm goin' to have to take a pass," Fly Ty lied because there was no way he would cheat on Tamiko with her.

Once he got rid of her, he walked over to JT and Mel's booth and slid in. "What's up Mel, JT."

"What's up wit' chu lil nigga?" JT arrogantly asked.

"What!?" Fly Ty asked with his face frowned up unable to conceal his anger. "Dig, I ain't one of yo' muthafuckin' niggas!" He glared at him. "Yo' lil nigga's is those lames you got out here runnin' 'round kickin' doors. So the next time you try to play me like I'm a ho ass nigga or somethin,' I'ma show you who the lil nigga is," Fly Ty finished the statement while staring JT in his eyes.

"Aw man, I ain't mean no funny shit, I was just hollerin' at 'chu," JT said feeling uncomfortable under Fly Ty's glare.

"Yeah Fly Ty, we here to talk about gettin' paper, playboy," Mel added.

JT watched as he thought it over. He didn't like how the young hustler called himself checking him but what could he do. He knew he couldn't beat him in a fist fight. Fly Ty was a four time national boxing champion before he put the gloves down to get deep into the game. He knew he couldn't risk trying to have him killed because, if it led back to him and Fly Ty's cousins found out, he would be as good as dead. So, he figured to let it slide for now.

"What 'chu need?" Fly Ty asked, getting over the remark.

"We need two and a half bricks. What's the ticket on that?" JT asked.

"Sixty two five."

"Damn, you can't give us a playa deal?" JT asked.

"It's tight out here. Y'all can take it or leave it," Fly Ty replied.

JT and Mel looked at one another, nodding their heads. "Cool. Give me a call tomorrow. I still have the same number," JT said.

"I'll call, tellin' y'all where to meet me," Fly Ty said, getting out of the booth heading to his next destination.

When he made it to Cha Cha's table, she was no longer by herself. Rose sat with her.

"You mind if I talk to your friend for a second?" he asked, standing over them.

"It's cool," Cha Cha reluctantly said as Rose looked at her. When she got up and left, Fly Ty took her seat.

"Hold this for me," he said, handing her the two wads of money under the table. She took them from him without thinking twice. "So you gon' spend the night wit' me or what?" he asked with a silly grin on his face.

"I don't know what you've been drinking but you're tripping," she responded, looking shocked by his question.

"I ain't drunk or trippin'. I wanna spend the night wit 'chu," he continued, staring intently into her eyes.

"I'm not up here by myself. I'm with my girlfriend," she said, trying to deter him.

"I'm wit' my homie so hook it up."

Cha Cha looked around nervously. "You're putting me out there Ty," she warned.

"Don't worry. We'll be real discreet 'bout it. You leave wit' Rose. Me and peeps will meet y'all up at the Marathon station, a few blocks over."

"When?" she asked, not believing she went for it.

"Now. I'ma go get my boy so I'll see you in about ten minutes," he said as he got out of the chair and headed toward the crap game.

Making his way back through the club, he spotted Young Curtis at the bar talking to one of his homies named Josh.

"What's good Josh," Fly Ty asked as he pulled up on them.

"Ain't shit homie. Just choppin' it wit' Young Curtis."

"Dig, I need to holla at Curt on the one on one," Fly Ty said.

"No problem." Josh nodded and gave each man dap before leaving to talk to a female.

"Let's get outta here," Fly Ty said with a smile on his face. Young Curtis looked up at him from the bar stool as if he was crazy.

"Man it ain't even one o'clock. This shit just started jumpin," he protested.

"Fam, I just set somethin' up for us."

"Who you hook us up wit'?" Young Curtis asked.

"Rose and her Puerto Rican girl."

"Quit bullshittin,'" Young Curtis said, not believing him. He could see Rose, but word on the street proclaimed Cha Cha only liked girls.

"On everything fam, it's goin' down. You gotta shoot yo' shot wit' Rose and I'm a shoot at her girl."

Young Curtis liked the arrangement. He knew he had a better chance at Rose than the lesbian. "How did 'chu get these hos to bite on this shit anyway?" he asked, suspiciously looking at Fly Ty.

"You know I got game." He smiled.

"Oh. You got game, huh?" Young Curtis asked then, without warning, he quickly tapped both of Fly Ty's pockets. "Mr. I Got Game, where the money you just won at?" He grinned at him.

"Man fuck all of that. Let's go."

"Ai'ight super trick," Young Curtis said under his breath while getting out of his seat.

$$$

Once inside the comfort of Young Curtis' Range Rover, Fly Ty realized something.

"Damn!" Fly Ty shouted.

"What the fuck!" Young Curtis shouted back, slightly startled by his outburst.

"I gotta call home and tell my girl something. What would you say?" he asked, turning to Young Curtis.

"I wouldn't say shit cuz Young Curtis ain't gotta check in wit' no broad."

"Okay mackin' gangsta," Fly Ty said sarcastically. "I know what I can say." He pulled out his cell phone and called home.

"Hello," Tamiko said.

"Hey baby," Fly Ty responded, trying to soften her up.

"Are you on your way home?"

"Nah baby, I'm up here in Detroit at the casino wit' Young Curtis. We've been drinkin' so we gon' wait 'til the mornin' to head back home."

Young Curtis shot him a look when he heard his name because Tamiko already didn't care for him. She thought he was a bad influence on Tyrone.

"Is that right?" she asked, instantly skeptical of his story.

"Yeah," he responded. "I'll see you tomorrow."

"Okay Tyrone. It seems apparent you've already had a good time. Now try not to do anything stupid," she said, stressing 'stupid.'

"I won't," was all he could manage to say.

"Well, I'll see you tomorrow. I love you, Tyrone," she lovingly said.

"Okay baby. I love you too," he replied, feeling guilty when he ended the call as Young Curtis pulled off.

$$$

Parked in the Marathon gas station away from the pumps, Rose looked in the vanity mirror on the passenger side visor, putting on her lipstick. When she finished, she rubbed her lips together before placing the lipstick back in her purse. "What's up with you girl?" she asked, pushing the visor up.

"What do you mean?" Cha Cha asked from the driver seat of her white Jaguar S Type.

"I mean, I've known you for close to two years and never seen you just wanting to hook up with some dude. So what's up?"

"Fly Ty just wanna to talk in private," she lied. "I know he wants some, but what a man wants and what he gets are two different things. Plus, he gave me a lot of money."

"I don't see why all of these trick ass niggas keep throwing money at your stuck up ass, knowing you ain't coming off of that big ass," Rose laughed.

"I don't know myself but, as long as they keep throwing, I'ma keep catching."

"I heard that girl but a bitch like me gotta work for mine," Rose said.

Cha Cha's heart sped up when she saw the platinum colored Range Rover pull up next to her car.

Fly Ty got out of the SUV and walked over to the driver's door of the Jaguar. He motioned for her to roll the window down. When she did, he looked passed Cha Cha to Rose. "You can ride in the Range wit' Young Curtis."

"I'll see you tomorrow," she said giving Cha Cha a hug

before grabbing her purse and getting out of the car.

Fly Ty stood outside the car smiling at Cha Cha. "Move over, I'm drivin.'"

She slid over to the passenger seat. Fly Ty got in and pulled off with Young Curtis following.

"Where we going?" Cha Cha asked.

"To the Hilton."

"Wake me when we get there," she said before reclining her seat and closing her eyes.

$$$

The two couples walked up the hallway together to their rooms three doors away from each other.

"Hey Young Curtis, I'll holla at 'chu in the mornin,'" Fly Ty said while opening the door.

"Ai'ight, in the a.m. homie," Young Curtis hollered back as he and Rose went through theirs.

Fly Ty held the door open for Cha Cha. When she walked passed him into the room, he looked at her big round butt. "J. Lo ain't got nothin' on you." He smiled as he closed the door. He then walked over to the bed where she sat with her pretty face frowned up. He knelt down to kiss her but she turned away from his advance.

"No Ty! I don't feel right being here with you." She got up from the bed and walked over to the dresser then leaned against it with her arms folded across her chest.

"What's wrong baby?" he asked, going over to her. But when he tried to hug her, she gently pushed him away.

"You're treating me like I'm a ho, Ty. Contrary to what you may believe, I'm not."

He stood there, looking confused and trying to figure out why she would say something like that. "What 'chu talkin' 'bout, I know you ain't no ho'," he said defensively.

She stood there, staring at him, unmoved by his words then looked at her watch and yawned.

At that moment, he knew his night wouldn't go as he hoped. "So what? You want me to take you home?" he asked, hoping she didn't but she quickly nodded her head. He looked at her with a smile on his face to hide his disappointment. "Let's go," he said, sounding defeated as he walked to the door and opened it.

As she walked toward him, he could see the smile she tried to hide. "Oh you think this a game huh?" he asked, smacking her hard on the butt as she walked passed.

She quickly turned around frowning at him. "*Estupido!* I know you better not hit me on my ass like that again," she angrily said, trying to rub the sting out.

"Yeah, whatever," Fly Ty laughed, following her up the hall.

CHAPTER 8
IT'S MONEY

Inside Club Caliente, Charm sat in the VIP suite with Omar and Pedro - two members of the Bolivian Cartel. But, this night wasn't about business. They were there to celebrate with him yet his mind wasn't on having a good time. It was on Asad and Ahmed.

Shortly before they were to depart for the club, Asad and Ahmed asked him to leave the keys to the Escalade and said they would meet him at the club later. When he asked what was going on, all they said was that they had to take care of some business. He could sense the two were up to something but couldn't figure out what.

$$$

Asad sat behind the wheel of the Escalade outside the parking garage where Ahmed entered three minutes earlier. Looking at his watch, he saw it was a little after 1 a.m. He smiled to himself, thinking Ahmed must be rusty. He remembered a time when his younger brother could steal any car in less than thirty seconds. As soon as he finished his thought, he saw Ahmed drive out of the garage in a gold colored Toyota Camry. Asad put the Escalade in drive and followed the Camry to Davie, FL, a suburb of Miami where Michael Guerrero lived. Asad's quick thinking paid off. The black Denali in the owner's parking space at M&S belonged to Michael Guerrero and they were paying him a visit.

$$$

"Oh yeah, baby! Ah, I love it," a fat, out of shape Mike Guerrero screamed at the TV. He sat at the foot of his bed naked, masturbating at the image of an older white man having sex with a little white girl.

Mike was so busy pulling on his penis that he didn't notice the two men peering at him through the first floor bedroom window. After seeing enough, they both ducked down. Asad looked around the dark backyard facing the woods. Mike's house set in a cul-de sac with the houses spaced widely apart. The only light in the backyard came from the kitchen and shined through the patio door.

"Let's go to work," Ahmed said, as he pulled out the long

flat screwdriver he used earlier to steal the car. Asad looked at him, nodding his head before going around to the front of the house.

It was one thing about Mike's house that stumped the brothers. There was an alarm system sign out front, but when they checked the box, it wasn't hooked up.

What they didn't know was that Mike had things in his house that he didn't want the police stumbling onto in case of a false alarm.

Stretched out on his bed, sweating profusely, Mike stared at the ceiling as a loud knock at the front door startled him. He got out of the bed, went to the closet, and grabbed his robe. *Who the fuck could this be*, he thought when he heard another loud knock. He quickly fastened his robe as he hurried to the front door.

When he got there, three more loud knocks sounded. He looked through the peephole and noticed it seemed unusually dark in the front of his house. He realized that the outside light was out. Then, he heard a noise in the kitchen. He turned around and headed back to his bedroom to retrieve his gun since he felt something wasn't right. A man with a gun met him in the hall.

"Open the front door," the man ordered in a cold voice.

Mike's heart dropped to his stomach as he found it hard to breathe but he followed instructions. He walked through the dark house with the gunman five feet behind. His hands shook so bad he could hardly grab the lock. Once he opened the door, another man seemed to appear out of thin air. Then, the shadowy figure stepped in, shut the door, and locked it.

Mike stood still in the dark house until he felt a hand roughly grab him by the collar of his robe and force him into the living room. He was pushed onto the sofa. Sitting in the darkness for a moment, he wondered what was going on before one of the intruders turned on a lamp.

He sat there, squinting from the light and trying to focus. When he regained his vision, he looked from one man to the other. "You're the two guys who were with Mr. La'Vette" he blurted out.

The brothers stared at him before Asad spoke his scripted lines. "Mike, there's only one way out of this. Tell us everything we need to know and you can make it on that plane tomorrow. But, if you lie, my brother will show you pain you never thought existed. First, he'll put that cigar out in both of your eyes."

Mike looked over at Ahmed lighting the Romeo & Juliet Cuban cigar he took from Charm's stash. He puffed on it, making the embers glow with a hot reddish orange hue. Mike instantly began to sweat. "If that don't work, I'll personally set your little penis on fire myself."

Mike looked the man in the eyes and knew he told the truth.

"Okay, what do you wanna know?"

Asad did all of the talking while Ahmed stood over the short, fat man. "Don't play games with me," Asad warned.

"I won't bullshit you guys," Mike promised, shaking his head with a frightened look in his eyes.

"Good, now tell us what's going on at M&S. Is it drugs or money?"

Mike's eyes got big as he let out a deep sigh. "I don't think you guys wanna do this."

Ahmed walked over to him and lightly touched his thigh with the lit cigar. "Let us be the judge of that."

Mike winced in pain rubbing his thigh. He could smell his burnt body hair. He meekly stared up at both of the men. "It's money," he said while dropping his head in shame.

"How much?" Asad asked.

Mike spoke with his head down. "Right now, it's probably a few million."

"What do you mean by right now?" Asad questioned.

"Because, today was the start of the ten day process of money collecting that goes on every three months," Mike answered. "Chico, the guy in the Aston Martin, works for my cousin Sereno Guerrero. He's here to get all of the money ready to be shipped to Colombia."

"How much money is it after the ten day process," Asad asked, feeling as if he stumbled onto something big.

"I'm not sure, but it's a lot."

"What, about ten million?" Ahmed said, getting in on the questioning.

"More, much more," Mike said, finding himself being overly helpful like all snitches.

The brothers shot one another a look. Asad grabbed a pad and pen off of the end table by the telephone then handed it to Mike. He told him to write down everything they needed to know from how many cameras to how many men and, most importantly, where the money was stored.

They waited patiently as he wrote down the information, giving them the layout of the facility. Once he finished, he handed the pad and pen back to Asad, who looked at it before putting the entire pad in his pocket.

"I've told you two everything, so you guys are gonna let me go right?" he asked, looking up at them.

"You have my word Mike. We're going to let you go," Asad convincingly said. "But we can't let you go right now. What would keep you from telling your cousin about our plan? This is what we're going to do. We're going to hold you until after the job is done then let you go."

Mike stared at him with a pitiful look in his eyes, not liking the idea.

"Hey Mike," Ahmed said about to ask a question that had been on his mind. "Why is the security so lax."

"This isn't Hollywood with a gang of armed men running around," Mike said, looking up at him. "You see it's all about discretion, not drawing attention to yourself. My cousin has been using M&S off and on for years without anyone realizing what was going on. You guys just got lucky."

When he said that, Asad thought of an old saying. 'Sometimes it's better to be lucky than good.'

"Do you have your bags packed for your trip?" Asad asked.

"Yes," Mike answered nodding.

"Go grab his bags and something for him to wear," he told Ahmed.

When Ahmed left the room, Mike sat on the sofa thinking

to himself, *if these guys were going to kill me they would've done it by now and they wouldn't bring extra clothes for me. I have a good chance to make it out of this alive.*

Ahmed entered the room with two suitcases and something for Mike to wear on his trip. He sat the luggage down then threw Mike his clothes.

"Go bring the car around," Asad told his brother.

Ahmed left as Mike started to dress.

$$$

It took fifteen minutes for Ahmed to make it back from the parking lot of the sports bar where he parked the Camry. When he pulled into the driveway, Asad took Mike through the patio door. Once they made it to the car, Ahmed popped the trunk from inside the car.

"Turn around," Asad ordered while pulling out a pair of handcuffs they had paid a homeless man to buy from a sex shop.

"Hold on," Mike protested. "You guys can trust me. I'm not going to try anything."

Asad turned the man around himself and slapped the cuffs on him then walked him to the trunk, ignoring his pleas as he forced him inside.

After shutting the trunk, Asad went back inside the house to get Mike's bags. He came back out, opened the back door of the Camry, threw in the suitcases, and shut the door before getting in on the passenger side.

"Take me to the Escalade. I'll follow you out to the Everglades. We'll dump this sick chump and the car there then change clothes and meet up with Charm."

Ahmed nodded in agreement, as he pulled out of the driveway.

$$$

Charm ignored the beautiful Black woman, who had been trying to get him to dance with her for the last hour. He wasn't in the mood. He stood at the large tinted window in his VIP suite and looked down at the people in the club. He had been waiting on Asad and Ahmed for close to three hours. *I hope they're alright,* he thought.

When he saw them making their way through the club a few seconds later, he felt relieved.

"Crystal, come here for a minute," he said without taking his eyes off of them.

"Are you ready to dance?" she asked, sashaying her way over to him.

Charm brought her closer to the tinted window of the VIP suite. "You see those two guys going over to the bar?"

She looked for a second, finally spotting them. "Are you talking about the ones standing next to the skinny ass blonde?"

"Yeah. Go down there and bring them up here."

"What's their names?"

"That's not important. Just tell them I sent you and I'm up here waiting."

"Okay," she said cheerfully before making her way downstairs.

$$$

Asad and Ahmed stood at the bar, facing the crowd. When the bartender asked, if he could help them, they politely waved him off and sent him to look for his next customer.

"I bet Charm is in the VIP," Asad said.

Ahmed agreed so they decided to make their way to the first floor VIP suite. As they navigated through the large crowd, a beautiful woman in a tight red, form-fitting dress approached them.

"Are you two friends of Charm?" she shouted over the loud music.

Ahmed who was in front nodded yes. She looked him up and down with a pleased smile on her lips. She motioned for them to follow her. When she walked away, she put extra emphasis in the sway of her hips. Ahmed watched her voluptuous derriere move from side to side. He looked back at his brother, giving him a wink and a smile as they followed her upstairs.

Stepping into the VIP suite, the brothers saw Charm sitting on a black, leather sofa. He wore an olive colored suit with gold pinstripes. His gold silk shirt had its top three buttons undone and his olive colored ostrich skin covered feet was on a black, marble coffee table. He had a champagne glass in his right hand with a dull look on his face.

Asad walked over, patting him on the leg as he took a seat next to him. Crystal could tell how Charm acted that he cared for these two men. She walked over to the mini bar in the room and poured herself a glass of the 1985 Dom Perignon.

Ahmed looked from his brother to Charm with a smile on his face. He walked over and sat down between the two. He put his arm around Charm's shoulder and pulled him closer.

"We apologize for being late but we had something to take care of. You know you're like family so quit looking so down. We're here now." Ahmed smiled.

Charm couldn't do anything but smile because he wouldn't have imagined becoming so close to the two. When he first met them they were so standoffish. They didn't want to hangout or get to know him. All they wanted to do was their jobs, leaving the relationship strictly on the business level. But over time, Charm proved himself worthy of being brought into their extremely small, close-nit circle. He was actually the only friend they had outside of each other.

"What about you?" he asked, looking over to Asad with his trademark smile.

"You know Ahmed speaks for me, as I for him. It's all love Charm," he said, flashing a rare smile.

Charm put his arm around his shoulder. "I know you boys love me," he said, only half jokingly. "Hey Crystal, go get your girlfriends and bring them up."

She put her glass down then walked to the door, stopping before opening it. She turned around and pointed at Ahmed. "Don't you go nowhere, handsome," she said in a seductive voice before leaving the room.

Charm sat between the two men, thinking this would be a good time to ask them what's going on. He quickly changed his mind, knowing it was against the rules of the game to question men like them about their personal business. He reasoned, if they wanted him to know, they would tell him.

"Hey Charm, who was that sista?" Ahmed asked.

"That's Crystal. She's a friend of mine. I met her down here some years ago. She's an interior decorator who worked on a few of my properties."

"So, she's not your girl or anything like that?"

"We tried that years ago but she's such an intelligent girl I figured it would be better to use her in a more important capacity. I didn't want a sexual relationship clouding our friendship. So, if you're interested, talk to her. She's a fun woman."

Ahmed nodded in agreement, wanting to find out if she was as fun as Charm claimed.

The door to the room opened and five of the most beautiful women Miami had to offer, entered.

"Five women?" Asad asked, looking over to Charm and thinking that was two too many.

"I had a couple of my partners up here but they had to leave on urgent business. So it's just us," he smiled at Asad.

After shutting the door, Crystal made an announcement. "The one in the light grey is off limits. He's all mine!" she said, walking over to Ahmed. Two Cuban women went to Asad while a blonde and a pretty light-skinned woman went to Charm.

CHAPTER 9
STARTED OFF AS FRIENDS

Fly Ty stood in a small room in the basement of the house on Gardner, in Warrensville, Ohio. He looked at his watch and saw that it was a little after one in the afternoon. He went to a large, blue chest in the corner of the room then took a key out of his pocket and opened it. He grabbed three kilograms of cocaine along with a digital scale before heading upstairs.

Once in kitchen, he sat at the table, putting the scale and drugs on the floor then opened the Sunday paper. He spread it across the table and picked up one of the kilos and the scale, setting them on the paper.

"Francisca, bring me a big knife and two Ziploc bags," he said.

She stirred the scrambled eggs one more time before turning the stove off and walking over to the kitchen counter to open a drawer. She had to move the black 9mm Beretta to get to the butcher knife.

"You got too many guns in this house, Tyrone," she retorted while shutting the drawer and handing him the knife.

He looked at her standing over him in a white oversized T-shirt that couldn't hide the shapeliness of her exquisite body.

"The last time I checked, all of the guns in this house was in your name." He smiled.

"Just because you told me to buy them don't make them mine," she countered.

"Okay baby, I'll move most of them by next week but I'm keeping at least two here."

"Okay Papi," she said, bending down and kissing him on his full lips.

"You forgot the Ziploc bags," he said, breaking their kiss.

As she turned to go get them, he slapped her on her butt. "Hurry up!"

She let out a squeal as she walked to the cabinet. After getting them, she took them to him while she trying to rub the sting out of her butt.

"Ty I told you about smacking me on my ass so hard. That shit hurts." She frowned.

"Come here," Fly Ty said.

Francisca walked over to him. He grabbed her by the waist, he turned her backside to him before lifting up her t-shirt. He then laid a soft kiss on her right cheek.

She looked over her shoulder at him with a wicked smile on her sexy wide mouth. "Now kiss the other one."

Fly Ty did as she desired. "Do they feel better now?" he asked, rubbing them.

"A little," she answered then turned around to kiss him.

She knew he had a woman but she also knew he loved her. Tyrone 'Fly Ty' Sparks and Francisca 'Cha Cha' Feliciano had been together in some sort of capacity, almost as long as he and Tamiko.

$$$

They met by chance, on a rougher part of the west side where he used to hustle, a few months after he met Tamiko. Francisca had just moved to Cleveland from Hartford, Connecticut, after her mother passed away from Cancer. Instead of going back to Ponce, Puerto Rico, where she was born and raised most of her life, to live with her grandmother, she came to Cleveland to stay with her aunt.

Fly Ty was on the west side to drop off three ounces of powder cocaine to a young hustler, who hustled on Clark Avenue. It was just starting to get dark when he parked his car on 33rd Street then walked up to Clark. When he turned the corner, he saw two vice cars and a black and white. Three detectives had eight boys from the block on the wall as the other detective and the officers from the black and white covered them. Fly Ty immediately turned around and began walking in the opposite direction. That's when he heard someone say, 'Hey you!'

With that, he took off running down 33rd Street. He ran past his car, up a driveway, and started jumping backyard fences. He didn't know how many fences he jumped or how many streets he crossed, but when he saw the tall wooden fence, he jumped it thinking it would be a good place to hide. Once he was back there, he realized it wasn't. The biggest Brindle Pitbull he ever saw charged at him. He tried to back peddle away but fell down in his haste. He quickly tried to get up but knew he wouldn't make it before the beast mauled him. But to his surprise, the animal stopped a foot away from him, growling and slobbering. That's when he noticed the big, rusty chain around its neck.

Hearing the back door of the house open, he and the dog both looked in its direction. A girl stood behind the screen door, shouting something to the dog in Spanish. The dog looked at her then ran around in a circle before stopping and glaring at her again, letting out a playful bark. The dog ears went up, hearing the crackling of a police walkie talkie behind the garage and took off in that direction barking.

Fly Ty got up from the ground and ran to the back security screen door. He tried to open it but it was locked.

"You ain't comin' in here," the girl said with a frown on her face.

He reached into his pocket and pulled out a big roll of money. "I'll give you a hundred dollars."

She then looked at the thick roll of money thinking she could get more. "Give me two."

Fly Ty looked over his shoulder, nervously, then turned back to the girl and agreed.

She opened the door in the nick of time. Just as she pulled the screen back, a policeman walked up the driveway.

"Miss, have you seen anyone back he... Wow, shit!" The officer shouted as the dog ran toward him before being stopped by the chain.

The girl shouted at the dog in Spanish again but, this time, he went into his doghouse.

"No, I haven't seen anyone. I heard my dog barking and came to check on him."

"That was me," another officer said, standing in the neighbor's yard. The officer in the driveway told her to be on the lookout for a Black male in a red, Ohio State jacket.

"What did he do?" she asked, not sure if she had just let a

murderer or rapist into her home.

"Suspected drug dealer," the officer answered.

"I'll make sure to call 911 if I see him," she said, shutting the door. She turned to Fly Ty who stood behind it pressed against the wall. "Gimmie my money," she demanded with one hand out and the other on her hip.

Damn, she's thirsty, Fly Ty thought while smiling as he took four fifty dollar bills from the roll of money and gave it to her. She took the money quickly and put it in her pocket as if he might try to take it back.

"You can't stay long. My aunt and cousins will be back in an hour so you'll have to leave within the next forty five minutes."

He nodded in agreement. "Do you know where 33rd Street is?" he asked.

"Yeah, I know where it's at," the cute Puerto Rican girl responded.

"Check this out," he said, going into his pants pocket and pulling out his car keys. "Dig, it's a purple Cutlass parked five houses from the corner in front of a white and blue house. Do you know how to drive?"

"Yeah," she answered with an attitude.

Not wanting to get on her bad side, he didn't say anything about it. "Can you go get my car for me?"

"What about the police?"

"They don't know it's mine."

She stared at him, for a moment, before leaving the room. He watched her as she walked away. *Damn*, he thought, noticing her body for the first time.

She returned, wearing her coat, and walked over to him then snatched the keys from his hand. "I'll be right back so don't steal nothing while I'm gone," she said opening the door.

She left before he could reply. Fly Ty walked around the living room, looking at the pictures on the mantle. He didn't see any of the girl who was helping him. He took a seat on the green sofa and thought about the dusty girl with the nice body. She was a little rough around the edges, had a terrible attitude, and her clothes were bummy. But, he pondered, if somebody cleaned her up, she could be the 'Queen of Dimes.'

His thoughts were interrupted by the sound of a slamming door. He got up to look out of the window and smiled, seeing his car in the driveway. She came through the front door, shutting it before walking over to Fly Ty and handing him the keys.

"The police are still riding around on Clark."

"Thanks," he said as he took off his coat and hat and gave them to her. She reluctantly took the items with the ever-present frown on her face. When he unfastened his corduroy pants, sticking his hand down in front, she took a step back.

"I don't know what you think you doin' but I don't get down like that."

He looked at her as he pulled the drugs out. "What's your name?" he asked.

"Francisca. What's yours?"

"Tyrone but everybody calls me Fly Ty," he replied while sticking his hand out with Francisca grudgingly shaking it. "Do you wanna make another two hundred?"

"Doing what?" she asked suspiciously, because she had noticed him checking her out since she returned.

"It ain't nothin' like that," he smiled, picking up on her thoughts. "Hold this stuff for me. When I come back through to pick it up tomorrow, I'll give you two hundred more."

It didn't take long for her to agree. She removed the coke from him, taking it along with the jacket and hat upstairs to the room she shared with her fourteen-year-old cousin.

When she came back down Fly Ty gave her his cell number. "Give me a call tomorrow," he said as she walked him out. He stopped at the door and turned around.

"Francisca, you're too pretty to keep your face all frowned up. Smile sometimes."

"What if I don't have anything to smile about?" she asked, staring at him.

He could see the loneliness and sadness in her pretty brown eyes. "You met me today. That should be worth a big smile."

She unknowingly started to blush, getting caught up in his eyes. When he spoke, it sounded like a player running game, but looking into his almond shaped eyes, they seemed so sincere and caring.

"You gotta go," she said, catching herself while coming out of the momentary trance.

"I'ma leave. But, before it's all said and done, I'ma see that pretty smile," he said, grinning at her as she pushed him out of the house.

After closing the door, she ran to the front window then watched as he got inside his car and pulled off. She smiled to herself, thinking, *he's kind of cute,* then she wondered what he saw in her. Feeling self-conscious, she looked down at her beat up clothes and raggedy Payless boots.

"I'm going to buy me some new clothes," she said out loud.

The money in her pocket gave her a newfound attitude. From that day on, Fly Ty and Francisca's relationship grew. At the time, he was the only person she knew in Cleveland outside of her family. They started off as friends.

At first, they would just hang out from time to time. He would take her shopping every week until her wardrobe got up to par. He even got her hair and nails done, claiming he wanted to show her how she looked in nice things. Part of him just wanted to show his appreciation because, without her help, he could've been doing four years in a state prison. The other part had more of a personal interest.

Their relationship started gradually changing when Francisca began to have a problem with her aunt's boyfriend. Whenever they were left alone in the house, he made subtle advances toward her until one day she woke up with him on top of her. Fearing something like this would happen, she slept with a knife. Before he had a chance to get her sweat pants off, she stabbed him in the chest and back then chased him downstairs and out of the front door. The wounds weren't life threatening but he never showed his face around there again. However, the incident made her want her own place.

She called Fly Ty and told him what happened. Ten minutes later, he picked her up. He set her up in the Marriott Hotel in downtown Cleveland for two weeks until her apartment in Lakewood, Ohio was ready.

At nineteen years of age, she moved into her new fully furnished rent-free apartment under a few conditions set by Fly Ty. One was he would stash his money and drugs there while no one was allowed in there but them. That didn't bother her because he was her only friend. The second one was more difficult. He said that, as long as he used her apartment for his stash house, no one could learn of their relationship. He didn't want the wrong people finding out where she lived. It would be safer for the both of them. Even with the new rules, they still spent a lot time with one another. Instead of going out in Cleveland, they would drive down to Akron, Ohio to eat or go to the movies. But they mainly stayed in the apartment, breaking down kilos into ounces and other small amounts or counting money.

For eighteen months their relationship remained platonic until, one night, the two celebrated him hitting one of his short-term financial goals. They set in the apartment and drank two bottles of Dom Perignon. She even took a puff of his blunt of 'Dro. The combination of the champagne and marijuana brought down her guard and she let her inhibitions be known. She told him she loved him. When he told her that he loved her as well, she was surprised—not by the fact he did, but that he admitted to it. Before either of them knew it, they locked lips in a long overdue kiss. From the day they first met, no matter how hard they tried to fight it, they knew their relationship would see this moment. That night, they made love, not knowing the complications their action would bring.

He was still madly in love with Tamiko and leaving her wasn't an option while Francisca thought the love they shared would end his feelings for his girlfriend, but it didn't. So, since she couldn't have him to herself, she didn't want him at all. She ended her relationship with him totally, not wanting anything to do with him. But, once he was out of the picture, it dawned on her that she had become dependent on the lifestyle he afforded her. To try and maintain it, she got two jobs but couldn't keep up with the bills.

It seemed like Fly Ty knew what was going on. One night, he showed up at her apartment, trying to give her money until she got on her feet, but her pride wouldn't allow her to take it. She told him again that she didn't need anything from him.

With the bills piling up and no money in sight, she watched a daytime talk show about exotic dancers. She was surprised by how much money they claimed to have made in a night. After a few weeks of convincing herself that she could do it, she chose an upscale club with a buffer zone - topless. It wasn't the job of her dreams but it paid the bills and Fly Ty hated it.

When he found out she was dancing, he was infuriated. He didn't want to have a confrontation with her about it because she would throw her new favorite line in his face. 'I'm not your woman.' So, instead of going through all the drama, he offered her a job that paid well. He started sending her to Detroit to pick up his packages of cocaine. From going out of town for Fly Ty, she earned enough money to buy a house, a Jaguar, and plus she had a nice nest egg put away in her bank account.

He paid her one thousand dollars for every kilo she drove back and she always moved between twenty-five to fifty each trip. However, the money she made from driving caused another problem. She needed to clean it. So his giving her the job backfired because she used dancing to clean up the money she earned from working for him.

Her stint as a drug runner only lasted ten months. One day, after her and Fly Ty made love, he apologized for even sending her to Detroit. He told her that he shouldn't have sent someone he loved to do those kind of things. She knew he still loved her but to hear him say it meant a lot. So she figured that sooner or later he would see she was the only one for him, and when that day arrived, she would be there.

$$$

Fly Ty put the half a kilo back in the chest in the basement before going back upstairs to give JT a call. They made arrangements to meet at the Open Pantry convenient store on a 131st Street in thirty minutes. Once he hung up the phone, Francisca brought him a plate of breakfast burritos filled with chucks of steak, scrambled eggs, and hash browns.

"You're not going anywhere until you eat," she told him.

"You know I love these," he said, sitting down at the kitchen table.

Before he could put one in his mouth, she bent down and gave him a kiss. She knew it was almost time for him to leave and this was the part of the relationship she hated. She stood there, rubbing his baldhead wondering when she would see him again.

Fly Ty stood up, pulling her into an embrace and giving her a slow passionate kiss as he moved his hand up and down her backside.

"I need you to drop me off at my mother's house," he said breaking their embrace.

"Alright, let me get dressed," she softly said then stared up into his eyes and kissed him once more before she left.

$$$

"JT!" Toi, his girlfriend, yelled from the front door.

"What!" he shouted back from upstairs.

"Your little friend Mel is down here."

"Hold on bitch," Mel said angrily. "Just cuz you fuckin' my nigga, you ain't gon' be playin' me like no lame."

"Boy, you better get outta my face."

JT came down the stairs when he heard the arguing. "Bitch, take yo' ass somewhere and sit down before I put my foot in it."

"Fuck you too, JT!" she screamed while leaving the room.

"Fuck wit' me you stupid ass ho'," he said, leading Mel upstairs. Once they made it to JT's bedroom, he turned to Mel. "You gotta quit arguing wit' Toi every time you come over."

"Man, that be her startin' that shit," he said in his defense.

"Fuck all that, you got those ends?" he asked changing the subject. Mel handed him a McDonald's bag with slightly over thirty-one thousand dollars in it. JT took the bag inside the closet with him to put his half inside it.

"Let's go handle this," he said coming out of the closet.

$$$

Francisca pulled up in front of Fly Ty's mother's house and put the car in park. He looked in the driveway and saw his mother wasn't home. He grabbed the door handle to get out of the car when Francisca's words stopped him.

"You're just gonna leave? No good bye kiss or nothing?" she asked, staring at him from the driver's seat.

He turned toward her giving her a short but passionate kiss. After they broke their embrace, all they could do was stare at one another. She wanted to tell him she loved him but she stopped doing that long ago.

"I'll see you soon," he said, picking the brown paper bag up from the floorboard.

"Okay, be careful," she said, watching as he got out of the car.

Fly Ty walked up the driveway to the candy painted, orange convertible Porsche. He got inside, put the paper bag on the seat, then let the top down. He looked through the rearview mirror, watching Francisca as she pulled off. He went in his pocket and pulled out his cell phone, putting in a call to Hollywood, one of his hustling partners.

"What's up?" he asked, answering the phone.

"Where you at Wood?"

"I'm over April's house."

"Good," Fly Ty said. April didn't live too far from his mother's. "I need you to get to my mama's house right now."

"I'm on my way," Hollywood said, ending the call.

Fly Ty hit end on his phone then dialed another number.

"Hello," Tamiko answered.

"Hey baby."

"Where are you Tyrone?"

"I'm at my mother's but I'm on my way home."

"Good, Ms. Kitty and I missed you last night," she said, referring to a certain part of her anatomy.

"Well, tell Ms. Kitty I'm on my way to take care of her." He laughed.

"She said hurry up," Tamiko giggled.

"I'll be there in a half an hour."

"Okay, I love you."

"I love you too baby," he said, ending the call. But, for some strange reason, Francisca's face appeared in his thoughts for a split second before Tamiko's replaced it. He shook his head as he backed out of the driveway.

$$$

Sitting in the parking lot of the Open Pantry, inside a burgundy Ford Expedition, JT and Mel waited for Fly Ty to show up.

"Where this nigga at," Mel said to no one particular.

"Here he go right here," JT said, watching a Porsche pull into the parking lot. JT got out of the SUV and walked over to the Porsche with the McDonald's bag in his hand.

"What's up Fly Ty? I see you ready to kill'em for another summer."

"Yeah," Fly Ty replied, not in the mood for small talk. "You got them ends?" he asked, looking up at him.

"Yeah. They right here," JT said, going around to the passenger side to open the door that was locked.

"Just drop the money on the seat. You don't gotta get in."

Not liking the young hustler's attitude, he stared at him for a minute. *Who this ho' ass nigga think he's talkin' to.* Then, he did as he was told. That's when a black '86 Regal pulled into the lot.

"My people got that. Just walk up to the driver's side," Fly Ty said before putting the Porsche in gear then pulling off.

JT walked over to the Regal, to get the bag from Hollywood before going back to his SUV and pulling off.

$$$

It was a short drive to a house off of 131st and Oakfield, where one of JT and Mel's many young soldiers lived. In the kitchen, he and Mel separated the cocaine and got it ready for distribution. They were going to rock up a kilo then break it down to all twenty-dollar rocks to be passed out to their young soldiers. They planned to sell the other fifty-four ounces in small weight, nothing over an ounce.

Mel and Ron Ron, whose house they were using, stood at the kitchen counter whipping the thirty-six ounces into fifty. Mel worked the blender like a pro as he told Ray Ray when to pour the cold water on it. The pungent smell of the good coke filled the air in the small kitchen.

JT sat at the table with a scale, breaking down the remaining cocaine into quarters, halves, and ounces. He scrapped a small amount of coke off the brick to test its potency. He laid the piece on the table, chopping it up real fine with a razor blade before he sniffed it. He leaned back in his chair and held his nostrils closed with his forefinger and thumb. When he let his nose go, he wondered where Fly Ty got his dope. As he started bagging it up, he thought. *Fly Ty is gonna have to get got.* Even with the Sparks being a large family spread all over the city, only two concerned him, Asad and Ahmed.

It wasn't that he feared them. He knew he could kill them just like they could kill him. But what separated them from everyone else was they weren't accessible. They didn't hang out or mess with women who everyone else associated with. So, it came down to how can you kill someone you can't see. On the other hand, people died every day from things they couldn't see and he knew he could definitely die by crossing their path.

They were like a Rolls Royce Phantom in the hood. People knew they existed but rarely ever seen them. So to go after them would be like committing suicide.

As he sat there thinking, it dawned on him. *Fly Ty would have to die.* He smiled at the thought.

***

CHAPTER 10
JUST KICKIN' IT

Missy was in the bedroom of her home in Louisville, Kentucky. She had just finished a call with Shukela, telling her that they were leaving for Cleveland the next day. She went around the room, gathering the things to take on the trip. She stared at two different dresses, trying to figure out which one to pack when she heard a car horn blowing in her driveway. She went to the front screen door and saw Daren sitting in his Ford F150 with Poo-Poo in his lap.

"Bring him inside!" she said before going back to her room.

After bringing his son in the house, he looked around for Missy. "Where you at?" he hollered while sitting Poo-Poo in front of the television.

"In my room," she answered.

He stepped in the room. "Where you goin'?" he asked jealously, already having an idea.

"To Cleveland for a few days," she answered as she folded a blouse and put it in the suitcase.

"I know you ain't goin' up there chasin' that nigga?" he asked, raising his voice.

"First of all, lower your voice in my house," she said while cutting her eyes at him. "Secondly, I'm not chasing some nigga. I'm going to spend some time with my man. And, if you don't like it, that's your problem."

"So where my son gone be while you up there fuckin' that nigga? Cuz I know you ain't takin' him..."

"Don't worry about where I'm taking him," Missy angrily said. "If I wanted to take my baby with me, I would, because I take care of him nigga. Not your sorry ass."

"You better watch yo' mouth," he warned with his face twisted up.

"Aw nigga you ain't gonna do nothing to me. This ain't the past when you use to beat me to make yourself feel like a man. You put your muthafuckin hands on me now and that nigga you keep referring to will be down here so fast to stomp a mud hole in your ass..." She stopped because he wasn't even worth it. She calmed herself. "He's going to be at my mother's because I know you don't wanna spend no real time with him anyway."

"You be on some bullshit, girl," he pitifully said.

"You ain't seen nothing yet, wait until I move."

"Where you going?"

"Don't you worry about it," she answered as finished packing.

$$$

Ducci pulled up to the stoplight on 116th and Union, waiting for it to turn green. He looked over at Young Curtis, who sat in the passenger seat yawning.

"So what did you do last night?" he asked as the light changed, before pulling off.

"Oh, it went down last night. Me and Fly Ty went to The Fame. We busted the dice game then hooked up with some ho's."

"Who y'all hook up with?" Ducci asked, turning onto Kinsman.

"We took Rose and Cha Cha to the telly," Young Curtis replied.

"Cha Cha, the Puerto Rican broad?" Ducci asked, glancing over to him.

"Yeah," he nonchalantly answered.

"Who was you with?"

"I was wit' Rose."

"Man, I've been trying to hit Cha Cha for awhile on the low but she wouldn't bite on my game."

"She ain't bite on your game 'cuz she likes pussy," Young Curtis said, laughing.

"Did Fly Ty say if he hit last night?" Ducci asked as they cruised around the hood aimlessly.

"I don't think he did cuz when I checked out this morning, they said I was the only one leaving. I asked about Fly Ty's room, the receptionist said they had to check out before five thirty this morning because that's what time she came in."

"That shit don't sound right. I've been doing my homework on girlie and forget about all that dyke shit you've been hearing. Girlie ain't on it."

"How you know?" Young Curtis asked, shooting him a look as if he didn't know what he was talking about.

"You know I know at least a few strippers in every club in the city. From the upscale ones to the grimy hood ones."

Young Curtis had to nod in agreement because Ducci was something like a player at one point in his life.

"I know a few cold broads who approached her on the lesbian side. One of them told me she checked her on some aggressive type shit and she sucka punched the other one. So, I know for a fact she's no slit licker."

As he drove, he started putting things together. This is what he did. He was an analytical person and that trait was probably the reason he and Young Curtis haven't come close to being caught on their robberies.

"You know what," he said, more to himself than to Young Curtis. "I knew she had somebody she was messing with on the low. That's why she's always turning niggas down. Name one nigga you ever heard she'd messed with? You can't," he said before Young Curtis even tried. "For a woman not to have a man or seem like they don't want one, why do she look so good every time she comes out. I'm telling you. Women don't go through all that primping for nothing. That's Fly Ty's broad." Ducci smiled to himself. "I always knew fam was thorough but not on no shit like this."

"Okay Sherlock. What about his woman Tamiko? I know for a fact he loves her to death. So, what do you have to say about that?"

"Damn, I forgot he messed with that broad. Don't she go to school in Columbus?"

"Yeah. To be a doctor. And, ain't no nigga in his right mind gon' take a stripper over a doctor."

Ducci had to admit, Cha Cha didn't seem like the type to share a man and he knew Fly Ty loved his woman, but even with all of that logic, he still believed the two were involved.

"Speakin of that ho, let me call Fly Ty," Young Curtis said, pulling out his cell phone.

Fly Ty took his phone off of his hip, answering it as he drove up the freeway. "Speak on it."

"What's good family?" Young Curtis asked.

"Nothin' much homie. I'm headin' back to the house wit' my lady. We just dropped her brother off at home."

"Oh! So ya girl put handcuffs on you from last night," Young Curtis laughed.

"Never that playboy. I'm just chillin' tonight."

"Ai'ight. I feel you fam but I didn't like how you just pulled out. You could've knocked on the door or somethin'."

Fly Ty looked over at Tamiko in the passenger seat. She had her eyes closed, listening to Alicia Keys 'So Simple' playing from the car radio. "My bad but dude wanted to go home. I guess he wasn't feeling the casino. We'll kick it on that later."

"Ai'ight fam. We'll hook in a few days."

"It's on," Fly Ty said, ending the call.

"Man, you over there with all of that Matlock shit. Girlie told fam she wasn't feelin' him. That's why they left."

Ducci just nodded, not wanting to talk about it anymore because it had to be a reason Fly Ty and Cha Cha was on the low and it wasn't his business to figure out why.

"Oh yeah. What's up wit' that bank in Indiana you was checkin' out?" Young Curtis asked.

"We gon scratch that one. It's located in a messed up spot. It'll take too long to hit a highway, so I'm not feeling it."

"Well fuck it. We cool for a minute anyway."

"Yeah. I forgot to tell you. Missy and your girl Shukela are coming in tomorrow."

"It's on now," Young Curtis said, rubbing his hands together.

"You feel like going to shoot pool?" Ducci asked changing the subject.

"Hell yeah, that shit gotta be betta then just ridin' around."

With that, Ducci headed to Julian's.

$$$

Standing at opposite ends of the pool table, Young Curtis watched as Ducci sunk the eight ball in the left corner pocket.

"That's three in a row. Do you wanna play it back?" he asked, looking up at Young Curtis with a smile on his face.

"Yeah. Rack'em up. You ain't did nothin'," Young Curtis said as his phone started vibrating. "What's up?" he asked.

"Hi Curtis, this is Shu."

"Oh, what's up baby?" he smoothly responded.

"I'm calling to let you know I'll be up there tomorrow. I'm packing my bags right now."

"I'm hip baby. I can't wait to see you again."

"I can't wait to see you either," she replied. "Where are you now?"

"Me and my homie up here at this pool hall, shooting pool… drinking… just kickin' it."

"Are we going to kick it when I get there?" she asked.

"Yeah. We gon' kick it. I'ma kick that muthafuckin' back door." He laughed.

"What?" she asked innocently.

"I'll hip you to that when you get here. I'm just trippin off this Remy right now."

"Okay, I'll see you tomorrow."

"Fo 'sho back door." Young Curtis laughed while ending the call.

After a couple more games of pool and a few more drinks, both Young Curtis and Ducci were ready to leave.

"Ducci, it's a wrap playboy. Take me to the house," Young Curtis said, drunkenly staring at him.

"You're going to have to use the spare room because I'm not riding through Solon like this.

Young Curtis thought for a second, knowing how strict the police were in the suburb where he lived. "Ai'ight, lets bounce," he said as he got out of his seat with Ducci doing the same.

CHAPTER 11
LOVE

Tamiko stood at the case in one of the finest jewelry stores in Northeast Ohio, trying to decide on which pair of earrings she wanted.

"Come look at these, Tyrone," she called. Fly Ty walked over to her and looked inside.

"I like those," she said, pointing at the two-carat diamonds set in platinum earrings.

"Those are nice," he said as a diamond and platinum necklace had caught his attention. "Can I see that tennis bracelet necklace," he asked the female sales clerk behind the counter.

She looked in the case confused until he pointed at it. She recognized the young black man from coming into the store, doing business directly with the owner Mr. Goldstein.

"Oh, you're talking about the Cartier Opera Necklace," she said while taking out a key to open the display case. She retrieved it and handed it to him.

Fly Ty held the opened black, felt box and stared. He figured it had to be about fifty, half-carat princess cut diamonds.

"Let me see it," Tamiko said, interrupting his thought and taking it out of his hands. She held it over the display case light causing the diamonds to sparkle brilliantly. "I like it and all but it's too expensive. I'll be fine with the earrings."

"Oh, okay," he said, looking at her as she gave it back to the sales clerk.

"We'll take the earrings," he smiled at the clerk.

"Good choice Mr. Sparks," she said, putting the necklace back and removing the earrings.

As Tamiko wandered around the store looking at wedding rings, Fly Ty followed the clerk to the register. He looked over his shoulder to make sure Tamiko wasn't close enough to hear him before telling the clerk he wanted the necklace and asking when Mr. Goldstein would be back.

The clerk knew what was going on. Since the necklace was

over seven thousand dollars, the purchase would have to be reported. But Mr. Goldstein routinely underwrote receipts for a handful of people. Fly Ty was one.

"He'll be back shortly."

"Just tell him I'll be back before closing to pick it up."

"I'll make sure to tell him Mr. Sparks."

$$$

"Shit, I gotta stop spending so much!" Francisca said to herself as she wrote checks for the pile of bills in front of her.

She sat on the sofa in her tight, unbuttoned jean shorts and a white halter-top. After she finished taking care of her bills, she ran her hand over her long, dark brown hair that was in a ponytail. She stood up from the sofa rubbing her stomach, thinking she should get ready for work. At this point, work just consisted of showing up. She figured she could write off twenty-five hundred dollars that night. She was booked at the Classy Kitty, in The Flats, an upscale club that catered to pro athletes and working professionals.

By her own accounts, this week would clean up the rest of the money she'd made driving out of town for Fly Ty. It didn't bother her that she lost a large chunk of it to taxes. It was more important for her to have money in the bank. With A-1 credit and a little over two hundred thousand dollars in saved, she would be able to get a loan to do almost anything she wanted in Puerto Rico.

Her ringing cell phone brought her out of her thoughts. She walked over and picked it up off the sofa then smiled as she read the caller ID.

"Hey *Papi*," she answered.

"What chu doin,'" Fly Ty responded.

"Getting ready to go to work. Why?"

"I need to see you tonight."

"Tyrone, you can't call me every time you get a jones and expect me to stop everything I'm doing to take care of it."

Fly Ty was silent. That gave Francisca time to finish her tirade. "Shit, it's not my fault you're not getting what you need at home."

"I didn't call cause I got a jones," he said in a low, calm

voice. "I called cause I've been thinkin' about you lately and I found myself missin' you."

Francisca leaned against the wall in the hallway to listen.

"If you don't wanna see me, I can't blame you. But, remember, you'll always have a place in my heart," he said, letting his words hang in the air.

She was quiet. *Ty will never realize I'm the only woman for him. I need to stop wasting my time, waiting for him to come around and start planning my life without him.* That thought alone brought tears to her eyes because it wasn't just about her anymore.

"Where are you?" she asked while wiping her face.

"I'm at the Embassy Suites in Beachwood, suite 3330."

"I'll be there," she said then hung up without waiting for a response. *Why do I keep falling for this,* she thought. "*Estoy consada de jugas con este pendejo!*" she screamed as she stomped off to her room.

$$$

Driving up E. 131st in Mel's metallic blue 64 Impala, JT turned the volume down on the music. "Check this out. I'm goin' to try a hook wit' Fly Ty tomorrow so we can put our plan in motion."

"What's the plan?" Mel asked, glancing over at him.

"You gon' cop from him but this time, after the play go down, I'ma follow him to his stash. I know it gotta be 'round here cuz he's too smart to be rollin' 'round wit' all that money in that hot ass Porsche. When we find out where, we gon' hit the spot."

"That's what I'm talkin' 'bout," Mel said, giving him dap before turning the sounds back up.

$$$

When Francisca knocked on the door, it took only a matter of seconds before he opened it. Fly Ty stood there in a white tank top, red velour jogging pants and white sweat socks.

"You look nice," he said to Francisca, who wore the same thing she had on at the house but with her hair down. He stepped to the side to let her in. She stared at him for a moment before entering. He shut the door, locked it, then turned around and watched as she sat her Louis Vuitton handbag on the coffee table. She turned toward him, folding her arms across her chest with an angry look on her face.

He ignored the expression as he walked over to the coffee table to turn on the radio he brought with him. "Come here," he said, holding his hand out.

She wanted to protest but did as he asked. When she reached him, Musiq's song entitled 'Love' started to play. He pulled her into an embrace and their bodies began to sway from side to side to the music. Everything she planned to say to him escaped her and all she wanted to do was get lost in the moment. She laid her head on his chest and felt his heart beating fast. She looked up at him as he stared down on her without saying a word.

"What's wrong baby?" she asked with concern.

"Nothin,'" he replied almost at a whisper.

Francisca gave him a long sensual kiss.

As they ended it, he told her the three words she had been waiting to hear. "I love you," he said, staring into her eyes.

"I've always loved you, Tyrone."

They held each other in a tight embrace until the end of the song. When he looked down at her, she turned her head.

"Are you cryin?" he asked.

"I'm not crying," she said then pulled away from him. She went to sit on the sofa, wiping her eyes, with her back to him.

Fly Ty went to the bedroom, returning with a black, felt jewelry box. "I got this for you today," he whispered as he sat down on the sofa and handed it to her.

She stared at him, smiling, before opening the box. She stared at the beautiful diamond necklace. "Thank you, baby," she said, leaning over to give him a huge hug and kiss. Then, she took the necklace out of the case and told him to put it on for her. She dipped her head and moved her hair out of the way, as he placed it around her neck.

She sat up straight and stared at him. It was her turn to surprise him. "I have something to tell you," she said nervously, taking his hand.

"What's up?" he curiously asked.

"I wasn't going to tell you at first but, now, I think you should know. I'm pregnant." She looked at his facial expression for a reaction but couldn't detect one.

Fly Ty wasn't really surprised. He never wore a condom when he had sex with her or Tamiko but they were both supposed to be on birth control.

"In case it's on your mind, I haven't been with anyone but you in the last eleven months. And, me and Tony always used a condom."

Fly Ty hated to even hear his name. Tony was a Puerto Rican from Lorain, Ohio. Her aunt introduced her to him. Fly Ty found it funny that he had Tamiko but hated for her to have anyone. There wasn't any doubt in his mind that he got her pregnant.

"Why weren't you going to tell me?"

"I thought you'd think I was trying to trap you or something," Francisca explained. "And knowing how you and your girl are, I didn't want to hear you tell me to have an abortion."

She looked away as an expression of disappointment appeared evident on his face.

"First of all, I would never accuse you of tryin' to trap me. And, as far as me tellin' you to kill my unborn child, I wouldn't do that for nobody."

Francisca knew he meant Tamiko.

"So what are we gonna do?"

"First, that dancing shit is over," he demanded.

"I know. This was gonna be my last week. I'm not going back," she continued then hesitantly switched gears. "So when are you gonna tell your girl?"

"She's goin' down to Columbus tomorrow. One of her sorority sister's is gettin' married. I'll tell her when she gets back."

"You know you have a decision to make. You can't be with both of us."

"But I love both of y'all," he said, not wanting to lose either of them. Then it dawned on him, he might end up losing them both, which was something he dreaded.

CHAPTER 12
SOMETHING NEW

Asad rushed down the stairs of the Hunting Valley townhouse he shared with his brother. He went into the family room where he saw Ahmed laying on the sofa, watching a nature show about their favorite animals, lions.

"Ahmed!"

"What's up?" he answered, lifting his head up so that he could see Asad.

"I have to make a run right quick. I'll be back in a few hours."

"Have you given any thought on who we can take to Miami?"

"I can't think of anyone off hand. But, if push comes to shove, we might have to do it ourselves."

"Whatever you decide, I'm with you but I think it would be better with two more men on the strength of how much stuff there's going to be."

Asad stared at him, knowing he was right. "We'll work something out. We still have time. We'll talk when I get back," he said before leaving.

Inside the garage, Asad slid behind the wheel of his S600 Mercedes Benz. He started the big V12 engine before hitting the remote to open the garage door. As it opened, he unclipped his cell phone from his hip and called the number on the card. After a few rings, a sexy, husky voice answered.

"Hello."

"Hi Dayna. This is Asad."

His name sent her heart racing. "Hi Asad," she said happily.

"I'm calling to let you know that I'm gonna be a little late. Give me thirty more minutes and I'll be there."

"Truthfully, I didn't know you were back in town and I'm really not prepared to go out tonight."

"I apologize for not calling earlier," he said as the feeling of disappointment washed over him. "We'll just set it up for whenever you find the time."

"Slow down, Asad. I said I didn't want to go out. Why can't we just eat at my place?"

Asad felt a smile creep across his lips. "I don't have a problem with that."

"Good, so what would you like?"

"Surprise me."

"Okay, let me get started. I'll see you when you get here," she said before ending the call.

$$$

Asad stood outside apartment door number 786 feeling like a sucker. He looked at the African Violets in his hands and thought about how it works in the movies before knocking on the door. It didn't take long for it to open. He looked at Dayna, who stood there with a smile on her face. Her beauty took him aback. The lighting inside the XO didn't do her the proper justice. "These are for you," he said, finding his voice and handing her the flowers.

"Wow, they're beautiful. Thank you Asad." They stood there looking at one another. "Oh, where are my manners? Come in while I put these in water." Asad followed her inside. "You can go in there and have a seat. I'll be with you in a second."

Asad walked through the nice, spacious loft on its polished hardwood floors. He stepped in the front room decorated with contemporary European style furniture. The red cloth sofa and love seat sat low and the complementary glass coffee table stood atop of a red, yellow, and white oriental rug. He walked over to the white Steinway Baby Grand Piano and gently tickled its ivory keys. He, then, stared at a beautiful piece of African art over the fireplace. It was a painting of a dark-skinned queen sitting on a huge, brown marble throne. The queen wore a long white flowing dress with a plunging neckline that exposed the sides of her breasts and, on her head, was an Egyptian styled head piece. Asad glared into the hazel eyes of the painting, thinking the queen looked a lot like Dayna. He then walked over to the large window, overlooking Lake Erie, and enjoyed the calming effect of the waves crashing into the breakwater.

"You like the view?"

"Its nice," he answered turning around to face her.

"Come on, dinner is ready," she said with a smile.

After a meal of Filet Mignon, baked potatoes and salad, Dayna and Asad went back to the front room to talk.

The sun had just started to set as the two sat on the sofa. Dayna folded her long pretty legs in front of her as she looked at Asad. "Can I ask you a question?"

Asad moved closer to her. "What do you wanna know?"

"This has been on my mind since I've met you."

He looked at her, wondering what could it be.

"You're intelligent, sweet, and good-looking… why haven't one of these sisters taken you off of the market?"

He smiled. "Truthfully, I've never had the time to put forth the effort to see what a woman really had to offer me. So I guess the answer is I never gave one a chance."

Dayna nodded slowly, liking his answer, but didn't quite understand it. "Why didn't you have time?" she asked, using the past tense and hoping he had it now.

Asad looked at her unable to tell her the true reason behind his decision for not being involved with a steady girlfriend. He couldn't tell her he and his brother came to the conclusion long ago that, while they were in the streets, it didn't make sense to have a women or children in their lives because the lives they led were too dangerous. They could end up dead, in prison, or on the run. And, not to mention the distraction a woman would cause. In their line of work, that could get them killed. However, Asad figured if the Miami thing went right, it might be time to try something new because he couldn't deny his interest in Dayna.

His mind shot back to question at hand. "Before I bring a woman into my life, I have to make sure I'm ready for that type of commitment. How I see it, in a relationship there's a lot of give and take," he said, looking at Dayna to make sure he had her attention. "To make one work, each person would have to relinquish a little control and power of themselves to one another. Plus, I haven't found a woman I would want in my life like that." Asad started to feel uncomfortable. He wasn't much of a talker but found himself talking too much.

"I understand what you're saying. Nowadays, speaking from a woman's perspective, a good woman has to go through a lot of jokers to find her king."

Asad nodded, understandingly.

They continued to talk throughout the night, with Asad opening up a little more. He briefly talked about his brother, Isis, and the grandmother who raised him. He didn't discuss his parents and she didn't pry. He told her he grew up on the Southeast side on Miles Avenue, but didn't bother to tell her where he currently resided.

After listening to him talk for a moment, she decided to question him about some of the things she heard.

"Asad," she started as he stared at her. "First of all, let me fill you in on something." She moved closer to him on the sofa and looked him directly in the eyes. "When a woman first meets a man, most can tell if she wants him in her life."

Asad listened intently, not wanting to miss anything.

She continued. "I can tell you, I would definitely like to get to know you a little better and see where we could go."

He looked at her, sensing there was more to come, so he waited.

"When I first saw you, I thought you were a hustler. After sitting with you for a few minutes, I knew you weren't. Most of them are arrogant and obnoxious but you were laid back, not wanting to draw attention even with half of the club sneaking peeks at you, myself included." She smiled.

"So what's your analysis?" he asked.

"In my heart, I feel that you're a good man but I heard rumors about you that were disturbing. I'd like to know if there's any truth to them."

"You can't believe everything you hear," he cautioned. "Just believe in what you feel and let's see where it goes from there. I can't lie. I'm feeling you Dayna and I hope you feel the same about me," Asad finished, feeling butterflies flutter in his stomach.

"I'm feeling you as well," she replied while moving closer.

Before either of them realized what happened, they locked in a long passionate kiss.

Asad thought it was the sweetest he ever had. It was his first time he ever let his guard down with a woman. This was something new for him and he liked it.

CHAPTER 13
CONFESSION

"Asad, wake up!" Ahmed said as he shook him out of his sleep.

"What's up?" he asked, yawning and looking up at Ahmed.

"I just got off the phone with grandma. I told her we would be over in an hour."

"What time is it?" Asad asked, sitting up in bed as he ran his hand over his face.

"A little after one," Ahmed replied then sat down on the edge of the bed. "When can I meet her?"

"Meet who?"

"The female you rushed outta here to see yesterday."

They stared at one another with smiles on their faces. "I bet it's the same female you called from Charm's house when we were in Miami. Listen, big bruh, there's nothing wrong with you finding someone you like. Man, that's one of the hardest things to deal with when it comes to us. You know how many good sisters I brushed off because I found myself really feeling them? That's why I can't wait until we walk away from this life. I look at Tyrone and Tamiko and that's what I want, a good woman I can go home to because I'm tired of coming home to your ugly mug."

They both laughed with Asad throwing a pillow at his younger brother.

"Get outta here so I can get dressed."

"I'm gone," he laughed, getting up from the bed. "But we're going to talk about this later," he said while leaving the room.

$$$

Inside Young Curtis' condo, he and Shukela laid across the sofa watching "Training Day" on his big screen TV. As he rested with her in his arms, he heard a knock at the front door.

"'Bout time," he said while lifting Shukela off of him.

"Damn homie," Josh stated when Young Curtis opened the door in nothing but a pair of wine colored Cavalier shorts. "It's after two in the afternoon and you still don't got no clothes on?"

"Just come in fool," he said, stepping out of the way.

Once inside, Josh followed Young Curtis to the living room where he saw Shukela on the sofa in a pair of form fitting white shorts with a red Louisville Cardinal T-shirt on.

"Shu, this my lil homie Josh. Homie, that's my girl Shu."

"Nice to meet you," Shukela greeted.

"Same here," Josh replied before following Young Curtis to the enclosed patio.

"Who was that," Josh excitedly asked.

"A broad I met in Louisville."

"What's up? Can I hit?"

"Hell naw, you little freaky ass fool. Get yo own."

Josh, who got tired of Young Curtis always referring to him as fool, shrugged his shoulder and sat down. He pulled a wad of money out of his pocket and put it in the middle of the table.

"You had two more weeks," Young Curtis said, staring at Josh before grabbing the money he loaned him with interest.

"Dawg," Josh said, leaning forward in his chair and staring Young Curtis in the eyes. "Check. Dig. I'm in heavy with this Nigerian nigga in East Cleveland on the dawg food side. This nigga's shit is fire. It's taking a three all day. Curt you ought to come in and we'll lock our side of town down wit' some of the rawest shit in the city."

Young Curtis sat there in silence, eyeing Josh and wondering was his proposition worth it. "I'ma think on it cuz I see how fast you got these ends back to me."

"C'mon in fam," Josh said, getting up and giving Young Curtis dap.

Young Curtis stood up and led him to the front door. "I'm havin' a cookout tomorrow so pick up some drank and drop by. We gon' kick it," Young Curtis said while opening the door.

"I got 'chu." Josh stepped out of the door and down the walkway to his car. Maybe it's time for me to change my game, he thought as he shut the door.

$$$

Ahmed pulled his black Hummer next to Fly Ty's orange Porsche.

“Why would that boy buy this loud car?” Asad asked as they got out of the Hummer.

“Because he’s Fly Ty.” Ahmed smiled.

In the daylight, it was easy to see how different the Sparks family home looked from the others, not only on their street but also throughout the entire neighborhood. The brick and white vinyl siding house was well maintained. In the backyard, their grandmother grew tomatoes and herbs in a small, fenced garden by the garage. The house itself had over a hundred-fifty thousand dollars worth of renovations, inside and out, completed over a three-year period. Unlike most houses on the street, it lacked security bars on the doors or windows. Their grandmother said she didn’t want to feel like a prisoner in her own home.

For the last three years, Asad and Ahmed tried to get their grandmother to move but she refused to leave her place on Miles. It never dawned on them that it held a sentimental value to her. It was the home she moved into forty-three years earlier when her and their grandfather moved to Cleveland from Selma, Alabama. It was where she raised three generations of Sparks.

The brothers walked around to the front. Stepping up on the porch, they saw Fly Ty sitting in a fold out lounge chair and talking on his cell phone. Asad couldn’t help but notice that his clothes matched his car. He wore a pair of orange mesh Nike shorts with an orange and white Tennessee Volunteer number sixteen football jersey. On his feet was a pair of orange and white suede Cortez Nike’s.

Fly Ty stood up, stopping his conversation, when he saw his cousins.

“When did y’all get back in town?”

“We’ll talk when you get off of the phone,” Asad said, nodding at the phone Fly Ty held with his right hand while covering the mouthpiece with his left.

“My bad,” he said, knowing he shouldn’t have put their business out there like that. “But, I wanna holla at y’all ‘bout somethin’ before y’all leave.”

“Alright,” Asad said as he and Ahmed went inside the house.

They went straight to the kitchen where they knew they would find their grandmother. Once there, they saw her standing at the sink cleaning greens. One went to her right while the other went to her left, both simultaneously kissing her on the cheek.

She smiled as she turned around, knowing it could only be them. They had been doing that to her since they were little boys.

"My grandbabies," she said, giving them each a kiss on the cheek. For as long as she lived in Cleveland, she managed to some how keep her Southern charm after all of those years.

Cynthia Sparks loved all of her grandchildren but favored Asad and Ahmed because they had such a hard life as kids. Leonard Sparks, the boys' father and her second oldest child, died on the job at a construction site when Asad was five and Ahmed was two. It was devastating to Asad because his little world revolved around his father. To make matters worse, shortly after the death, their mother dropped them off one day and never returned. Grandma Sparks wrote it off as Staci, the boys' mother, still being a young attractive woman and two little boys wouldn't do anything but hold her back. A couple of years after she abandoned them her conscience must've got the best of her. She called and told Grandma Sparks that, once she got herself together, she would be back but Grandma Sparks didn't want to hear it. She told her to stay wherever she was because running in and out of her sons' lives wouldn't do anything but hurt them more.

Yet and still, she sent the two birthday and Christmas cards postmarked from Oakland, California, every year for the last twenty years. Asad always discarded his, never forgiving his mother for leaving him and his brother, and whatever he did, Ahmed followed suit.

Grandma Sparks watched the boys closely as they grew up. But, one thing struck her as odd. From being the mother of seven, she was quite familiar with sibling rivalry yet never once heard the two argue or fight. She remembered when her son taught them how to box. He would try to get them to spar until Asad told him he would never fight his brother for real or for sport and never did.

"How my grandbabies?" she asked, wiping her hands on her apron.

"We're good grandma," Ahmed answered with a smile.

"How are you doing?" Asad asked. "Isis told me you're still having dizzy spells," he continued with a look of concern.

"That child talks too much," Grandma Sparks said with a smile on her chubby face.

"Well, just to make sure, I'm going to have her set up an appointment with Dr. Robinson," Asad insisted.

"Bless your heart but I'm okay," she said. She walked over to him then kissed his cheek.

The brothers just stared at her. She glared at the two, as they had this look they inherited from her deceased husband, so she couldn't do anything but cave into their demands.

"Okay," she said somewhat annoyed. "I don't need to see no doctor. But, if it will put you boys' hearts at ease, I'll go."

They both smiled at one another, knowing how much she hated doctors.

"I need y'all to run to the supermarket for me," she said while going over to the refrigerator and pulling a list off the door. She handed the piece of paper to Ahmed.

"We'll go now," he said, giving her a kiss on the cheek with Asad doing the same before they left.

She stood there watching the two as they walked out of the kitchen, thinking what good grandsons they were.

Stepping out of the house, they saw Fly Ty in the same spot and still talking on the phone.

"Where y'all goin'?" he asked as the two went down the stairs. "To the store for grandma," Ahmed answered while pulling his car keys out of his pocket.

"I'm goin,'" Fly Ty said as he ended his call and got up from the lounge chair. After they all piled into the Hummer, Ahmed pulled out of the driveway.

"What's been up with you?" Asad asked, looking over the headrest of the passenger seat at Fly Ty.

"I'm 'bout to be a father."

Both Ahmed and Asad gave their congratulations. "How's Tamiko doing?" Asad asked.

"Oh, she's doin' good. The only problem is she's not pregnant."

"I know you didn't let one of these lost sisters mash a baby on you?" Ahmed asked through his laughter.

"Nah, it ain't like that. Francisca ain't even that type of woman. Me and her have been kickin' it every since she moved here."

"Is this the same woman you were sending to Detroit?" Asad asked, putting two and two together.

"Yeah, I met her a few years ago. At the time, me and Miko was still building so I put her on the back burner but I couldn't stand that shit. Over time, we got closer and whenever I needed her she was always there. But, after awhile, the dancing got to me..."

"You mean she's a stripper?" Ahmed asked from the driver seat, looking through the rearview mirror. "Ty, I know we raised you to have more sense than that."

"I said it ain't like that!" Offended, Fly Ty got somewhat aggressive.

"Whoa! Calm down killer," Ahmed smiled.

"How do you feel about her outside of being pregnant with your unborn child?" Asad asked.

"I love her but that's fucked up 'cause I still love Tamiko."

Ahmed pulled into the parking lot of the supermarket, shaking his head in disbelief.

"Have you told Tamiko?" Asad asked.

"Not yet. She went to Columbus this morning and won't be back until next week."

"Well, it looks like you've painted yourself into a corner," Ahmed said as he parked. "The only thing I can say is you've put a Sparks' seed in that woman so you have to make sure her and the child are taken care of."

Fly Ty shook his head in agreement.

"Sooner or later, you're gonna have to get her and Tamiko together and work something out," Asad reasoned. "Like Ahmed said, you take care of the bloodline no matter what."

"Enough about that," Fly Ty said, tired of the conversation. "How was Miami?"

"It was cool," Asad answered as they all got out of the Hummer and headed for the store.

"I want y'all to come out with me tonight," Fly Ty informed them.

"Yeah. Since it's a special occasion, we'll come and hang out with the father to be, especially since Tamiko is gonna kill you when you tell her this," Ahmed said. He and Asad started laughing.

Fly Ty couldn't find the humor in it. The only word in his mind was "Damn."

$$$

JT hung up the phone and looked over at Mel. "It's on, I just got finished talkin' to Fly Ty's bitch ass. I told him to raise it by half and he said seventy-five."

"Damn, that lil nigga is tryin' to dick us," Mel complained.

"Yeah, but its all good," JT said. "Cuz once we find his spot, we gon' dick him right back. The nigga supposed to call in a few hours. So, when he do, you gon' meet him while me and Ron Ron try to follow him."

"It's on," Mel said, giving him dap.

"Let me go get this money and go holla at Ron Ron. We'll hook back up later," JT said, then left.

$$$

Asad, Ahmed, and Fly Ty all grabbed a bag of groceries from the back of the truck before heading inside the house through the back door. Grandma Sparks stood at the stove over a pot of boiling greens, stirring them as she talked on the phone. Fly Ty put his bag on the table then walked over to her and kissed her on the cheek. "I'm 'bout to leave grandma."

"Okay baby," she said, covering the phone with her hand. "I love you, and tell your mama to give me a call tonight," she said before returning to her conversation on the phone.

"Don't forget, we're goin' out tonight," he said to his cousins on his way out of the door. "I'll call y'all around eleven."

"We're not going to stand you up," Ahmed assured before biting into an apple that he took out of one of the grocery bags in front of him.

Fly Ty nodded before stepping out of the back door heading for his car. When his cell phone rang, he reached into his pocket and pulled it out. "Speak on it," he said into the phone.

"What's good playboy?"

"What's up Curt?"

"Ain't shit. Where you at?"

"My grandmother's but I'm 'bout to ride' out cuz I got somethin' to handle in a few hours."

"Come swoop me. I need you to drop me off at my mama's. Plus, I need to holla at you."

"I'll be there in 'bout twenty minutes," Fly Ty said, ending his call before getting inside his car.

$$$

Fly Ty walked up the walkway to Young Curtis's door and knocked twice. After waiting a few seconds, he was just about to knock again when the door opened.

Young Curtis, who was on the phone, motioned him in. He stepped inside going straight to the living room where he picked the remote up from the coffee table then sat down on the red Italian leather sofa and turned the TV on.

Young Curtis walked in the room, holding up one finger before disappearing into his bedroom. Fly Ty remained, channel surfing. When Young Curtis reentered, he had a good looking light-skinned woman with him. She wore a tight fitting blue jumpsuit.

"Who's your friend?" Fly Ty asked.

"Oh, this is my Southern Bell, Shukela," Young Curtis replied.

"How ya doin? My name is Ty."

"Fly Ty," Young Curtis interjected.

"Pleased to meet you," she smiled.

After the greetings, Fly Ty looked at his watch. "You ready to go playa?"

"Yeah," Young Curtis answered before turning around to kiss Shukela on the lips. "My sister will be here in about a half hour to take you to the mall, so pick out something nice," he said as he and Fly Ty left.

Fly Ty drove up the freeway with the top down, bumping Jay-Z's "Allure." He turned the volume down.

"You heard what that nigga said?" Before Young Curtis could answer he continued. "That shit is real. The allure of the game is a muthafucka!"

Fly Ty glanced over to Young Curtis before returning his attention back to the road.

"Ty, didn't you use to fuck wit' that heroin a minute ago?"

"Why?" Fly Ty asked with a quizzical look on his face.

"Dig, I've been loan sharkin' these fake ass dope boys money when they fall off. I'll give a nigga up to ten G's but he gotta have my ends back to me within a month plus thirty percent interest."

"Shit that's good if you can find some dummies to go for it," Fly Ty smiled.

"Well, it's a lot of dumb muthafuckas out here cuz I'm gettin' it off. But anyway, Josh came and borrowed some paper from me 'bout two weeks ago. The lil nigga brought me my ends in half the time. So, he tells me 'bout this Nigerian nigga he's fuckin' wit' on the heroin side. He told me the dope is fire and takin' three on the cut side. Is that good?"

"Yeah, it's cool," Fly Ty said, switching lanes.

"I'm thinkin' 'bout takin' fifty stacks and seein' what's up wit' that shit."

"Fam, you ain't no dope boy," Fly Ty laughed.

"I know. But I ain't gon' be out there. I'ma let Josh down it for me."

"Dig Curt, don't fuck wit' that shit. You good at what cha do. You a take money boy. This dope game is so fucked up nowadays it seems like the in thing to do is to snitch on a nigga. Now just think 'bout how many niggas you know gettin' major cake and don't got dirt on their names? Niggas get picked up by the Feds and out in two weeks. Next thing you know, niggas around them start fallin.'"

Young Curtis nodded in agreement. "They say the nigga Jazz the police." After thinking for a second, he looked over to Fly Ty. "Why you still in it?"

"What you ain't peepin is I'm on my way out."

"Straight up?"

"Fo' sho. I'm over this shit. I got my paper. It ain't nothin' else fo' me to do."

"What 'chu gon' do after this?" he asked, looking at Fly Ty from the passenger seat.

"Dig Curt, you know I don't like puttin' my business in the streets but I know what I say to you won't leave this car. I got over three hundred fifty thousand dollars in my savings account and another hundred fifty in Miko's."

"Damn fam! How you pull that off without the Feds and IRS runnin' down on you?"

"My dude in Detroit turned me on to this investment banker in Michigan that he fucks wit'. He told me about a white boy who could clean up to a million for a nice fee. So I took my money up there one weekend along with me and Miko's account numbers. After 'bout a month, we got bank statements showing the money was there."

"I wonder how dude did that?" Young Curtis said, more to himself.

"When I step away from the streets, I'ma get into the real estate game like Ducci. First, I'ma start a small construction company, laying asphalt and concrete. After a couple of years of learning the game, I'm gonna do what I always wanted, become a developer. That's where the real money at," he said while pulling into Young Curtis' mother's driveway.

"That's a slick ass plan playboy," Young Cirtis said, giving him dap.

Fly Ty turned his attention to Young Curtis' mother coming down the porch stairs. "Hi Ms. Houston."

"I told you about calling me Ms. Houston. You make it seem like I'm an old woman," she said as she walked up to the passenger door of Fly Ty's Porche.

Terri Houston was a sexy thirty-nine-year-old woman with the face and body of a twenty-five-year-old. It was easy for people to mistake her for Young Curtis' sister instead of his mother.

"Let me get outta here," Young Curtis said to his mother, who stepped back as he opened the door.

"The Water is jumpin' tonight," Fly Ty said. "Why don't you and Ducci come through?"

"I'll see what's up wit' him. He got his girl up here so he might wanna stay hugged up wit' her."

"Well if you come through, I'll be there."

"It's on," Young Curtis replied as Fly Ty backed out of the driveway.

"What's up, Ma?" Young Curtis asked, turning to her.

"My damn dryer went out again. I called Henry's shop and he supposed to be sending someone over."

"Mama, I told you 'bout messin' wit' those fake ass Maytag niggas."

"You better watch your mouth Kentonio Curtis Houston."

"C'mon ma! What I tell you 'bout sayin' my name in the streets?" Outside of his family, very few people didn't know that his first name wasn't Curtis.

As a child, he had such a hard time pronouncing it when Terri enrolled him into preschool so she asked the teachers to call him by his middle name and it stuck through the years. Now, he treated it as a closely guarded secret.

"Boy I just got that washer and dryer last year. Now, the people don't wanna honor the warranty."

"Ma, once you let those clowns go inside it, you killed the warranty. Don't worry 'bout it. We'll go up to Sears this weekend and get a new washer and dryer."

"I'll give the old ones to Ms. Tolbert and let her deal with it," Terri said as she followed her son up the driveway.

Young Curtis opened the garage door and stood there for a second, staring at his car. "You ain't been drivin' my car stuntin' on your friends have you?" Young Curtis jokingly asked.

"Hell nah! I'm not trying to get car jacked in that thing."

Young Curtis got inside his car and let the top down. "Ma, I'ma have a Bar-B-Que tomorrow, so don't plan nothin.'"

"I won't," Terri said leaning down to give him a kiss before he drove off.

CHAPTER 14
I FOUND IT

Fly Ty sat on the the pink leather sofa inside Francisca's living room, staring at the three tightly wrapped and compressed kilos of cocaine on the coffee table in front of him. He was thinking about calling off the deal with Mel and JT because he didn't feel like going out. *Man, I betta get this money while the gettin' is good*, he thought. He picked up the 9 millimeter Berretta and pulled the slide back, chambering a round into it before putting the safety on and laid it on the sofa.

"Where you going?" Francisca asked as she stood in the entryway of the living room, wearing a short pink silk robe while drying her hair with a rose-colored towel.

"I got some business to handle," Fly Ty answered, nodding to the drugs on the table.

Francisca smacked her lips. "I knew you didn't come over here to be with me," she said, pouting as she stepped into the room and leaned her back against the wall.

Fly Ty stood up and walked over to her. He pulled her into an embrace and gave her a sensual kiss on the lips.

"Soon as I take care of this, I'm comin' right back," he said as he laid soft kisses on her neck.

"You better," she replied. A smile crossed her wide beautiful mouth before she returned his kiss.

As their tongues wrestled in one another's mouth, Fly Ty's manhood started to rise from the feel of her warm body under the silk robe. Francisca couldn't help but notice his erection as he leaned against her body. Then, the casual display of affection quickly erupting into something more as both of their breathing turned heavy with lust. With both hands, Fly Ty frantically unfastened the belt on her robe as she pulled down his shorts. He broke their kiss by cupping her breast as he ran his tongue over her erect nipples. Once he pulled his mouth from her breast, he used his right hand to guide his swollen penis into her dripping wet vagina. As he entered her, moans escaped both of their mouths. Fly Ty lifted her up using the wall for support.

Francisca tightened her grip around his waist with her thighs and wrapped her arms around his neck as she slowly moved up and down on him while talking dirty in Spanish. Even though he didn't understand a word she said, he loved when she did it.

From the constant humping, his legs began to buckle as they got tired from holding her up. He eased her off of him but they both knew it wasn't over. He turned her toward the wall and re-entered her from the back then wrapped his arm around her waist to give him more control as he went to work on her.

"This how you like it, Mami?" he asked as he hit her with hard, quick strokes.

"Ah, *Papi*… Oh, you gettin' it!" she hollered as she threw it back to match his thrust.

"Look at me Mami," Fly Ty said gripping her hips as the clapping sound of their bodies got faster and grew louder.

"*Te amo! Te amo*!" she screamed as she looked over her shoulder at him then salaciously licking her lips. That pushed him over the edge. He couldn't hold on any longer. He tightened his grip on her hips as he reached his climax, shooting his semen into her.

"Got damn baby! You gotta have the best pussy in the whole wide world," he laughed as he held her against the wall, trying to catch his breath.

"This isn't comfortable," Francisca complained, straight-faced in pain, from all of his weight resting on her. Once he stepped back, she turned around and kissed him. "I love you."

"I love you too," he said, kissing her back.

As they stood there hugging, he felt his cell phone vibrating in his shorts' pocket. He pulled them up and reached for the phone. "Speak on' it," he said.

"Hey! This ya boy. I'm at the spot on pause, holla," Mel said.

"I'm on my way," Fly Ty shot back before ending the call. He walked over to the sofa and picked up his gun before grabbing the bag with the kilos.

"You're not gonna wash up?" Francisca asked while watching him move around the room.

"Nah, I'll be right back."

"You nasty."

"I'm cool. Plus, you know your stuff don't got no smell to it."

"Just hurry back and I'ma definitely have a bath waiting on you," she said, ignoring his comment and disappearing into the master bedroom.

He followed and gave her a kiss before exiting through the side door that led to the attached garage. Once inside his car, the thought of not going crept back into his mind so he drove around and toiled with the idea of actually meeting JT. He knew it wasn't smart for a young black male in a hundred-thousand dollar Porsche, with three bricks and a gun, to do something like this. Just as he was about to call it off until the next day, he looked at the bag next to him, and realized he was half way there. He figured it would be best to take all of the back streets to the gas station on 131st and Harvard and wished Bay Bruh and Hollywood wasn't in New York on a shopping trip.

"Fuck' it," he said to himself, pressing the garage door opener.

He couldn't have known at the time that this rash decision would cost him.

$$$

Fly Ty made it to the gas station on a 131st and Harvard without any problems. As soon as he pulled into the lot, he spotted Mel standing beside a green late model Monte Carlo that sat off to the side. Fly Ty nodded to him as he slowly drove pass before parking at the last island of pumps. He turned the car off then getting out, walked into the Mini Mart to pay for his gas.

It was just a little past six in the evening but there were only a few customers behind Fly Ty's Porsche. Mel quickly made his move. He reached into the open window of his car, taking a Foot Locker bag off of the driver's seat before walking over to the Porsche. He went around to the passenger door and got inside. He looked in the brown paper bag at the taped kilos. He closed it and picked it up, leaving the Foot Locker bag in its place. Mel got out of the car and closed the door before heading toward his own.

Fly Ty watched the whole scene through the Mini Mart window. When the transaction was complete and Mel pulled off, Fly

Ty hurried out and pumped five dollars worth of gas into the car that was already practically full. After fueling, he got inside his car and looked inside the bag Mel left. Shifting through the stacks of money, he was pleased with how it looked then put the car in gear and pulled off. *I'll never do this dumb shit again,* he thought, chastising himself. The only thing on his mind as he drove up Harvard was getting back to Francisca's house. As he made it closer to his destination, he kept looking in the rearview mirror because he thought a blue Honda Civic followed him. But, when it turned on Lee Road, putting his mind at ease.

"I'm trippin,'" he said out loud as he continued to Francisca's. It didn't take long for him to make it back to the house. Once there, he waited in the driveway as the garage door slowly raised. When it was fully open, he drove inside while pressing the button on the remote.

As the door closed, he didn't notice the gray Ford Taurus slowly driving pass.

$$$

Mel sat on the black, leather sofa in a house on Melzer that JT owned, rolling up a blunt. When his cell phone vibrated on his hip, he quickly answered it.

"Yeah, what's up?"

"I found it," JT stated.

"Good, hurry up to the spot so we can kick it," Mel said before hanging up.

$$$

"I'll get it!" Missy said as she picked up the phone. "Hello."

"Damn, you answerin' my peoples phone already?" Young Curtis asked.

"Curtis, what do you want?" she asked, trying not to laugh.

"Where Ducci at?"

"He's in the shower."

"Dig, tell him we're goin' out tonight."

"I'm with it," Missy happily said because she felt like going out herself anyway.

"Tell him we're going to The Water. Me and Shu will come

through around eleven so y'all can follow us up there."

"Alright, I'll tell him."

"Cool, I'll holla when I see y'all," Young Curtis said, ending the call.

$$$

Mel sat at the kitchen table in the house on Melzer, breaking down the bricks of cocaine he had just copped from Fly Ty. When he felt his cell phone vibrating, he tried to ignore it because it had been going off all day from clientele calling and begging for work. As he sat at the table, JT came in the kitchen through the back door. He walked over to the table that had four lines of coke on it ready to be snorted. He quickly grabbed the rolled up hundred dollar bill and did two lines before passing it to Mel, who did the remaining two.

"So when we gon' hit the nigga?" Mel asked as he sniffled.

"Give me a few days to watch the spot to make sure everythin' is everythin,'" JT said, staring at Mel through glossy eyes.

"You betta have this shit planned good. Cuz, if this gets out, it can get ugly," Mel said with a sniffle. "You know that nigga's people are some serious dudes," he warned while wiping his running nose with the back of his hand.

"Man fuck them niggas! We serious too!" JT shouted angrily.

"Do you have the masks and vests?" Mel asked, changing the subject.

"Yeah."

"Who we takin' wit' us?"

"I got Ron-Ron on deck. He's fresh out from that juvenile life bit so he's ready to put in some work to get his pockets right."

"Good, cuz I'm tired of frontin' that fool anyway," Mel said. "C'mon and help me break the rest of this shit down," he told JT, who took a seat at the table, ready to help.

CHAPTER 15
CUT FROM THE SAME CLOTH

It was a little past midnight and The Water was packed to capacity. The Water was one of the most popular nightclubs in the city with a strict dress code. No jeans, sneakers and especially no broke hustlers.

The decor was that of a club in South Beach, Miami, blue fluorescent lights glowed all around the otherwise dimly lit room. The black and light gray walls with the matching carpet gave The Water a classy look. The large polished circular wooden dance floor was surrounded by numerous tables and booths. Farther away from the dance floor in one of the six elevated VIP booths that over looked the entire club sat Asad, Ahmed and Fly Ty Sparks.

On the tables sat a bottle of Dom Perignon in front of Fly Ty and glasses of apple juice in front of Asad and Ahmed. Fly Ty picked up his champagne glass and started to bounce to the beat of Lil Jon and the East Side Boys hit single. He looked over at his cousins who sat there like statues.

"Damn... Ahmed, Asad. Y'all need to loosen up, sittin' over there all stiff and shit," Fly Ty said, turning his glass slightly too fast and spilling a little champagne on himself. He jumped up quickly wiping it off of his peach colored silk shirt. When he sat back down, he saw the stern face of Asad staring at him.

"Slow down with the drinking, Tyrone," Asad warned.

I'm cool cuz. I'm just relievin' a little stress." Fly Ty thought for a moment. *Shit, I got future baby mama drama slash woman problems on the way.* He stared into his empty champagne glass as if looking for an answer to his problems. He glared over to his cousins with a dreadful look in his eyes. "How can I tell the woman I love I got another woman pregnant? Not only that but I love her too." He thought for a second before continuing. "And Francisca knows damn near all my business. Shit!" He slapped the table.

"Pick your head up little cousin, however it turns out it's meant to be," Asad said.

"I guess you're right," Fly Ty said looking, over at his cousin.

"Enough about that, we're here to kick it. I ain't gon' burden y'all wit' all of my problems." He stood up and glanced down at the lounge area then motioned for a waitress. He sat back down when he saw her coming.

"How may I help you?" the attractive, brown-skinned waitress asked.

"I need another bottle of Dom P," Fly Ty answered.

The waitress wrote down his order before turning her attention to the other two men. "Can I bring you anything?"

"No, thank you, sista," Ahmed said. The waitress smiled before going to fill Fly Ty's order.

$$$

Ducci, Missy, Young Curtis and Shukela entered The Water at close to one in the morning. Both couples were decked out. Missy wore a black, short backless dress with a pair of four inch, open toe, black heels on her feet. Ducci matched her with a white short sleeve silk shirt and white linen pants. On his feet were some black and white gator shoes.

Young Curtis was dressed in all burgundy from head to toe. He wore a long sleeve silk shirt with hidden buttons with a pair of matching silk slacks and big block gators. To top it off, he wore a burgundy Dobb's hat. He let Shukela walk in front of him. She wore a shoulderless, silk ruffle top and a tight, white skirt that stopped at her knees and clung to her body.

Young Curtis walked over to Ducci. "Find us a booth. I'ma look for Fly Ty."

Ducci nodded and lead Missy and Shukela through the crowd. As they made their way, a big, light-skinned guy in a played out Versace shirt stopped Shukela.

"I ain't gonna let you pass unless you holla at me." The man smiled.

Shukela could tell by his breath that he had been drinking. Not knowing that she was being held up, Ducci and Missy continued making their way through the crowd.

Young Curtis happened to look back in search of Ducci and the women. He saw Shukela trying to make her way around a man but he stood in her path every time she took a step. Seeing this, he muscled his way back toward her. He quickly returned to her side.

"What's the problem?" he rhetorically asked the thug.

The man glared at him with a frown on his face. "Lil nigga, what you want it to be," the man menacingly said.

Young Curtis stepped in front of Shukela, ready to do whatever. "What you tryin' to get into?" he asked as he got into a fighting stance. The troublemaker looked over his shoulder then back at Young Curtis. That's when he saw three other men coming his way. But, to his surprise, Ducci appeared at his side.

"What's up with these lames?" he asked, sizing them up.

"I don't know and don't give a fuck," Young Curtis said feeling better about the odds. "We can tear this bitch up!"

Only eight feet separated the men from one another but, before anything could happen, security rushed over as a spotlight from the DJ booth beamed down on the area.

$$$

"I wonder what's going on down there," Asad said seeing the commotion.

Fly Ty stood up to take a look at what was happening. "What the fuck! That's my fam," he excitedly said as he headed for the stairs.

"Ty! Where are you going?" Asad asked.

"That's my fam down there," he said before rushing off.

Asad shook his head in disapproval at his younger cousin's actions. "Go make sure Tyrone is straight," he told Ahmed, who left the booth without saying a word.

When Ahmed approached the scene, people made room for him to advance through the crowd. The closer he got, he could hear his cousin's voice. He stood in front of a large group of "Up The Way," thugs. "UTW" was a make up of main streets on the city's Southeast side. Miles, Harvard, Union, Kinsman, Buckeye, 116th, 131st, and 93rd collectively made up "UTW."

"Me and you can go outside and shoot the fair," Fly Ty said, pointing over the bouncer to the light-skinned thug who caused all of the trouble. "We don't need to get everybody caught up? What's up?" He nodded at the man for an answer.

Shukela looked at Fly Ty, thinking he wasn't big enough to fight the oversized trouble maker until she heard people in the crowd making bets that Fly Ty would knock the man out.

When Ahmed made it to the front where he took his place at his cousin's side, he looked at the men who started all of the drama and could tell by the fear in their eyes that they wanted a way out so he gave it to them. Ahmed walked over to the eight bouncers at the scene to squash the beef.

"It was just a misunderstanding. Everything is cool now," he said to the head bouncer.

The man looked nervously at the large group of thugs who gathered, before motioning for Ahmed to come closer. "Man, if these boyz wanna go off it ain't no way my team could stop them," he said into Ahmed's ear.

Ahmed turned and looked at Fly Ty. "Is your dude cool?"

"What 'chu wanna do?" he asked Young Curtis.

"It's cool homie. I came up here to kick it," he answered but inside he wanted to get at them.

Ahmed turned to the bouncers. "Everything is everything." With that, he looked at Fly Ty and his partners, telling them to follow him. As they left the scene, heading for the stairs everyone else dispersed, giving the four men a chance to exit the club without incident.

Inside the VIP booth, Fly Ty introduced Young Curtis and Ducci to his cousins. In turn, they introduced Missy and Shukela. Once everyone was comfortable, Young Curtis ordered two bottles of Dom Perignon as he, Ducci, Fly Ty, and the women kicked it. When the champagne arrived, he poured everyone a glass except Asad and Ahmed, who didn't drink.

Missy, who sat across from the brothers, took a glance at the two when she took a sip of her champagne. *Damn, they look just alike,* she thought of the two attractive men but that wasn't the reason she kept looking. It was something about them that demanded attention. She reflected on how everyone reacted when Ahmed approached the scene with Young Curtis. Everyone showed him the utmost respect.

After finishing his drink, Young Curtis suggested to Shukela to hit the dance floor. He grabbed her hand and led her to the dance floor.

"C'mon baby," Missy said to Ducci as she got out of her seat.

Asad watched as the two couples left before turning his attention to Fly Ty. "Listen Ty. You can't run around here like some nobody, getting into childish beefs. You're a millionaire, Tyrone. You have to think. Now what if it had gotten out of hand and we had to down one of those fools. Is your dude worth you going to the penitentiary for?"

"Hell yeah," Fly Ty answered without hesitation. "Young Curtis has been my friend since we were in the fifth grade. Him and Ducci is two of the realest dudes I know outside of y'all."

"The dude Ducci and I went to Kennedy at the same time," Ahmed said.

"You hustle with them brothers or something?" Asad asked, somewhat surprised by his cousin's loyalty to Young Curtis.

"Nah," Fly Ty laughed. "Young Curtis and Ducci ain't no dope boys. Y'all all cut from the same cloth. They take money," he smiled.

Asad looked over at Ahmed, who stared back at him. "What, they rob cats in the city?" he asked.

Fly Ty knew something was up because his cousins didn't concern themselves with other peoples' business. "Nah, they hit banks."

When Fly Ty's friends made it back to the booth, Asad watched the two men closely for the rest of the night. He even laughed at some of Young Curtis' jokes. He could tell Ducci was the more calculating, laid back one of the two while his partner appeared to be the more arrogant and brazen one. They seemed like an odd couple. But like the old saying goes, "opposites attract." The time for the Miami job was nearing and, since he couldn't think of anyone else, he figured the two men would be a perfect fit. Not to mention, Tyrone spoke highly of them. Plus, he figured that if anything went wrong and he had doubts about them, he would just kill 'em.

"Are y'all ready to blow this spot?" Fly Ty asked looking at his watch.

"Let's blow this bitch before the parkin' lot gets crowded," Young Curtis suggested. Everyone agreed with his logic and gathered their things before heading for the exit.

"Are y'all hungry?" Asad asked once they were in the parking lot, heading to their cars.

Fly Ty was the first to answer. "I'm hungrier than a muthafucka."

Asad was looking at Ducci and Young Curtis when he posed the question.

"Where y'all wanna go?" Young Curtis asked, stopping in the parking lot.

"Send your women home and let's meet up at the Steak House. We'll eat some good steak and discuss some things."

I wonder what he wanna holla' at us about, Ducci thought. *Fly Ty's people must have something they want to turn us on to.* Ducci handed his car keys to Missy and told her to go out to Young Curtis' condo that they would be there later.

Send my bitch home? Shit, she gotta eat too, Young Curtis thought.

Ducci saw Young Curtis wasn't catching onto what Fly Ty's cousins insinuated. "Dig Curt, Missy and Shukela have to fall back on this one. I think this might be about some business so let's go listen to what they have to say."

"Yeah, I feel you," Young Curtis said before he walked over to Shukela and passed her his house keys. He kissed her on the cheek, telling her to leave the key in the mailbox before walking off.

$$$

Shukela watched as he and Ducci got into his SL 500 then fell in line behind Asad in his black Viper and Ahmed, who drove Fly Ty's white CL 55 with him in the passenger seat.

"Who does that man think he is telling them to send us home?" Shukela asked as Missy pulled out of the parking lot in Ducci's SS.

"Shu don't worry your little soul. They're probably going to talk business or something."

"What business?" she asked, staring at Missy. "It's past three in the morning and you know what they say."

"What they say, Shu?" Missy asked, glancing over to her.

"The only thing open for a man after three is some female's legs."

Missy let out a laugh as she got on the freeway.

$$$

Inside the Steak House, The Sparks, Young Curtis and Ducci sat at a table for five in the back of the restaurant. When Asad saw the waitress coming their way, he waited for her to clear the table before filling Young Curtis and Ducci in on the nature of the impromptu meeting.

When the waitress walked away with the tray full of dirty dishes, Ahmed looked around the almost empty restaurant. He knew the place would be filled up with the after the club crowd in about ten minutes so he got down to business. "First of all, let me say that no matter how this turns out, it was good meeting you brothers," he said, looking from Ducci to Young Curtis.

"Same here," Young Curtis said. "You and your brother are some good dudes and it's truly an honor to kick it wit' y'all."

Asad looked over to Ducci who nodded his head in agreement. "My cousin speaks highly of you two. After spending a little time around y'all, I can see why," Asad said.

Ducci sensed this could be the big one, so he sat quietly to hear what they had to say.

Asad continued, "I asked the both of you here tonight to offer y'all an opportunity to take some money with me and my brother. Fly Ty stared at his cousins. A look of shock became evident on his face because he knew they never partnered with anyone in the past. *Shit, Young Curtis and Ducci are the best picks they could've made*, Fly Ty thought.

"What? Is it a bank?" Young Curtis asked Asad.

Ahmed shook his head. "No. Some major money getting Colombians."

"We've done our homework on them," Asad interjected. "But I haven't quite decided on how best to move on them. What we do know is this. We all have to be in Miami by Saturday."

"What's the risk and the reward," Ducci asked after thinking for a moment.

"The risk is three to four men armed with assault rifles. The reward is a one-third cut to you and your partner," Asad answered.

"A third?" Young Curtis questioned in dismay.

Ahmed looked to him. "We're not trying to take advantage of you brothers. We're trying to turn you and Ducci on to some major paper."

That's when Ducci asked. "What would a third be?"

Ahmed smiled. "We're not sure but you two should be guaranteed to come out with at least two to three million each."

Young Curtis and Ducci stared at one another, caught off guard by the figures.

"So are you two in?" Asad asked, staring at them.

Young Curtis looked at the Sparks brothers with his face twisted into a Tony Montana mask and in his best Scarface accent said, "I hit banks for fun but, for them millions, I'll bury those fuckin' Colombians."

Everyone at the table burst into laughter.

"Man, you're silly," Fly Ty said, smiling before throwing his cloth napkin at Young Curtis.

"Alright, let me get y'all cell phone numbers. When it's time, I'll give y'all a call."

After programming both of their numbers into his phone, Asad called for a toast. The five men held their glasses up over the center of the table and toasted. "Take Money," Asad said with the others repeating after him as he stared at Ducci and Young Curtis.

"You drive," Young Curtis said while handing Ducci his car keys as they walked to his car.

$$$

Once inside, Ducci pulled out of the parking lot in route to Young Curtis' condo in Solon, Ohio. "After we make this move, it's all over homie. A brother can settle down and live life right," Ducci said as he glanced over at Young Curtis in the passenger seat.

"I think I'ma open up the hottest club in the city wit' my

ends. I was choppin' it up wit' Fly Ty and he was talkin' 'bout steppin' away from the game too."

"That's the best thing any smart cat can do," Ducci said. "We can't make a career out of hustling. That's the reason penitentiaries are full. Dudes didn't know when to get out, and in this life, it's only a matter of time before a dude ends up in there."

"After this, our only problem is goin' to be where to stash all of the chips," Young Curtis laughed.

"Man, talking about all of that money got me feeling real foxy. I'm about to go a make love to my woman," Ducci smiled.

"You can do all of that soft shit if you want to but I'm 'bout to go in here and hit Shu's back door," Young Curtis said, getting a laugh out of Ducci.

CHAPTER 16
THE COOK OUT

Down in the lower level of their Hunting Valley townhouse, the brothers had just finished their high intensity workout. "C'mon, push it!" Ahmed said, standing over the weight bench, motivating his brother. Asad's arms shook from the weight of the two hundred and sixty five pounds as he forced it back up for the tenth time. "Good work, big bruh," he continued while helping him put the weight back in the craddle before sliding under it himself. He lifted the weight as if it was nothing, doing fifteen quick reps.

"You showing out." Asad smiled as he spotted him.

"I'm just feeling it today," Ahmed responded as he got up from the bench.

"That was some good work, but tomorrow, I'm driving. We're doing squats, calf raises, lower back and sit-ups."

Ahmed nodded his head as he took off his damp T-shirt and wiped the sweat off of his muscular body with it. Asad, who sat on the weight bench, did the same.

"Hey Asad. Think those two brothers we met last night might work out well?"

"Yeah, they seem like some solid dudes." Asad looked over to his brother.

"That Young Curtis is a character though."

Asad smiled. "Yeah, he's a work of art but don't get too attached to them dudes," he said as his smile faded. "If they show any signs of weakness or flaws in their character, you know they'll have to go."

"I'm with you on whatever but I'm with Ty. I think they're good people. Like last night, Young Curtis wanted to tear those chumps' heads off in the club. I saw it in his eyes but he let it ride because he didn't want to drape a whole bunch of people off into it. My man swallowed his pride and let it ride. That right there showed me he was solid people. If he was a lame, he would have just set it off because he knew he had a gang of people riding with him, not caring what happened."

"I feel you. I just hope they're as solid as I think they are but in case their not..." Asad let his words hang in the air.

"Okay bruh, but I think those two are goin' to surprise you."

Deep down inside, Asad felt the same way but it was only one person in the world he trusted wholeheartedly and he was looking at him.

"I'm going to give Buzz a call later to see if we can hook up tonight."

"Okay. I'm about to hit this shower. When I'm done, I'm going to cook some steaks and brown rice," Ahmed said while heading for the stairs.

"Hook some french fries up too," Asad yelled.

"Alright, take them out of the freezer," Ahmed replied.

$$$

"Here you go Curtis," Shukela said, putting a glass of orange juice in front of him as he watched TV in the enclosed patio.

"I'm hungry. Not thirsty!" he said as he looked from the glass to Shukela.

"Your breakfast will be ready in a minute." She bent down to give him a soft kiss on the lips. "Are you still mad at me about last night?" She stared at the side of his face as he ignored her by watching the television. "Don't be mad, Curtis," she pleaded before going back into the kitchen.

"Good morning Shu," Missy happily said as she entered, wearing oversized sweat pants and a white T-shirt.

"Hey Missy, I'm almost finished with breakfast. When is Ducci coming down?"

"What's up? Here I go," Ducci said, stepping into the kitchen with a smile.

"It looks like you had a good time last night." Shukela grinned at Ducci.

"Let me go holla at my boy," Ducci said. He smiled at Missy before going out to the patio.

Once Ducci left, Shukela looked over at Missy. "You my homegirl, right?"

"Yeah, what's up," Missy answered with a confused look on

her face.

"Well, why didn't you tell me that Curtis is crazy?"

"Shit, it was obvious," she chuckled.

"Girl you won't believe what he tried to do to me last night."

"What?" Missy asked with concern in her voice.

Shukela looked over her shoulder into the enclosed patio to make sure neither Young Curtis nor Ducci could hear. When she saw the two sitting at the table, she turned to Missy going into a whisper. "That boy tried to stick his thang in my butt."

Missy stared at her for a few seconds then burst out laughing, slapping the kitchen counter. "Yeah girl," she said through her laughter. "Don't let that little freaky fool do you any kind of way, especially if that's not you."

"That's definitely not me," Shu assured. "But now he's mad at me."

"Believe me baby, he'll get over it. He's just spoiled and used to having his way with everybody." Missy stared at Shu, wanting to tell her that Young Curtis wasn't serious about relationships so there wasn't any reason to get too attached to him but figured she would find out sooner or later.

$$$

"What's up homie?" Ducci asked staring at Young Curtis, who watched TV.

"What's up wit' chu?" Young Curtis shot back not in the mood to talk.

"Why you out here acting all dry. What's wrong?"

"It ain't shit, homie," Young Curtis said feeling bad for giving Ducci the cold shoulder. "I'm just over that bitch in there," he said, pointing his thumb over his shoulder in the direction of the kitchen.

"You're talking about Shu?" he asked, leaning forward in his chair.

"Yeah," he answered without taking his eyes from the movie.

"What she do?" Ducci asked, sounding suspicious, because he was willing to bet she did nothing.

"I don't want to talk about that shit right now."

Ducci already knew what was going on. It happened every time Young Curtis started liking a woman. "Check this out homie. What I'm about to say, you're not gonna wanna hear but I don't care because you need to."

Young Curtis finally turned his attention from the television to Ducci.

"Dig, you're living so far in such an opposite extreme of your true self when it comes to women it doesn't make any sense."

"What chu talkin' 'bout?" Young Curtis asked with a frown on his face.

"I'm talkin' about, every time you start liking a female, you always find a way to get rid of them."

"Man, that's becuz I don't give a fuck about no ho," Young Curtis said in his defense.

"That might work on people who don't know you but I was there when you first started messing with Shannon." Ducci saw the angry look in Young Curtis' eyes but wasn't deterred. "Don't forget, I was the one you used to call every day asking me to take you over her house. I saw how you used to treat her like a queen. That's why you use to stay broke back then. Always giving her your money..."

"What 'chu tryna say. I was a trick or something," Young Curtis asked with his face twisted up.

"Hell nah," Ducci said, dismissing him. "That's what men do. We give our women money and anything else they want or need. But what I'm saying to you is, you were young when you met her and she used you up Curt."

"Man I don't want to hear this shit."

"Dig Curt. All I'm sayin' is tone it down some before you miss out on a good woman, playing that playa role."

"Man you got me fucked up. I don't bar these hoes fo' real."

"Okay." Ducci smiled. "I'm telling you. One day, you're goin' to meet your match and I'm goin' to laugh every time she puts it down on you."

"The only thing a bitch gon' put down on me is this dick," Young Curtis laughed.

"Yeah. Okay, super playa. We gon' see." Ducci chuckled.

"Enough about that big homie," Young Curtis said, wanting to change the subject. "Man, I was up all night thinkin' 'bout what we talked about wit' Fly Ty's people."

"I couldn't sleep myself. I laid up for an hour thinkin' about it too."

Young Curtis stared at Ducci with a puzzled look on his face. "Didn't you used to go to school wit' one of Fly Ty's cousins?"

"Yeah, I went to Kennedy with the one named Ahmed."

"What's up wit' them cats? They don't seem like street dudes. You hear how proper they sound when they talk?"

"Yeah, that's how ol' boy used to talk back then and he used to get straight A's in the two classes I was in wit' him."

"What's up wit' all of that brother and sista talk they be on?"

"I don't think they like being called niggas. I remember when Ahmed beat the fuck outta this dude after school who kept saying, 'what's up my nigga' to him."

Before they could continue their conversation, Missy and Shu, brought them their plates.

"I see you made yourself at home," Young Curtis said to Missy, who wore his clothes.

"I didn't have anything to wear," she responded, shrugging her shoulders.

"It's cool," he said as she sat down to eat.

"What we doing today?" Missy asked as she buttered her toast.

"I was thinkin' we could stay out here for the day and throw some meat on the grill," Young Curtis replied.

"That sounds like a good idea," Ducci said. "What time you want to get started?"

"Round three or four, cuz I told my mother to come out here. She doesn't get off from work until about three. And, before she comes, I'm going to tell her to pick Amani up." He turned to Ducci. "You should pick AJ up after school and bring him out here too."

"Yeah, since we're gonna hit the road in a few days I need to spend some time with my lil man."

Surprised, Missy looked at Ducci with a frown on her pretty

face. “Where you going?”

“I have some business I need to take care of,” he replied. Missy left it at that for the time being, thinking they’ll talk later.

“Are you going also, Curtis?” Shu meekly asked.

“Yeah,” he answered, still not making eye contact with her.

After breakfast, the women put the dishes into the dishwasher before using Ducci’s SS to go grocery shopping for the cook out. Ducci and Young Curtis got in his Range Rover, headed toward to neighborhood to see what was going on and to find some good marijuana for the nights festivities.

$$$

“I’m tellin’ you, Fly Ty, they got some of the finest broads in the world runnin’ ‘round New York,” Hollywood said as he drove up Warrensville Center Road in his pewter colored Escalade EXT.

Fly Ty looked through the rearview mirror at Bay Bruh, who was in the back seat playing NBA Jam on the PS2. “What Wood talkin’ ‘bout Bay Bruh?”

Bay Bruh was a reddish brown complexioned brother with natural curly, black hair and light brown eyes.

“Any broad that smiled at him he was ready to trick wit ‘em,” Bay Bruh said.

Fly Ty laughed. “I see you takin’ your show on the road. It ain’t enough that you tricked off with every female in the city. Now, you going nationwide.”

“Man… y’all trippin,’” Hollywood said as he pulled into Sandra’s Soul Food parking lot.

Once inside, they were quickly seated at a table in the back. And, within a few minutes, an older black waitress was there to take their orders.

Hollywood spoke for the group. “Give us three orders of fried chicken, catfish, macaroni & cheese, sweet cornbread and mashed potatoes. I want the gravy brought separately, along wit’ a side order of mustard and turnip greens.”

“And would you like anything to drink with that?” the waitress asked as she wrote.

“Yes ma’am, a pitcher of ice tea,” he answered before she left to fill the order.

Fly Ty looked around the half full restaurant at the late lunch crowd before turning his gaze on his two-man hustle team. He could remember when they all used to hustle on the same block on the corner of 114th and Miles. When they first started, they all had different goals in terms of getting money.

Bay Bruh, the smallest of the crew, just wanted to make enough money to buy the flyest clothes and some decent jewelry. Hollwood, the biggest of the three at 6'1" 235 pounds, all he wanted to do was come down in a nice Cutlass or Regal with some sounds and rims on it. Fly Ty, on the other hand, saw the game for what it was worth. He figured that if he did it right, he could walk away with a million dollars providing he hustled hard. So when his cousins turned him on, he went back to his block and got the two best hustlers he knew – Hollywood and Bay Bruh. It took no time for the trio to lock down their side of town. Fly Ty showed them a higher level of the game and, in return, they gave him their complete loyalty. Even when they started making serious money, unlike most guys who would have used their earnings to start their own operations, the two men stayed true to him.

"Fly Ty, what's up wit 'chu? You ain't heard shit Hollywood said."

Fly Ty looked over at Bay Bruh, "I was just thinkin' 'bout somethin.' Check this out," he said, leaning forward over the table with them doing the same. "I got twenty-five more of those thangs left. I'ma give y'all twelve and a half a piece. All I want is fifteen off of each one. When that's done, it's game over for me." Fly Ty leaned back in his seat, looking from Bay Bruh to Hollywood.

"Like Jay-Z said on 'Allure,' I've just been playin' it to play it. I know y'all money should be right," he said, looking at the two men who nodded in agreement. Fly Ty continued. "If y'all get on the grind right now while it's dry out there and load your block boys up, along wit' sellin' small weight… nothin' over an ounce, y'all could make about two hundred G's."

Both men nodded in agreement with Fly Ty's idea.

"So what 'chu gon' do after this?" Bay Bruh asked, curiously.

"I'ma try my hand in real estate."

"What made you wanna walk away all of a sudden?" Hollywood questioned with a puzzled expression.

"It's a number of things but the main one is my mind ain't into it no more. Plus, I'm gettin' sloppy. Listen to this. I served Mel the other day in my Porsche."

"What!" Hollywood shouted as if he couldn't believe it. "Aw, homie, you was trippin hard. You know better than that. You the same one who told us to leave fly rides at home when we're hustlin' and to always ride wit' back up when doing heavy weight deals."

"I know, homie. That's why I'm over this..." He stopped talking when he saw the waitress coming with their orders. They all watched as she laid plate after plate of food on the table. Hollywood licked his lips at the sight of the fried chicken and catfish that smelled so good.

Once the waitress cleared the tray, she told the men to let her know if they needed anything else before walking away.

"Well Wood, it looks like our man is leavin' at the top of the game like a true hustler should," Bay Bruh said.

"Yeah, he's through," Hollywood replied before biting into a drumstick.

They all started to eat when Bay Bruh asked Fly Ty his perfectly-timed question. "You wanna get in on this record company me and Hollywood is about to start?"

Fly Ty smiled. "Y'all still on that?"

Hollywood looked at him before he took a sip of his ice tea. "Hell yeah we still on it! That shit that happened last year was a learning experience."

Fly Ty thought about last summer. It seemed like every car and club in the city was playing the single 'Money Men' from the CD Bay Bruh and Hollywood's little independent label put out. They had two nice rappers named Fatty and Nick who could give anybody a run for their money lyrically. Fly Ty had to admit the song was hot. Plus, they had a local producer who was on par with anyone in the majors. But, with all of that going for them, the label crumbled from bad business practices.

"What are y'all gonna do different this time to make it work?" Fly Ty asked.

"Man, we've bought every how to book and DVD dealing with the record industry. Plus, we're about to start going to those Hip Hop conventions to link up wit' people already in the game so we can learn from them," Bay Bruh said.

"And, a dude gotta be dedicated to this," Hollywood added.

"Now, that we're gonna have the time, we'll have no limits," Bay Bruh continued.

Fly Ty laughed. "Ai'ight, y'all sold me. I'll come in as a silent partner but don't expect me to do anything becuz I don't know shit about the music business. But, to get our feet in the door, I'ma holla at my dude who is connected in the industry."

"Well… it's on," Bay Bruh smiled. He picked up his glass of ice tea feeling this thing was going to blow up.

$$$

"What's good, baby?" Young Curtis said as he walked up to Shu in the kitchen and kissed her on the neck.

"You're not angry with me anymore?" She smiled at him.

Young Curtis, who was half drunk, stared at her through slanted eyes. "Nah, I ain't mad at 'chu. If you ain't on it, you ain't on it. But dig, I gets down like that every now and then. So that's all part of being down with a dude like me."

"So you're saying… if I don't let you treat me any kinda way, I can't be with you?"

Young Curtis laughed. "Baby girl, don't take what I'm sayin' as me tryin' to press you into doin' somethin' you don't want to but we'll kick it on this later," he said when he heard his sister shout from the front door. "I'm in the kitchen, Tiff."

Tiffany Houston came into the kitchen with her niece and daughter in each of her arms.

"There goes my baby." Young Curtis smiled, taking Amani out of his sister's arm. "Gimme kiss," he said to the grinning little girl before giving her a peck on the lips.

"I miss you, daddy," she said while wrapping her little arms around his neck.

"I miss you too, lil lady," he smiled, kissing her on the cheek.

"Give me kiss, Uncle Curt-Curt," his niece Indigo requested from her mother's arms.

"Look, this is daddy friend Ms. Shu." He handed Amani to her. "Hey, lil pretty girl," he said, taking his niece from his sister and kissing her on the cheek.

"Shannon said tell you don't have Amani drinking any pop, don't have her up all day, and you bet not bring her home late," Tiffany warned.

He frowned his face up about to say something but caught himself.

"Grandma outside," he told Indigo before putting her down. "How did mama get here? I didn't see her car outside?" Tiffany questioned.

"She came with Ducci's mother," Young Curtis answered. He looked over at Amani, who was laughing in Shu's arms as she tickled her. "Put her down, baby, so she can go see her grandma."

$$$

"Boy you're going to burn that meat," Rita Martin said to her son, Ducci.

"C'mon ma, let me do this," Ducci pleaded.

"Hey mama" Tiffany said, heading into the backyard with Amani and Indigo.

"Hey, there go my girls." Terri beamed. She squatted down, giving each of them a hug and kiss.

"Hi Ms. Rita," Tiffany said while walking past her mother.

"How have you been," Rita asked, giving her a hug and a kiss.

"I'm good."

"Have you met my future daughter-in-law?"

"No, but I've heard about her."

Missy walked pass Ducci extending her hand to Tiffany. She shook it.

"What's up Tiff?" Ducci asked from the grill.

"Nothing much. I just saw your lil look-a-like in the house playing a video game."

"Oh, that's where AJ ran off to," Ducci replied before hearing a loud, thumping car system.

Young Curtis rushed out of his front door when he heard the loud music playing. "Man, turn that shit down!" he shouted at his cousin, Doughboy, who parked in his driveway with the doors of his blue candy painted '75 Caprice open, and the radio bumping TI.

"Turn that off before you get out, Duka," he told his seven-year-old son.

"Man, fuck these people. They can give me a ticket. Fuck 'em!"

"Yeah, fuck 'em," Duka said just like his father.

"Ai'ight, my mother is in there and she gon' whup yo' bad ass if she hear you," Young Curtis warned.

Duka looked around then said, "I ain't gon' cuss no more."

Doughboy and Young Curtis glared at each other and laughed.

As day turned into night, the people at the house broke off into groups. Duka and AJ were in the lower level playing PS2. Terri and Rita sat inside the enclosed patio with Amani and Indigo fast asleep in their arms, while Missy, Shu and Tiffany sat in the kitchen engaged in girl talk. Inside the garage, Young Curtis, Ducci, Doughboy, and Josh – who stopped by – were drinking shots of Quavo Gold, sipping Heinken, and passing a blunt around.

When the time neared eleven o'clock, Rita and Terri told their sons that they were leaving. The two men kissed their mothers goodbye before Young Curtis helped his sister carry their daughters to her car and put them in their seats. He gave his sleeping daughter a kiss on the lips before shutting the door. He stood there and watched as Tiffany backed out of the driveway followed by Ms. Rita and his mother. As he walked back inside the house, he noticed everyone leaving.

"Where the fuck y'all goin'?" he asked as they all walked past him.

"I'm going home," Ducci answered on his way out of the door.

"Hold on… y'all muthafuckas ain't gon' help me clean up?"

He could hear Josh and Doughboy snickering as they got to their cars.

"Ai'ight, that's how y'all wanna play it. Ain't no more muthafuckin' cookouts over here. The next time, y'all will be in the park gettin' ate up by them mosquitoes."

"Chill out fam. Call Minute Maid in the morning," Ducci said before he jogged off to his car. Young Curtis watched everyone pull off. *Them no good muthafuckas, he thought before slamming the door.*

$$$

Shortly after eleven, Asad and Ahmed pulled into the alley behind the Rocky Tavern. They both got out of the car and walked over to the steel plated back door that was immediately opened by a white man. The brothers walked past Buzz, who shut the door before leading the two to the storeroom.

"How have you guys been?" Buzz asked once they were in the storeroom.

"We're good and yourself?" Ahmed asked.

"I can't complain."

Matthew 'Buzz' Polanski, who everyone called Buzz was a fifty-three year old, white man with salt and pepper hair that he wore in a military style buzz cut and a matching goatee. His gray hair was the only thing that hinted at his true age. He was in phenomenal shape. Buzz was a short, stocky man with a big barrel chest and a hard flat stomach. As an ex-marine, he fought in Vietnam from 1970-72. He was only seventeen when he went to fight for the country he so loved. Now, even though he still loves his country, he hates the government. Buzz believed in a conspiracy called the New World Order. He claimed a group of elite, super rich people were trying to rule the world. He'd pointed out a lot of things in recent history that he thought proved the U.S. Government was being used to further this plan. Buzz, who thought of himself as a true patriot, said he and his friends across the country would fight any enemy of the U.S., including the government.

The brothers followed Buzz to the corner of the room, where he asked them to help him move the freezer. As they moved it, Asad could hear the people in the bar above them listening to country music and having a good time. After moving the freezer, the brothers stood back as Buzz pulled the cellar door up revealing stairs. They all went down them into the darkened cellar. Once they reached the floor, Buzz hit the light switch.

The small underground room looked like a military armory as racks of assault rifles and handguns lined the walls. There were numerous wooden crates on the floor and designated explosives on the side of them. Buzz went to the back room to get what the men came for.

Asad went to a rack of guns and grabbed the odd looking Steyr Aug carbine assault rifle. Unlike most assault rifles, the Steyr Aug clip went behind the guns handle instead of the front and had a built on scope. Ahmed stood at the side of the menacing looking Beretta M82 .50 caliber sniper rifle that sat on a tripod. He stared at the huge gun, guessing it had to be at least five and a half feet long. He wondered what kind of kick it possessed.

"I shortened the sound suppressors on all the weapons," Buzz said as he came back into the room with a black duffel bag.

He laid it on the metal table in the center of the room and pulled out one of the Heckler & Koch MP5-K's submachine guns then handed it to Ahmed.

"Won't this make it louder?" Ahmed asked, looking at how short the silencer appeared.

"C'mon, how long have you known me? I just learned this new technique from a friend of mine, and believe it or not, they're almost soundless. Oh, before I forget," he said reaching back into the bag. "Knowing what big fans you guys are of Heckler & Koch's, I found you these," he said pulling out one of the USP .40 cals already silenced.

Asad took the gun with a smile on his face. He pointed it across the room and looked down the sight. "This is slightly heavier than the Glocks."

"Yeah… but it's just as good, if not better," Buzz shot back.

Asad put the HK back in the bag with the others then reached under his shirt, pulling out a manila envelope filled with hundred dollar bills. "Here you go," he said, handing it to Buzz.

"Until next time, you two be careful," Buzz warned as he took the money. That was something he said every time he and the brothers parted ways. He walked them to the back door then watched as they got into their car and pulled off.

During the time he had done business with them, he never asked what they did. But, it was obvious. He knew that only professionals used the type of weapons they purchased. He liked the two men's style. They never carried themselves as hitters. They never talked too much. And, they always watched everything around them. As he stood at the door, he thought about the first time he met them at a gun store in Parma, Ohio that his buddy owned. It seemed like every time he was there, they showed up. They never attempted to purchase anything. It seemed as if they were there just to study weapons. They would look at the guns then ask a clerk a few questions and leave. After seeing this a few times, Buzz approached them as they looked at a post-ban mini-14. He told them they wouldn't want that piece of shit, and if they wanted to see some real weapons, to give him a call.

A few months went by before they finally contacted him to check out his hardware. Later, they told him they didn't know if he was the Feds or what, but figured it unlikely for the Feds to hang out in a gun store soliciting customers. Over time, Buzz took to them and it didn't have anything to do with all of the money they spent. He liked their style and hoped whatever it was they were doing wouldn't catch up with them someday.

CHAPTER 17
GIRLFRIENDS

Francisca laid on her sofa getting worked up from the Spanish soap opera she watched on Univision. *"No te vallas con el,"* she said out loud to one of the female characters. When Fly Ty stepped into the room fully dressed with his car keys, she stared at him.

"Where you going?"

"I gotta hook up with Hollywood and Bay Bruh."

"Didn't you spend the whole day with them yesterday?"

"Yeah, but today is different," he said walking over and giving her a kiss. Before he could pull back, she grabbed his shirt.

"I'm hungry baby."

"Well get off of that big ass and go cook you somethin' to eat!" he jokingly exclaimed.

"I don't feel like cooking. I want you to go to that Chinese restaurant on Kinsman and get me some shrimp fried rice and two egg rolls."

"You know you workin' me," Fly Ty said, staring at her.

"I'll pay you back tonight, Papi," she seductively said.

"You got me," he smiled. "I'll be back in twenty minutes. He gave her another kiss before leaving the room, heading for the side door.

Fly Ty looked at his watch. It was 8:25 p.m. He pulled out his cell phone and called Bay Bruth to let him know he would be thirty minutes late. After dropping Francisca's food off, he headed to his house in Bedford, Ohio to get the drugs for Hollywood and Bay Bruh. *Well this is it. Game over,* he thought. But, little did he know, it wouldn't end as he planned.

$$$

Inside a posh upscale restaurant in German Village, a district of downtown Columbus, Ohio, four intelligent, beautiful, black women sat at a table in the dimly lit eatery, finishing off a bottle of red wine.

"You're not nervous about this weekend, Janet?" Mary, a dark-skinned woman with dreads asked.

Janet, a light brown-skinned woman smiled, nodding her head. “I am but in a good way. I’m just ready to get the wedding over with because all of the scheduling and planning is really a headache.”

“You haven’t felt pain yet,” a high yellow woman named Alexis retorted.

“What do you mean by that?” Janet asked with a puzzled expression.

Alexis sat her wine glass on the table before making her point. “First off all, you’re about to marry DeAndre Johnson, the first running back taken in the draft. Everyone at this table knows about his doggish behavior during his three years at school. And now that he’s about to sign a big contract, he’s going to have every floozy in every city he stops in throwing themselves at him.”

“DeAndre and I have worked through his past infidelities,” Janet meekly said. “I believe him when he says all of that is behind him.”

Alexis picked her wine glass back up and took a sip. She turned her legs out toward the aisle and crossed them. She swung the top one back and forth, as she stared at Janet. “If you believe that, I feel sorry for you. Once a dog, always a dog.”

Hearing all she could take, Tamiko came to Janet’s rescue. “That’s enough Alexis. You need to put that glass down and apologize to Janet.”

Alexis took another sip of her wine and hunched her shoulders. “Why must I apologize for giving my opinion?”

“Because you’re talking about the man she’s marrying in a few days,” Tamiko said, angrily.

Alexis rolled her eyes and waved Tamiko off.

“You’re just so cynical when it comes to men.” Mary shook her head in disapproval.

“Excuse you?” Alexis contemptuously cut her eyes at Mary.

Not wanting to get in a long drawn out argument, Mary leaned back in her seat and ignored Alexis.

“I think you’ve had enough wine for the night, Alexis,” Tamiko suggested.

Alexis stared at Tamiko with a smirk on her face before

finishing her drink. "That might work on that little boy you're seeing but I am an adult." She giggled at her own comment. "By the way, how old is he again?" she asked, feeling as if she found a new target.

Tamiko quickly became angry but calmed herself. "He's twenty."

"He was only seventeen when you met him?" Alexis asked after a quick calculation.

"Yeah, so what are you getting at?" Tamiko questioned.

"Oh, its nothing. I just wanted to point out to our girlfriends how smart you are when it comes to men.... See girls," Alexis said while turning her attention back to Janet and Mary.

"Instead of dealing with a corrupted man, our friend went out and got herself a little boy she could dominate and train."

"Alexis!" Janet said, in hopes of getting her to apologize.

Alexis looked at her for a moment then turned her attention to Tamiko who seemed unfazed. "I have to be honest with you Tamiko. I wouldn't trust leaving him by himself this long. For all you know, he could be with another woman as we speak."

Janet and Mary sat quiet, knowing how protective Tamiko was of her relationship with Tyrone. She stared at Alexis with anger in her eyes. "I don't know what your problem is, but if you don't stop this right now you're going to have another one. Me! So, while you're sitting over there trying to tear everyone's relationships down, you need to get over your past experience and realize that all men are not out to hurt you."

All the women at the table knew what Tamiko alluded to. It was two years earlier when Alexis skipped a class, went back to her off campus apartment, and found the only man she ever loved in bed with her roommate. The sight devastated her and she vowed to never be hurt again.

Alexis finally put her empty glass down and looked at her sorority sisters with a somber expression. "Tamiko is right. I've had too much to drink. Janet, you know I wish you the best."

Janet gave her a smile, letting her know that none of this would be held against her.

Alexis turned her attention to Tamiko. "You know I love you

like a sister. I'm sorry for what I said about Tyrone."

"Say no more," Tamiko said as she leaned over and gave Alexis a hug. As the two women embraced, Alexis' statement weighed heavy on her mind.

CHAPTER 18
SHOTS RANG OUT

The cool night air hit JT's face as he sat on his porch, smoking a Newport and waiting for Mel and Ron-Ron to show. *Bout time*, he thought when he saw Mel's Denali coming up the street.

JT stood up, when the SUV pulled into his driveway, and waited for the men. Mel and Ron-Ron got out of the car and stepped up onto the porch, following JT inside the house.

They all went to the dining room where they saw an oak table with three Smith & Wesson, 9mm's and bulletproof vests.

"Dig, I've been watchin' that house Fly Ty bitch ass went to," JT informed as the three men sat down at the table. "You won't believe who lives there," he said, looking to Mel.

"Don't tell me that's his cousins' spot."

"Nah, scary ass nigga. It's that bitch Cha-Cha's."

"You're talkin' about the stripper bitch?"

JT nodded before laying out the plan. "Check, for the last two nights Fly Ty has been going to that house. Tonight we're goin' to lay on him and, if he shows up, we move on him," JT finished, staring at the men.

"How we gon' do it?" Mel asked.

"We're goin' through the attached garage. When the nigga pulls up, he always uses a garage door opener. So once he's in, y'all have to get under the door before it closes. Once y'all got the nigga, open the garage door for me."

"Where are we gon' hide 'til he comes home?" Ron-Ron asked.

"Behind the garage. They have some bushes back there."

"Damn man, we gotta lay in some bushes," Ron-Ron whined.

"What's up?" JT asked looking at Mel, ignoring Ron-Ron's complaint.

"We gon' smoke the bitch too?" Mel asked.

"Nah, two bodies bring more heat than one. I'ma just smoke Fly Ty's punk ass." JT didn't tell them his plans to hook up with Cha-Cha after all of this was over. The way he saw it, Fly Ty was in his way. Once he was out the picture, Cha-Cha would be his.

"Shit, ain't no sense in waitin' and fakin.'" Mel said, standing up. "This sounds like a plan to me." He grabbed one of the vests and put it on. He picked up one of the 9mm's and chambered around with JT and Ron-Ron doing the same.

They all left the house with Mel going to move his car while JT and Ron-Ron went to the garage and pulled out the rented, gray Ford Taurus. Once JT pulled out of the driveway, Mel pulled back in and parked. He got out then ran and jumped in the front passenger side seat.

"Let's get it," he said, amped up as JT drove off.

$$$

"Hey Curt, it's goin' down," Josh said, hitting the end button on his cell phone as they waited at a red light.

"What's goin' down?" Young Curtis asked from the passenger seat of Josh's new creamed colored '03 Lexus SC430.

"Rob set up a big boy dice game at his barber shop," Josh answered while pulling off.

"I'm tired," Young Curtis said, not in the mood. "I've been wit' you since ten this mornin.' I took you to pick up your ride. I went wit' you to lace it wit' shoes and I've been ridin' 'round wit' you all day, stuntin' on these fools. I'm over this," he said, leaning back in his seat and closing his eyes.

Josh could hear it in his voice but continued to push. "You know Rob said some big hat St. Clair boyz is there."

This caught Young Curtis' attention. "Who is it?" he asked, looking over to Josh.

"He said Choppa and Lil' D."

"What!" Young Curtis said, excitedly.

"Yeah... and Rob say them boyz got so much money their pockets look like they're 'bout to bust."

Young Curtis looked at the clock on the Lexus' dashboard and saw that it was shortly after eleven. "Take me to my mama's house so I can get some ends and my truck. I'm 'bout to bust those chumps then shoot home to my broad."

Josh smiled. "Good, 'cause I didn't feel like goin' to the game by myself.

$$$

Fly Ty drove up Harvard Avenue with the top down on the Porsche, listening to 50 Cent's "Many Men." When he pulled up to the light on Lee Road at Harvard, his cell phone started to vibrate.

"Speak on it," he answered.

"What did I tell you about answering the phone like that?"

Fly Ty smiled, hearing her voice. "Fall back wit' that," he said.

Tamiko laughed. "What are you doing?" she asked from the phone in her hotel room as she undressed.

"I'm on my way to my mother's." He lied.

What's going on over there?"

"Nothing, I'm just staying over there 'til you get back home." The light changed and Fly Ty continued on his way to Francisca's.

"Sometimes, I forget how much of a mama's boy you are."

"It ain't nothin' wrong wit' that is it?" he asked, making small talk because he started to feel guilty.

"No. there's nothing wrong with it."

"Oh yeah, I got some good news for you," he said.

"What is it," Tamiko asked, pulling the covers back on her bed.

"I've finally did what you've been asking me to do since we first met."

"What's that?"

"I'm finished with the streets," he said proudly.

"Are you serious?" she questioned gleefully.

Hearing the happiness in her voice made him smile. "Yeah, that chapter in my life is closed, baby."

"I'm so glad. Now you can do your real estate thing."

Fly Ty became silent for a moment. "I got somethin' else I wanna tell you but I don't want to do it over the phone."

For some reason, she didn't like how that sounded. "What is it?"

"We're gonna talk when you come home, baby." He really wanted to tell her about Francisca, to get it off of his chest, but he knew it had to be done face to face.

"Okay babe," she said, before changing the subject. "Do you miss me?"

"I miss you like crazy," he answered, sincerely.

She smiled at his words. "I'm coming home right after the wedding Saturday. There is no need for me to stay the entire weekend."

"I'll see you Saturday, My Special Lady," he said, smiling as he called her by his personal nickname for her.

"Alright. I love you, Tyrone."

"I love you more," he said then ended the call. He turned onto Francisca's street. *I really do love you Miko*, he thought. He stopped three houses from Francisca's then leaned over and opened the glove box to retrieve the garage door opener before he continued. He drove up the driveway then hit the button and watched as the door slowly opened.

$$$

JT sat in the Taurus on the other end of the street. "Get ready, Mel," he said into the small yellow and black walkie-talkie.

Mel, who listened through an earpiece tapped Ron-Ron and motioned for him to follow. The two masked gunmen made their way around the garage as quietly as possible.

JT watched Fly Ty pull into the garage. When the door started lowering, he pressed the button on the walkie-talkie. "Go now, Mel… Go now!"

The two came from the side of the garage and slid under the door, little over half way down.

$$$

Fly Ty caught a glimpse of something in his rearview mirror. Instead of getting out of the car, he continued to look through the mirror. His heart dropped when he saw the two masked gunmen rise up from the garage floor with their guns pointed at him. He became a sitting duck in the Porsche with the top down.

One of the men snatched him out of the car and put the gun to the side of his head. The second reached inside the car and grabbed the garage door opener and hit the button. Fly Ty thought about making a run for it but that idea escaped him when he saw a third masked man step from the darkness into the dimly lit garage. Right then and there, he knew this didn't look good. He started trying to pick up on anything that could help him identify them. He could tell that they all wore vests under their jogging suits.

"Face the door, bitch ass nigga." One of the men demanded. Fly Ty complied.

Earlier, it was agreed that Ron-Ron would do all of the talking, saying everything they told him to say. "Open the door," Ron-Ron said in a terribly disguised voice.

"I don't have a key," Fly Ty said calmly, even with his heart racing. He hoped they would go for this because Francisca would know whoever was on the other side without a key wasn't suppose to be there. Hearing the knock, she would respond with gunfire. Fly Ty figured the sound of gunshots would cause enough confusion to provide him a getaway or run the robbers off. He stared straight ahead, praying to the 'Game God' they would knock on the door.

Ron-Ron looked to JT, who stood between the Porsche and Jaguar, wanting to know what to do next. JT walked over and went through Fly Ty's pockets. He pulled out a little over two hundred dollars and a lone key.

When Ron-Ron saw the key, he smacked Fly Ty on the side of his face with the gun. "Nigga lie to me again and you dead."

The blow didn't draw blood but Fly Ty could feel his face starting to swell. He watched as the one who took the key from him stuck it into the lock and slowly opened the door. The men all positioned themselves behind Fly Ty using him as a shield.

They marched him up the three stairs that lead to the kitchen, listening for any movement in the house. Once inside, he tried a last ditch effort to alert Francisca. "Ain't nothing..." But, before he could finish, he took a hard punch to the ribs.

The gunmen moved Fly Ty to the living room where a lamp was on. One of the men pushed him down on the sofa as the shortest of the three motioned for his partners to stay put.

Fly Ty's heart dropped as he watched the man disappear around the corner in the direction of the first floor bedroom. He looked at the two men who stayed with him. *These niggas are on top of their game*, he thought. He could tell that they had done this before by how they positioned themselves around him and held their guns. It wasn't any of that sideways garbage you see on TV or in the movies. The one who did all of the talking held his with two hands like a cop while the other held his like a guy in an old school gangster flick. His elbow was tucked close to his body with the gun pointed at Fly Ty. The style might have looked funny to a square but Fly Ty knew that it was an old stick-up man move. They would hold the gun that way in case a fool wanted to play hero. If someone rushed them, they could fend them off with their free hand and shoot with the gun hand.

Fly Ty sat there wanting to try the men but it looked ugly and he didn't want to risk getting Francisca and their unborn child killed. He decided to play it by ear before making a move.

$$$

JT stood with his ear to a bedroom door and listened for any movement but all he heard was the sound from a TV. He slowly turned the doorknob, gently opening the door. He peaked inside and saw the light from the television illuminating the room. He then pushed the door farther and saw Cha-Cha asleep in the bed. He stepped into the room and felt the wall for a light switch. Instantly, he found one and turned it on.

The room lit up and he could see her clearly. She slept on her stomach under a crisp, rose-colored satin sheet that partly covered her naked body. The sheet imprinted every crease and curve of her luscious buttocks. Her long full hair flowed behind her as she faced him. *Damn, she's gorgeous*, JT thought. He walked over and shook her shoulder with his free hand.

"What do you want, Ty?" she asked in a sleepy voice while rolling over onto her side with her eyes still closed.

JT said nothing, just stared at her exposed breasts.

Feeling something wasn't right, she opened her eyes and looked up at the masked gunman who stood over her. She blinked a few times to make sure her eyes weren't playing tricks on her.

JT motioned for her to get out of the bed. She slowly got up with the sheet held in front of her. As she stood there, she thought he would rape her. But, when he made no attempt to grab her, she knew it was a robbery.

"Can I put my robe on?" she asked with a slight tremble in her voice, signaling toward the closet.

He quickly nodded yes. She walked over to the closet holding the sheet around her body. When she reached the door, the masked man stopped her. He opened it, grabbed a short pale pink robe, and handed it to her. As she slipped the robe on, she thought about the Glock inside the closet but the masked man led her out of the bedroom to the living room. When they turned the corner, she saw Fly Ty sitting on the couch with two armed, masked men standing over him. She immediately noticed a large bruise and swelling on the side of his face. She went to him, ignoring the three men.

"Are you okay?" she asked while sitting down and taking his face into her hands.

Her actions surprised everyone in the room except Fly Ty. He always knew she was a ride or die type woman.

"I'm cool," he said.

"Nigga, you ain't gon' be cool if you don't tell us where that shit is," the gunman, who did all of the talking, warned.

"Man, I told y'all ain't nothin in here," Fly Ty said defiantly, watching the men for a reaction.

"Okay, we gon' see how much you know after I make you watch me fuck yo' ho,'" Ron-Ron said. He had been watching her every since she came into the room and he wanted to get between her thighs. He walked over and grabbed her by the arm to lift her off of the sofa.

As soon as he touched her, Fly Ty jumped up to go at him but, as quickly as he moved, all the guns in the room pointed at him.

He stared at Francisca, feeling in his heart he would die that night because no one was going to do anything to her as long as he was alive.

Seeing the look on Fly Ty's face, she snatched away from the masked man and sat back down on the sofa. She wasn't even scared anymore. If it was meant for it to end like this, she was ready.

Frustrated by her reaction, Ron-Ron changed his tactics. "Oh, you love this bitch huh? Well since you love this bitch so much... if you don't tell me where that shit is, I'ma blow her muthafuckin' brains out in front of you." Ron-Ron placed his gun to the side of her head as he stared at Fly Ty.

It didn't take long for him to break. "I'll show you where it's at," Fly Ty quickly responded.

"C'mon nigga," Ron-Ron said after getting the nod from JT.

Fly Ty walked to his capturers. On his way past Francisca, she grabbed his hand and told him she loved him. He nodded his head and walked to the two men, leading them to the basement. *If I get out of this, all three of these niggas is dead,* Fly Ty thought as he took them down the stairs. He never shot or killed anyone in his life but he knew he could murder all of them if he ever got a chance.

$$$

JT, who stayed in the room with Francisca, lowered his gun when Mel and Ron-Ron left with Fly Ty. He stared at the beautiful Puerto Rican woman sitting on the sofa, staring straight ahead. He admired the heart she showed with Ron-Ron. He figured, after this, he would lay low for a couple of weeks then find her and fill in where Fly Ty left off. He reasoned with himself that it was only because of Fly Ty and his tricking ways she never hooked up with him. He couldn't help but notice all of the expensive furniture and electronics in the bedroom and living room.

JT was glad Ron-Ron didn't attempt to rape her because he would've come to her defense. *That rape shit is for lames anyway. I ain't never had to rape a bitch so why start now?* Once he finished thinking, his gaze fell back on Cha-Cha.

$$$

Down in the basement, Fly Ty told the robbers where they could find the drugs.

The quiet one went into the small room and opened up the chest, finding five and a half kilos.

"Where's the money?" The masked man in the room came out and asked in a muffled voice.

"It ain't none," Fly Ty replied.

Mel went back into the room, turning boxes over and looking through bags of clothes.

"Hurry up!" Ron-Ron screamed.

"Shut the fuck up, Ron-Ron." Mel was so caught up in looking for money it was too late when he realized his mistake.

Ron-Ron looked toward the room over his shoulder while still holding his gun on Fly Ty. "Why you say my name?"

Bingo, Ron-Ron off 'The 1st, Fly Ty thought.

"It don't matter. The nigga is dead anyway," the muffled voice from the room said.

When Fly Ty heard that, he knew it was time to shoot his shot. While Ron-Ron looked over his shoulder toward the room, Fly Ty hit him with a crisp right cross that landed more on his jaw than his chin.

As Ron-Ron fell back from the blow, Fly Ty went for the gun on the laundry room shelf.

Everything happened so fast. Before he could reach the room, seven rapid-fire shots rang out, while Ron-Ron pulled the trigger again and again, Fly Ty hit the floor.

Mel came running out of the room with his gun at the ready. "What happened?" he asked as Ron-Ron picked himself up from the floor.

"That bitch ass nigga took off on me," he answered rubbing his jaw.

Mel walked over to Fly Ty's body. Blood oozed from his back and the side of his head. "He's dead," Mel declared before rushing back inside the room to get the bag with the kilos in it.

$$$

When she heard the shots from downstairs, Francisca's hands covered her mouth. She hoped Fly Ty got to one of the guns he had stashed throughout the house.

JT instantly knew something was wrong because he was supposed to kill Fly Ty. He looked in the direction of the kitchen then back at Cha-Cha, making a gesture for her to stay seated before he went to see what was going on. As soon as he left, she rushed to her bedroom.

JT met Mel and Ron-Ron coming up the stairs, noticing a bag in Mel's hand.

"What happened?" he asked as they stood at the top of the stairs.

"He's dead," Mel answered.

They all headed for the back door, but just as they opened it, they heard a barrage of gunfire coming from behind them. Mel turned around and fired blindly back into the house as JT helped Ron-Ron, who was hit, to his feet while Francisca emptied the Glock at the fleeing men.

Once the return fire stopped, she quickly shut the back door before going to the knife drawer. She pulled out a 9mm and cocked it. She then grabbed the cordless phone off of the counter before running down the basement stairs and dialing 911.

At the bottom of the stairs, she found Fly Ty in a pool of blood.

"911, what's your emergency," the operator asked.

Looking at Fly Ty's body, Francisca felt herself losing it. "Send an ambulance to 3818 Gardner. Someone broke into my house and shot my boyfriend," she said before dropping the phone. She went over to Fly Ty, laid the gun down, and turned him over. As she held his lifeless body, it felt like her soul was being snatched out of her body. She lifted him up in her arms with tears streaming down her face. *"Oh dios mio. Porfavor no lo dejes morir, salva su vida senor,"* she prayed then rocked him back and forth in her arms. When she felt him move, she almost dropped him. Looking down, she could see his eyes semi open. "Ty, Tyrone. Say something, baby," she cried.

With a pained expression on his face, he managed to say, "Tell my cousins Ron-Ron off the 1st." Then, his speech was cut off by the blood he started to cough up.

"I love you baby. Just hold on. Help is on the way."

"I... love ya..." was all he said before his body went into a violent convulsion.

She quickly checked him for a pulse and found a weak one. She went into the laundry room and got some towels to put under his head. When she heard sirens outside, she rushed up the stairs and out of the front door covered in blood. She ran out to the curb, franticly waving down the ambulance that stopped in front of her house.

One of the paramedics jumped out and quickly approached her with his medical bag in hand. "Where are you bleeding from ma'am?"

"It's not mine! Its boyfriend's! He's been shot. He's in the basement not moving," she informed in a trembling voice.

"John, grab the gurney!" the paramedic said to his partner before hurrying inside the house.

$$$

The police arrived on the scene as Fly Ty was loaded onto the ambulance. Francisca wanted to go with him but the police said they needed to question her and that his family was already notified. She watched with tears in her eyes as the ambulance pulled off before being escorted back inside the house by officers.

$$$

Ron-Ron sat on the couch in the living room of JT's house, drinking Hennessy and Coke while licking his wounds. "Man, that bitch tried to do me," he said looking at the large deep dark bruises on his side from where the bullets impacted on the resistant vest. He could feel two more on his middle and lower back. The Hennessy and two lines of coke made him feel a little better but he was still in pain.

"Man, I think that bitch broke my ribs," he whined, easing his way into the living room where JT and Mel sat at the table. "Why didn't you tie that bitch up or something?" he asked JT as he took a seat at the table.

JT didn't answer. He just nodded his head to the sound of Tupac's 'Outlaws.'

"Hey J, you should've seen how your young nigga lit Fly Ty's ho ass up."

JT stared at Ron-Ron through glazed eyes, listening to the replay.

"That bitch had some pop on that punch but I took it like a true "G" and tore his head off."

JT smiled, thinking about Cha-Cha. "We might as well celebrate. Let's hit the Mirage."

"I'm wit' it," Mel said, taking a look at his watch.

"I'm cool," Ron-Ron said. "I'm bout to go over my girl's house and get some pussy. Let me get them ends so I can get up outta here."

Mel looked at JT with a smile on his face.

"Hold on," JT said before going upstairs. When he came back down with a stack of money in his hand, he sat at the table and placed it in front of Ron-Ron. "Grab that half outta there," he told Mel.

Mel reached in the bag, pulled it out, and handed it to him. "This you, homie. That's ten stacks," JT said as he slid the half a key to him.

Ron-Ron looked at the ten thousand then the half of kilo, inwardly happy, but he knew they were trying to play him. "What the fuck is this?"

"Nigga, your cut!" Mel said, flipping gangster on him.

Sounding like a kid, Ron-Ron put up a weak protest. "It was five and a half birds in there and this all I get?"

JT jumped in to smooth things over. "Look Ron-Ron. This was our lick. I brought you in becuz you're my little nigga and I wanted to put some paper in your pockets since you're fresh out the pen." He could see his words were having the affect he wanted so he continued. "That should hold you over 'til the next one I'm plannin.'"

Ron-Ron smiled wide. "Y'all know y'all my O.G's," he said walking around the table giving JT and Mel dap. "My bad, Mel."

"It's all good my young nigga."

Ron-Ron wrapped the drugs and money inside his jogging suit jacket before following JT to the door.

"Don't forget, keep your mouth shut about this," JT warned as he opened it.

"Believe me, this shit ain't gon' get out."

JT watched Ron-Ron go down the stairs before he shut the door, smiling from getting out on the young thug.

CHAPTER 19
AWKWARD MEETING

It took Francisca over three hours to make it to the hospital. The detectives who questioned her kept asking if Tyrone was involved in drugs and couldn't think of any other reason why someone would do this to him. She constantly told them no.

After answering all of their questions, she took a quick shower and packed some clothes then headed to the hospital. The police told her he was still alive but just barely. When she arrived at the waiting area, outside the ICU, she noticed three women sitting together holding hands. As she watched them from across the room, the woman in between the other two looked familiar. It dawned on her that she was Tyrone's mother. She looked at the other two females and correctly guessed they had to be his grandmother and cousin. Even though she never met them, Tyrone talked about them so much it was like she knew them. She wanted to go over and introduce herself and find out how Tyrone was doing but felt awkward under the circumstances. Just when she thought about how to approach them, a doctor came out and briefly spoke with the women. She couldn't hear any of the conversation so she watched the women's body language for any hint as to what was going on. When the doctor stopped talking, the women followed him through the double doors of the ICU. She watched the doors, for over five minutes, hoping Tyrone was still alive.

The doors to the ICU opened and the youngest of the Sparks' women came through them. They both locked eyes as the woman made her way to her.

"Are you here for Tyrone Sparks?" The woman asked standing over her. Francisca stared up at her nodding yes.

"I'm Isis Sparks," she said sticking her hand out.

"I'm Francisca Feliciano," Francisca said.

"Were you with him when this happened?"

Tears instantly filled her eyes. "Yes, how is he?" she asked, longing to know.

"He's not doing too good right now but us Sparks' are strong.

He'll pull through. I know he will." The statement was more to herself than Francisca.

As Francisca stared up at Isis, she noticed that something had caught the girl's attention. She followed Isis' line of sight and saw a woman she knew had to be Tamiko coming up the corridor.

Tamiko wore a pair of scarlet running shorts and a gray Ohio State sweater. She had on a pair of white running shoes and no socks. Her long jet-black hair was pulled back into a ponytail. Looking at her, you could tell she just threw anything on to get there.

The closer she got, Francisca could see she had been crying.

She walked up and gave Isis a hug then looked at the pretty woman talking to Isis. At first, she mistook Francisca for one of her own friends, but when she saw the woman's neck, anger instantly shot through her mind. Knowing it wasn't the time or place to address the issue, she held her emotions in check.

"Hi, my name is Tamiko," she said extending her hand out.

"I'm Francisca." The two women shook hands.

Isis looked at them both and figured they would be smart enough not to start anything.

Tamiko slowly pulled her hand back from Francisca but it took her a little longer to break her gaze on the diamond necklace. She turned back toward Isis. "I received a call from Joy telling me to get back to Cleveland ASAP because Tyrone had been hurt. Tell me, what's going on," she pleaded.

"Ty was shot three times. He's back there fighting for his life."

Tamiko looked as if she went into shock as the words registered. "I need to see him," Tamiko cried. Isis took her hand and walked her through the double doors.

Francisca wept silently when they vanished through the doors because she wanted to see him as well. She picked up her Prada handbag and pulled out some tissues to dry her face. When she looked up, she saw them.

Asad and Ahmed walked up the corridor in a smooth, controlled pace. They both looked straight ahead without much sign of emotion on their faces. She thought about stopping them, but when she was about to get their attention, Isis came out of the ICU doors to greet them. They went to her, walking past Francisca. She saw the slightly shorter of the two looking at her as they followed Isis into the ICU.

Once at Fly Ty's bedside, Asad and Ahmed consoled their aunt and grandmother. Asad didn't want to ask them what the doctors thought of his chances because he could see they were hurting. He looked over at his cousin, lying in the bed with his head wrapped up and face swollen. He stared at the I.V. in his arm and the tube in his mouth then shook his head in disbelief.

Ahmed stood over Tamiko, who sat at his bedside, and rubbed his hand. When he saw Asad and Isis walk out of the room, he followed.

"What did the doctors say about, Tyrone?" Asad asked once they were away from the receptionist desk.

"He's not doing well right now," Isis sadly answered. "He was shot three times, twice in the back and once in the head."

The brothers stared at her expressionless, waiting to hear the rest. Isis continued. "From what the doctor said, only one bullet is causing all of the trouble. The one to his head was more of a flesh wound. They say the angle the bullet entered caused it to ricochet off of his skull. Grandma always said he was hardheaded," she joked, trying to lighten the mood. The brothers smiled.

"They took another bullet out of his back but the other one tore into his lung so it collapsed. The doctors are trying to save it but said if he continues having trouble breathing, they might have to take it out."

"Where was he when this happened?" Ahmed asked, apparently hearing enough.

"Over her house." Isis pointed into the waiting area at the woman in the pink Baby Phat jogging suit.

Asad and Ahmed walked over to her and sat down.

"Francisca right?" Asad asked in a friendly voice. She shook her head yes. He took her hand in his as if they were old friends. "Did you speak with the police?"

"Yes, but I didn't tell them anything."

"Don't worry Francisca. Everything is going to be all right. Just tell us everything that happened."

Francisca sat up straight to clear her mind so she wouldn't leave anything out. After twenty minutes, she recounted the night's events in great detail.

"You're sure he said Ron-Ron off 'The 1st?'" Ahmed asked.

"I'm positive."

"When you shot at them, did you hit anyone?" Asad asked.

"I had to but I think they had something on under their clothes because they all looked bulky."

"Kevlar?" Ahmed surmised, looking at his brother. She watched the two men who were in deep thought.

"Have you seen Tyrone yet?" Asad asked.

The question caught her off guard. She looked at him through saddened eyes. "No, I didn't want to cause any trouble."

"You have just as much right to be back there as anyone else. Tyrone loves you," Asad said.

That brought a smile to her lips. She was surprised that he told his cousins about her.

"And you carrying his unborn child," Ahmed chimed in. She looked at Asad who stood up and took her hands, leading her into the ICU.

When they entered the room, Ahmed walked over to Tamiko and whispered into her ear. She looked from him to the woman standing next to Asad. She got up from her seat without saying a word and followed Ahmed outside.

Francisca walked over to Fly Ty's bedside and gently kissed him on the cheek. Asad went to the family and explained to them Francisca's connection to Tyrone. Both his grandmother and aunt walked over to where she stood and gave her a hug.

Asad stepped out of the room and saw his brother talking with Tamiko. He approched them.

"Listen, you're a smart woman," Asad started. "You can see what's going on. This is something you'll have to work out with Ty if he pulls through." Ahmed's jaw tightened at the last comment.

Asad continued. "I want you to know that my family and I love you and we're were not taking sides but Francisca needs to be in there also."

Tamiko's mouth said nothing but her eyes screamed "Why!" Asad took her in his arms, wanting to tell her everything but it wasn't his place as long as Tyrone remained alive.

The two men hugged her once more before they headed toward the exit. Neither spoke until they were in the parking lot.

"I'm going to find Ron-Ron," Ahmed said, not bothering to wipe away the tears that started to fall. Asad put his arm around his brother's shoulder to comfort him.

"You're going off emotion, Pook," Asad said, calling him by his childhood nickname. "If you go looking for this chump, word will get back to the other two. Remember. It was three, from what Francisca told us, I don't want none of them to get away."

"So how are we going to play it?" Ahmed asked, seeing the logic in what his brother said.

Asad looked at him before reaching for his cell phone. He pulled a number out of its memory and pressed send. After the third ring, someone answered.

"Who this?"

"Is this Young Curtis?" Asad asked as he got in the passenger seat of the Hummer.

"Yeah… who this?" he asked, a bit annoyed as he watched one of the St. Clair hustlers crap out.

"This is Asad."

When he heard the name, he dropped the attitude. "My bad, Asad. I thought you were one of these simple lames who found my number in their baby mama phone," Young Curtis laughed.

Asad ignored the joke. "How fast can you meet me at the all night restaurant on Lee Road and Harvard?"

Young Curtis became serious because he knew something was going on. "I can be there in ten minutes."

"Okay… I'll be up there waiting."

"Cool, I'm on my way," he said before ending the call. He walked over to Josh to let him know he was leaving and then moved out.

* * *

$$$

Young Curtis pulled into the parking lot of the restaurant shortly after the brothers arrived. He pulled his truck up next to Ahmed's Hummer and got out. Ahmed motioned for him to get in the front seat. Once inside, he was surprised to see Asad in the back seat. He turned his back to the door so that he could see both of the men. He looked from one man to the other and could see the seriousness in their demeanors so he became solemn. "What's up?"

Asad did all of the talking. "You know that my cousin has a lot of love for you and I feel Ducci and yourself are solid brothers."

Young Curtis nodded his head, not wanting to interrupt.

"To make a long story short, Curtis, we need your help to find a guy name Ron-Ron off 'The 1st.'"

"Do you know him?" Ahmed asked from the front seat.

What the fuck they want wit' Ron-Ron, he thought, noticing how intently the brothers were watching him for an answer.

"Yeah… I know him. He just got out from doin' juvenile life about a month ago. At least that's what I heard. I ain't seen him yet but what's up?" Young Curtis asked, sensing something major.

"What I'm about to tell you doesn't leave here," Asad said.

"Yeah… ai'ight… so whats up?"

Ahmed spoke from the front seat. "Late last night, someone moved on Tyrone. They robbed and shot him up real bad."

"What?" Young Curtis shouted, instantly losing his cool.

"He's... he's still... you know," Young Curtis said, scared to ask.

"It's hard to say right now but we're all praying," Asad answered.

Young Curtis, who tried to hold his composure, stared at Asad. "So this bitch-ass nigga Ron-Ron had somethin' to do wit'it?"

"Yeah, that's the name he told his girl before he lost consciousness," Asad answered.

"When I find this nigga, I'm smokin' him on sight," Young Curtis said through clenched teeth. He abruptly reached for the door handle to get out of the car but Ahmed grabbed him.

"Look Curtis, we know how you feel about Ty but you can't

do that. We need to talk to him because two other chumps were involved. We have to find out who they are," he said before letting Young Curtis go. "When you find Ron-Ron just give me a call and we'll handle it from there."

"I feel you. When I find the bitch, I'll call you," he somberly said before getting out of the car. He went to his Range Rover and pulled off.

Asad got out of the car and returned to the front passenger seat.

"I hope Young Curtis doesn't do anything stupid." Ahmed started the Hummer.

"He won't," Asad assured.

"You know, when we find these chumps, an example will have to be made out of them."

"It will," Asad replied as they pulled out of the parking lot.

CHAPTER 20
ROCKED TO SLEEP

Young Curtis rode around for most of the morning looking for Ron-Ron to no avail. He could have easily told Asad and Ahmed where his mother lived but he wanted some time alone with him before he turned him over to the brothers. He stared at Ron-Ron's mother's house until the sun started to come up. He remembered how he, Fly Ty and Ron-Ron all went to A.B Hart middle school together back in the day. Even then, Fly Ty and Young Curtis didn't hang with Ron-Ron, they were cool because they were all from 'Up The Way.' It had been years since Ron-Ron had got locked up for killing a dope fiend who tried to run off with a twenty dollar rock. *Now he's out here robbing and shooting dudes he grew up with*, Young Curtis thought. He started the Range Rover, putting it in drive and pulled off.

$$$

Ducci and Missy both woke up when they heard loud knocking on the front door.

"Who can that be," Missy groggily asked.

"It can only be one person," Ducci said, getting out the bed.

On his way to the door, he heard five more loud knocks. Once he made it there, he looked through the peephole. "Go back to sleep baby, its just Young Curtis!" Ducci hollered toward the bedroom before he opened it.

Young Curtis walked past him with a troubled look on his face.

Ducci shut the door then turned to him. "What's up? Don't you know it's not even six in the morning yet?" Ducci asked wiping the sleep from his eyes.

Young Curtis went and flopped down on the Caramel colored sofa. "Fly Ty got robbed and shot last night." As soon as the words left his mouth, he dropped his head.

"Damn!" That was all Ducci could say because he knew how Young Curtis felt about Fly Ty. "Does anyone know who did it?"

"Yeah," Young Curtis said, looking up at him. "I met up wit' Asad and Ahmed a few hours ago. They told me to find this nigga,

Ron-Ron off 'The 1st.' They said Fly Ty gave his his girl that name before he went out. A thought crossed his mind. *Man, I could've sworn Fly Ty said Tamiko was outta town.*

Ducci walked around the cherry wood coffee table and sat next to Young Curtis. "Why they got you looking for him?"

"Becuz, if they go lookin' for him, they'll spook the other two niggas that was wit' him."

"Who was the other two?"

"I've been thinkin' 'bout that all morning and the same two names keep poppin' up in my head, JT and Mel."

Ducci thought for a moment. It's true those two who controlled the young dudes on 'The 1st.' "You think they'd do something that stupid, knowing how his people play?"

Young Curtis sunk in his seat. "They could've got away wit' it if Fly Ty wouldn't have said Ron-Ron's name. But I ain't even sure if them niggas had anything to do wit' it." Young Curtis thought longer. "I know don't nothin' go down wit' them '1st' niggas unless Mel or JT give 'em the green light.

"I'm with you on whatever but we have to be careful dealing with Asad and Ahmed," Ducci warned, staring at Young Curtis.

"What'chu mean by that?" he asked vexed.

"Dig Curt, those two don't leave loose ends from what I hear. All those rumors out there about them are just that, rumors! There is no one who can say what those dudes really did. You know why?" Ducci asked, staring at him.

"Why?"

"Because… they don't leave witnesses."

Young Curtis thought about it and understood what Ducci was saying. They would either have to gain their trust or leave them alone. *Ron-Ron is the way in,* Young Curtis thought.

$$$

In the waiting area of the Intensive Care Unit, all the women who loved Tyrone Sparks remained from the previous night. Grandma Sparks and Isis sat on each side of Joyce, who read her Bible. Francisca, who was physically and emotionally drained, slept on a love seat with her head on the armrest. Tamiko stood in a corner away from the rest of the women, quietly talking on her cell phone, explaining to Janet that she had to leave on a family emergency and wouldn't be able to attend the wedding. She chose to not tell her the emergency concerned Tyrone.

After the brief conversation, she ended the call and walked over to the Sparks women.

"Do any of you want something out of the vending machine?"

"Nah baby, we're alright," Grandma Sparks spoke for everyone.

Tamiko walked over to the vending machine and stood there for a second trying to decide on what she wanted. She put her money into the machine and got two cherry Danishes then went to the beverage machine and bought two orange juices. She put both of the pastries in the microwave. Once they warmed, she walked over to where Francisca slept. She nudged her on her on the knee, with hers, waking her. Francisca sat up straight.

"They didn't have much of a choice," Tamiko said, handing Francisca a juice and Danish.

"Thank you."

"Tyrone sure do have a thang for beautiful women," Grandma Sparks said.

Isis looked over at the two sitting together. Joyce also looked on as the women talked.

"I like your necklace," Tamiko started.

"Thank you," Francisca said softly, fingering the necklace.

"I was with him when he was looking at in the jewelry store."

Francisca stared at her, knowing Tamiko was going through it. Francisca thought it was best to let her vent, just as long as she didn't get out of hand with it.

"You won't believe this but I thought he wanted to buy it for me." Tamiko nervously smiled. Both women stared at one another during the awkward encounter.

"How long have you known him?" Tamiko asked.

"I met Ty a few months after y'all met."

So he discussed me with this woman, Tamiko thought. She couldn't believe her eyes.

Francisca continued to talk. "Once I realized he would never leave you for me, we went our separate ways."

If they went their separate ways, what is she doing here, Tamiko mused to herself.

"I know this might sound strange coming from me, but Ty would never do anything to purposely hurt you. He loves you. When I first met him, I was new to Cleveland. Young and lonely. At first, we were strictly friends for close to two years..." She stopped to find the right words. "When you spend a lot of time with someone, things happen and I fell in love with him," she said bluntly but with tact.

It was strange for Tamiko to hear another woman say she loved Tyrone. She didn't know how to respond. Part of her wanted to scream 'Bitch! What do you mean you love my man?' Instead, she stared at Francisca with tears in her eyes, shaking her head in disbelief.

"Does Tyrone love you?" she asked.

"That's something you'll have to ask him when he wakes up."

Tamiko looked at the necklace again, believing she already knew the answer.

$$$

Driving up Buckeye, Young Curtis and Ducci rode around the hood all day and night searching for Ron-Ron. Just when they started to think he might have gone into hiding, Young Curtis' cell phone rang.

"Yeah," he answered. Listening to the caller on the other end, he excitedly started to tap Ducci.

"If he tries to leave stall him," he said before ending the call.

Josh just saw the nigga go into the Arab store on Kinsman," Young Curtis said as he accelerated through Cleveland's streets.

When Young Curtis made it to 119th off Kinsman, he saw Josh parked on the street in his Lexus with the top up. Young Curtis turned his headlights off as he pulled his Range Rover up next to

Josh's car. He pressed the power button for the passenger window.

"Where he at?" Young Curtis asked past Ducci and through the open window.

"He still in there hollerin' at some boppa," Josh answered.

"Good lookin' out homie but remember don't say shit 'bout this to nobody."

"Man, I'm true to this, not new to this," Josh shot back.

"Stay up, my thorough young homie." Ducci smiled at the young hustler.

"No doubt," Josh said, pulling off.

Young Curtis parked on the opposite end of 119th, giving him and Ducci a better view of the store.

"There that nigga go right there," Young Curits said, seeing a shadowy figure coming out of the store.

"What, you just wanna snatch him up?" Ducci asked as Young Curtis put the truck in gear.

"Nah, just follow my lead."

He pulled his SUV up next to Ron-Ron, who stood next to a light blue Honda Civic and blew his horn. Ron-Ron, just about to open the driver's side door, turned around and squinted his eyes to see who drove the Range Rover.

"Who dat?"

Young Curtis let the passenger window down. "Ron-Ron, what's up my nigga!" he happily shouted out the window.

It was so dark in the SUV, he couldn't make out the faces inside. "Who dat?" he asked again, apprehensive about approaching.

"Nigga, it's me," Young Curtis said as he leaned over Ducci.

"Oh shit! What's good my nigga?" Ron-Ron smiled as he walked up to the Range Rover. He stuck his hand through the passenger window and past Ducci to give Young Curtis some dap. He stepped back from the Range Rover to admire it. "Damn, this you?"

"Yeah," Young Curtis answered with a smile.

"I see you got spinners on this bitch!"

"You been locked up too long, we call 'em Hard Heads."

"Hard Heads?"

"Yeah… cuz… when a nigga stop, they keep going."

"I like that." Ron-Ron laughed.

Ducci sat there with a fake smile on his face, hoping Young Curtis would hurry up and get him in the truck.

"I see you got some blunts," Young Curtis said, noticing the box in his hand.

"Yeah, these are for me and my niggas. We suppose to go out and kick it tonight."

"Well shit, I got some blunts of good Haze. Get in so you can blow a stick or two wit' me."

Damn, I ain't never had no Haze and this might be another way in with some money gettin' niggas, Ron-Ron thought. "It's on my nigga. Let me take my girl her car," he said.

Young Curtis instantly protested. He didn't want him to go home and tell his girl who he was with. "The car is cool right there. We just gon' bend a few corners, blow on these good trees, and talk 'bout gettin' some paper together."

Shit, if this nigga pushin' a Range and wanna holla at me about gettin some bread together, I'm with it,' Ron-Ron thought. "Let's roll," he said, going for the back door.

"Nah playboy. You ride up front," Young Curtis said, stopping him. "Let my dude ride up front, Ducci."

Ducci got out and Ron-Ron got in.

This nigga Young Curtis is good people. He recognizes a real nigga when he sees one, Ron-Ron said to himself, as he got comfortable in his seat. He ran his hand over the wood grain and soft leather in the luxury SUV, liking everything about it. "I might get me one of these."

"Oh yeah," Young Curtis said, staring at Ducci in the rearview mirror as he slowly pulled off. At the same time, Ron-Ron had no idea he was being 'rocked to sleep.' By the time they'd reached the four suite apartment building on Union, Ron-Ron had unknowingly finished off the first blunt of potent marijuana by himself. When he tried to pass to Young Curtis, he would tell him "I'm driving." When he passed it to Ducci, he would just puff on it then blow it out. As soon as the first one was finished, Ducci handed him another.

Young Curtis pulled up in the driveway of the apartment building and parked in the back.

Ron-Ron lit the blunt, taking a long drag on it. "Gon' hit this," he said holding the smoke in while trying to pass it.

"Get high, my nigga," Young Curtis insisted.

Ron-Ron continued to hit the potent weed before realizing he smoked most of the blunt.

"I got some Henn up in the apartment," Ducci informed.

"Let's go down some," Young Curtis suggested.

"I'm high as fuck right now!" Ron-Ron said, already gone off the Haze.

"C'mon playboy, we kickin' it," Young Curtis said, giving him a playful push.

Ducci was the first to exit. Young Curtis climbed out, walked around the front of the Range Rover, and met Ron-Ron getting out.

"Damn, that Haze is a muthafucka," he said, stumbling a little as he shut the door. When he looked at Young Curtis, he saw the stainless steel semi-automatic .45 in his hand.

"Damn playa, put that shit away before police ride down on us," Ron-Ron warned in his drug induced stupor.

Ducci stepped up on the side of him and threw a hard right hand that landed on his mouth.

Ron-Ron hit the ground, trying to figure out what happened. He laid there high off of the weed and drunk off the punch with his eyes wide open and a bloody mouth.

Young Curtis walked over and kicked him in the face.

Ron-Ron lay there, moaning, before Ducci helped him to his feet. He had to hold him up because his legs still wobbled from the punishment he received.

Young Curtis pointed his gun at Ron-Ron and told him to walk.

"Why y'all playin' me like this," he cried, still not understanding why this was happening to him.

For his question, Young Curtis slapped him in the back of the head with the pistol, telling him to shut up and walk.

They walked him to the chain-linked fence behind Ducci's building, where they went through the hole in it. They marched him to the abandon house right behind the building. Once inside the back door, Ducci felt around on the floor for the bag they stashed earlier.

Young Curtis stood behind Ron-Ron with him in a choker. He held his gun against his temple. Ducci found the bag then took the large yellow, square-shaped flash light out. He turned it on, not worried about anyone in the streets seeing it because all the windows were covered with plywood. He led the way through the house to the living room.

"Get in the corner," Ducci ordered Ron-Ron.

"What Curtis… what type of shit you on?" Ron-Ron asked, staring at Young Curtis.

"Nigga, if you don't sit down. I'ma lay you down right now!" Young Curtis threatened.

Ron-Ron stared at .45 in his hand and thought it would be a good idea to do what he said.

When he sat down in the corner, Ducci walked over with a roll of duct tape and quickly tied his right wrist to his right ankle and his left wrist to his left ankle. Young Curtis pulled out his phone once Ron-Ron was secure and made the call.

CHAPTER 21
SENDING A MESSAGE

Asad and Ahmed sat on the couch in the furnished basement of their grandmother's house, hoping to hear from Young Curtis. They knew, no matter what, they had to start planning for Miami. The guns had already been shipped so they just needed to get down there with Young Curtis and Ducci.

Ahmed looked at the clock on the wall. It read 10:03 p.m. He stood up from the couch to go get something to drink. "Do you want anything from the kitchen?"

"No, I'm alright," Asad answered. As he sat there thinking, his cell phone suddenly rang. "Hello," he quickly answered it.

"This ya dude," Young Curtis said on the other end. "I found that CD you were lookin' for. If you wanna listen to it meet me at the spot I told you about earlier when we kicked it."

"I'll be there in ten mintues," he said before hanging up. He snatched the black book bag off of the couch and ran upstairs to the kitchen. "I just got the call. They got'em... Let's go!"

$$$

Ahmed pulled the rented black Honda Accord up behind the Range Rover. When they got out of the car, they saw Ducci coming their way.

"Where's Young Curtis?" Asad asked.

"He's in the house back there."

Asad looked in the direction Ducci pointed in then reached inside the car, pulling out two wooden bats and a book bag. "Let's go and find out what he knows," Asad said to his brother.

Inside the old abandoned house, Ducci turned on the flashlight and led the brothers to an upstairs bedroom. Ducci opened the first door they came upon. Inside, Young Curtis held a smaller flashlight on Ron-Ron, who sat in the corner, looking scared to death.

By now, he had figured out this was about Fly Ty because that was the only thing he done since he'd been home that could've brought all this heat.

Asad and Ahmed stepped into the room with Ahmed

dropping the book bag on the wooden floor. When the bag hit, the sound of metal could be heard.

He stuck his hand out for Young Curtis to give him the flashlight. Once he had it, he walked over to Ron-Ron and pointing it in his face. Ron-Ron squinted from the bright light then turned his head.

"Your name Ron-Ron?" Ahmed asked.

"Yeah," he answered in a trembling voice while trying to see.

"Could y'all go downstairs and watch out?" Asad asked.

Young Curtis looked at the two bats in Asad's hands and tapped Ducci's back, indicating it was time for them to leave.

As soon as they left, Asad laid the bats against the wall then pulled a black folding knife out of his pocket and walked over to Ron-Ron. His eyes got big when he saw him coming his way. Asad used it to cut off his restaints.

"Take off all of your clothes," Asad demanded as he stepped back.

When he stood up, Ron-Ron thought about trying his assailants but he knew he couldn't take both of them plus Young Curtis and his partner downstairs.

"What's goin' on brothers," Ron-Ron said, as he started undressing. "I don't even know y'all. Why y'all wanna do me like this?"

Neither of the brothers spoke. When Ron-Ron finished taking off his clothes, he stood in the room naked.

Ahmed gave Asad the flashlight then went to the book bag and unzipped it. He pulled out what looked like a small sledgehammer and four rusty, sharp railroad spikes.

Ron-Ron couldn't see what was happening. The flashlight blinded him.

"Turn around," Asad ordered.

Ron-Ron did as he was told.

Asad looked at the bruises on his side and back. "You see them Ahmed?"

"Yeah, I see them Asad."

Ron-Ron closed his eyes after hearing the names. He knew

for sure now this was about Fly Ty but wondered how they found out so quickly.

"I ain't do shit," he said, turning back around to plead his case. "I'll tell y'all everything… just let me go." He looked at Asad who set the flashlight on the floor and pointed it toward Ron-Ron, giving the room a dim glow.

"No deal," Asad said to his offer. "You're going to tell everything anyway."

Ron-Ron didn't notice Ahmed creeping up on him. That's when everything went black.

"Let's hurry up," Asad said to his brother, who stood over Ron-Ron's unconscious body with one of the baseball bats in his left hand.

$$$

Ducci stood in the front room of the abandoned house, looking out onto the street through the crack in the plywood that covered the window.

He quickly turned around to face Young Curtis. "You hear that?"

Young Curtis heard a hammering sound.

"I wonder what they are up there doing to that fool." Ducci thought out loud.

"Whatever they doin,' that nigga had it comin,'" Young Curtis said matter-of-factly.

They listened as the hammer sound stopped for a few seconds then started back.

$$$

Ahmed got the first spikes through Ron-Ron's wrists easily. But, when he started putting one through his right ankle, Asad had to hold Ron-Ron's legs down since he had regained consciousness.

After putting the railroad spikes through both ankles, Asad ripped the duct tape from Ron-Ron's mouth. It was covered with a thick glob of saliva. He looked down at Ron-Ron who was sobbing in pain with tears in his eyes.

"Who else was with you when you moved on Fly Ty?" Asad asked in a calm, emotionless voice.

Ron-Ron didn't even think about staying strong. He told them everything, how JT set the lick up, and even lied by saying JT was the one who killed Fly Ty. He also told them he was supposed to meet JT and Mel that night.

Asad stared at him for a moment. "By the way, Fly Ty isn't dead."

Ahmed walked up to his brother and handed him one of the two bats.

As they approached, Ron-Ron began to beg for his life. "Please man don't do me like this." Before he could say anymore, Asad placed a piece of duct tape over his mouth.

The brothers stared at one another for a second then went to work. They started on his lower body with each working a side. They commenced to breaking every bone in his body. The sound of the breaking bones in his legs could be heard as they viciously brought the bats down over and over again.

Ron-Ron's screams were muffled as he tried to struggle but the spikes were driven deep into his wrist and ankles.

Asad and Ahmed worked their way up to his torso, caving his ribs in with the violent blows. They said nothing as they methodically beat him.

Ahmed and Asad tried to cave in Ron-Ron's chest plate. Ahmed put all he had into a swing that broke his collar bone. That's when Ron-Ron's bowels let loose, human waste began to seep from under him. The brothers ignored the foul smell and continued. Ahmed stood over Ron-Ron's head, staring down at the badly beaten, barely alive man. He swung the bat like a golf club and a loud cracking noise filled the room as Ron-Ron's jaw dislocated from the socket.

$$$

The thudding sound could be heard downstairs along with Ron-Ron's agonizing muffled screams. Young Curtis and Ducci listened.

"Let me go get these dudes. It's time to get up outta here," Young Curtis said.

Young Curtis stepped inside the room and was shocked by

the sight of Ron-Ron's nude and badly beaten body. He looked to the brothers, who stood over him glaring down at the dying man, with blood smeared bats in their hands. For some strange reason, Young Curtis couldn't take his eyes off of Ron-Ron. This was the most disturbing sight he'd ever witnessed in his life. He could hear a low constant moan coming from the almost lifeless man.

"Y'all find out what y'all needed to know?"

"Yeah," Asad answered, still staring at Ron-Ron breathing heavily.

Young Curtis walked up to him and saw he was still alive. His face was swollen to about twice its normal size and covered in blood. His jaw hung grotesquely to the left. Young Curtis looked into Ron-Ron's one good eye that stared back at him. Every time he breathed, bubbles of blood came out of his nose and mouth.

Seeing enough, Young Curtis quickly pulled his gun and shot him once in the forehead.

As soon as Asad and Ahmed saw Young Curtis pull his gun, they both covered their ears with their hands. The thunderous sound of the big handgun in the small enclosed, empty room was deafening.

"Shit!" Young Curtis shouted with his face in a grimace as his free hand shot to his ear in an attempt to stop the ringing in it.

That wasn't smart, Asad thought as looked at Young Curtis, who still tried to get over the ringing in his ears.

Asad turned to Ahmed. "I'm going to talk with Young Curtis. Grab everything and make sure dude is gone!" Ahmed nodded in agreement.

As Asad went to Young Curtis, Ahmed pulled out a silenced .40 caliber and shot Ron-Ron twice in the head.

Young Curtis watched him as he picked up the two shell casings and put them in his pocket.

"Check this out Young Curtis," Asad said, getting his attention.

"What's up?"

"My brother and I don't get down like this with no one," he said while motioning to Ron-Ron's dead body. "It should go without saying, outside of Ducci and yourself, no one should ever hear of this."

"I feel you," Young Curtis said, staring him in the eyes.

"Good," Asad smiled. "I need your help one more time tonight. I got word on where the other two suppose to be."

"Me and Ducci is wit' y'all on whatever. Just say what need to be done," Young Curtis replied.

Asad looked over to his brother and saw that he had everything together. "Let's get out of here. I'll fill you in on the way to the car," he said while collecting the bats on their way out of the room, leaving nothing but Ron-Ron's dead body behind.

$$$

Young Curtis pulled into the parking lot of the Play Pen, a popular strip club in Warrensville Heights. He circled the lot looking for any sign of JT and Mel.

"Ain't that's JT's car right there?" Ducci asked.

Young Curtis looked past Ducci, out the passenger window at a black, kitted up S430 Mercedes sitting on twenty-two inch Lexani rims. "Yeah, that's his shit."

After parking, Young Curtis pulled out his cell phone and called Asad to let him know they spotted JT's car and was on their way inside. When he finished, he looked over to Ducci.

"I've heard rumors and stories about Asad and Ahmed but homie its official. Them dudes ain't to be fucked wit.' Man, they had ol' boy up there assed out, nailed to the floor taking it to him wit' those baseball bats."

"And, now, they wanna hit these niggas in a packed club," Ducci added.

"What trips me out is they seem like some square type dudes from how they talk but them niggas is crazy."

"They're not crazy Curt," Ducci offered. "They're just sending a message to the streets. If you fuck with a Sparks, you die."

Young Curtis stared at him for a moment. "Well shit, I might change my name to Sparks." He and Ducci both laughed as they exited the car and headed toward the club.

Before they could enter, Ducci and Young Curtis were stopped at the door, where a bouncer ran a hand held metal detector over them.

"Oh, my bad," Young Curtis said when the detector picked up on something. He pulled out his cell phone. The doorman ran it over him again. Not detecting anything, he let them in.

The club was filled with hustlers, ballers and half-naked women. Ducci looked at the two woman act on the center stage as he made his way through the crowd looking for JT and Mel. Young Curtis went to the rest room to set the plan in motion. Inside, he saw two men in the last stall smoking a blunt. He acted as if he was taking a piss. When he finished, he went to the sink to wash his hands. He tried to wait the smokers out but, when he heard one say 'fire up another one,' he left on his mission. He stepped out into the hallway then looked toward the show area. When he saw no one coming, he ran to the fire exit at the other end of the halls. He opened the door and put a folded piece of paper in it to keep it from locking. With the door rigged, he ran back up the hallway but stopped before he got to the show area then casually walked out.

Ducci exited the VIP suite, looking for Young Curtis. When he saw him coming out of the restroom area, he walked over to him.

"JT and Mel are in the back, the last room on the left."

"How you know?" Young Curtis questioned.

"I was just back there. I heard some broads going in the room telling her girl that Mel and JT spend good money." Young Curtis pulled out his cell phone.

"It's a big ass bouncer back there as soon as you come through the curtain," Ducci warned.

Young Curtis made the call and relayed all of the information to Asad.

$$$

"C'mon, lets see who can make it clap the best," JT said to the two strippers in the VIP.

A cute light-skinned stripper with ass for days, named Kola, turned around and started making her butt bounce.

"Can't nobody do it like me," she said, looking over her shoulder at JT.

"Damn! Look Mel," JT said, excitedly.

Mel sat on the other end of the black, leather couch with his pants to his ankle as two strippers gave him head.

"That's cool but I got a real serious dick suckin' contest jumpin' off right now."

JT looked over and saw a brown-skinned stripper going to work on Mel.

A beautiful, dark skinned stripper in a red thong and matching top, name Dime, stood over Mel and watched the competition technique. "She ain't even doing it right," she protested.

From the look on Mel's face, no one could tell the difference.

"Hold on, Bubbles," he said, stopping her. "Let's see what Dime talkin' 'bout."

Bubbles took his piece out of her mouth and gave Dime the evil eye as she got up. Bubbles knew her head game was tight but Dime was called the 'Head Doctor' so she knew she wouldn't win the two hundred dollar prize.

That nigga Ron-Ron don't know what he's missing, JT said to himself. He pulled his penis out. "Kola, show these ho's how to eat a dick."

Kola smiled as she got on her knees and began to perform oral sex on him.

$$$

Outside the club's back fire exit, Asad and Ahmed pulled down the ninja style ski mask. Asad, in the lead, opened the door and peeked inside. Seeing the hallway empty, they both entered and made their way to the front. Asad looked around the corner at the entertainment area. He saw a large crowd at the center stage watching two strippers freak with one another. He looked to his right and saw a straight path behind the ten-foot high DJ booth to the VIP suite. He spotted Young Curtis sitting at a table by himself, away from the show. He held up a clinched fist.

Young Curtis saw the signal and stood up to put his play into effect when he saw a stripper walking up the aisle.

"Bitch, you stole my money!" he said, snatching the woman by the arm.

"Nigga, you betta to get your damn hands off of me!" The

half-naked woman screamed as she snatched away.

The scene accomplished its intended affect. All of the bouncers rushed to the woman's aid. As they arrived, Ducci intervened by grabbing Young Curtis.

"My dude is just a little drunk. I'm going to get him out of here."

The four bouncers looked on in anger at Young Curtis, as they escorted him and Ducci out of the club.

The staged scene was enough of a diversion for Asad and Ahmed to make it to the VIP suite without being seen. As soon as they stepped behind the curtain, they were confronted by a huge bouncer who sat in a chair in the hallway.

"Hey!" The bouncer said, getting up from his seat. When his mind registered what was going on, it was too late. Asad raised the HK and tapped the trigger once sending a bullet through the bouncers head.

As he made his way down the hallway, Ahmed stood over the fallen bouncer and fired two shots into his face before quickly catching up to his brother who stood outside the last door on the left.

Asad put his ear to it and could hear the giggling of women. He grabbed the doorknob and slowly turned it. He looked back at Ahmed, who stood in position. He had the stock of the HK against his shoulder while looking down the sights ready to shoot anything that moved. Asad opened the door and stepped inside followed closely by his brother.

JT and Mel didn't have a clue what was going on. They both sat on the couch with their heads back and eyes closed as the strippers sucked them off. Jackie and Bubbles, two of the strippers not participating, froze at the sight of the two masked, machine gun toting gangsters. Jackie let out an involuntary gasp that drew the attention of the other girls performing the sex act. They took JT's and Mel's penises out of their mouths and stared up at the gunmen with sheer horror on their faces.

JT opened his eyes. "What type of games y'all ho's playin?'" he said but, when he looked toward the door, he saw death.

"All you females face the wall. If anyone turns around,

everybody dies," Ahmed said.

The strippers rushed to the wall and buried their faces in it.

Mel watched as one of the brothers approached and stood in front of him. The gunman stared hard at him, through his mask, with the other one doing the same to JT. They both had their pants down to their ankles. It wasn't anything they could do.

Asad and Ahmed looked at one another for a second then back at their victims. Ahmed used his right hand to lift the mask, exposing his face, with Asad following.

JT and Mel knew who it was before they showed their faces.

Mel swallowed hard. "We fucked up homie," he said to JT without taking his eyes off of Ahmed.

Without a word, the brothers opened up on the two men, emptying clips into their faces and upper bodies of their victims. The brothers watched over the muzzle flashes as Mel and JT's torsos were violently shredded from the impact of the bullets ripping into their flesh. It wasn't the dramatic jerking like in the movies. After the first few shots, they went limp as the brothers continued firing into them. When the gunfire ceased, a thick cloud of gun smoke hung in the air. The brothers quickly reversed the clips and chambered rounds back into the HK's. They pulled their masks down and headed out of the door.

On their way up the hall, they stepped over the dead bouncer with the pool of blood around his head. Just as they got to the curtain, a thick stripper in a white thong came through it, escorting a trick to one of the rooms. They were so busy freaking, they never noticed the body in the hall until it was too late. When they saw the bouncer, they looked up and saw machine guns pointing at them.

"Go in one of those rooms and don't come out," Ahmed ordered.

The stripper and the trick tip-toed over the body with the trick saying "Thank you, man," before disappearing.

Asad peeked out the curtain. He noticed no obstruction and motioned for Ahmed to follow. They casually walked from the curtain toward the fire exit. Once in the hallway, they saw three men talking.

"Up against the wall," Asad said, pointing his gun at them.

The three men all raised their hands with frightened looks on their faces.

Ahmed ran down the long hallway as Asad covered him. Once at the door, he held it open with his back as he pointed his gun up the hall at the men on the wall. When Ahmed was in position to cover, Asad lowered his gun and ran down the hall and out the door followed by Ahmed.

$$$

Ahmed pulled into his grandmother's driveway while Young Curtis parked on the street. Ahmed got out of the car with the two HK's wrapped in a towel as he headed inside the house to destroy the guns. Asad walked over to Ducci and Young Curtis, who were getting out of the Range Rover.

"That was good looking out at the club," he said, giving both men dap.

"Man, you don't even gotta mention it. We all just ridin' for Fly Ty," Young Curtis said.

Asad smiled. "I understand you but that's something I had to say. It's rare for real brothers to connect out here in these streets. I'm not only speaking for myself. I'm speaking for my brother as well. You two keep it pure with us and we'll do the same toward you." He stared at them.

Despite all of the killing that occurred that night, this was the first time Ducci felt comfortable around the brothers. He felt like everything Asad said was real.

"That's what it is then," Ducci said, sticking his hand out. Asad stared him in the eyes as he shook it before doing the same to Young Curtis.

Asad looked at his watch and saw that it was quarter to midnight. "You two ready to go to Miami?" he asked, looking up.

"What? Right now?" Ducci responded, somewhat surprised.

"Yeah, you have two hours to handle whatever business you need to get in order. Then we're outta here."

Young Curtis laughed. "Shit, since you just sprung it on us. We ain't got no choice but to be ready."

"Good," Asad smiled. "I'll see you two in a couple of hours

and don't forget to pack light."

$$$

Young Curtis and Ducci got back in the Range Rover then Young Curtis pulled off.

"Missy is gonna trip," Ducci said.

"Dig. I'ma drop you off then shoot out to my spot to pick up Shu and some clothes. I'm coming right back," Young Curtis informed him.

"That sounds cool. By the time you make it back, I'll be ready."

$$$

At the Play Pen strip club, all of the dancers and customers were outside observing the overwhelming police activity. As soon as the first officers made it on the scene, the club was ordered to shut down and the VIP section taped off.

When homicide detectives Meyers and O'Malley arrived, they were quickly escorted to the crime scene by a patrol officer. The officer pulled back the curtain to the VIP suite, giving the detectives their first look.

They both stopped and stared at the body of the bouncer in the hallway.

"What's his name?" O'Malley asked the patrol officer.

"That, sir, was Danny Sanders. He was an employee of the club."

The detectives examined the dead man's body, staring at the bullet holes in his face and head. They rolled him over onto his side. That's when detective Meyers noticed two bullets lodged into the concrete floor.

"It looks like, as soon as the shooters encountered this guy, he was shot. Then, to make sure he was dead, they pumped two more bullets in him."

O'Malley nodded in agreement before turning his attention to the patrolman. "Where's the other two?"

The patrolman pointed down the hallway to where another officer stood in front of an open door. The two detectives walked up to the room, stopping in front of the officer.

"How many ass holes have been in this room, fucking up the crime scene?" O'Malley asked in his gruffy voice.

"Sir, the room was sealed off as soon as we saw the situation."

The detectives entered the room that still smelled of gunpowder and saw all of the spent shell casings covering the floor.

"Damn, it looks like close to a hundred rounds were fired," Meyers said. They eased their way to the black, leather couch shredded from the gunfire along with the victims' faces. They were so mutilated that chunks of flesh stuck to the blood splattered walls.

"It looks like the poor bastard in the hallway got off easy compared to these two," O'Malley said.

"That's because, more than likely, these two were the real targets. The guy in the hall was just in the wrong place at the wrong time," Myers added.

After taking notes the detectives came out of the room. "Where are the witnesses?" Meyers asked the officer at the door.

"Talking to them won't do you any good," the officer said. "The four women, who were in the room when it happened, said two masked gunmen entered then ordered them to face the wall. After that, they heard one of the victims say 'we fucked up' and that's when the women heard shells hitting the floor.

"Shells hitting the floor? What about the gun shot?" Meyers asked.

"It's believed the gunman used silencers because no one in the neighboring rooms heard shots," the officer said.

"Did anyone see the shooters?" Meyers asked.

"Yeah, a guy and a girl, but those two refuse to talk. The guy said they could've killed him if they wanted to but, since they let him live, he'll let them live. In his words, I quote, 'I ain't seen shit.'"

"Are they still here?" O'Malley questioned.

"The girls are out front but the guy got to screaming about lawyers and, that if he wasn't being arrested, he wanted to leave so we took down his information and let him go."

"I guess we'll talk to him tomorrow. Let's see what the women have to say," Meyers said to his partner.

$$$

Asad stood in the basement of his grandmother's house, watching his brother destroy the last HK. Ahmed had already broken the guns down and removed the firing pins. Now, he stood in the corner with welding goggles on, taking a blowtorch to the barrel of the guns. The weapons were so badly damaged that, even if they were ever found, running ballistics on them would be impossible.

Asad stripped down to his black boxer briefs and put all of the clothes and the shoes he wore during the murders in a bag with his brother's clothes and shoes. Once Ahmed finished destroying the guns, he put them in the bag with the other items and left the house to get rid of everything.

Asad went upstairs to his old room to get ready for a shower when his cell phone started vibrating. He picked it up from the bed and answered it.

"Hello."

"Hi Asad. This is Dayna."

When he heard her voice, he smiled. "Hi, how are you?"

"Oh, I'm fine. Just suffering from a bout of insomnia. I've been laying here for the last few hours unable to go to sleep."

"You must have something on your mind."

"Yeah… you," she laughed.

Asad smiled and shook his head. He couldn't believe how this woman made him feel like a little school boy.

"What are you doing?" she asked.

"I was just about to get in the shower."

"Mmm," she moaned "What do you have on," she asked in a seductive voice.

"What?" Asad laughed, nervously.

"You heard me. What are you wearing?" she continued in an even sexier voice.

"I have on a pair of black boxer briefs. What do you have on?"

"Do you really want to know?" she teased.

"Yeah," Asad answered as he caressed himself through his underwear.

"I don't have on anything," she whispered. From her words, she could hear his breathing pick up and it excited her enough that she slid her hand under the sheet. She knew she shouldn't be doing this but couldn't help it.

"You mean nothing at all," Asad asked as he squeezed himself.

"Mmm, nothing," she said, losing herself for a second.

"I wish I could see you." He stood there imagining her sexy body naked.

Dayna stopped what she was doing and regained her composure. "If you want, you can come over and keep me company. We can talk or watch a movie."

Asad let out a sigh. "I would love to come over and spend some time with you but I'm on my way outta town."

"When are you leaving?"

He heard the disappointment in her voice. "In about an hour but, when I get back, I'll have all the time in the world for you."

She smiled to herself. "Well, I'm looking forward to that. Where are you going?"

"To Los Angeles," he lied. Outside of Isis, he never let people know what city he would be in during a job.

"Well, I'm not going to hold you up. I'll see you when you get back."

"Okay, I'll be back in a few days."

"Asad!" she said before he hung up.

"Yeah."

"I miss you already, bye," she said, quickly hanging up.

Asad smiled as he threw the phone on the bed and picked up his towel.

$$$

"They should be here any minute," Young Curtis said while lying on the sofa with his head in Shu's lap.

Ducci sat on the love seat with Missy. "Don't forget to drop my keys off at my mother's hair salon when you leave tomorrow," he said to Missy, who still was upset.

"I won't baby," she replied then gave him a kiss.

The sound of a car horn made Ducci break their kiss. He got up and looked out of the front window to see a Ford Windstar in the driveway.

"I guess this them," he said, looking back at Young Curtis.

"I'll call when I get back," Young Curtis said before giving Shu a kiss.

Ducci grabbed his duffel bag and followed Young Curtis to the door.

"Ducci!"

He stopped at the door and turned around. Missy walked up and gave him a hug and a kiss. "Be careful," she said.

"I will," he replied, walking out of the door.

Ducci got in the back of the van and pulled the sliding door shut. "What's up with y'all?" Ducci asked once seated.

"Just ready to hit the road," Ahmed replied while backing out of the driveway.

"I see Young Curtis worked you out of the front seat," Ducci said, looking over at Asad.

"It's not like that," Asad lied. "This is going to be a long ride and I can get more comfortable back here."

Ducci knew that wasn't the sole reason he was back there. He knew he was watching him and his brother's back.

"This is our travel plan," Ahmed said as he drove. "First, we're going to stop in Ann Arbor. From there we'll head out to Miami."

Ann Arbor, Ducci, thought. "You mean Michigan?" he asked.

"Yeah," Asad said from the back.

Young Curtis looked back, over the front seat. "Why we gotta stop in Ann Arbor?"

"I put a call into this brother I know. Since he was going down there, I figured we could catch a ride with him," Asad answered.

Shit, we won't make it to Miami until around this time tomorrow, Ducci thought to. He leaned back in his seat to get settled in for the long ride.

CHAPTER 22
MIAMI

Charm pulled his silver Lexus LX 470 into the parking lot of the Friendly Inn motel in Ann Arbor. He parked next to the Ford Windstar, got out of the Lexus, and went to room number 19, where he knocked twice. Asad opened the door and quickly shut it behind Charm.

Standing in the room, Charm took off his Cartier sunglasses turned to Asad and shook his hand. Ahmed stepped out from the bathroom, brushing his teeth, and nodded a hello to Charm then returned. Charm walked over to the nearest bed, picked up a pillow, and propped it against on the headboard. He sat down and leaned back. "I called the Charter late last night after I got your call. We have an hour to get to the airport. It takes off at eleven forty-five," Charm said as he looked at Asad with his ever present smile.

"That's good."

Charm shrugged his shoulders. "It's nothing. Was gonna fly down Monday anyway. Oh yeah. My people had been calling Fly Ty for the last two days. He got something Ty wanted but haven't heard from him. He's not locked up or anything?"

Ahmed stepped out again, pulling a gray Polo shirt down over his head.

"He's in the hospital," Ahmed answered.

Charm stared at Ahmed, who seated himself on the bed across from him. "What happened?" Charm asked with a look of concern.

"Some lames moved on him. They robbed and shot him three times," Asad answered.

"How is he?"

"Talked to my grandmother this morning. She said they upgraded him from critical to serious condition. The doctor said that the first twenty-four hours were crucial. He's passed that." All the men sat silent for a moment.

"Y'all got any word on who could've done it?" Charm asked.

"Yeah, we found out and put a straightening on it," Ahmed

offered.

Charm knew whoever moved against Fly Ty was already dead. "Hey Ahmed, why don't you go get Ducci and Young Curtis out of their room. Tell them we're leaving."

"Alright," he said then got up from the bed and went out the door.

Once the door was shut, Asad went and sat on the bed with Charm to fill him in on what was going on.

"Did you get your yacht from that spot yet?" he asked.

"Yeah, it's already at the marina. Had it sent there a few days ago." He smiled. "I know y'all didn't call me just to ride on that yacht?"

"No." Asad laughed. "But, check this out. When you took us to M&S, Ahmed and I noticed something strange so we did some homework. We found out that M&S is a stash spot."

"How did you find that out?"

"Mike Guerrero told us."

That's where they went before they came to the club, Charm thought.

Asad ran down everything to Charm that Mike told him. "So what do you think?" Asad asked.

"Sounds like this might be the jackpot. Let me make some calls when we get down there about this Sereno dude. You know if he's connected to my people, I'll have to ask y'all to call it off?"

"If it will jeopardize your situation, I'll let it go," Asad said with all sincerity.

Charm smiled, shaking his head in agreement. "Right now, I think it's a go. I never heard of this dude. Plus, Bolivians and Colombians typically don't care for one another so my people shouldn't have any interest in this."

At that point, the conversation stopped as Ahmed entered with Ducci and Young Curtis. Ahmed introduced the men to one another. Charm got off of the bed and went to them. "How are you brothers doing?" he asked as he shook their hands.

Ducci looked at the short man, clad in low top, white Air Force One's, blue jeans and a long sleeve, white, button up shirt and instantly liked him. He could sense Charm was an important man by the aura around him.

"These two are solid brothers," Asad informed Charm.

"They have to be, if you two are with them," Charm replied, looking at his watch. "It's time we get outta here."

"Can we stop at McDonald's," Young Curtis asked. "So I can get somethin' to eat?"

"Yeah, we can swing by there. I haven't eaten either."

When they got outside, Charm told Ahmed to leave the keys in the Windstar. He would have someone pick it up. Ahmed went to the Windstar, put the keys in the glove box, then ran back to the Lexus and got in the back seat.

"Miami, here we come." Charm smiled as he pulled off.

$$$

After landing in Miami and picking up a black DTS Cadillac from the rental agency, they dropped Charm off at his Villa. Once they arrived, Charm got out and stood at the back passenger door talking with Asad.

"You know all of you are welcome to stay here."

"We'll be better off in a motel," Asad declined

"Oh, hold on for a minute," Charm said before going inside the house. He returned with two small, silver Nokia cell phones and handed one to Asad.

"The number to this one is programmed into the one I gave you. Both of these are clean so we'll use them to communicate."

"We have to get outta here," Asad said as he put the phone in his pocket. "Give me a call as soon as you find something out."

"I'm on top off it," Charm said as he walked toward his home. "I'll call you in a few hours."

"Where to now?" Ahmed asked as he put the car in drive.

"Head to M&S Yacht Sales," Asad answered from the back seat.

Seventy-five yards away from M&S Yacht Sales, in the parking lot of an auto body shop, the four men watched the establishment. Asad looked at his watch. It read 5:30. "This is the time they usually close on Saturday. They should be pulling up any moment now," he informed them.

Fifteen minutes later, Ahmed got everyone's attention. "Here they go."

The men all watched as a blue Cadillac Seville turned into the back driveway of M&S. A few seconds later, a white cargo van did the same.

"You saw that van?" Asad asked Ducci and Young Curtis.

"Yeah," they answered in unison.

"That means they're still collecting. And, from what I heard, the money won't be moved until Tuesday. So, we're going to hit them Monday." With that said, he tapped the front driver seat, signaling Ahmed to pull off.

$$$

Once the huge garage door came down, Chico got out of the Cadillac and was met by Raul, Jose, and Roberto.

"Get the money outta the van," he ordered before going back inside the office.

Roberto removed the strap of the AK-47 from over his shoulder. He leaned the rifle against the wall then went to the van. Raul stood in the back of the van, passing out large burlap sacks with the word coffee printed on them.

"This thing is heavy," Jose said as he hoisted it up to his shoulder. He took it in the back office. Raul and Roberto followed suit.

"Come and move these stools," Chico ordered from behind the mini bar.

Jose and Raul rushed over and did as they were told. After getting the stools out of the way, Chico knelt down and undid two latches on each side of the bar. He looked up at Jose and Raul and nodded. The two stood on each side of the mini bar and pulled it forward. The entire mini bar and a section of the floor came up as they laid it down on the carpeted floor.

Raul stood over the 6X6 hidden compartment in the floor and motioned for the bags. After dropping three in, they had a total of eight. Raul stepped back as Roberto and Jose put the mini bar back in place.

Chico sat behind his desk smoking a fat Cuban cigar. He

ordered Jose and Roberto to leave the room. He wished to talk to Raul in private.

Once they left, Raul walked over and sat on the edge of Chico's desk.

"What is it?" Raul asked.

Chico blew out a thick cloud of smoke. "We have a small problem that needs taking care of."

Raul knew right then that someone needed to be killed. "Who is it?"

"It's an earner of ours," Chico said, taking another puff from his cigar. "A Cuban by the name of Luis Nunez. It came to my attention that our friend Luis has been using Sereno's money to further his promising heroin business. Twice I've gone to collect money and the guy keeps slow walking me. He was supposed to have had a mil-five for us this time. But, I only got a mil."

"So where's the rest?"

"He claims he'll have two fifty for me tomorrow and he'll get the rest to me next week."

"But the money will be shipped outta here by then."

"I know. That's why Sereno wants this to be taken care of. An example must be made of anyone who attempts to fuck with Sereno's money.

$$$

Inside their office, at the district headquarters in downtown Cleveland, Meyers and O'Malley sat at their desk shifting through statements and photographs. The photographs were of a deceased black male named Ronald Tate, known on the street as Ron-Ron.

When the news came in of a young man found nude, beaten, and shot to death in an abandoned house off of Union, the two detectives had no interest in the case. But, all that changed when detectives assigned to the case told them Tate's girlfriend said he was supposed to have been with Jayson Taylor and Melvin Carter, aka JT and Mel.

As they looked at the photos, they couldn't get over the brutality.

"This son of a bitch must've pissed off the wrong people,"

O'Malley said as he placed the picture on the desk. Meyers, leaned back in his chair with his fingers interlocked behind his head, thinking *three bodies in one night and all the men knew one another.* Suddenly, a puzzled look appeared upon his face.

"Bill, do we still have the Feliciano report and statement from the robbery at the house on Gardner?"

"You're talking about the one when they thought the guy wouldn't make it. They sent us to get a headstart?"

"Yeah."

O'Malley dug through the paper work in his file. "Here it is," he said passing it to Meyers.

"There were three masked men," Meyers read from the statement of Francisca Feliciano. He looked up at O'Malley. "Three!" He then went through the autopsy photos of Ronald Tate and found the one with the victim on his stomach.

"Remember when they found him, he was nailed belly up to the floor."

O'Malley shook his head in agreement as Meyers pointed at the bruises on Tate's body with a pen.

"You see them?"

"I see 'em," O'Malley answered.

"I'm no expert but I've been shot while wearing my Kevlar vest and those look like impact bruises to me." He looked at Francisca's statement and read. "I shot at them when they were going out the back door. I thought I hit one of them but I guess I didn't!" Meyers emphasized. "I think these might be retaliatory killings for the shooting on Gardner."

O'Malley picked up the police report from the shooting on Gardner and read the victims name. "Sparks!" he said, excited. "You might be onto something Paul. If this guy Tyrone Sparks is related to the family I'm thinking of, we might be on the right track. I should've picked up on the name earlier!" O'Malley said, angry at himself. "Let me give you a run down on this family." He looked at Meyers. "Do you know Robert Sparks?"

"Yeah, he's the guy that owns the temp service and donates a lot of money at the F.O.P fundraisers."

"Yeah, good man and he has two other brothers that are just the same. Then, there's his two other brothers James and Raymel Sparks, two real bad asses in the early eighties. They used to rob after hours joints and shake down drug dealers. Those two names came up in over a half dozen murders back then. In '84, they went down on a manslaughter charge. Did three years."

"Just three?" Meyers questioned.

"They both had a really good mouth piece. After they got out, they terrorized the entire city again until they caught ten years Fed time for robbing an undercover agent during a drug deal."

"How do you know so much about these guys?"

"The Sparks name is almost legendary in the annals of the streets. It all started with Julius 'Country Slim' Sparks back in the late sixties. Country Slim was a feared and respected numbers man who made a name for himself as a tough guy when he took on a group of extortionists. My uncle spent three years of his life trying to bust his operation until Country Slim died in a shootout. Now, it seems that every generation a few bad asses comes outta that family. Right now, its two brothers. I don't know if they're the sons of James or Raymel but they killed two intruders in front of their grandmother's house years ago. Robert called around to his friends on the force, asking could they help the kids. Since then, there's been rumors about them involved in murders, nothing concrete but whispers. So we might be right about this but it'll never stick. We got suspects but no proof," O'Malley said.

"That's what we get paid for, to find proof," Meyers reminded his colleague.

CHAPTER 23
KEEP IT PURE

"Okay, I'll be there in a half hour," Ahmed said before he hung up the motel's phone. He looked over to the bed where Asad and Ducci played chess then to Young Curtis, who was on the other bed in front of the TV, playing a PS2 he'd bought.

"Hey Asad, I'm on my way to pick up that package."

"Want me to go with you?" Asad asked, without looking up from the game.

"I'll go wit 'em," Young Curtis offered, getting up from the bed. Asad looked to his brother.

"It's cool. I'll take him with me. I can see he's restless."

Asad nodded his approval then turned his attention back to the game.

"Let's get outta here," Ahmed said to Young Curtis on his way to the door.

"Where we goin," Young Curtis asked.

"To South Beach, to see a friend of mine," Ahmed answered as he got in the car.

$$$

Ahmed and Young Curtis stood outside the door of a luxury condo. Ahmed was about to knock again but it suddenly opened. Standing in the doorway wearing an open, short red robe, Crystal quickly covered herself when see saw Ahmed wasn't alone.

Damn... girlie is thick as fuck, Young Curtis observed as he followed Ahmed inside.

Crystal shut the door with one hand while holding her robe with the other. "I wasn't expecting you to bring anyone with you," she said with an embarrassing smile.

"Oh, I apologize. This is my cousin, Reggie," Ahmed introduced Young Curtis by a false name. "Reggie, this is my friend Crystal."

Crystal stuck out her hand. "Nice to meet you, Reggie."

"Same here." He fought the temptation to look down the sexy woman's robe.

Crystal turned toward Ahmed. “I have your things in the bedroom. Come on. I’ll help you get them.”

Ahmed could tell by the smile on her face and the look in her eyes what was about to happen so he walked over to Young Curtis. “Dig, I’ll be out in a few minutes.”

“Handle ya business.” Young Curtis knowingly grinned as he gave him dap.

When Ahmed stepped in the room, Crystal stood by an open closet door. “You know you have to pay shipping and handling,” she said, breathingly while taking off her robe.

Ahmed felt himself stiffen at the sight of her sexy body. “I can’t stay long... have to drop my cousin off.”

“So, you’re telling me you don’t want another taste?” she inquired as she put her right foot on one of the boxes he came to pick up.

Ahmed took in the sight of her shapely legs and thighs. Her breasts were small but, with Black women, small breasts gave way to big butts and that’s the body type Crystal flaunted.

“We can both play that game.” Ahmed smiled, pulling out on her. “I already told you I can’t stay long.” He stroked himself and stared Crystal in the eyes. “No pun intended.”

Crystal glared at his piece. She grew so aroused by watching that she caved in and rushed over to him. “You win.”

$$$

“Checkmate,” Asad declared.

Ducci stared at the board. “Damn, you got me again.”

“Wanna play another one?”

Ducci turned the board around and started setting his pieces up. “Hey Asad.”

“What’s up?” He looked up from the chessboard.

Ducci couldn’t think of a better way to say it so he just threw it out there. “I know you and your brother don’t fuck with dudes in the city. That’s pretty much like me and Curt. We know most of them are snakes that can’t be trusted. They’ll sell a dude out in a heartbeat.”

Asad listened, waiting to see where Ducci was going. He stared Asad in the eyes. “I noticed that you still don’t trust me and

Young Curtis. I saw how you were looking at your brother earlier when he was playing the video game with Young Curtis, laughing and having a good time. You looked like you were disappointed in him for letting Young Curtis get in with him."

Asad didn't expect this conversation but he couldn't do anything but respect how Ducci came at him. So he put his cards on the table. He stared at Ducci without any sign of emotion on his face or in his words.

"Dig Ducci, I'm gonna give it to you raw and uncut."

Ducci nodded his head in approval.

Asad continued. "I like you and Young Curtis. I think both of you are stand-up brothers. But, *thinking* and *knowing* are two different things. The only thing I take at face value is money. With people, it's a little different. It's a wait and see thing. But, like I told you before we left Cleveland, just be the real brother you are and we'll grow and build from there."

"Yeah, like you said," Ducci smiled. "Keep it pure with me and I'll keep it pure with you."

"Exactly," Asad smiled as they pounded fist over the chessboard.

When Asad heard the knock at the door, he got off the bed to answer it. "Yeah."

"It's me," Ahmed's voice called out from the other side.

Asad opened the door. Young Curtis and Ahmed carried in Sony TV boxes.

"Put 'em on the dresser," Asad directed.

Ahmed set his box on the dresser with Young Curtis doing the same. Ducci got up off of the bed and joined the other men, standing at the dresser.

"I see she didn't open them. Did she even ask what was in them?" Asad looked to Ahmed.

"Nope," Ahmed smiled. *Those boxes was the last thing on her mind*, he thought.

Asad turned back to the boxes and pulled out a black folding knife. He cut the tape off the first box and opened it then pulled out one of the HKs. He handed it to Ducci.

"Damn, what is this?" Ducci asked as he looked at the German made firepower in his hand.

Ahmed opened the other box and gave Young Curtis a HK before taking the last one for himself. Asad went back in the box and started passing out silencers.

"How you put this on?" Young Curtis asked.

Asad and Ahmed looked over at him and burst out laughing. "You have it backwards," Ahmed said, taking the silencer and gun from him. He put it on correctly and handed it back.

Mimicking Al Pacino in the movie, "Scarface," Young Curtis looked in the mirror and held the machine gun waist high. "Say hello to my muthafuckin' friend," he said, getting a laugh out of everyone in the room.

"Tomorrow, we gonna take you two out to shoot them," Asad said, getting back serious.

"They don't have too much of a kick and they shoot really smooth," Ahmed added.

"Oh yeah, Charm will have vests for all of us too," Asad said. He went back to the boxes and took out four packs of 9mm ammunition. He gave Ducci and Young Curtis one each.

"Those are the bullets you'll practice with. So, tonight, in your room, get a feel for reversing the double clips and get comfortable with your weapons."

Asad unfolded the stock on his HK and gave a demonstration. "See, I like coming from the shoulder." He put the stock of the submachine gun against his shoulder and looked down the sight as if he was a Navy Seal or something. "This style is for more precise shooting." He looked over to Young Curtis and Ducci. "You can also go from the hip but that style is more for a large group of people in a small area."

Ducci nodded, understanding everything Asad showed them. *Damn, dude knows a lot about killing. I wonder how many people him and his brother murdered,* he thought.

After a few more demonstrations, Young Curtis and Ducci put their guns back in the empty box and went down four doors to the room they shared.

"Man, I'm tellin' you. We rollin' wit' some paper chasers now," Young Curtis said after shutting the door. "These dudes are 'bout their business. Like that boy, Charm. That cat gotta have long paper. You see his mansion?" he excitedly questioned.

"Yeah, I peeped dude. When I first saw him, I could tell he was 'bout his business. But, I didn't know it was on some private jet, big mansion type shit."

"I think dude Fly Ty's connect."

"What made you think that?" Ducci asked, staring at him.

"The last time I kicked it wit' Fly Ty, he was tellin' me 'bout his dude in Detroit who hooked him up with this white chump who could clean up paper and I doubt if it's a coincidence that his cousins just happen to know another ballin' ass nigga outta the same city. Charm gotta be the dude Fly Ty was talkin' 'bout."

Ducci went in the box and took out the guns. He handed one to Young Curtis.

"Whatever Asad and Ahmed wants us to know, they'll tell us so let's stop speculating and get familiar with these straps."

"Yeah, you right," Young Curtis agreed as he put an empty clip into the HK.

$$$

"That's all I needed to hear. I'll talk to you tomorrow," Asad said, ending the call with Charm.

"What he say?" Ahmed asked as he lay on the bed.

"It's a go. Charm gave the green light. M&S is not connected to his people. We're going Monday for sure."

"I think I know the best way to hit 'em," Ahmed said as he set up in the bed.

"What's on your mind?"

Ahmed smiled. "What's a drug dealer's biggest fear?"

"I guess the Feds."

"Exactly. We can probably gain entry if we roll down on them like we're the D.E.A.

A smile spread across Asad's face. He liked the idea. The way he saw it. The fake DEA gear would give them enough time to get the drop on the men at M&S.

He grabbed the clean cell phone Charm gave him and called him to run down everything he needed by Monday afternoon.

CHAPTER 24
MY SON

It was early Sunday morning so the hospital had very little traffic. Joyce's insurance covered Tyrone, which afforded him a private room. He was out of critical condition but still in bad shape. They removed the tube out of his mouth and he breathed on his own. He still had a catheter stuck in his left side to drain the excess blood from around his lungs. He also had a catheter stuck in his penis to collect the urine as well as a colostomy bag for his bowel movements. The doctors strapped him down to the bed for his own protection. They said, often times, when people come to their senses after a traumatic event, their first instinct is to pull the tubes out of their body.

Only Joyce, Tamiko and Francisca remained at the hospital. Isis took Grandma Sparks home to get some rest. Isis had also tried to talk Joyce into going home but she refused. Both Tamiko and Francisca left for a couple of hours to shower and change clothes when he was upgraded to serious. Since their talk, neither woman said a word to the other. They spent most of their time worrying about Tyrone and sizing one another up. Francisca couldn't get over how statuesque Tamiko appeared. She figured her to be close to 6'0" tall and weighed about 165 pounds. From the looks of it, most of her weight was in her hips, thighs and butt. Francisca had to admit that Tamiko was pretty but felt she was prettier.

Tamiko subtly checked Francisca out over the few days. Likewise, she considered her an attractive woman. She had a pretty smile and nice eyes. Francisca's body seemed slightly overweight, not to mention the big bubble butt she drug along behind her. Tamiko knew men considered that 'thick.' She reasoned that Francisca was good looking but, by far, she looked better.

The women remained in the private room, trying to keep themselves occupied. Joyce read the Bible while Francisca leafed through an art book and Tamiko listened to her MP3.

Then, suddenly, the door opened and the nurse ushered in Raymel Sparks.

Tamiko and Francisca stared at the handsome, light brown-skinned man with the thick mustache and eyebrows, wondering his identity.

They both watched as he went to Joyce. He gave her a long hug and a kiss on the cheek.

"How's our boy?" he asked.

"He's fighting, Ray."

Francisca and Tamiko were shocked to learn that the strange man was Raymel Sparks, Tyrone Raymel Sparks' father. He looked ten years younger than his age of thirty-nine. What the women didn't know was that prison stints have a way of preserving men who take care of themselves while locked up. Both of the women knew Tyrone and his father weren't close, due to Raymel's recidivism while Tyrone was a kid as well as his tendency to put his mother through marital hell. The constant separation for years at a time wore on Joyce. Every time Raymel went away, she was always taken care of financially, but left empty emotionally. After Raymel's second prison sentence, she gave him an ultimatum. It was either her and their son or the streets. For close to two years, he chose them then it happened again. A five-year stint in a federal prison. The day he was sentenced, she filed for divorce and Tyrone sided with his mother.

When released from prison, Raymel relocated to Atlanta with his brother James to get away from his past and start over. He and his brother opened their first J&R RIBS, a popular chain of restaurants in Atlanta and Decatur, Georgia. He started a new family as well. Tyrone never met his younger brother and sister, Raymel and Sade.

The older Raymel got, the more he wanted to explain to Tyrone that he was eighteen when Joyce gave birth to him and he was too caught up in the streets to be a good husband, let alone father.

After talking with Joyce, he walked over to his son's bed and looked down on him. Even with his back turned, the women could tell he was crying. He wished he could've been a better father, that he and his first born was closer.

Raymel dried his eyes before he turned around. "Where's Asad and Ahmed?"

"Mama said they're outta town," Joyce answered.

Raymel, just about to ask another question, was interrupted by two unexpected guests opening the door.

Detectives O'Malley and Meyers entered the room introducing themselves and flashing their identifications. Meyers did all of the talking. "Sorry to disturb you all at this time but we've been looking all over for Ms. Feliciano."

Joyce and Tamiko both looked at Francisca. "Why are you looking for Ms. Feliciano?" Joyce asked.

"We just need to do a follow up on the report she gave the detectives the night of the shooting at her house."

"Are y'all robbery detectives?" Raymel asked as he stepped away from his son's bed. To his experienced eye, they looked like homicide.

"And what is your name, sir?" O'Malley inquired.

"Mr. Sparks," Raymel answered staring at the older detective.

"I didn't catch the first name."

"I didn't throw it." Raymel's dislike for the police was evident. Both men stared at one another with contempt in their eyes. Seeing enough of the macho bravado, Meyers turned to Francisca.

"Do you mind following me outside so we can talk Ms. Feliciano?"

"Anything you wanna ask me, Francisca said still seated, you can do it right here."

Meyers wanted to talk to her alone but, since he didn't have good enough cause to drag her down to the station, he had to talk to her in front of everyone.

"Well Ms. Feliciano, when the report was taken on the night of the shooting, you said there were three men who entered your home?"

Raymel wanted to tell her not to answer any questions but he wanted to know what happened and what the police knew. He figured if they started asking questions he didn't like, he would stop her.

"Yeah, it was three masked men."

Meyers nodded his head in agreement. "You also said you fired sixteen rounds at the men as they fled out the back door?"

"Yes, one of the men stayed with me when the other two took Tyrone down to the basement. A little after that, I heard a lot of gun shots so the guy with me ran to the basement. That's when I ran to my room. By the time I made it to the kitchen, I saw them going out the back door and shot until the gun was empty."

Raymel looked at the beautiful Puerto Rican woman and smiled inwardly.

Tamiko stared at her, not knowing she had shot at someone. She wondered if she could have done it.

"Did you hit anyone?" Meyers asked.

"That's enough," Raymel jumped in. "It seems like y'all know all of this already so what's going on?"

"Well Mr. Sparks… we think we might have found the three men who shot your..." He said but left the end opened for Raymel to fill in.

"My son."

"Are they in jail?" Joyce asked.

"No," O'Malley enlightened. "All of 'em have been found murdered. Two were machine gunned to death in a strip club and the other was found beaten and shot to death in an abandoned house."

Meyers stared at O'Malley in disbelief, wondering why he gave the family those details.

The two younger women looked genuinely shocked by the news. The older woman shook her head in mock disappointment. O'Malley could see that Mr. Sparks was doing his best to stifle the smile playing on his lips. All of Tyrone's love ones had the same thought on their minds. *Asad and Ahmed must've found them.*

"What makes you two think," Raymel asked, "those guys had something to do with my son laying in that hospital bed?"

"Well, first of all, Mr. Sparks, we're not one hundred percent sure they are the men. That's why we wanted to talk to Ms. Feliciano to piece this thing together."

"Look detective," Francisca said, rising from her seat. "The only man I'm concerned with is in that bed over there." The more she talked, the angrier she got, causing her accent to become more pronounced. "So if it's not about him, I'm through talking. And if you wanna talk to someone..." She quickly went to her handbag and plucked out a card. "This is my attorney, Jerry Greenburg's number. If you have anymore questions, they can be directed at him." She walked over and handed the card to Meyers. With that said, she once again seated herself.

Hearing that, Raymel stepped in. "Well, the lady is done talking. And, since this is a private room, I'm telling you two to leave."

"It's time to go Paul," O'Malley said, as Meyers stood there dumbfounded.

As soon as the detectives left, Raymel shut the door behind them then turned to Francisca. "You handled yourself well, Tyrone should be proud to have a woman like you in his corner."

The room fell under an awkward silence. Raymel looked from Francisca to Tamiko. He hadn't paid any attention to the two women before but quickly realized they were both there for his son.

"I'm not Tyrone's girlfriend," Francisca shyly offered. "I'm just his friend."

He could see in the woman's eyes that she was much more than a friend.

"Ray, that's Tamiko over there," Joyce tried to fill him in. "Her and Tyrone live together."

Raymel noticed the fury on Tamiko's face as he walked over and shook her hand. He went back to Joyce's side to get away from the angry looking woman.

"You look tired. How long have you been here?"

"Since early Friday morning."

Raymel stared at her and could see she needed to rest. "C'mon and get your things. I'm taking you home."

"No… you're not!" she protested. "I'm staying here until my baby wakes up."

"Just go home and get a few hours of good sleep and come back. Tyrone will be in good hands with these two women."

"Yeah mama, you need some rest," Tamiko agreed. "If anything changes, I'll give you a call."

Joyce looked over to Francisca who nodded in agreement. She got up from her chair and walked over to her son's bed. Staring at him, she gently rubbed his face. She then bent down and kissed him softly on his chapped and cracked lips. She stared at him a litte longer before turning to Tamiko. "As soon as there's any change, you call me."

"I will." Tamiko nodded and gave her a hug."

"I'll see you in a few, baby," Joyce said to Francisca as she walked pass.

"Okay, Ms. Sparks." Francisca smiled as Tyrone's parents left the room.

$$$

During the drive back to the station, Meyers was still furious with O'Malley for giving the family details about the murders. He wanted to see how much information he could glean from them. Obviously, one of them tipped off the killers.

"Why tell them about the murders?" Meyers sighed from the driver's seat.

"I just wanted to see their reaction. For all we know, that asshole back there could've been involved," O'Malley said, referring to Raymel.

"What!" Meyers shot him a look.

"Don't get your panties in a bunch, Paul. First of all, we don't have anything to support my theory. No evidence. No witnesses that we can use to actually identify anyone. All we have is a hunch. The only way we'll be able to solve this case is if someone starts talking and, truthfully speaking, I don't see that happening."

Meyers thought about it and knew his partner was right. The first twenty-four to forty-eight hours are crucial in any investigation yet they were well beyond that timeframe and still had nothing.

"So what do we do now?" Meyers asked.

"There's nothing we can do but wait."

CHAPTER 25
ANOTHER ARIZONA

"What do you brothers wanna to eat?" Charm asked the small group of men as they sat at an outside table at a popular South Beach restaurant.

"Just order me whatever," Young Curtis answered as he watched the beautiful women of Miami walk up and down the strip. "As long as the shit taste good."

The temperature was 87 degrees without a cloud in sight and most of the women wore next to nothing.

"Since you eat here, just order for me," Ducci yawned, still tired from the morning activities.

Asad and Ahmed woke him and Young Curtis up at six o'clock and took them to a wooded area, not far from the motel, to practice with the Heckler & Koch weapons. Asad was surprised by how well they handled the weapons. So when Asad received the call from Charm, offering to treat everyone to lunch, he figured it would be good for them to get out of the motel room for a few hours.

Asad watched as three women exited the restaurant. One of them stopped and looked toward the table. *That's why I didn't want to eat out here. It's too easy for people to spot you,* Asad thought.

"Hey Charm, how you been?" When the woman got closer she took off her Gucci sunglasses. The men instantly recognized the hot, young R&B starlet. Charm stood up and gave her a friendly hug. He held her at arms length. "You've grown up and filled out since the last time I saw you," he said.

She smiled at his words then waved over her two friends. "Girls, this is Charm. He's the only big concert promoter to ever work with me when my first album dropped."

Her girlfriends, Veronica and Sharon, listened but Asad and Ahmed caught their interest.

"What's up wit y'all," the two women greeted in unison.

The starlet noticed that she didn't have their undivided attention so she finally looked down at the other men seated at the table. First, she noticed the cute, light-skinned boy with French braids and reasoned that he could not have been more than sixteen years old. Next, she took in the dark-skinned man with quite possibly the nicest set of eyes she ever saw. Then, her focus went to the men who sat right under her. *I see why Veronica and Sharon were so distracted. These two are fine*, she thought.

She looked at the brothers' clear, caramel skin and medium-sized full lips that seemed so kissable. Their brush-waved hair shimmered from the little sunlight making its way through the canopy. The longer she stared, the more she liked what she saw. However, she didn't like how neither of them paid her any attention. *I know these niggas know who I am.* She tapped Ahmed on the shoulder then put on her best smile and thickened her New York accent.

"Are you two bruh'fahs or sumthin? Cuz, y'all look just alike."

Ahmed looked at the shoulder she touched then glanced up at her. "No!" he answered as dry as possible then returned his attention back to watching the people walking pass the eatery.

She looked over at the other guy, who she knew had to be his brother, but he didn't even bother to glance up at her. She thought about giving the two arrogant men a piece of her mind but quickly changed her mind. It was something about the two that told her she wouldn't want to get on their bad side. Feeling eerie, she looked over to Charm and told him it was nice to see him. Before walking away, she waved goodbye to Ducci and Young Curtis then made one more attempt to capture the brother's attention. But, to no avail, it didn't work.

"Let's go Veronica and Sharon!" the disgruntled star barked at her friends before she stomped off. Her friends followed with smirks on their faces.

"Man, y'all are too gangsta for T.V. Why y'all play that broad like that?" Young Curtis asked once the girls left.

"First of all," Ahmed answered. "She came over here on that star garbage, thinking we're all supposed to stop what we were doing to ogle over her. Then, to top if off, she touched me. You don't run around putting your hands on people you don't know."

Charm laughed. "You two are something else," he said before changing the conversation. "I got the jackets, stencil and acrylic paint in the car. I'll have the other things you wanted by noon tomorrow."

Asad nodded his approval.

$$$

After the late lunch, the brothers, Young Curtis, and Ducci went back to the motel. Inside Asad and Ahmed's room, four dark blue windbreakers were spreaded out with two on each bed. The letters D.E.A were painted on the back of the jackets in dark yellow.

"Ducci, grab those smaller stencils off the dresser for me," Asad said.

Ducci took the three-inch letters off the dresser and handed them to Asad.

"They're almost dry," Asad said as he touched them. He turned the jackets over and laid the stencils out. It read DEA over the chest area. He then sprayed the letters onto the jacket. He did all of this as the other men watched. When he finished, he stood back and examined his work.

"They're not authentic but they should buy us enough time to do what we have to do."

"What's up wit' the vests?" Young Curtis asked as he sat on the dresser.

"We'll get them tomorrow when we pick up the cars," Asad informed. He sat on the edge of the bed and told the other men how the move would go down. "Who's the better driver outta you two?"

"I am," Ducci answered.

"Well dig, it's me and you in one car and Ahmed and Young Curtis in the other. On weekdays, M&S doesn't close until nine o'clock. So, when the guy followed by the van drive up, we're going to follow them in. Ducci, we're going to come from the opposite end of the street, the same spot we watched them from the first day we got here."

Ducci nodded his head, letting Asad know he understood.

Asad continued, "As soon as we see the van pull into the driveway, you floor it. Get us back there fast as possible. Hopefully, the police dash light will buy us enough time to identify ourselves as drug enforcement agents. Dig, it's a lot of room inside this spot but there's an office about thirty-five feet away from the entrance. Stop the car a little ways from the door but make sure you leave Ahmed enough room to pull in behind us.

"I'm going to be right on your bumper when you pull in so don't play," Ahmed informed him.

"I got 'cha," Ducci replied.

"Dig, Young Curtis," Asad said, turning to face him. "Just before we go in, have your window rolled all the way down and be ready to lay anyone down who looks like a threat. It's a good chance they might not go for this DEA stuff and open up on us. With me and Ducci going in first, we'll catch the brunt of whatever they got. If you see it going down like that, don't panic. Stay calm as possible and pick out your target quickly. Your first target should be..."

"Whoever is the biggest threat to you and Ducci," Young Curtis interrupted.

Asad looked at Ahmed with a smile on his face.

"I told you these two would surprise you," Ahmed said.

Asad looked back at Young Curtis. "You're right little brother. You down anyone who's shooting at us."

Young Curtis nodded his head.

Asad started again. "All of that is worse case scenario. If it goes as planned, we should get in without a gunfight. If that happens, as soon as we're back there, I'm out of the car screaming DEA. So when you get out of the car, get the guy out the van."

"How many people gonna be there?" Ducci asked.

Asad thought for a few seconds. "Five. The guy Chico. Then, it's the three guards and the van driver."

Damn, that's a lot of people, Ducci thought.

"Hey Asad, once we got all these muthafuckas, what we gon' do wit 'em? Tie 'em up or what?" Young Curtis asked.

"No. These aren't the type of people you tie up. Once we get them all in the back, my brother and I will give them all 'Coup de Grace,' get the money, and get out of there," Asad said.

"Coup de what?"

"That means we're gonna kill all of 'em," Ahmed explained.

"Anyone have a problem with that?" Asad asked, looking from Young Curtis to Ducci.

"Naw, we know what we signed up for," Ducci answered. "I know you don't take the type of paper we're talking about without droppin' bodies."

The men stayed in the room talking and planning for hours before Ducci and Young Curtis left.

$$$

Ahmed sat on the bed across from his brother. "After hearing everything, this can easily turn into another Arizona," he said.

Asad rubbed the scar on his face.

Arizona was the only job where one of the brothers almost lost his life. It started when they kidnapped a postman and used his truck to approach a ranch on the outskirts of Tucson. The target was a white biker named Gator. He got on Charm's people's bad side by cutting them off and dealing with some Mexican drug runners from across the border. It was believed that the ranch was his gang's stash house. It was a little past noon when the brothers drove up the long dirt road. Once in front of the house, Asad got out in the postman's uniform with a large cardboard box with the bottom cut out to conceal the Heckler & Koch.

After knocking on the door, a skinny pale white girl with dirty blond hair who looked like she had not slept in days opened it. What the brothers didn't know was there had been a coming home party the night before for one of Gator's old prison buddies.

There wasn't anyway for them to have known a group of people were in the house.

In a flash, Asad quickly discarded the box and revealed the HK in his right hand. He grabbed the white girl with his left and forced her back inside. To his surprise, the woman screamed. When they entered the living room, he saw six people. Some slept on the floor with others on the couch and love seat.

Before Asad could process his next move, all hell broke loose. A bare foot, shirtless, jean-wearing, bald white guy with a red goatee stormed out of the kitchen brandishing a stainless steal .44 Desert

Eagle. Before Asad could do anything, Gator opened up on him screaming "Die you fuckin nigger!"

The skinny white woman, he held in front of him, caught the first barrage of bullets. She dropped at his feet. The third bullet zipped pass, grazing the left side of his face. When it hit, his adrenaline kicked in instantaneously so he didn't feel it. He leveled the HK at Gator and caught him with eight shots in rapid succession, dropping him where he stood. By this time, of course, the people asleep were up and hastily pulling guns from everywhere. Asad racked the room with a fully automatic burst from the HK and bailed.

Before he could make it to the door, a long, dark haired biker set his sights on him but, before he could pull the trigger, Ahmed materialized from around the corner and gunned the man down. That bought his brother enough time to make it to the postal truck.

As Asad drove up the dirt road, Ahmed hung out the side door ready to blast anyone who followed, but to their amazement, no one did.

When Ahmed sat in the passenger seat, he studied at his brother's face. What happened?"

"It got ugly," Asad answered as he drove off.

"I'm talking about your face."

At first, Asad thought the wetness he felt was sweat from all of the action. But, after he touched his face, he looked at his hand and saw blood. Then, he peered in the rearview and saw a huge gash.

"We have to find a place to drop the postman off," Asad said.

After dropping the postman off on a deserted road, they torched the truck.

Asad, reluctant to risk going to a hospital in Arizona or its surrounding states, drove the day and a half journey back to Ohio. By the time he made it home it was too late for stitches. Instead, he went to one of the best plastic surgeons in the state of Ohio, located in Avon Lake. His expertise was worth every bit of the money spent. The work was so good, the scar became barely visible.

After reminiscing about Arizona, Asad turned to Ahmed. "All of the jobs we've done could've turned into Arizona. That's why we have to be on top of our game every time."

Looking at his brother, Ahmed nodded in agreement.

$$$

Ducci lay on his bed, gazing up at the ceiling in deep thought about the job and how it wouldn't be a cake walk. To him it sounded way more dangerous than he expected.

"Ducci, what 'cha thinkin' 'bout?" Young Curtis asked as he cleaned the dismantled HK.

"I'm thinking about those ends we gon' knock tomorrow. After this, ain't no looking back. I'm even thinking about marrying Missy."

Young Curtis stopped. "You serious?"

"Yeah homie. I've laid enough broads in them streets. When we get back home, I'ma be ready to build up my real estate business and settle down."

"On the fo' real, Missy's a good girl and y'all two are good for each other. So, I wish you the best on whatever you do."

Ducci couldn't believe it. This was the first time Young Curtis didn't clown him about getting married. "You need to find a woman and settle down too." Ducci stared at him.

Young Curtis blinked, looking over at him as if he was crazy. He laid his gun on the bed and stood up.

"Man, you got me fucked up wit' a sucka. If Young Curtis take this dick off the market, you best believe hoes all over the country will riot."

Ducci couldn't help but laugh.

"Yeah, that's what I'm on," Young Curtis continued. "Every bitch in America gotta take all this work!" He pumped the air.

Ducci couldn't stop laughing for close to two minutes because he knew Young Curtis was as serious as a heart attack.

CHAPTER 26
THE NUNEZ FAMILY

"Listen to me, Alfonzo. I need this stuff in New Orleans like yesterday," Luis Nunez said over the phone to his trusted transporter as he paced back and forth in the spacious kitchen of his Pinecrest, Florida home.

"Okay, Luis, meet me at our usual spot tomorrow morning at 8:30 a.m. and I'll take care of everything from there," Alfonzo replied.

"See you in the morning," Luis smiled as he hung up.

He walked over to the black, leather briefcase on the kitchen counter and opened it. He stared at the quarter million dollars. *This should hold Chico off,* he thought. He reasoned some money beats no money. Luis knew using Sereno's money to help build up his heroin ring could be dangerous but he felt his connection to Santiago would protect him as long as he returned it. He figured, after dumping the twenty pounds of pure heroin, he wouldn't have to tap into Sereno's funds anymore.

He moved from the kitchen into the family room where his two beautiful daughters colored in one of their coloring books.

"Maria, Isabella, you two have one minute to get to bed."

The eight-year-old Maria protested. "Come on, daddy. Just one more page."

"Please, please, please daddy," cried the six-year-old Isabella.

"Okay," Luis said, giving in. "Only under these conditions. You can stay up thirty more minutes and finish but you'll have to do it on the lower level, in your playroom."

The girls' eyes lit up as they smiled at their father.

"Remember, don't come upstairs and don't be too noisy because your mother will make the both of you go to bed."

"Okay daddy," Maria whispered as if she was on a top-secret mission.

The girls gathered their crayons and coloring book then headed downstairs. Luis smiled.

The knock at the door took Luis' attention from the thought of his daughters. He briskly walked to the foyer and opened the door.

"Hi Chico. For a second there, I thought you weren't coming," Luis smiled.

"I'm only a half hour late. You of all people can understand being late."

Luis smiled but he didn't like the overtone of Chico's last comment. He stepped out of the way to let him in, but was surprised by the huge man who appeared out of what seemed like nowhere.

Raul stood on the side of the door out of sight during Chico and Luis' conversation. When Raul entered the house, Chico looked back at Luis and told him Raul was an associate of his. Luis shut the door and thought that this was strange. Chico never brought anyone in the past and he didn't like the look of this guy.

"Who's in the house with you?" Chico asked as he looked around.

"My wife..." Luis said, catching himself because he started to get a bad vibe.

"I have the money in the kitchen," Luis said, before he walked off with Chico following.

Once in there, he grabbed the briefcase off of the counter. When he turned around, he found Chico holding a black 9mm Ruger on him.

"What's going on?" he asked with a terrified look in his eyes.

"Our dealings have come to an end," Chico said as Raul took the briefcase from Luis then marched him into the living room and made him sit down on the sofa. Chico took a seat on the white, micro-fiber recliner positioned right across from him as Raul stood at his side.

Chico pulled a cigar out of his shirt pocket and had Raul light it. He took a puff and calmly exhaled the smoke.

"Luis, Luis, Luis. Did you think we wouldn't find out about your budding heroin venture?"

Luis said nothing. He looked at Chico with a blank expression, wondering how he found out.

Chico continued. "It's not the fact that you found a way to make extra money on the side. What pissed me off was that you used money that didn't belong to you to purchase that stuff. What do you have to say for yourself?" Chico paused for effect.

"I'm sorry. I promise I'll have the other two hundred and fifty thousand by tomorrow morning."

Chico laughed, looking up at Raul. "Now he says he can make the money appear like that," he said, snapping his finger. Raul laughed with him.

"I have the stuff upstairs right now or I can go to the bank and get the money outta my safety deposit box." Luis said, trying to convince the men he could come up with the money.

Chico took another puff from his cigar. "Where is the stuff?"

"It's in my bedroom, under the bed."

"Go get it," Chico said to Raul.

"Let me go. My wife is up there..."

"You just sit there. Raul will go get it."

Raul pulled out his gun then headed upstairs.

Luis watched then thought about his two daughters and prayed they would stay downstairs until Chico and his goon left.

Raul went to the first door he came to on the second floor. Then, he entered the master bedroom with his gun ready. It was illuminated by a lamp on the nightstand. He looked around the room decorated in all white from the carpet to the walls. As he stood there, he could hear the shower being turned off in the adjacent bathroom. He eased his way over to the slightly open door and peered in at a naked Christina Nunez, drying off with a large white towel. Raul watched intently as the voluptuous yet semi-chubby, Cuban American woman ran the towel over her body. He felt his manhood rise as he lusted over the average looking woman.

Christina, sensing someone watching her, looked toward the door. Then, it suddenly flew open and a huge man with a short haircut and thick mustache rushed in and grabbed her. When she screamed, he smacked her with the gun and told her to shut up. He dragged her into the the bedroom then threw her on the floor.

"Reach under the bed and grab the suitcase," Raul demanded.

Frantically, she did as told while wondering if the girls and Luis were all right. The sight of her reaching under the bed, on all fours, excited Raul.

She pulled the suitcase from underneath then looked up at him. He told her to open it. She continued to obey. Once the case was ajar, the pure heroin was so strong Raul could smell it in the air.

"Shut it," he ordered as he approached her. She zipped it back up then he grabbed her with his powerful hands and roughly threw her onto the bed.

She watched as he laid his gun on the nightstand then went into his pocket and pulled out a buck knife. He unfolded it and moved toward the bed while unfastening his pants. Holding the knife in his right hand, he got on top of her and forced her legs open.

"I haven't had a woman in over a week," he said, ramming his manhood in her.

Luis could hear what was happening to his wife upstairs.

"What the fuck do you guys think you're doing?" Luis said through clenched teeth. "When Santiago hears about this bullshit heads will roll," he continued as tears of anger ran down his face.

"Santiago already knows about it. He'd never go against Sereno for you," Chico said, smugly. He then looked toward the stairs. "Hey… hurry up, up there!" Chico smiled as he stared at Luis.

Raul grunted like an animal as he drove in and out of Christina. When he finished, he got up from the bed and pulled his pants up.

"You were good chica but now it's over. He grabbed her by the hair with his left hand then cut her throat with his right. Blood shot forward onto the white wall from the large gaping slash. Raul watched as the blood rushed out of her neck, turning the white sheet a dark red. Knowing she was dead, he picked up the suitcase and headed down stairs.

Raul entered the family room with the suitcase in one hand and a bloody knife in the other.

"Where's my wife?" Luis asked with a horrified look in his eyes.

"She's sleep," Raul smiled.

"NO! NO! NO!" Luis shouted as he dropped his head into his

hands. Luis' chest heaved up and down as he stared at the two men before he snapped. He sprung up from the sofa so quickly he caught them off guard. He went straight at Raul, raining punches down on him until one single shot rang out. Luis' body gave out under him. As he lay on the floor, he couldn't feel any of his extremities. The bullet shattered his spine. All he could do was watch as Raul walked over with a knife and started viciously stabbing his head and neck.

"Daddy!"

Chico and Raul both looked back and saw two little girls in nightgowns, standing in the entryway of the room and holding hands.

"Give me the knife and go take care of them," Chico said.

Raul handed him the knife then went after the little girls. They took off running back down to the lower level with Raul in hot pursuit.

As Chico cut Luis' throat, he heard two shots. He quickly went to work on Luis' dead body. When he finished, he left the dead man with a signature Colombian Necktie. Chico then casually walked to the kitchen and washed his hands in the sink. Raul entered from the stairs of the lower level with a gun in hand.

"Go grab the suitcase," Chico said as he picked up the briefcase from the kitchen counter.

Once Raul returned with the suitcase, the two men went out of the front door, leaving the carnage of an entire family behind.

$$$

Chico pulled into the garage area of M&S to drop Raul off. He told him to take the money and the heroin and put it with the rest of the stash.

"What are we gonna do with the drugs Chico? You know we can't put it on the ship with the money."

"I'm going to give Sereno a call and ask, so just hold it 'til tomorrow."

Raul got out of the car and went in the back with the briefcase and suitcase.

Once the office door closed, Chico blew the horn for Roberto to open the garage. After pulling out, he drove toward his rented South Beach penthouse.

CHAPTER 27
CONFRONTED

Tamiko, who slept in a chair by Tyrone, woke up to the sounds coming from his bed. She looked over at Francisca, who slept in a chair across the room, then got up and moved closer to Tyrone. He moved slightly while mumbling something. Her heart raced because this was the first time he showed any sign of life. The doctor told her the previous night that, as soon as the sedative wore off, he should be able to talk within a day or two after.

As she approached his bedside, she started making sense of his words. He spoke Francisca's name. She didn't like it but knew from her medical training that, when victims of traumatic events regained consciousness, they normally recall the name of the last person they saw.

As Fly Ty came to, he started to struggle against the restraints. Tamiko rushed over and hit a button on the wall then turned back to Tyrone, who was now in a violent rage. She grabbed both of his arms in an attempt to hold them down. By this time, Francisca rushed over.

"What's happening?" she asked.

Before Tamiko could answer, the door opened and two nurses ran over to the bed. Francisca stood back as they tried to calm him but she kept hearing him call her name.

One of the nurses pulled out a hypodermic needle, ready to inject it into his I.V.

"Don't stick that in his I.V.," Tamiko said as she held him down.

"Miss, this is just a sedative," the nurse responded.

"He doesn't need it," Tamiko angrily said. She knew he was still in a dream like state. "Tyrone. Tyrone. Wake up baby." After doing this a few times, he stopped his struggle completely then opened his eyes. Tamiko smiled at the sight.

Still weak and dazed, he blinked his eyes to focus them in the dimly lit room. As he lay there, he wondered why his body was sore and his head ached. When he tried to lift up, Tamiko held him down.

"Just relax, baby," she said.

He looked up at her then tried to touch her face. That's when he saw the restraints. "What the fuck is this," he uttered.

"Baby, you're in the hospital," Tamiko answered in a soothing voice. "They'll take those things off of you in a minute. Just stay calm."

He laid back and that's when everything rushed back to him. The robbery. The name Ron-Ron. And the shooting. He then thought about Francisca, he hoped that she was all right and vowed to kill Ron-Ron and the other two men if anything happened to her.

"Hi Ty," Francisca said.

He thought he was dreaming when he heard her sweet voice. He looked to the left of his bed and saw her beautiful face staring down on him. "Francisca?" he asked as if he couldn't believe his eyes. She nodded her head as she smiled down on him. He flashed a weak smile back.

"Are you okay?"

"I am now," she replied while fondly gazing down on him.

Tamiko could see the love in Francisca's eyes for Tyrone and heard the concern in his voice. It hurt.

"How do you feel?" Tamiko asked as she rubbed his face softly.

When Fly Ty turned from Francisca to Tamiko, his faculties restored and he realized they were in the room together. Before he could say anything, a doctor entered.

"Excuse me, can you ladies step out for a little while. I would like to examine Mr. Sparks and take those restraints off of him."

Both women nodded but, before leaving, Tamiko lightly kissed him on the lips.

As soon as she got into the waiting area, she pulled out her cell phone and called Joyce. The phone rang five times before she answered.

"Hello," she sleepily answered.

"Mama, this Tamiko. I have good news. Tyrone just woke up..."

"I'm on my way," she said then hung up. Tamiko returned to the room.

$$$

Fly Ty lay in his bed, listening to the women make small talk. He found it highly uncomfortable to have Francisca and Tamiko in the same room together. Then, what he knew expected to happen occurred.

"Can you step out the room? I need to talk to Tyrone in private," Tamiko said to Francisca.

Francisca, not liking the tone, was about to say no but, when she looked at Tyrone, he gave her a slight nod. She gently rubbed his arm before leaving.

Fly Ty turned to Tamiko and looked up at her. He could see the storm building in her eyes. She was hurt and upset, wanting an immediate answer.

She pulled her chair closer to his bed then sat down. She stared at him for a moment, trying to find the right words to say. "Tyrone, I thought you loved me?"

Tamiko must really be pissed to come at me with this, now, Fly Ty thought as he stared up at her.

"I do love you," he said through sincere eyes.

"How in the hell can you lay there and say that when that woman is pregnant by you?" She saw the surprised expression on his face and knew the assumption she made days earlier stood correct. From his silence, she dropped her head into her hands. "I knew it," she said looking back up at him.

"Who told you?" he meekly asked.

Tamiko stared at him, doing everything in her power to keep from slapping him.

"No one told me Tyrone. I'm not fucking stupid! I just used logic. One day. Out of the blue. A woman, who no one in your family knows, shows up, then all of a sudden they're treating her like one of the family.

"I was gon' tell when you came home," Fly Ty said, trying to ease her pain.

"You have one more time to say something stupid to me and I'm going to knock the shit out of you," Tamiko said as she reared her fist back. "What… your telling me when I got home was going to make me feel better?" She put her arm down and unballed her fist.

He didn't know what to say because he never saw her this angry. It was as if he could feel the hurt coming off of her body as she stood over him.

"You know what, Tyrone? I always had a feeling you were messing around. I couldn't prove it but I knew how much you liked sex and, with me being down in Columbus, I kinda knew. But, I thought that whoever you were probably screwing was just a plaything for you and, in time, you'd grow out of it. Then I thought I might just be paranoid because, as long as we've been together, there has never been any other female drama. Now, I see I was just being a damn fool."

She bowed her head and shook it in disbelief. Fly Ty knew there wasn't anything he could do to fix the problem as he watched her attempt to leave.

"Miko," Fly Ty called out. When she turned to face him, he saw the tears in her eyes. He lifted his arm and held it out. Tamiko put both of her hands around his.

"I know its nothin' I can say to make this better. But… I'm so, so, sorry baby and please believe me when I say I love you and always will."

She stared down on him and felt in her heart that she would never stop loving him then took one of her hands and wiped the tears from her eyes before staring at Fly Ty.

"As long as we've been together, I never cheated on you, Tyrone. Never! I've might have flirted with a few guys but I never betrayed nor dishonored our relationship."

Fly Ty noticed the words she chose to use and they both stung because he never looked at it that way. She was right.

She continued. "What's done is done. We can't change the past. The only thing we can do is work on the future. So answer this, Tyrone. Do you want me in your future?"

"Yes," he answered without any hesitation.

She bent over and kissed him softly on the lips. She pulled back just a little, staring him in the eyes. "I know that you are a man and will take care of the child that woman is carrying."

Fly Ty recognized how she didn't even want to say Francisca's name. He continued to listen.

"I'm willing to put all of this behind us," she said squeezing his hand. "We can fix this baby. All you have to do is clarify one thing for me and I promise we can move on and I won't hold this against you."

He stared at her, wondering what it could be.

"Just tell me you don't love her. I need to hear you say it," Tamiko pleaded.

They both stared into one another's eyes for a long moment, without either saying a word. He didn't say anything because he couldn't bring himself to say what she wanted to hear. He watched as the expression on Tamiko's face went from anticipation to understanding.

"You love her Tyrone," she asked with a pained expression on her face. She hastily snatched her hand away from his and gazed at him for a moment as he silently stared back.

"Well," she said with a nervous smile as tears welled up in her eyes. "As intelligent as everyone thinks I am, I see I've been playing the fool for you. But, no more. I'm going to get out of the way so you and that woman can be a family and live happily ever after."

"Miko, don't do this."

"Don't do this!" she shouted with a look of disgust on her face. "Tyrone I haven't done anything… you have!" She headed for the door then turned around. "Give me a few days to get out of your house and I'm leaving the car there with anything else you ever bought me. I'll have the money in my account that belongs to you transferred as soon as possible."

Fly Ty quickly pressed the button to raise his bed and grimaced from the pain as he propped himself up.

"Tamiko!" he said in the strongest voice he could muster. "You can knock that bullshit off, like I need or want any of that stuff. I gave them things to you. You can have the condo, car, and the money in your account. Everything I ever did for you was out of love. So, if you ever loved me, keep it all."

Tamiko stared at him from the door. "I still love you and

probably always will but its over," she said as she exited. Once outside the room, she saw Francisca leaning against the wall. Tamiko looked in her direction and the two women locked eyes. At first she wanted to run over there and slap her but knew it wasn't her fault. The blame fell squarely on Tyrone. Tamiko broke her glance then made her way to the exit.

Francisca stepped inside the room and saw Fly Ty still propped up. She walked over to the bed then pressed the button to lower it. She looked down at him, seeing the blank expression on his face.

"Are you okay?" she asked in a caring voice.

He said nothing as he stared off into space.

"What happened in here?" she asked.

"She's gone," he answered as a lone tear crept down his left cheek.

Francisca saw it and quickly wiped it away. She knew whatever decision he made would be rough on him but she also had to set him straight. "I'm sorry that you had to go through this, at this particular time, but you're not going to treat me like some secondary option. So, make this the last time I see you shed a tear for her." She gave him a kiss on the lips as if that would soften her words.

Fly Ty lay there, thinking about how vicious women could be when they're hurt. Here he was in a hospital bed, his first time conscious in days, and this was what he woke up to.

$$$

Tamiko stormed out of the hospital into the parking lot with her mind racing. As she headed through the lot, she heard her name called. She looked over the cars and saw members of Tyrone's family. She turned around and went to Joyce. As she approached, she tried to put on a strong front.

"What's wrong, baby," Joyce asked with concern.

Tamiko looked at her and lost it. She started to cry as Joyce took her into her arms. She turned to the family and told them to go inside. She'll be there in a minute. Joyce walked Tamiko to her red V7OR Volvo.

"Do you want to talk about it?" Joyce asked, already suspecting the problem.

"Mama, right now, I just need to get my thoughts together. But, whatever me and that son of yours is going through, it won't change how I feel about you," Tamiko said, giving her a kiss on the cheek. Tamiko got inside her car and pulled off.

Joyce watched, hoping Tyrone could live with his decisions. When she entered the hospital room, she saw the family around the bed smiling and laughing. Francisca sat alone in one of the chairs off to the side. "How you doing?" she asked, making it to him.

"I'm alright mama," he smiled. "The doctor told me I'm going to be here a month or two but I'm going to make a full recovery."

"Praise Jesus," Joyce interjected.

Fly Ty looked around the bed at his family. Happy to see them all.

"Grandma, when I'm able to eat solid foods, will you cook for me?"

"Bless your heart child. I'll cook for you everyday and will send Isis up here to bring it to you."

"I'm not coming up here every day, bringing this boy food like I'm his slave," Isis said while playfully cutting her eyes at him. The family laughed at her remark.

Fly Ty looked at his father who he had ignored since the man entered the room.

"What's up wit' you Raymel?" Fly Ty asked. Raymel didn't like how his son addressed him but lived with it.

"I had to come up here and see how my boy was doing," he answered.

Fly Ty shook his head in approval, then a puzzled look crossed his face. "Where's Asad and Ahmed?"

"Oh, them two are outta town again," Grandma Sparks replied.

"Oh yeah, Tyrone," Isis said, getting his attention. "Since you've been in here, people in the hood been dropping like flies."

He looked at her, wondering what she was talking about. She

saw the look on his face then explained. "You know some guys named JT and Mel?"

"Yeah."

"Well, somebody ran down on them in a strip club and killed them."

Fly Ty's eyes got wide from the news.

"And some other guy off 'The 1st' named Ron-Ron was found dead in an abandoned house."

After hearing what Isis said, it was as if a veil lifted from his eyes. *JT and Mel were the other two niggas with Ron-Ron. Damn, those bitch ass niggas tried to take me out the game*, he thought. Then his mind went to his cousins. He smiled, remembering that they were in Miami with Ducci and Young Curtis.

CHAPTER 28
OUR PHILOSOPHY

The knock on the door broke Ahmed's attention from the noon news broadcast. He got off of the bed with his eyes still glued to the television. When he made it to the window, he looked out and saw Young Curtis and Ducci. He let them in and sat back down. Ducci came in first followed by Young Curtis.

"What's up Asad, Ahmed?" Young Curtis spoke.

Asad held his hand up for Young Curtis to be quiet. He shut the door then went and stood next to Ducci. Everyone in the room watched the pretty Latina anchorwoman as she described the horrific discovery in the quiet suburb of Pinecrest, Florida.

"There is a total of four victims," The anchorwoman said. "Two children ages six and eight, and two adults. From what our police sources tell us, the adults' throats were slashed and the children were shot. All of the victims have been identified but we will not release the names until the families are notified."

Ducci watched the brothers throughout the entire newscast and noticed they seemed sickened by the report.

Ahmed got up from bed and turned the television off.

"That's fucked up," Young Curtis said. "But, somebody put some gangsta shit down on those people."

Asad and Ahmed both turned to face him.

"Dig this, Young Curtis," Asad started. "There isn't anything gangster about the murder of innocent kids."

Young Curtis looked Asad in the eyes and nodded in agreement.

Ducci on the other hand seized the moment to get into the brothers' mind set. "Man, it ain't no telling what those people did to have somebody do 'em like that."

Asad, who sat up on his bed stared at Ducci. "Whoever did that had to be some sick coward types. It doesn't take a gangster to kill a kid."

"Man, y'all should know how it go. Y'all probably had to do things, y'all ain't wanna do," Ducci pushed on.

"Ducci! Knock off those games you're playing," Asad said, standing up. He knew Ducci's intentions. He wanted to know what made him and his brother tick or how far they would go. Asad told Young Curtis and Ducci to have a seat. Ahmed moved over on his bed to give them enough room to sit.

"You want to know our philosophy on what we do," Asad asked as he sat on the edge of the dresser. Ducci nodded yes.

"See my brother and I are warriors. Not much different than say a person in the military. The biggest difference is we pick and choose what battles to fight. We don't let the government tell us that it's cool to kill the enemy as long as it's for them. Dig, my brother and I have never killed anyone who wasn't game related. Everything we ever did was within the confines of the game. It's not like were out here canceling civilians."

"Well, what about the bouncer at the strip club?" Ducci asked.

"That man wasn't a civilian. He was back there to protect those lost sisters selling their bodies. So don't believe he was some square type dude."

Ducci thought about it and reasoned Asad was right.

"Ducci, all I'm saying is that Ahmed and I have morals and killing a kid would go against that. I'll risk going to prison before I do that. You want to know why? Because when I stand before the Most High, I will have to answer for all the things I've done in my life and doing something like that I'll never have to answer for."

Everyone in the room was quiet for a moment, lost in their own thoughts until the cell phone on the nightstand rang. Asad walked over and answered it. He hung up after a brief conversation. He turned to the other men in the room. "That was Charm. He has a place set up for us so you two go to your room and pack all your things because we're not coming back."

$$$

The small group of men met Charm in a grimy section of Miami called Liberty City. Ahmed drove into the driveway of a single house that looked damn near abandoned. The white paint chipped and the gutters looked like a good rain would send them to the ground.

Asad surveyed the scene and thought to himself that Liberty City looked like my other ghetto in America.

On their way inside the house, Asad noticed five young thugs sitting on the porch drinking forties and smoking weed. They all stared at him as he entered.

Once inside, the contrast from the interior and exterior became immediately apparent. The interior was plush from its wall-to-wall, black carpet and leather furniture to the large plasma screen TV in the living room.

Asad shut the door and watched as Charm greeted everyone. "How did you get here? I didn't see a car outside," Asad asked Charm.

"I drove one of the cars you wanted. Both of them are in the garage. I figured you didn't need the Caddy any longer so I'm going to take it back to the rental agency."

"Did you get everything I asked for?"

"You know it," Charm smiled. He walked around the couch and picked up one of the four bulletproof vests.

"This thing is heavy," he said, handing it to Asad.

Asad inspected the vest then placed it on the couch.

"Let me see the cars?" he asked Charm.

"C'mon," Charm said. He led the men through the house, out the back door, outside, and then through a side entrance to the garage.

Young Curtis and Ahmed walked around the dark blue Ford Crown Victoria as Asad and Ducci got in the black one parked next to it.

"Where the keys at?" Asad asked.

"Look in the driver's side visor," Charm answered as he leaned in through the open door.

Asad pulled the visor down and the keys fell out. He looked over at Ahmed in the car next to him. He held up his own set.

"Look under the driver's seat!" Charm hollered at both men.

Asad felt under the seat and pulled out a blue, dome-shaped police light then placed it on the dash. He flicked the switch on the side and it started flashing. Ahmed put his police light on the dashboard, flashing, as well.

After checking everything out, they all went back inside the house. Once everyone was seated, Asad looked over at Charm, who sat next too him.

"Do you have transportation set up to take us outta town after we take care of this?"

"Yeah, just how you asked." Charm pulled a folded piece of paper from his shirt pocket then handed it to Asad. "I know how you two are about meeting new people so I'm going to handle this myself."

Asad looked at him, wondering if they were letting him in too deep.

"Don't worry about me," Charm said, seeing the look on his face. "The part I'm playing is very minimal." Truthfully, he enjoyed it. He had never been involved in the planning stages of any of the brother's jobs. To him it was interesting to see all the things they went through to pull off a move. He had a new respect for what they did because he realized there weren't many stick-up men from the streets who could do what they do.

"Charm, whose house is this?" Ahmed asked.

"This young brother that's on my team."

"And he lives here?" Ahmed asked in dismay.

"Well, he really doesn't live here. He has a beautiful home in Coconut Grove but he thinks keeping a house in the hood is keeping it real." Charm laughed.

"We won't have to worry about him pulling up being nosy, do we?" Asad asked.

"No, he's the one who drove the other car over here. I told him I needed to use the house overnight so he's not coming back," Charm assured.

For the next two hours, the men went over the plan from beginning to end a number of times. Charm, who heard enough, stood up. "I better get outta here," he said.

The brothers walked him to the front door, but before Ahmed could open it, Charm turned to face them.

"I expect to see you two tonight," he said.

"We know," Ahmed smiled.

Charm smiled back then his face took on a serious expression. "What I'm really trying to say is be careful because this shit sounds dangerous as hell to me."

Ahmed laughed. "Don't worry, Charm. This is what we do."

He stared at the two with an uneasy smile. "You two are like brothers to me. Without y'all, I don't know what I'd do."

"You're killing me with this bad vibe you're putting out in the universe, Charm," Asad said. "So take our word. We got this Big Bruh."

He stared at the brothers for a few seconds then gave each of them a hug. "I love y'all."

"Same here," Ahmed smiled.

"Well, I'll see you tonight," Charm said as he opened the door and left.

$$$

"Si, todo va acuerdo al horario, Mr. Guerrero," Chico said over the phone to his boss Sereno. He filled him in on everything, letting him know they were on schedule. He told him everyone on the list showed up at the restaurant and he was on his way there to make the last pickup as well as talk with Santiago.

"Si, Mr. Guerrero," Chico said before he hung up the phone. After the call, Chico walked through the luxury penthouse to the master bedroom. "Hey you," he said to the tall, slim, beautiful, naked, blonde woman in his bed. He walked over and kissed her. "I have some business to attend to and I won't be back until around eleven. So, do you wanna stay here or go home?"

"I'll stay here and wait for you." The woman smiled.

Chico grinned because that's what he wanted to hear. "Make yourself at home. When I get back I'm going to show you a night out on the town," he said before leaving.

Inside the underground parking lot, Chico chose his black Aston Martin. He got in, then pulled out his cell phone and placed a call. "Meet me at the restaurant," was all he said before he hung up. He looked at his watch and saw that it was 7:26 p.m. *I still have enough time to eat,* he thought as he started the car and pulled out of the parking garage.

$$$

Inside the small house in Liberty City, Asad stood in front of his team going over what everyone needed to do. They wore identical clothing – black, military style pants and boots with black, long sleeved T-shirts. Young Curtis sat on the sofa wearing his black, ninja style ski mask.

"Could you take that off so I can see your face while I'm talking to you?" Asad asked.

Young Curtis pulled the mask off like a restless little kid. "Man, we've been goin' over this all day. I'm tired of talking it. I'm ready to do this."

Asad looked at him and smiled. He liked the brash, youthful exuberance he displayed but it was his job to let him know this wasn't going to be easy.

"Dig, Curtis, I know you're the youngest in this room and I don't doubt that your heart is just as big as anyone's in here but you have to remember the brave dies first and the smart survive."

Ahmed and Ducci nodded their heads in agreements as Young Curtis fiddled with his mask while listening to Asad.

"This lick we're about to hit is nothing like hitting a bank. Its a hundred times more dangerous." Asad paused to let his words take affect. He could tell by Young Curtis' expression he was beginning to understand that one of them could easily die.

Asad turned to Ducci and Ahmed, both sitting on the sofa. "Ahmed, I know you already know this but I'm just making it clear." He looked over at Young Curtis, who sat in a chair, to make sure he was listening. Thankfully, he was. "If gun play jumps off, the main thing to remember is don't panic!" He looked from Ducci to Young Curtis. They nodded, concurring with Asad.

"And, don't forget. If one of us goes down, looking at him or rushing to him won't do anything but get you killed. So stay focused on your target and do your man. Oh, before I forget," he said while walking over to the black duffel bag where he pulled out small cardboard boxes. He handed two boxes to Ahmed, who passed them to Ducci, who passed them to Young Curtis.

Once Asad distributed them all, he sat down on the love seat with his and told everyone to load their clips with the bullets he had just given them.

Young Curtis was the first to open the box without any markings on it. He pulled out the Styrofoam tray and dumped the bullets in his lap then picked one up and stared at it. Never seeing anything like it before, he glanced over at Asad who loaded the clips to his HK.

"What type of bullets are these?" Young Curtis asked.

"They're a special blend. This guy I know made them. They'll go through a vest and any other light armor," Asad answered.

Damn! Young Curtis thought as he proceeded.

After everyone finished putting the new loads into their clips, Ducci sat his gun down on the floor before getting up to make a call. He picked up the cordless phone and started dialing a number when Asad walked over to him.

"Don't use that phone."

Ducci stared at him and saw the cell phone in his hand. He put the cordless phone back and took the cell phone from Asad. "What's wrong with that phone?" Ducci asked, nodding toward the land line.

"We don't want to leave anything down here that can lead back to us," Asad answered. "No phone records, no nothing. Just use the phone Charm gave us." With that said, he walked off.

I never been around no dudes this thorough, Ducci thought as he dialed a number. He walked in the kitchen to get some privacy.

"Hello."

"What's up baby?"

A big smile went across Missy's lips as soon as she heard his voice.

"Why haven't you called me?" she angrily asked, getting over her initial joy.

"I'm sorry baby but I've been concentrating on this thing I have to take care of. I wasn't going to call until I got back home but I couldn't stand another day without talking to you." She smiled on the other end of the phone, forgetting she was supposed to be mad at him.

"So when will you be home, boy?"

"Late tomorrow night."

"That's good, because I'm taking off Thursday so we can spend a long weekend together."

Ducci grinned. "I'll come down Wednesday night but I wanna go somewhere for the weekend."

"Where you wanna go now?" she asked with an attitude, thinking he would leave her alone again.

"The Bahamas or Hawaii," he said.

"You mean this weekend?" she asked, excitedly.

"Yeah, I figured me, you and Poo-Poo could go on a quick vacation."

"Why don't you bring AJ with you?"

"Monica won't let me take him outta school. Plus, I'm taking him to Disney World this summer."

"Well where you wanna go?"

"You decide baby. Just make sure everything is first class."

"Okay, I'll take care of this in the morning. Oh yeah, where's Young Curtis crazy ass?"

Ducci looked out of the kitchen, into the living room where he saw Asad talking to Young Curtis.

"He's talking with one of our dudes," Ducci answered.

"He got that girl Shu wide open."

"Yeah, my little homie knows how to put it down," Ducci laughed.

As he carried on with his conversation, Ahmed stepped into the kitchen. "It's about that time," he whispered.

"Here I come. I gotta go, baby. I'll call you when I get in tomorrow."

"Okay, I love you, boo."

"Yeah, I love you too." Ducci hit end on the cell phone before walking into the room with the other men.

Asad pulled the heavy drape back and looked out the window. To his surprise, the once sunny day turned into a wet, gloomy one. For some reason, he thought it to be some type of omen. He quickly shook the idea off before picking up one of the duffel bags with him and Ducci's gear in it. Ahmed grabbed the other one.

A light constant drizzle fell from the sky as they walked out the back door. Ahmed, Ducci, and Young Curtis went into the garage through the side as Asad lifted the door up. Ahmed drove the dark blue Crown Victoria out first with Young Curtis riding shotgun. They stopped a ways down the driveway to wait for Ducci, who pulled out behind them.

Asad opened the passenger door then set the duffel bag on the floor. He went to the garage and pulled the door down before getting back inside the car. He positioned the bag on the floor then wiped the rain from his face. He leaned forward to look out the windshield at the dark, gray sky.

"Let's go," he said. Ducci tapped the horn once and watched as Ahmed pulled out of the driveway then he put the car in gear and followed.

$$$

Inside Sabor A Cuba, a restaurant located in Little Havana, Chico sat at his table full from the meal he just ate. *A cigar would be good right now*, he thought.

He watched as a cute waitress approached. "Mr. DeJesus, Mr. Moya would like to see you in the back." Chico stood up and followed the young woman through the double doors that led to the kitchen. Once inside, he noticed all of the action as people ran around with pots and pans while five cooks in white stood over the grills and stoves preparing various dishes.

He eased his way through the kitchen, into the storeroom, where he saw Mr. Moya.

Santiago Moya was the owner of the restaurant and a good friend of Sereno Guerrero. He was known as 'The Miami Strongman.' At 6'4" and of Cuban decent, one look into his cold, hard, wrinkled face, it was easy to tell he was a dangerous man in his past.

Chico greeted him with a hearty hug.

"Did they take care of you out there?" Santiago asked.

"As always, the food was great. You should think about opening a chain of these restaurants," Chico suggested.

Santiago smiled and shook his head no. "I only do this becuz my papa. Rest his soul. He started this place forty years ago when he came here from Cuba. But you know what my real business is," he grinned. "Those are the last two," he said, pointing to the burlap sacks in the corner.

Chico looked at his watch that read 8:36 pm. *He should have been here by now*, he thought. He sat on one of the many boxes in the storeroom and pulled out a cigar. Santiago grinned at him and pulled out less than half of one before lighting it with a wooden match. He walked over to Chico and lit his also. Chico inhaled the smoke as he looked around the storeroom. He had been in every day that week. The restaurant was used as a drop off. Once the money would arrive, Santiago would count it then wrap it and pack it into the burlap sacks. The money was never left overnight for security purposes just in case one of the guys who dropped it off got the idea to come back and rob the place. Chico came by every day and picked the money then took it to M&S for safekeeping. Hearing a knock, Santiago stood up from his crate and opened the back door.

"I know I'm late, Chico, but an accident had traffic backed up for miles," Miguel said, shaking the rain off in the doorway.

"Just load the money up so we can go," Chico ordered, taking another puff from his cigar.

After loading the van, Chico sat in the front passenger seat since the rain started to pour.

"Take me to my car around front."

Miguel turned the lights and windshield wipers on as he slowly dove up the alley.

CHAPTER 29
GUNS BLAZING

Seventy-five yards away from M&S Yacht Sales, parked in the parking lot of an auto body repair shop, the four-man team sat in the dark, waiting to make their move. The two Crown Victorias didn't look out place, sitting out front, because the shop was already overcrowded with cars needing repair. Asad looked at the clock on the dash. It read 9:05 pm so he wondered if they missed the last drop off. He could see all the way up the long dark, deserted street and hadn't witnessed a car drive up it since they parked.

Over in Ahmed's and Young Curtis' car, Ahmed sat silently as he listened to Young Curtis recite Juvenile's verse form the Hot Boy "Let 'em Burn." *Whatever it takes to get a brother's mind right*, Ahmed thought as he continued to listen.

All four men sat in their cars with the same anxious and nervous feeling in the pit of their stomachs that always came before hitting a score.

"You think we might've missed them?" Ducci asked as he looked over to Asad.

Secretly, he had the same thought but knew they couldn't have because they had been waiting since 8:30 p.m. and Mike Guerrero said they always drop the money off after closing.

Just when he was about to answer, he saw a pair of headlights turn onto the dark street.

"I think this might be them," he said quickly. He pulled the ski mask down over his face and Ducci did the same.

Asad watched as the car stopped a little ways from M&S. That's when he saw the white cargo van turn the corner. He looked over to the car next to him then rolled his window all the way down. Ahmed and Young Curtis had their masks on as well. His heart raced as he checked to make sure the Heckler & Koch had a round in the chamber. He turned to Ducci. "When I say hit it, hit it."

Ducci and Ahmed started their vehicles. Asad watched as the car moved again, followed by the van. He waited until both vehicles pulled into the driveway.

"Hit it!" he yelled.

Ducci throw the car in drive, stepped lightly on the gas then harder. The car bounced and fishtailed out of the parking lot.

"Don't forget to hit the light as soon as we get to the entryway," Asad said.

Ducci nodded his head as they sped up the street.

Ahmed was right on Ducci's bumper as they turned into the driveway of M&S. He took the corner so fast that Young Curtis, already out the window with the HK, almost fell out. As the cars stormed up the driveway, Asad could see the van was barely in the shop when they pulled up.

Chico looked in his rearview mirror at the two dark police sedans rushing toward the shop and thought, *damn.* Raul and Jose were about to reach for their guns but, when they saw the blue flashing lights approaching fast, they both knew killing a police officer or an American Federal Agent wouldn't be a good idea from the heat it would put on Sereno's organization.

Ducci pulled into the shop and came to a screeching halt three feet behind the Aston Martin. Even before it stopped, Asad was already out.

"DEA, DEA, Get outta the car!" he screamed at the driver of the Aston Martin, while pointing the machine gun in his face. Chico slowly got out of the car with his hands up and backpedalled to Raul and Jose who had their hands up as well.

Young Curtis who was out of the car, a fraction of a second behind Asad, snatched the driver of the van. He forced him to go stand with the others.

Inside the office, Roberto ran around with his AK-47 assault rifle unsure of what to do. *Should I throw my gun down and surrender with the others or should I just let the police find me back here.* He looked around the room that didn't have windows and knew he was trapped. He crept closer to the door, hoping he could pick up on something from either Chico or Raul.

Raul watched as one of the assumed agents checked the van then hollered clear. That's when something caught his eye. He noticed all of their weapons had silencers then realized that they weren't agents.

As he stood there, with his hands up, he watched one of the armed men press the button on the wall to close the garage door and started shouting in Spanish.

Asad, who stood ten feet away with his gun trained on the men, told Raul to shut up but the big Colombian stared back with death in his eyes. Asad instantly noticed the change in the men's body language.

Raul, continuing to speak in Spanish, stared at Young Curtis as he walked past the office door with Ducci pulling up the rear.

Ahmed, who stood by the car to switch from covering his brother to covering Young Curtis and Ducci, was ready to open fire on the group of men.

"Y'all muthafuckas shut up!" Young Curtis demanded as he approached them. That's when Ahmed saw movement behind the frosted glass window of the office door.

"Office door! Office door!" Ahmed hollered.

Young Curtis' reaction wasn't fast enough. Instead of turning his whole body toward the door so he could get a shot off, he just turned his head. It seemed like eveything happened in slow motion. He saw a shadowy figure level a gun at him. *Damn, I'm dead.*

Ahmed couldn't get off a clear shot with Young Curtis in the way but a fraction of a second before it went off, Ducci closed the distance between Young Curtis and himself. Without thinking, he pushed him out of the way with his left hand as he raised the HK with his right but it was too late.

The gunman opened up with a fully automatic AK-47, shredding Ducci's bullet prove vest. After that the M&S erupted into an all out gun battle.

As soon as Ducci's body hit the floor, Asad and Ahmed simultaneously sprung into action.

Asad saw three of the four men he had his gun trained on reach for theirs. Miguel quickly stepped forward, trying to pull the weapon from the small of his back but Asad fired on him, sending four shots through his chest.

Miguel's act of bravery gave Raul and Jose enough time to

pull their weapons. They both opened fire. Jose, in a panic, shot wildly at Asad and missed all three shots. Asad quickly crouched down, took aim, and pulled the trigger on the HK. He saw Jose go down from the hail of bullets ripping into his torso. He turned to Raul and Chico but couldn't get a good shot off because both men ran around a yellow speedboat as Raul continued to shoot.

When Ducci went down, it gave Ahmed a clear shot at the shooter in the office window, who still wildly sprayed the AK-47. Ahmed pulled the trigger on the fully automatic Heckler & Koch, sending a fifteen shot volley through the broken glass with eight shots finding their mark.

Roberto never heard the shots that killed him. As he stood in the office, spraying the area with bullets, Ahmed's shots hit him in rapid succession. Three tore through his stomach while another three bore into his chest. The last two pierced his skull, leaving him dead in the office doorway.

After taking care of the shooter in the office, Ahmed heard shots and felt something hit him in the side. As he turned toward the sound, three more bullets hit him. One in the shoulder and two in the chest. He went down.

Once the sound of shooting stopped, Asad got away from the Aston Martin and took a wide angle in the large storage area to try and get a shot around the speedboat at Chico and Raul. Chico's once calm and suave demeanor immediately transformed him into a scared and nervous wreck.

"What are we gonna do Raul?" he asked.

Raul quickly tired of Chico's cowardice, he was already thinking about killing him if they got out of this alive.

Ahmed regained his composure and rolled over on to his stomach into the prone position.

He pointed his gun toward the speedboat then motioned to Young Curtis, who had been pinned down during the exchange of gunfire to get up and flush the two men from around the boat.

Young Curtis eased his way toward the boat. "Bring y'all punk ass from back there!"

Raul fired three shots that harmlessly flew over his head.

Young Curtis ducked. "Oh bitch! You wanna play!?" Young Curtis asked. He sprayed the side of the speedboat with gunfire.

Raul was surprised when bullets came through the boat just missing him. He backed away from that end of it, which exposed his legs to Ahmed.

Ahmed pulled the trigger, letting off a five round burst.

Raul legs gave out on him from being splintered by the bullets. He hit the floor in pain. When he looked from under the speedboat, he saw one of the mask men take aim. All he saw were the muzzle flash and knew he was dead before the bullets hit.

Chico, on the other end of the boat, hid behind the tire of the trailer. He watched Raul's head exploded. Blood, bone chips and pinkish looking brain matter blew four feet from his head. He knew it wasn't safe behind the boat so he picked up the gun Raul dropped. As soon as he touched it, he was shot once in the leg. He limped back to the end of the boat and, just when he was about to make his move, one of the masked gunman popped up out of nowhere. Chico pulled the trigger twice before being mowed down by a barrage of bullets from Asad's gun.

As Chico lay dead, Asad fired two more shots into his head. When he stepped to Raul, he knew there was no need to do him. He walked over to the bodies of Miguel and Jose, shooting them both twice in the head as well.

As he made his way toward the office, he saw a truly sad sight.

Young Curtis was on his knees, cradling his dead partner in his arms. "C'mon, big homie! Get up! Get up!" He repeated himself as he rocked back and forth.

Asad went to his brother and could see the holes in his jacket.

"Are you alright?"

Ahmed turned to him with a saddened look in his eyes through the ski mask.

"I'm cool Asad, but he's not," Ahmed said, nodding to Young Curtis.

"C'mon, get yo' ass up. I can't tell yo' mama and little Abdullah, I got you killed."

Asad knew it was time to take control before it was too late to bring Young Curtis back. He let the HK hang from the shoulder strap on his shoulder as he walked over to Young Curtis and pulled him up. "Come on, little brother. He's gone and we have to get outta here before the police show up. Ahmed will take care of Ducci." Young Curtis stared up at Asad with tears in his eyes as he led him inside the office.

When Asad opened the door, he stepped over the body inside, Young Curtis stopped. He put the silenced HK an inch from the dead man's face and held the trigger until the clip emptied. "Come on so we can get this and be gone," Asad called from the mini bar.

Young Curtis looked down at the Roberto's bloody mush of a face before stepping over him.

When he got to the mini bar, Asad was already under it. He told Young Curtis to find the latch on his side and pull it. After undoing the latches, they both stood up then pushed the bar over to reveal the secret compartment.

They stared down at the burlap sack before Asad pulled one up. It was a lot heavier then he thought it would be. Once he sat it down, he pulled out a black folding knife and cut the sack open.

He looked inside and a warm exciting feeling consumed his body as he found money wrapped in plastic. He reached back into the compartment and pulled out a black suitcase. He handed it to Young Curtis. Before helping him put one of the sacks on his shoulder, he told him to put everything in the van and hurry back.

Asad went back to the compartment and pulled the sacks out, stacking them up in the room. It took close to ten minutes for him and Young Curtis to load them all in the van.

Ahmed put Ducci's body in the back seat of his car so Young Curtis wouldn't have to see him.

Young Curtis got behind the wheel of the car Ducci and Asad came in.

Asad walked over to the wall and hit the button to open the garage door. When it opened, they all backed out with Asad stopping the van outside the garage door. He got out with a can of gasoline and went back inside. He poured it on all the places Ducci bled before dropping it and hitting the button on the wall to let the door down. He quickly stepped outside. As the door came down, he turned around and fired the HK at the concrete floor, which caused a spark and ignited a fire. As the door nearly closed, Asad jumped back inside the van and followed his brother and Young Curtis out of M&S driveway.

$$$

Charm looked at his watch and noticed it was almost a half an hour past the meeting time. He paced the large warehouse he normally used to store his drugs when they came in from the Bahamas. He started to wonder would he ever see the brothers again. The thought of calling the cell phone came to his mind but he reasoned that wasn't the smartest thing to do. As he walked around, hoping Asad and Ahmed were all right, he heard a car horn. He rushed to the two large double doors and pulled one open then stepped outside and saw Ahmed in the first car. He pushed the other door open, letting the cars enter. When they were inside, Charm pulled the doors shut then hurried to the cars with a smile on his face. He watched as the men exited their vehicles and observed the holes in Asad and Ahmed's jackets. He could see in their faces that something went wrong.

Asad walked over to Ahmed and helped him take his jacket off. Ahmed winced with pain when he had to move his left arm. Asad inspected the vest and saw that the two bullets in the front were stopped cold but the one on side almost went through. He looked at his shoulder and saw an entrance and exit wound.

"It looks like a flesh wound," Asad said.

"Yeah, that's what I figured but it still hurts like hell," he smiled.

"But are you alright?" he asked, seeing the holes in his brother's jacket.

"Yeah, I'm good. I didn't know I was hit until the drive over here."

Charm looked over to Young Curtis, sitting on the hood of one of the cars with his feet on the bumper and holding his head in his hands. He had been so concerned with Asad and Ahmed, he didn't noticed Ducci missing.

"Where's the other guy?" he asked Asad.

"He's in the back of the car. He didn't make it."

Charm found it hard to believe that a guy he was just with earlier laid in the back of a car dead.

Asad told Charm to take the car that Young Curtis drove up in and to go buy twelve bags of ice, peroxide and extra strength Motrin.

Charm could understand everything but all the ice. He followed Asad over to the car then watched him talk to Young Curtis for a second.

Once they finished, Young Curtis got off the car, walked over to the black and gray Renaissance Coach Tour bus, and went inside.

"Hurry back, we need to get outta here," Asad said.

"I'll be right back," Charm said while getting in the car. Asad opened the doors for him. He slapped the back of the car as Charm drove past.

After shutting the doors, he went to the van then started taking the money out of the van and putting it in the bins of the tour bus. Ahmed watched as his brother loaded up the bus with the large sacks and a black brief case. When he finished, he leaned his back against the bus with his younger brother.

"I think it's at least twenty million in those bags and it was two more hidden in the van under a black tarp."

"We messed up Asad. We should have gone in shooting like always. If we would have done that, we all could have made it outta there alive," Ahmed said.

Asad put his arm lightly around his brother. "Hindsight is 20/20. Ducci gave his life saving Young Curtis' and I would've done the same thing for you. We can't second guess ourselves. We lost a good brother and believe me… I'm feeling it because I took a liking to both of them. But, what can we do? It played out how it played out."

Ahmed knew his brother could sound cold at times but he was right. You can't change the past and they were lucky because it could have been worse.

"Why don't you go get that vest and jacket from Young Curtis," Asad said.

"Alright."

Before Ahmed could move, Young Curtis exited the bus while taking off his jacket. And, as he got closer, he unfastened the Velcro straps on his vest then lifted it over his head.

"I heard y'all talkin,'" he said, looking from one to the other.

"It's not much a man can say under these circumstances," Asad said as he glared at Young Curtis.

"I'm hip," Young Curtis replied, sadly. "I want y'all to know this wasn't y'all fault. If I would've been on top of my game, Ducci would still be alive."

"Its not your fault so don't think like that," Ahmed said.

"We all knew what we signed up for. And, that could've happened to either of us. So, don't put that on yourself."

Young Curtis thought on it for a second and knew it was his fault.

"I'm not leaving Ducci down here," he stated.

"We're not leaving him," Asad assured.

The men stood there consoling Young Curtis when they heard a car horn blow twice. Asad opened the double doors to allow Charm in. He pulled all the way up to the tour bus where Ahmed and Young Curtis stood.

He got out of the car with a white drug store bag in his hand and handed it to Ahmed.

"All the stuff your brother asked for is in there." He then turned to Young Curtis. "I'm sorry about what happened to Ducci," he said sincerely before giving him a hug. "Anytime you wanna get away from Cleveland and come down here to kick it, just give me a call and I'll set it up. We can go out on my yacht or something," Charm smiled.

Young Curtis flashed a weak smile. "I'm gon' take you up that one day."

"Hey Asad, make sure you give this brother my number when y'all get back home."

Asad nodded in approval as he pulled the black tarp out of the van before walking over. "We're about to move Ducci. You might not want to see him like this," he informed Young Curtis.

"Yeah, you right. I don't," Young Curtis responded.

Charm put his arm over his shoulder then walked him to the farthest end of the warehouse.

Asad watched then grabbed the tarp and took it on the bus. When he came back out, he grabbed four bags of ice out the car and took them on the bus. After setting up the back room on the bus, Asad and Ahmed went to the car to get Ducci's body. They opened up the back door to the dark blue Crown Victoria and pulled him out.

Once they had him in position, they took his jacket and bulletproof vest off. They looked at the five bullets holes in his chest and stomach, which was covered in dried blood. Asad surmised that one of the bullets must've hit his heart because there wasn't a lot of blood lost. Ahmed stared at Ducci's face and, even though there was nothing physically wrong with it, you could see death all over it. They laid his body on the ice-covered tarp before Asad went and got more. This time they placed a sheet over him then dumped the rest of the ice over it.

When they finished, Asad wrapped the tarp up tight with duct tape.

He exited the bus, went to Young Curtis, and told him they would be leaving in five minutes. He then turned to Charm. "After we make it home and count the money, we're going to throw you something."

"Asad, I have more money than I know what to do with. That's y'alls. I'm cool. All I want is for y'all to make it home safe."

Ahmed stayed back at the warehouse while his brother, Young Curtis, and Charm went to get rid of the guns and clothes used in the robbery. They also burned the van and the car with Ducci's blood in the back seat. It took close to an hour for them to make it back.

They all got out of the car then walked over to the tour bus where Ahmed stood.

"Dig, Charm, make sure you get rid of that car as soon as we leave," Asad said.

"Don't worry. I'm on top of it."

After talking a little longer, the men all said their farewells as Young Curtis and the brothers boarded the tour bus.

Inside, Asad got in the driver's seat as Ahmed laid on one of the two couches. Since cleaning his wound and taking the Motrin, his shoulder felt better but he knew it would be sore the next morning. Young Curtis lay on the couch across from Ahmed with his eyes closed but he wasn't sleep. He was thinking about his friend.

Asad knew taking Ducci's body back, like this, was dangerous but this was all he could come up with. He didn't want to take the chance on leaving the body in Miami to let the police match ballistics or something else that could lead them back to Cleveland. If they would have got a hold of his body, the investigation would have definitely shifted to Cleveland and they would start searching his running buddies. Young Curtis' name would surely come up and all types of things could unfold. He also knew that Young Curtis wouldn't just let them leave him. Plus, he was a stand-up brother and his family should have a chance to give him a proper send off.

Asad turned the large bus around in the warehouse as Charm opened the double doors. Asad hit the horn once as Charm waved goodbye with his ever present smile.

CHAPTER 30
MIKE'S HOUSE

It was 11:53 a.m. and M&S Yacht Sales was besieged by law enforcement. All of the alphabet boys were present. The DEA was on the scene because Chico started drawing a lot of unwanted attention when he came to town. The ATF was there because four fully automatic weapons were found. The FBI showed up when it was realized that three of the deceased men weren't supposed to be in the country since 9/11. And, when that happens, it's their job to figure out how it occurred.

A representative from each agency stood in an upstairs office, along with Ricardo Garcia, a Miami-Dade homicide detective. They all watched the surveillance video for the fifth time, trying to see if they could pickup on anything else. The pictures on the monitors were crystal clear. M&S security cameras were state of the art and top of the line equipment.

After watching the video, they realized two things: the men who did this were pro's and to, everyone's surprise, they all agreed the men were Black. It was unclear if they were of Latin decent or African Americans but they were sure Black males were their suspects. The exposed skin around the eyes of the ninja style ski masks tipped them off.

The question puzzling everyone was the contents of the sacks they carried.

Detective Garcia pulled out his cell phone and called the station.

"Yeah, this is Garcia. I want you to call all the hospitals and city morgues to find out if any unidentified Black males were dropped off or found dead last night or this morning." Detective Garcia ended the call and told the rest of the lawmen if they hear anything, to give him a call because Miami-Dade was still the lead team on the homicide investigations.

It seems like Miami is going back to the fucking eighties, Detective Garcia thought as he drove back to headquarters. When his cell phone rang, he quickly answered it.

"Hello, Garcia speaking." He listened to the dispatcher for a few seconds then responded. "Tell them I'm on my way." He ended the call then made a wild u-turn and rushed to Davie, Florida, a Suburb outside of Miami.

Detective Garcia arrived at the scene and was met outside by a Black homicide detective named Kevin Phillips.

"What we got Kevin?" he asked.

"We sent a patrol car over like you said to check the place out. When the patrolman pulled into the driveway, he noticed the front door partly open. So, he called for back up. Once they entered, they saw it had been ransacked. That's when I was called to the scene."

"Did you find anything?"

"We did but we didn't."

Garcia stared at him with a puzzled expression on his face, so Phillips explained.

"When we searched the house, we found a sophisticated surveillance system in the basement. The strange thing… the entire inside of the house has hidden cameras throughout but all of the tapes are missing."

"What do you mean they're missing?"

"Well, a neighbor from across the street said, about an hour before the patrolman pulled up, three Latinos entered the house. She said she didn't think of calling the police because she knew Guerrero was a Latino."

Garcia couldn't believe his ears. The only possible lead in a quintuple homicide was gone and only God knew where.

$$$

Santiago Moya set in his office and watched the tape of the two men putting the squeeze on Mike Guerrero.

It was a good thing he sent his men to Mike's house after receiving the news about what happened at M&S Yacht Sales. He figured, with Mike being the only person who knew what was going on, it would be a good idea to check his place out and it paid off... He still wished Jim would have followed protocol and called him before he called the police once he found the bodies of Chico and the others, but he panicked.

Santiago looked at the tapes from different angles of the two Black men. He knew Mike was dead by how they handled their business at M&S. He looked at the rest of the tapes on his desk that were of Mike and underage girls. He figured the video surveillance was there so Mike could record his sick act without the kids knowing. His thoughts went back to the two Black men. He knew if they weren't local, it would be even harder to find them. He reversed the tape and watched it once more, knowing he had to find the men.

$$$

It was midnight when the brothers and Young Curtis pulled into the auto body customizing shop off 131st and Miles. Young Curtis called his cousin Doughboy as soon as they entered Ohio and told him he needed to use the garage to park a motor home until the morning. At first, his cousin protested, saying he didn't want to get caught up in any of Young Curtis schemes. When Young Curtis told him he would throw him some money, Doughboy instantly agreed.

The men all exited the bus with Young Curtis in the lead. Asad and Ahmed stood by the bus as he went to talk to his cousin. Young Curtis saw the look on his face when the brothers got off the bus. He walked Doughboy out of hearing range of Asad and Ahmed.

"I'm gon' need the keys so, when I leave, I can lock up."

"Why you wanna stay here?" Doughboy questioned with a suspicious look in his eyes.

Young Curtis, not in the mood for his cousin's questions, flipped gangster.

"Look you petty ass nigga. Just let me use the spot and quit askin' all these muthafuckin' questions!"

Doughboy stared at him, realizing he really needed the garage. "Man, you can use it. But what 'chu doin' with them?" he asked in a whisper.

"Quit being so muthafuckin' nosy," Young Curtis replied. "Now c'mon and drop me and my dude off," Young Curtis said before walking off. Doughboy just shook his head before following.

$$$

After having Doughboy drop them off at Asad's

grandmother's house, Asad went in the garage and got Ahmed's Hummer. He drove Young Curtis to Ducci's house where he got Ducci's Impala and followed Asad back to the garage.

Once inside, they loaded the Hummer up with the twelve sacks and the suitcase. Then, the brothers went to the room on the bus to get Ducci's body. The room was so cold from the air conditioner being on high that, when they unwrapped the tarp, they could see that a lot of the ice didn't melt around the body. They removed the sheet and the ice then lifted his cold stiff corpse. They took it off of the bus and put it in the back seat of the Impala.

"You don't have to go," Young Curtis said to Ahmed. "I'm gon' take him."

"Alright bruh."

Asad and Young Curtis got inside the Impala and drove to St. Luke's Hospital. They chose St. Luke's because it was one of the only hospitals in Cleveland without cameras in the receiving entrance. They waited in the parking lot until it was clear then drove up to the entrance. They both quickly got out of the car and pulled Ducci's body out of the back seat and laid it down in front of the entrance before jumping back in the car and pulling off.

Young Curtis looked back as they pulled off, not liking how they just left his partner's body laying out there like garbage but understood they had no other choice. And, as hard as that was, he knew it would only going to get harder because he still had to tell Ducci's mother and Missy.

When they got back to the garage, Asad and Young Curtis got out of the car and walked over to Ahmed.

"If you want, you can stay the night out at our place and we'll all count the money tomorrow," Asad suggested.

"If y'all ain't crossed me by now, y'all ain't gon' cross me," Young Curtis said, staring at him through tired eyes. "Y'all count the money and I'll pick up me and Ducci's shares later. I got a lot of things to do tomorrow."

"We got you little brother," Ahmed assured. The brothers got inside the Hummer and headed home, leaving Young Curtis with thoughts of his fallen partner.

He looked up toward the heavens. "I'll give all that money back just to have you by my side, Big Homie," Young Curtis wept as tears ran down his face.

CHAPTER 31
THE TAKE

Asad and Ahmed woke up at 6:30 a.m. They went to the lower level of their townhouse to tally up the take from M&S. Asad picked up one of the sacks then carried it to the sofa, where Ahmed setup two money counting machines on the coffee table. After sitting down, Asad cut open one of the sacks and started taking out blocks of money wrapped in plastic. Once he emptied the bag, the brothers fed bills into the machine.

After the third one, they realized it came out to three million, just like the two before it. Asad got up from the sofa and arbitrarily picked up another one then pulled it back to the sofa. The lower level resembled a Federal Reserve. Stacks of money littered the floor, sofa, weight benches and the pool table. Asad cut the forth burlap sack open and pulled out a block of fifties and hundreds wrapped in plastic. After counting all of it, the forth bag came out to three million as well.

Shirtless, with his left shoulder heavily bandaged, Ahmed stood over his brother. "I don't think it's a coincidence Asad but we can count another one and I'll bet it comes out to three too."

Asad looked up at him. "If that's right, we're sitting on thirty six million dollars in cash!"

"We're sitting on twenty four after we give Young Curtis him and Ducci's cut," Ahmed corrected.

"He has that coming. He deserves it," Asad said.

Ahmed looked at his watch. "It's almost eleven. Let's put this money up and go see what's up with Tyrone."

"Okay, I'll take care of this. You go upstairs and get ready and make sure you take another antibiotic before we leave," Asad said. Even though his brother's wound looked clean, he still wanted to make sure it didn't get infected.

When Ahmed went upstairs, Asad remembered the suitcase. He thought it contained another half a million. Once he had it, he laid it on an empty spot on the floor and opened it. The smell that came rushing out caught him off guard. He stared at the heavily wrapped heroin and wondered why it was stored with the money. He remembered Mike Guerrero told him that only money was stored at M&S. He shut the case and seriously thought about flushing it but he reasoned that he should see if Young Curtis wanted it first.

He picked the suitcase up and slid it under the sofa then ran upstairs to get ready to leave.

$$$

Young Curtis stared at Rita Martin's house from the driveway for close to fifteen minutes. He sat in the SUV wondering how he could tell the woman, like a second mother to him, that her only biological child was dead. He sat there a little longer before finally building up the courage to get out. When he did, he looked up at the sun shining in all its glory. Even though it was a nice warm, bright day, it was the darkest in his life.

As soon as Young Curtis stepped onto the porch of the well-maintained Cleveland Heights home, the front door opened. "Boy, I was wondering were you going to come in," Rita greeted as she gave him a hug and a kiss.

Young Curtis followed her into the house, shutting the door behind him.

"You hungry baby," she asked as she went into the kitchen. Young Curtis said nothing as he stepped into the living room. He stood in front of the mantel and his emotions erupted from looking at the pictures of Ducci.

The pictures showed a baby grow into a man, from a missing front tooth elementary kid to an acne faced teenager then finally the handsome thoroughbred he turned out to be. Young Curtis stared at the picture of him and Ducci on the block when they both had nothing but each other. He shook his head in disbelief.

Rita came out when she heard his sobbing. She studied him standing in front of the mantel staring at the pictures as tears ran down his face. The realization of what happened instantly hit her like a ton of bricks. Her heart raced so fast it felt as if it was going to burst out of her chest.

She slowly walked backed to Young Curtis as her body trembled. "Curtis baby, where is Abdullah?" she asked with a shaky voice.

He turned to her with tears streaming.

"Mama..." he started then paused just as his chest uncontrollably heaved up and down.

"Come on, baby. I got to hear you say it," she pleaded as she began to cry.

"Mama..." he said again as he shook his head from side to side. "Ducci is... Ducci is gone." When the words left his mouth, Rita pulled him close and held him tight as they both cried.

After what seemed like an eternity, she walked Young Curtis to the sofa and sat him down.

"What happened?" she asked.

He told her everything. He felt he owed her that much but he did alter a few of the facts. He told her that they were in Detroit and left Asad and Ahmed's name out of it.

"I knew you two were out there doing dangerous things," she said as she got up from the sofa. She slowly walked around and spoke in a distant voice. "Like the times y'all would go out of town and come back with all of that money for me to put up in the safe at the salon." She shook her head in disapproval. "Abdullah told me a long time ago not to question him about what he did in the street." She always knew death or prison was a possibility for her son and Young Curtis.

Rita Martin was far from a square and a lot of the men she dealt with in her younger life were 'Street Players.'

Ducci's father, Abdullah 'Cash' Martin, was a hustler. Growing up on Hough Avenue, in an Islamic family, Cash was a good kid. But, when the streets called, he answered. Cash and his three-man crew became the most prolific jewelry store robbers in the Midwest, in the late seventies and early eighties. The life was fun and exciting to Rita. It was rumored that her husband and his crew stole over five million dollars worth of jewels during their run. For back then, that was a lot. When they married, Cash bought the Cleveland Heights home for her as a wedding present.

By the time Ducci came along, Cash had all the money a man could want back then. Rita suggested it was time for him to leave the streets alone and spend more time at home with his small family. Cash looked at her as if she was crazy then told her "Woman, you worry about my son and the house and let me worry about everything else."

That's when she realized a woman could never stop a hustler from hustling. They had to do it themselves.

Except in Cash's case, the police stopped him.

Coming out of an upscale jewelry store in Deerfield, Illinois. Cash and his men were confronted by the police and a shootout ensued. Two officers died at the scene and an ABP was put out on Cash and his crew, or better yet a hit. The police had no intentions of arresting four 'niggers' who killed two white officers.

When Cash and his men came to a roadblock after changing cars, a state trooper approached and looked inside. He then walked back to the other officers who ended up opening fire on the car, killing Cash and his crew.

When the troopers removed the bodies from the car and searched it, they found no guns or jewelry. In the report, they claimed the men tried to run through the roadblock but there wasn't any proof of it. Charges were never filed against the officers because all of the men were identified as the people who killed the patrolmen.

After hearing the news, Rita didn't know what she was going to do. Ducci wasn't even a year old at the time and the little money Cash kept in the house wouldn't last long. She couldn't except help from Cash's family because they wrongly believed she was behind his descent from Islam. Without any help coming from family or so called friends, Rita thought about selling the house in order to get a small apartment for herself and her new baby.

But, a day before Cash's funeral, a postman came to the house with a package postmarked from Chicago for her to sign. After doing so, she took it to her room and opened it. Inside the large box was another box with an envelope on it. She pulled it out. It was a letter from Cash.

Hey baby, if you're reading this, it can mean only two things. I'm either locked up or dead. Whatever the case may be I'm cool with it. The only regret I have is, I'll never see you and our son again as a free or probably a living man. I'm sorry, baby. Just remember, I loved you like no one before and everything I ever did right or wrong was for us to have a better life. Let my son know when he's old enough that his father was a real man who took care of his family, in life, in prison or death. I love you Rita.

Rita's tears fell on the letter as she read it. She sat it down then picked up the box. When she opened it, she stared inside at a large eleven-carat diamond ring, four carat matching earrings and an assortment of expensive jewelry from watches to necklaces. She stared at the missing loot from the jewelry store robbery and thought, *even in death Cash is still taking care of me and our son.*

Young Curtis watched Rita as she paced back and forth with tears in her eyes as a smile went across her lips.

"Mama, you alright?"

She was so lost in her feelings that she forgot he was there. "Yeah, I'm alright baby," she answered. "Ooh, I got so much to do," she said as she wiped her eyes. "I have to call and find out where they have him and to make funeral arrangements."

Young Curtis stood up and went to her. She hugged him.

"Curtis, whatever you do, don't hold yourself responsible because God does everything for a reason." She broke their embrace then wiped the tears running down his face. "Go home and try to get some rest. I'll break the news to everyone."

He kissed her on the cheek. "You and AJ will never have to worry about nothing, mama."

Rita hugged him once more then walked him to the door. She stood there, watching him get in his SUV and pull off. *God works in mysterious ways*, she thought. That day, she lost her son but knew in her heart she gained another.

$$$

When Asad and Ahmed entered Fly Ty's hospital room, they saw Francisca sitting in a chair away from the bed, reading a magazine while Fly Ty slept. She looked up when she heard them enter and set the magazine down. She got up and walked over to the brothers.

"How's he doing?" Asad asked, giving her a hug. He couldn't help but notice the softness of her body as they embraced.

"He's doing a lot better from the last time you two seen him," she answered as she moved to hug Ahmed.

"Ahhh," he said as she touched his shoulder.

"Are you alright?" she asked stepping back.

"He's cool," Asad answered before he could. "Do you think it'll be alright if we wake Ty up?"

She looked over at Fly Ty. "He's been sleep all morning. Its time he wake his butt up anyway. When y'all wake him, tell him I stepped out to get something to eat and will be back in about fifteen minutes."

"I'll tell him," Asad said.

When she left the room, the brothers made their way over to his bed. Ahmed tapped him on the shoulder twice to no response.

"You know this boy is a hard sleeper," Asad said before he shook him with a little more force.

Fly Ty slowly opened his eyes. When he focused on his cousins, he smiled. "What's up with y'all two?" he asked in a sleepy voice.

"I don't know what these people did to you," Ahmed started. "But your breath smells like four different types of animal shit."

The room instantly filled with laughter from the Sparks men. Asad laughed so hard he had to hold on to the rail on the side of the bed to keep from falling over. Fly Ty laughed then grimaced in pain. "Ahmed, chill out with the jokes before you fuck around and make me bust something."

Once the two men got their composures back, Fly Ty called them closer to his bed.

"Good lookin' out on those lames who tried to do me," he said.

"We don't know what you're talking about," the two replied in unison with smiles on their faces.

Fly Ty knew how they were when it came to murder. They never talked about it once it was done.

"So how did everything go in Miami," he asked, changing the subject.

The brothers looked at one another, thinking of the best way to break the news to him about Ducci.

"Things didn't go as planned," Asad started. "Ahmed caught one in the shoulder."

Fly Ty looked at him for any sign of injuries. "Us Sparks and bullets are having a bad week."

"Yeah, but we're all still here," Ahmed replied.

Fly Ty nodded in agreement, because he should've been dead.

Asad, not knowing how to tiptoe around the issue put it out there. "Your boy Ducci didn't make it."

"What 'chu mean?" Fly Ty stared at him.

"He died down there."

Fly Ty laid back in his bed, glaring up at the ceiling. Asad and Ahmed noticed the tears forming in the corners of his eyes. Neither said a word. They both gave him a moment to mourn a friend.

"What's up wit' Young Curtis?" He looked at his cousins.

"He's cool physically but, emotionally, he's going through it. He lost a friend who was more of a brother than anything else." Ahmed answered. *If anything ever happened to Asad, it would be no reason for me to continue living,* he thought.

"Let me use one of y'alls phone," Fly Ty said.

They both reached for their phones with Asad pulling his out first. Fly Ty took it and dialed the number.

When the phone was answered, Fly Ty knew immediately Young Curtis wasn't himself. "What's up, Curt? This Fly Ty. I'm just calling to check on you."

Hearing Fly Ty's voice instantly brought a smile to Young Curtis' face, knowing he still had one brother to lean on.

"What's up my fly fam?" Young Curtis asked. "I see you pulled through that shit. How you feel?"

"I'm still a little sore but I'm cool. I ain't paralyzed or anything, and they said I'ma make a full recovery."

"That's good. I want you to know, even though I don't believe in that fake ass religion shit, I prayed to the Most High for you every night."

Fly Ty smiled. "Good lookin' out." Fly Ty closed his eyes. "My people told me about Ducci. God bless his soul."

"Yeah, the big homie is gone, fam," Young Curtis said in a sober voice.

"Where you at?" Fly Ty asked, not wanting to carry on the conversation over the phone.

"Homie, I'm just drivin' around the hood thinkin.'"

"Why don't you come up to the hospital so I can see you?"

"Yeah, that sounds like a good idea. I'm on my way now."

"I'll see you when you get here," Fly Ty said, ending the call.

Asad and Ahmed stood around his bed not sure of what to say.

"I saw your girl Francisca when we stepped in," Asad said. She told me to tell you she was going to get something to eat and would be back in a few minutes." He stared at Fly Ty curiously. "So, what happened with you and Tamiko?"

Fly Ty squirmed in his bed, attempting to put up a strong front.

"Man, she made my decision for me. As soon as I came to, she was mashin' the gas on me. And, when I couldn't tell her what she wanted to hear, she told me it was over then left. I haven't seen or heard from her since."

The brothers could hear the heartbreak in his voice and see it on his face.

"You'll be alright," Ahmed said, putting his hand on Fly Ty's shoulder.

Just as they finished their conversation, Francisca came into the room. As she walked toward the bed, a smile spread across her wide sexy mouth.

"I see you finally woke up," she whispered before kissing him on the lips.

"Yeah, I'm up," Fly Ty smiled.

Francisca jumped back and put her hands over her nose then looked at Asad and Ahmed.

"Y'all been talking to him all this time with his breath smelling like this?"

Fly Ty looked over at his cousins, who tried to keep straight faces, but couldn't.

They both started laughing hysterically, grabbing on to one another to keep from falling over.

Francisca couldn't help but laugh from watching two of the most feared men in the city, chuckle like two little schoolboys. She wondered how many people had a chance to see this side of them.

"You ridin' wit' these two clowns," Fly Ty asked, looking over at her in mock anger.

"*No bebe*," she responded as she tried to control herself. "I'm riding with you but let me get you together."

She went to the small table next to his bed and grabbed a bottled water and unused plastic bedpan. She opened the water and told him to swish it around in his mouth before she gave him a sip. After swishing the water around, he spit it into the bedpan.

Francisca then grabbed a bottle of mouthwash from the table and had him repeat the act. Once he finished, she put all the items back on the table.

"Now, you're so fresh and so clean." She smiled before leaning over and giving him a passionate kiss.

Asad and Ahmed observed the scene of affection with different thoughts on their minds.

Asad thought about Dayna. He knew he had to see her.

Ahmed looked at Francisca, admiring her beauty. He considered her a perfect ten. From her sun kissed skin to her long flowing dark brown hair, he even found the fine, dark brown hair on her arms sexy. He couldn't help but notice her cleavage in the gold spaghetti strapped, silk blouse while the diamond necklace further attracted his attention. Ahmed smiled to himself, wondering where his cousin found such gorgeous women.

Everyone turned toward the door when they heard it open and saw a nurse escorting Young Curtis into the room.

Ahmed noticed that he still had on the same clothes he rode back to Cleveland in as he approached the small group around Fly Ty's bed. He stepped to Asad and Ahmed, showing them love.

"What's up with y'all?" he asked after breaking his embrace from Ahmed.

"We're alright. Just wondering how you were doing," Asad

answered.

"I'm gon' be a'ight. I ain't got no choice. It's a lot of people I gotta step up for and I ain't gon' let my big homie down."

"I know it's hard but that's what separates the strong from the weak. Anyone can handle things when it's easy but only the strong can handle the heavyweight," Ahmed said, putting a hand on his shoulder.

Young Curtis nodded his head in agreement before turning to Fly Ty.

Fly Ty looked up at him. "Let me properly introduce y'all." When Young Curtis looked up, it was the first time he paid attention to the woman standing over Fly Ty.

"Man, that's Cha-Cha," Young Curtis said somewhat surprised.

"This ain't Cha-Cha. Her name is Francisca," Fly Ty corrected.

"What's up?" Young Curtis, confused, stuck out his hand out.

"He hates that name," she informed Young Curtis as she shook his hand.

Fly Ty, who knew Francisca would talk a person to death, stopped her before she got warmed up.

"Hey baby, why don't you step out for a few minutes so I can holla at my peoples."

Even though she wanted to stay and be nosy, she knew her place. "Alright, I'll be outside if you need me." She leaned over and kissed him before she left.

Once out the room, Young Curtis stared at Fly Ty with a smile on his face. "Ducci was right again."

"What 'chu talkin' 'bout?" Fly Ty asked.

Young Curtis sat on the side of his bed. "When I told him we kicked it with Rose and Cha-Cha, he knew that shit ain't add up. He told me that he would bet that y'all was fuckin' around." Young Curtis smiled, thinking of Ducci's sharp mind.

Ahmed tapped him on the shoulder to get his attention. "We counted the money and you and Ducci's cut comes out to twelve million."

"Oh yeah," Young Curtis managed to say. He knew that was more money than he ever expected. But, instead of having that warm feeling inside, his heart was still saddened from the loss of his best friend, brother, and confidante.

"You mean twelve million dollars?" Fly Ty asked, excitedly.

"Yeah and you have a cut coming from turning us on to some real brothers," Asad replied.

"What 'chu gon' do wit' all of that money, Curt?" Fly Ty asked.

Young Curtis thought about it for a minute. "I don't know what I'ma do wit' mine but I'ma give Rita four point five, three for AJ and one and a half for herself. Then, I'ma give Monica a million to take care of her and AJ until he grows up. And, I'ma give his girl in Kentucky a half a million because that's how he would've wanted it."

All the men stared at Young Curtis with admiration in their eyes. Asad and Ahmed were surprised by the young man's act of nobility. They both thought he would give Ducci's family most of his share, but they didn't think he would give it all to them.

"Oh yeah," Asad said to Young Curtis. "Remember that black suitcase from the spot?"

"Yeah. What's up wit' it?"

"I opened it this morning and it's filled with heroin. I was going to flush it down the toilet but I thought I should see if you wanted it."

Young Curtis contemplated on saying 'flush it' but a thought came to mind. *Ducci gave his life for that, get everything you got coming.* "I'll take it," he finally said.

All right, you can hook up with Ahmed tonight and he'll have everything for you."

"Ai'ight but what time is it goin' down?"

Asad looked to Ahmed, not sure.

"I'll give you a call around nine."

Young Curtis nodded his head in agreement.

"Well, Ty," Ahmed said looking at his watch. "Asad and I have to leave. We told grandma we'd stop by but you know we'll be up here every day until you come home."

"I wouldn't have it any other way," Fly Ty smiled.

As the brothers headed for the door, Young Curtis stopped them. "Are y'all coming to Ducci's funeral?"

The room fell silent as Ahmed and Fly Ty looked at Asad. They both knew he hated funerals to the point he didn't even attend his beloved grandfather's. He stayed in the car until it was over. Grandma Sparks said that he'd been like that since his father died. As a kid, he always related funerals to the loss of his dad and created some sort of phobia he refused to shake.

"Dig, Curtis. I'm speaking for myself. I can't make it. I would like to honor Ducci's memory but going to the funeral isn't an option."

Young Curtis stared at him, seeing he was rattled. *This is the same dude that didn't mind goin' into a situation that could've got him killed, but he's scared of a funeral,* Young Curtis thought.

"I'll be there," Ahmed said, seeing the confused look on his face.

After saying their farewells, the brother left. Fly Ty and Young Curtis were alone.

Young Curtis turned to Fly Ty with a sorrowful look in his eyes. "You the only fam I got now."

Fly Ty put his hand on Young Curtis' and looked him in the eyes. "I got 'chu fam, but I ain't the only real dude on your team. You still got little CCW, and Asad and Ahmed are ridin' wit' you."

Young Curtis laughed. "I like your people and I really like Ahmed. But from kickin' it wit them the last few days, I realized they're some different type of dudes. You know, they don't kick it like us and I can respect that."

"Man, I'm tellin' you those two are wit' you," Fly Ty said. "I can tell they took a likin' to you. They just don't show it like the average dudes."

"Oh, I know they like me fo' sho. We bound by blood and, if that didn't prove it, it ain't no doubt in my mind they would've left me in Florida with two holes in my head. All I'm sayin' is they too strict and disciplined for a dude to try and hang out wit.' On the fo' real, I didn't even know niggas like them existed." Young Curtis chuckled.

Fly Ty smiled, knowing exactly what he meant.

"Oh yeah! What's up with your girl Cha-Cha?" he asked, changing the subject.

Fly Ty shook his head in disapproval. "Quit callin' her that. Her name is Francisca," he said before he ran the whole story down to Young Curtis.

"What, I ain't sleep too! You have a lot of your cousins in you," Young Curtis said, referring to Fly Ty's discipline on keeping secrets.

"So you think it's over wit' you and Tamiko or does she just need some time to cool off?"

"I think its over, Curt," he answered in a low voice. "She's one of those women you can only cross once." After the word left his mouth, he lay in his bed with a far off look in his eyes.

Young Curtis knew how much Fly Ty loved Tamiko and even felt sorry for him. Then, the real came out.

"Man, quit laying there like a sucka. If she's gon, she gon. You gotta remember dudes like us are the catch and, if a bitch can't get in line and go for what we puttin' down, fuck'em!"

Fly Ty couldn't do anything but smile. It was good to see Young Curtis getting back to his old self. He thought, *it's easy for a dude to give that type of advice, especially when it wasn't their feelings involved.*

Young Curtis sat on the bed looking at Fly Ty. He was glad he came, because this time with Fly Ty helped clear his mind and made him feel better.

CHAPTER 32
DAYNA

"So, how was your trip?" Dayna asked Asad as they sat at their table in an upscale Italian restaurant in downtown Cleveland.

"I wish it could've went better but I guess it was all right."

"Where did you go again?" Dayna inquired as she finished off her Chicken Alfredo.

Asad took a sip of water, "I went out to L.A."

"Oh yeah. You did tell me that. Did you get a chance to see any stars?"

Asad smiled. "The only star I was thinking about was you."

"Oooh, that's so sweet, Asad." She leaned over the table and gave him a quick peck on the lips.

When their lips touched, it was electric. Dayna knew she had to have him that night, no matter how wrong it seemed.

After dinner, they sat and talked for closed to twenty minutes then Dayna looked at him with a mischievous grin. "Do you want to spend the night together?" she shyly asked.

Asad's heart rate involuntarily sped up at her question. He wanted her more than he ever wanted any woman in the past. He gazed at her for a moment, not wanting to appear too anxious.

"Yeah, I would like that."

"Well, let's get outta here, Mr. Sparks," she said in her low sexy voice.

Asad signaled the waiter then paid the bill. He stood up then helped Dayna out of her seat. The waiter just stood there and watched as the beautiful Black couple left.

Once inside the luxury confines of Asad's Mercedes, Dayna looked over to him from the passenger seat.

"Are we going to your place?" she asked.

Asad glanced over at her somewhat caught off guard by her question. He knew they were just a few blocks from her apartment. He reasoned that she just wanted to see where he lived.

"We can't go to my place. Like I told you before, I live with my brother and he's entertaining company tonight. We have a rule, if one is having a guest over, the other gets lost," Asad lied.

The brothers never brought women to their home for security purposes. They figured the less people who knew where they lived, would make it harder for them to be found.

Dayna laid back in her seat and turned her head to face him. "I'm just so tried of being in my apartment. I was hoping I could spend the night somewhere different."

"You still can." Asad smiled as he pulled off from the curb.

$$$

It was almost eleven o'clock when Fly Ty checked the time on the wall-mounted television. Everyone he loved had stopped by to see him, but every since Francisca left, he found himself bored and feeling lonely. He couldn't stop thinking about Tamiko. He lay there a little longer then made up his mind. He leaned over and grabbed the phone.

Tamiko went around the bedroom, collecting everything she needed putting them in two large suitcases placed on the bed. She had already gathered most of her belongings when the phone rang. She picked up the black, cordless phone from the nightstand. She thought it to be her mother calling to see what took her so long.

When she answered and heard his voice, she immediately wanted to hang up. "What do you want, Tyrone?" she asked in her most unfriendly tone.

"I just wanna talk, Miko, cuz I ain't like how our last encounter ended," Fly Ty somewhat passively answered.

"You're not the only one," she shot back.

He could feel the venom in her voice through the phone and it hurt.

"Miko, you didn't give me a chance to explain myself or the situation. For the last couple of days, I thought about what you said. I know my betrayal toward you should be punishable by death..."

"Well why don't you kill yourself?" she said, pouncing on his last comment.

Fly Ty closed his eyes and shook his head as he held the receiver to his ear. "Oh, that would've made you feel better if I had died?"

Tamiko was silent on the other end of the phone. They both knew that was last thing in the world she wanted.

"Look Tyrone! I don't want to play this game. You can try and make yourself out to be the victim all you want, but you and I both know that this is all your fault." She let out a sigh, finally realizing for the first time that it was truly over between them. She felt the tears coming and tried everything in her power to stop them to no avail. Her voice cracked as soon as she spoke. "Tyrone, you had a good thing. And, like all stupid men, you ruined it," She wiped her tears away. "Just to let you know, the only reason I'm at your condo is to collect my things. Once I'm done, I'll be gone."

Before he could say a word, she continued. "I'd really appreciate it if you made this the last time we talk. And, please don't call my mother's house looking for me."

Fly Ty listened on the other end of the phone feeling physically ill. He thought, if he gave her a couple of days to cool down, they could remain friends. But, realizing she wanted nothing to do with him crushed his heart.

Tamiko listened to the silence on the other end of the phone and knew she had him right where she wanted him. Part of her wanted to give him a second chance but her vengeful side wanted him to suffer and that won out.

"Well, Tyrone, I said all that I have to say." With that, she hung up.

Fly Ty held the phone to his ear, listening to the dial tone. He angrily snatched it from his ear and dialed the number again. But, this time, he got the answering machine.

"Miko… Miko… Tamiko! I know you still there. Pick up the phone so we can talk."

Tamiko sat on the bed, staring at the answering machine doing everything in her power to keep from answering it.

"Miko! I just wanted to apologize for all this shit I put you through. God knows I never meant for this to happen. I have to be real. Knowing I'll never have you in my life again is the worst thing I've ever had to deal with. Knowing my Special Lady is gone. Special Lady was a nickname he'd given her a long time ago. "I want you to know I still love you and I'll miss you as long as I'm breathing. Bye Miko."

When the answering machine clicked off, Fly Ty looked at the phone in his hand then threw it at the TV. He watched as it bounced off and hit the floor. He stared up at the ceiling with his teeth clenched, welcoming the pain in his back from aggravating his wounds as the feeling of loss consumed his thoughts.

Tamiko sat on the bed and played Tyrone's message twice more. She couldn't stop herself from crying. She thought for a moment that maybe she was being too rough on him then from somewhere inside her the word "No!" exited of her mouth. She got up from the bed and went to the dresser mirror. She stared at her reflection.

"There's no need to cry for the man who betrayed your heart," she said to herself as she wiped the tears away. She stood in front of the mirror, straightening herself up by wiping away the remnants of tears. Once pleased, she took a deep breath then slowly exhaled. She got the suitcase off of the bed then headed downstairs.

When she got to the front door, she put one of the suitcases down to reach for the knob. When she turned around to pick them back up, she looked over the place where her and Tyrone lived, loved, and laughed together. She instantly felt the tears reform and hurried to leave behind memories of the one man she ever truly loved.

$$$

"This is nice Asad," Dayna said as they entered the suite in the four-star Renaissance Hotel.

Asad shut the door and followed her into the living room area.

"This is a classy place," he said as he looked around at the Victorian style furnishings.

"Let's see what the bedroom looks like," Dayna seductively suggested while looking back over her shoulder.

When Asad entered the room, he saw Dayna standing at the foot of the bed. It had a dim, romantic glow from the moonlight entering the window through the open drapes. Asad stood there, watching Dayna as she slipped out of her pumps and skirt. She motioned with her finger for him to come to her.

She put her hands on her hips, staring at his handsome face as he made his way to her. She just loved his boyish shyness as he approached her. When he finally made it within reach, she stroked his cheek then pulled him closer and kissed him. She could tell he hadn't kissed a woman like that in a long time because, when she pushed her tongue in his mouth, it felt like he wanted to pull back but didn't. When she broke their embrace, she rested her hand on his chest and felt his heart racing.

"You're not scared are you?" she teased, looking up at him.

He glanced down at her with a shy smile and shook his head from side to side. That's when she started unbuttoning his shirt as he did the same to her. Once she got his off, she gasped at the sight of his upper body. She ran her hands over his shoulder and arms, feeling every cut and ripple of muscle. She traced his eight-pack physique with her index finger.

Asad pulled her shirt off then removed her black Victoria Secrets bra, revealing her coco colored breast with large dark nipples. Dayna quickly loosened his belt and unbuttoned his pants while telling him to take his shoes off. After he removed them, she pulled his jeans down then off. Slowly, she went back up to his boxers and couldn't help becoming aroused from looking at the bulge.

She helped him out of them with a smile on her face. She stared at his erect penis, wanting to put it in her mouth but knew it was too soon. She had to continue to play to his fantasy as the perfect woman. She stood up and slipped out of her black thong then all of a sudden things changed.

Instead of her being in control, Asad took over. He started running his hands lightly over her entire body, sending what felt like an electrical charge through her. He cupped her breasts as he kissed her while rubbing his thumbs back and forth across her nipples. He sent her into the abyss of ecstasy. He stopped her long enough to turn her around then started softly kissing the nape of her neck. Dayna, who felt the warm flesh of his manhood pressing against the cleft of her butt, pushed back on him as he continued to expertly manipulate her body with his hands. Asad ran his hands lightly over her stomach then gripped it tightly. When he stuck it between her legs, she couldn't take it anymore.

She turned around and wrapped her arms around his neck before frantically kissing him. She pulled him down onto the bed with her as he kissed her neck before lightly biting down on her collarbone, which sent a tingle through her body. She reached between them and grabbed Asad's penis, guiding it inside her. She released a moan.

After a perfect balance of sensual lovemaking and hard sex, Dayna lay awake in Asad's arms as he slept. She still felt the buzz from the after glow of their sex escapade. She thought about Asad, wanting to believe he was an innocent man. From the first time she'd laid eyes on him, she felt a spark. But, after talking to him, she knew it would be hard for her to do her job. She thought that her professionalism would override her physical attraction. She never counted on becoming emotionally attached to the handsome, soft spoken, intelligent, somewhat shy man.

Now, she questioned herself, wondering if she was cut out for this type of assignment fresh out of the FBI academy at Quantico. She ran over the facts. She knew, from the active file on the Sparks, all of the men knew Ellery 'Charm' La'Vett, one of the biggest drug traffickers in the United States. Two informants planted deep inside his criminal organization, identified Tyrone 'Fly Ty' Sparks as a player. The only problem… With Tyrone Sparks hospitalized, the joint task forces of the FBI and DEA, didn't know how long it would take to get the concrete evidence they needed to link him to La'Vette.

Dayna then thought about the brothers. When their pictures were shown to the informants, neither knew the brothers. Both said they never saw them. The FBI and DEA noticed Asad and Ahmed in two different surveillance videos with La'Vette which led them to believe the two were somehow linked to his organization. Whatever the case maybe, it was Dayna's job to find the link. And, since she found her way in, she planned to do it.

She stared at Asad as he slept, hoping they were wrong about him. She kissed him on the lips, thinking she was just playing her part and hoping she wasn't playing herself.

CHAPTER 33
MADE IT OUT

It was the morning of Ducci's funeral and Ahmed was in the kitchen of his home rushing to finish breakfast so that he would make it on time. After cooking a breakfast of scrambled eggs, turkey sausage, and toast, he set a plate in the oven for Asad. He went to the small oak table in the kitchen then took a seat and started eating.

"What did you cook?" Asad asked as he came into the kitchen, still wearing his black pajama bottoms, house shoes, and white tank top.

"Yours is in the oven."

Asad went to the oven with a smile on his face because he was hungry. He pulled out the plate and was pleased to find it still warm. When he went to take a seat at the kitchen table, he noticed Ahmed watching his every move.

"Why are you watching me like I stole something," he smiled.

Ahmed looked at him shaking his head. "I see you've stayed out two nights this week and, every time you come home, you smiling from ear to ear." Ahmed paused to let his words sink in. "I know you aren't getting serious with that woman you've been seeing already?"

Asad looked at his younger brother from across the table and laughed. "You're not jealous are you?"

Ahmed stared at him, not finding a bit of humor in what his brother said.

"Dig, Asad, I'm just saying don't fall for the first woman who sparks your interest."

"Come on." Asad knew it was more. "What's on your mind?"

"All I'm saying is since we've been back, you've been running around like nothing happened."

Asad stared at his brother, trying to figure out what he referred to.

"Today is Ducci's funeral," Ahmed said, seeing the look on his face.

Asad knew where he was going. "That's not going to happen.

I feel for him and his family but I'm not going."

Both men stared at one another for a long moment without either blinking.

Ahmed shook his head in dismay. "You're wrong, Asad. Ducci gave his life, possibly saving all of ours and now you're telling me you can't put your thing with funerals behind you for fifteen minutes to pay homage to a good brother who's no longer with us?"

Ahmed looked into his brother's eyes and could tell everything he'd just said went in one ear and out the other. He stared at him a little longer, shaking his head in disappointment before he got up from the table to go get dressed.

On his way out of the kitchen, the phone rang. He went over to the counter and answered it.

"What's up? No. Not yet. You're sure? Okay. I'll be there in about forty five minutes," he said before ending the call.

Asad watched as he went around the corner and thought about how forceful he spoke to him. *Ahmed's tripping,* he thought before he started eating.

$$$

Young Curtis sat in one of the front pews of the Prince of Peace Baptist Church along with Rita Martin on his left and Abdullah Martin Jr. on his right. Monica sat next to her son, hugging him as they both cried. Missy sat further down the pew next to Rita, holding her hand as she rocked back and forth with tears running down her face. Everyone in the front pew was dressed in black.

Young Curtis looked back and saw that the church filled with mourners. It seemed like people from all around 'Up The Way' was there. The homies from the hood was about fifty deep, all wearing red and white RIP T-shirts with Ducci's image on the front.

He watched as the last few people walked past Ducci's opened casket to say their last good byes and wondered about Ahmed's whereabouts. *He practically gave his word he would be here.* He looked back at his mother and sister who were both silently mourning. He thought about how he had to convince Missy and Monica to take the money Ducci left them. Neither wanted the very thing that cost the man, they cared for, his life. Young Curtis told them if they didn't take it, Ducci's life would have been lost in vain because everything he ever did was to make sure his loved ones would be better off.

As he watched the last young woman walk away from the casket, he heard what sounded as if everyone in the church began to talk in hush tones. When he turned around to see what was going on, a big smile went across his lips. He watched as the Sparks' made their way up the center aisle.

Both Ahmed and Asad wore black suits with black button up shirts without ties. Young Curtis looked at Fly Ty in his wheelchair being pushed by Asad. He could tell Fly Ty was in a lot pain from the expression on his face. He wore a black robe over his hospital pajamas and a black skullcap over the bandage on his head. He was still hooked up to an IV attached to his wheelchair.

Once they made it to the front, Ahmed walked over to the casket and bowed his head, paying his last respects. When he stepped back, Asad pushed Fly Ty as close as he could get. Fly Ty touched the casket and closed his eyes as he said a prayer. He hoped Ducci was in heaven, where he belonged. When he finished, Asad pushed him toward the family, not even wanting to look at Ducci's body. He stopped the wheelchair in front of Ducci's mother. She leaned over and gave Fly Ty a hug and kiss on the cheek.

Since there wasn't anywhere to sit, Asad and Ahmed stood in the center aisle on each side of Fly Ty's wheelchair. Ahmed looked at Ducci's family and his heart went out to them. Another son and father's life was lost to the streets while in the pursuit of the 'all mighty dollar.' As he stared at all the tear stained faces in the front row, he experienced a sorrow he never felt in the past. He was willing to bet that all the money in the world wasn't worth the pain and suffering they went through.

He looked from his cousin to his brother and thanked the Most High that they all had made it out before one met the fate of so many others before them.

$$$

In Miami, Santiago Moya sat in his office, upstairs over the restaurant. He watched the videotape from Mike's house for about the hundredth time. He viewed it so many times. He could easily spot the twins in a crowd. He prided himself on knowing everyone and everything that went on in Miami but the last few days turned up no leads on the guys who hit M&S. He suspected the men were out-of-towners because there wasn't a Black crew working Miami who could have pulled off a job like this without leaving a trace. He remembered some Jamaicans pulling a job like this in the eighties but they were all dead or in jail. Santiago thought about all the people he had on the streets, who all brought back the same bad news… No one knew anything. That bothered him more than anything. He came to the realization he may never find the men who killed Mike and robbed Sereno.

The news of Mike's body being found in the everglades, shot twice in the head, erased the idea that he was involved. As he sat there lost in his thoughts, the phone rang…

"Hola."

"Santiago, *dime que mierda este pasando alla arriba?*"

This was the call Santiago had waited for but dreaded. He explained everything to Sereno, from the videotape to the murder of his cousin.

Sereno stood on the second story balcony of his large estate, which overlooked a lush tropical forest that was part of his land. He took a puff of his cigar, thinking about how to get his money back and avenge his cousin's murder.

The two men talked a little longer with Sereno telling him he didn't care how long it takes but he wanted the men responsible found and killed.

Santiago placed the phone in the cradle then grabbed the remote. He rewound the tape to the best shots of the two men. "I'll find you two and when I do, you're dead..."

The End

THE FAMILY SPARKS

FOLLOW-UP TO TAKE MONEY

…..COMING OCTOBER 2012

An Excerpt From

RIDDLES

The Upcoming Novel

By RHONDA CROWDER

Tony Moda

Chapter One

"She's dead! She's dead!" some girl cried out just as rapper Fat Joe's "Make It Rain," stopped abruptly after Lil Wayne's lyrics "I'm in dis … with da terror."

From there, I heard loud yelling and screaming while feeling like I had awakened from a long dream that, at times, seemed a little nightmarish.

"Call the police!" a baritone voice demanded over the mayhem.

"We did!" a sassy alto exclaimed.

But, those words were not music to my ears.

My customer, a middle-aged male, looked at me and I glared at him. *Wha da hell*, I thought. And, according to the perplexed expression on his pale pie face, I reasoned he pondered the same thing but in the King's language. I quickly jumped off his lap. He snatched his hand from inside of his underpants then stood up, moving away from the dingy loveseat.

I immediately exited the stale, dimly lit, medium-sized, closet-like space we had been tucked away for at least forty-five minutes, leaving him and the full bottle of Verde in the sweated metal ice bucket sitting atop of a small round table behind while thinking… *Something like this could only happen on Friday the 13th. And, while it is April, I ain't up for some fool's jokes.*

Standing there completely naked, my eyes scanned the club.

With body parts jiggling, girls scattered and screamed while almost one hundred men desperately hurried to the nearest exit like someone yelled “fire.” I turned around to see the gentleman who just paid me over two hundred dollars for the private session that simply consisted of me watching him masturbate, trying to ejaculate, knowing good and well he was high off cocaine. Hell, I was too for that matter but not as much as him.

We looked at each other again, perceiving what was understood didn’t need to be explained, and he headed toward a group of men trying to exit through club’s main entrance. I, on the other hand, had to be nosy, so I roamed to learn more about the situation while a crowd gathered at the oppose end of the bar. At the same time, strippers scurried and hollered as if they were actresses in some horror flick.

“UGGGGGH,” a few cried out while loudly sobbing and slobbering. In my mind, I could imagine one of them tripping over their feet and falling at any moment because they could be that clueless and clumsy, especially when drunk and hysterical.

Now, the last thing I needed to see was a dead body. But, for some strange reason, I felt compelled to view it. I never knew a girl to be dead in a strip club, passed out drunk; or P.O.D. as they say, but not dead. Unfortunately, the floor men directed all the dancers to the back and secured the main doorway as they refused to allow anyone to enter or exit. However, I did see the night manager ushering a few select guys through the curtain, which covered one of the two entrances to the dressing room, then out of the emergency exit. The chaos as well as the night manger’s desire to help his friends afforded me the opportunity to ease closer to the corpse.

“Tee, just let me get a peek,” I said, trying to convince the bouncer guarding the room to grant me a chance to view the body. “Who, Tee?”

“Malibu. And, no,” he replied while I sniffled.

"*Malibu*?" I gasped then grasped my mouth and paused for a few seconds. "Tee? Malibu?" I leaned forward onto my toes and tried to look beyond his big Jethro Bodine of *The Beverly Hillbillies* country built frame. "Ahh, come on, Tee. You gotta let me see her. That's my gurl... Wuz's up?" I shrugged and turned my hands upward, exposing my empty palms, knowing the gesture wouldn't bring about any results, but I felt it was worth a try.

"Riddles, if I let you peek, somebody else gone *wanta* peek and then there'll a roller coaster ride line over here. Besides, boss man wants ya'll girls in the dressing room, right now, anyway. We don't need all that extra noise round here. This is some serious shit!"

"Uh, Tee, I can take it," I continued, but with his arms crossed, he shook his head from side to side. "And, everybody else going to the back. C'mon."

"No," he said with the same mannerism of his television counterpart.

Truth was, sadly to say, I thought I could stomach the sight. Where I came from, it was common to see a dead body if you walked through the right alley at the wrong time. Maggots started to eat away at the worst case I observed to date and my intestinal contents became an added topping on their entrée so, unless Malibu was worse off than that guy, I figured I could take it. Suffice to say, Tee wasn't hearing it, so I had to resort to monetary persuasion, which always worked on his kind.

I looked at my thigh, plucked a single twenty-dollar bill from my garter and pointed it to him. He took it. "Hurry up! Then get your ass in dat dressing room. And, I mean hurry," he said as he quickly shoved the money in his front pants' pocket.

Broke, thirsty ass, I thought.

Now, although I did manage to maintain my composure, I couldn't believe my eyes. It seemed as if I saw myself… As if I looked at my own image reflecting from a mirror. See, people always said Malibu and I looked alike but I never really paid them any mind or at least wanted to admit it. I like to think I look like myself. I simply shrugged the comments off as, "whatever." Some white people think all Blacks look alike so, most of the time, I figured they were just saying that because we were close to the same size and the only dark-skinned, African-American girls working at Joker's Gentleman's Club. But, to me, that was the extent of the resemblance because our eyes were very distinctly different. Hers were round and mine were slanted, which gives me a more exotic appearance as they complemented my oval face, high cheekbones, narrow nose and full yet pouty lips.

The resemblance often caused those who knew us individually to take a double look when seeing the other. And, for the first time since I've known the girl, I actually saw it. I saw myself in her as she lay stretched out in the chair with her head cocked to the side and arms limped along her body. The sight slightly overwhelmed me because her mouth and eyes were wide open while her two black nipples, protruding from her perky breasts, stood at attention.

There was no sight of blood or an obvious struggle. It appeared as if someone simply placed her in the small chair, after putting her to rest, like a slick stick up kid who got the ups on a sleeping hustler. I wondered if she just died and the customer left her in there or if foul play was involved. I would've liked to think he would have told someone if she merely passed as a result of circumstances beyond his control. But, as I looked around the very small room, just as dingy as the one I exited, I noticed the garter around her thigh was empty and a broken rubberband hung from it.

DESCRIPTION	PRICE	QTY	TOTAL
TAKE MONEY by TONY MODA	$15.00		
FREE SHIPPING and HANDLING			0.00
TOTAL			

NAME: ______________________________________

ADDRESS: ____________________________________

CITY, STATE, ZIP: _____________________________

MAIL MONEY ORDERS OR CERTIFIED CHECKS TO:

StoryLine Books
P O BOX 608987
CLEVELAND, OH 44108

TO ORDER BY CREDIT CARD OR FOR MORE INFORMATION, CONTACT US AT:

Website: www.storylinebks.com
Email: storylinebks@yahoo.com
Phone: (216) 220-3162 Ext. 101

Made in the USA
San Bernardino, CA
09 March 2016